KALEIDOSCOPIC
SHADES

DAVID A. NEUMAN

KALEIDOSCOPIC SHADES

Within Black Eternity

Kaleidoscopic Shades: Within Black Eternity

First published 2021
by Gatekeeper Press
2167 Stringtown Rd., Suite 109
Columbus, OH 43123-2989
www.GatekeeperPress.com

This edition published 2023
by Rowanvale Books Ltd
The Gate
Keppoch Street
Roath
Cardiff
CF24 3JW
www.rowanvalebooks.com

A CIP catalogue record for this book is available from the British Library.
ISBN: 978-1-914422-44-7
eISBN: 978-1-914422-43-0

CONTENTS

TIME

~

Suppose, just for a moment, that time does not merely exist on a single plane, but is multi-layered; and what we see, what we experience, is to the exclusion of a vast majority of possibilities. Like a multi-storey edifice erected in haphazard fashion, there are time zones merrily ticking away in the past, present and future.

Suppose also, just for a moment, that this disparate conglomeration, whilst generally hidden, allows a glimpse into such layers, a peek through a doorway between dimensions. And in each exists an Earth, or perhaps many hundreds of Earths... of the past, the present... the future. Each presenting realities and possibilities—where wonders exist only if one cares to open their mind and accept what sits beyond sound reasoning and logic.

In the late 1930s, Ivan Sanderson, a scientist who just happened to share an uncanny resemblance to the late actor Vincent Price, stumbled through one such inter-dimensional doorway. Suffice to say that this was far more than just a peek. This was the whole shebang.

Whilst conducting a research expedition through the jungles of Haiti to gain further knowledge of the diverse biology of the country, his investigations gave way to the truly bizarre. Lucky for us, his character lent his mind to accepting those things beyond sound reasoning and logic.

However the unfolding events are recounted, whether it involves Ivan's car breaking down or becoming bogged, the main thread holds true: he, his wife and assistant became stranded in the Haiti jungle due to vehicular inconveniences. From this point forward, the assistant faded from the picture—which one might think of as typical in a mystery worth its salt—whilst Ivan and his wife Alma pressed on, seemingly oblivious to the well-being of their lost comrade.

Making their way along a road that cut a swath through the jungle's thick vegetation, and supposedly heading for home base, it's hard to imagine the Sandersons' shock as benighted trees and undisturbed undergrowth gave way to the French city of Paris. But this was no ordinary Paris: candlelight flickered through windows of multi-storey houses, whilst lanterns lit the street below. They swung gently in a breeze that somehow didn't exist, catching the grooves of the cobbled street below. It was covered in patches of mud, as well as piles and piles of horse shit.

Upon contemplation, the Sandersons concluded on having been transported back in time to Paris of some five hundred years earlier. Of course, this drew its share of believers as well as cynics.

And so the debate began in earnest on the veracity of such an 'extraordinary' event.

But if the Sandersons had walked, as they claimed, the streets of Paris five hundred years before, had they themselves been seen? And what of it if they had been? Had a keen-eyed Parisian glimpsed them as ghostly figures? A snapshot that had somehow become buried and encapsulated in the ether of time? Or men from the future come to do some mischief? Creatures from *outer space*, perhaps?

～

People like the Sandersons—though, perhaps, not as famous or notorious, depending on what side of that debate you stand— commonly find themselves lost.

The sudden substitution of another time and place can rarely find satisfactory reasoning for those affected. We hear suggestions of hallucinations, perhaps too many drugs or too much booze, followed by whiffling laughter, either nervous or disparaging.

But do we, more often than we care to admit, experience such inter-dimensional doorways, bearing witness to strange if not downright peculiar unknowns?

～

The great man of science himself, Albert Einstein, concluded that time is not a constant, that it forms part of multiple dimensions and is, therefore, able to be transgressed. Albert went on to say: "*The distinction between past, present and future is an illusion, although a persistent one.*"

"Tonight the monkey takes its final breath.
Tonight we will see evil.
We will hear evil.
And we will speak evil."

SOLAR FLARES – 2011

~~~

In the year 2011, a brutally dark storm threatened to envelope the entire world.

All communications went down. Life ground to a halt over the state of South Australia, and in particular, Adelaide.

And people began losing their lives.

The technological age was rendered utterly useless.

Some twelve years on, one fact stood firm: despite a total shut-down of communication across continents, all systems had either maintained the capacity to function or—as in the case of the horde of satellites whizzing around Earth—were in fact still functioning. Their electronics had not been fried into a gooey mess by a massive belching of solar flares; they'd been simply unable to penetrate the storm's density.

The "event" was not without precedence. In the year 1859, a similar occurrence had unravelled. However, its impact on the crude technology of the time, whilst disruptive and somewhat unnerving, had lacked the cataclysmic destruction of 2011. As well, it had remained localized, without the slightest hint of global catastrophe.

These discrepancies gave rise to voices of consternation.

But as the debate continued, people became increasingly desperate for an answer, and such voices were gradually silenced.

And an answer that provided solace was as good as it would get.

∽

With the debate concluded, the "*Perfect Storm*" was hurriedly packaged up and trundled off to some hidden vault, residing amongst other such infamous conundrums, such as: What really happened at 7:17 A.M. on June 30, 1908 over Tunguska, Russia? (Alien technology gone askew… or did a meteorite detonate above the ground, laying 32 square kilometres of forest flat?) And whose face was that on the Shroud of Turin? (Jesus' or merely what people wanted to see?) Whatever became of Amelia Earhart after her fateful flight in 1937? (A strong activist for woman's rights, who disappeared while circumnavigating the Earth, did she die? Or did she live her life out in America as an unknown?) And what was at the bottom of an entire crew's disappearance on the seaworthy American brigantine *The Mary Celeste* in 1872? (One theory had exploding barrels of denatured alcohol forcing Captain Benjamin Briggs to send his men, his wife, and his young daughter scrambling overboard. But others claimed mysterious interventions precluded them from ever arriving at their destination in Italy.)

Despite these conundrums, life went on, and people were happy in their knowledge…

∽

In another dimension, the message, surely struck by the hand of Death Itself—

00:01

—continued beating like a malevolent heart. Only instead of pumping blood, it propelled the ultimate extinction of mankind throughout the universe.

For some tens of thousands of years, untold Earths, and the lives that they had supported, had been lost to this other dimension.

The message reinforced its desire to feed without cessation.

And while the human toll mounted, the madness within it strengthened.

BROKEN CHINA

~~~

Wednesday, March 9, 2022

> *In a place far over the rainbow*
> *The Boogaloo is out of sight*
> *In a place far over the rainbow*
> *Everyone's lost in a lullaby...*

Yet another stirring within this lull of some twelve years started with a rip-roaring smash 'em up demolition derby at Number 47 Gordon Street, Surrey Downs, England. It was generally a quiet suburb of megalomaniacs and stockbrokers, as if there was a difference. And one demented lady.

Exposed like a mutant light globe with one enormous crack through the centre, her fanny hung from the toilet's ceiling, her nightie providing a flannelette shade. Tighter and tighter the flesh compressed, squeezing through the plasterboard, her cheeks dimpling heavily with an overabundance of cellulite. Her face, pinched within the roof cavity, looked not dissimilar to a death mask. It glowed with the light of the balloon-things attached to every part of her torso and arms. Several festooned her head as if she'd taken to wearing some sort of outrageous laurel.

But then, for a long time, Ruby Jenkins had been given to doing some crazy shit.

And though Ruby was having a decidedly rough end to the day, these balloons laughed with what might have been mistaken as cruel delight.

A fine mist of white plaster-powder cascaded in disturbed swirls to the toilet floor. Her legs thrashed uselessly, surrounded by the agitated daisies of her nightie. A pair of ten-gallon panties scissored violently around her ankles. Stretching and contorting, they worked free to flutter down and drape over the rim of the toilet bowl, with all the grace of having been deliberately placed there.

Diseased by advancing dementia, the clouds of befuddlement had parted and allowed crystal clear thoughts to shine through for the first time in an age. She saw it all: her life past, her life now, and what was to become of her future.

In that moment of merciless clarity, Ruby hollered while her surroundings of some sixty years literally slipped away. Here she had lain beside her lover and best friend and had worked to raise a family of five, three boys and two girls. Her children had long flown the coop. Five years ago her devoted husband, Horrie, had also flown the coop. Snatched by the insidious hand of prostate cancer, he'd been taken from her forever.

Now, it seemed it was Ruby's turn to do the proverbial flying. Or not so proverbial.

The curtains of dementia pulled tight once more, closing out the last insight into clear thinking.

Her screams echoed dully through the roof cavity, and drifted like ghostly plasma into the starry night.

Amongst the constellations and twinkling, however, there was movement. Not all the stars were still. Some whirled about in packs, like small dogs on the prowl.

Kicking frantically on autopilot, the bare soles of Ruby's feet and somewhat hairy lower legs were pulled up through the ceiling, gradually and with absolute inevitability.

There was no fairytale ending here.

There was only the darkness in which the Boogaloo cast its deadly strum of 00:01.

The house was scattered with ruin, its former décor smashed to smithereens. No room had been spared, but the parlor was where the brunt of this mayhem seemed to have been applied. An antiquated telephone sat on a small table next to the couch, its hand-piece swinging on its cord against the floor's field of flowers.

In the main traffic areas, the design had been worn down to vague representations washed of color, the carpet's nap trodden down over the decades to its hessian weaving.

Surrounding the hand-piece was an explosion of Royal Doulton slivers and an array of shattered and discarded knick-knacks. From its miniature holes, through which voices of the outside world had travelled since the far distant day of instalment—although with decisively lessening frequency over the past few years—an emptiness stole into the darkness. It nourished the brooding atmosphere, pervading the house's deepest recesses.

Not a thing stirred.

Then, like a candle burning black, a Royal Doulton cup, having seemingly evaded the destructive swipe of Ruby's straw broom, suddenly cracked in half. It emitted one final delicate *tink* into the parlor before falling silent forevermore.

The balloons pressed suffocatingly around Ruby Jenkins.

Their smooth round bodies squeaked the way balloons rubbed together do. They laughed—unlike any balloon ever did or would ever do—sticking their tiny stretched faces into Ruby's. She was in a mad, mad circus room of mirrors, and everywhere she looked were tiny eyes and tiny noses and tiny mouths, each drawn in crude stick-figure fashion.

And Ruby Jenkins was heating up. By God, she was on fire.

Her screams snuffled amongst the mad ones attached to her, layer upon layer. For a ninety-year-old who had lost her mind, she still sported a good set of bellows. Her false teeth clattered in the cavity of her mouth like reeds in a wind instrument, the vibration of the mad ones' smooth bodies like mosquitoes on the wing.

But, as it always was when the mad ones came calling, the fight was wasted effort.

Currently on Black Eternity Flight of No Return, Ruby Jenkins slipped through the terrazzo tiles of her roof, like Casper the Friendly Ghost, and rose higher and higher above the skyline of Surrey Downs, until she was a speck against the constellation of Cancer. Further out in the cosmos, a shooting star streaked across the velvety landscape, parting a hunting pack of star-dogs.

At some point in the flurry and bluster, Ruby stopped screaming herself hoarse and began laughing. This, too, was as it always was when those dinky little bastards from another dimension took a fancy that they couldn't control. Her false teeth flew out, smacking a mad one square on, creating a tiny puncture in its rubbery skin. It started making a noise, as one might do after a night on raw onion, and Ruby could see its mean little face fold in on itself. Suddenly she got the joke, and starting farting herself, the pressure of laughter building up inside faster than she could release it. Tooting her way through the atmosphere's upper layers, Ruby was like a rocket with a dodgy power booster.

Laugh? She hadn't laughed like this since Methuselah was in diapers!

Oops! Did I just wet my panties? Oh, hang about—I'm not wearing any panties!

They had been left behind on the toilet rim in Surrey Downs, where they finally slipped from the rim and bundled up on the large tiles below.

Something jabbered momentarily through the tiny holes in the phone's receiver lying on the living room floor.

At the third stroke, the time will be twelve… twelve o-one A.M.…
Beep! Beep! Beep!

It then stopped.

Further along the hallway, standing at one of its doors, was a diminutive creature. It appeared to be a dwarf harlequin, a jester of medieval times, Its body silhouetted in the mutely lit darkness. It wore a three-pinnacled hat, one pointing to either side, another directly atop like an upside-down ice cream cone. At each tip was a tiny bell. On Its feet were ridiculously long shoes, curled at the toes. They too terminated in a bell.

Whatever this creature was, It appeared stunned.

The woman couldn't be snared in her dream. She was different. Her mind was different. This, of course, It had witnessed before, on countless occasions stretching impossibly far into the past.

With a suddenness of microseconds, It darted into the darkness, Its shoes and hat tinkling as It went, becoming fainter... ever fainter... finally fading altogether...

From its sixty-watt globe, the toilet cast feeble light into the oppressive solidarity of shadows. And besides the steady metronome of a clock somewhere in the house, Number 47 Gordon Street, after some sixty years, became deathly quiet.

Sometime in the year 2022

One hand turned an unfriendly card.

Though portraying every characteristic of human appearance, the being to whom the hand belonged was alien through and through. And it was here for one purpose: to guide this Earth to its annihilation, just as multiple Earths before it had been guided to theirs by others of his kind.

"Seems I hold all the aces," one Dark Suit commented brashly to the other four, seated stoically at the table.

Two fluoros burned overhead. The room lacked windows. And on a bad day, it had been fancied that one could actually feel the distant furnace of Earth's magma core seeping through its walls. This room wasn't merely underground; it was buried to the fathoms, using what had been the best of their modern technology.

They had been on this Earth for a very long time.

The oldest of the Dark Suits replied in cold, calculating tones, "If I thought you were trying one on me, Jimmy my boy, I would get to thinking that the mission doesn't need your involvement. Two empty chairs already reside amongst us; it would be a pity if I were forced to make it a third."

Jim Gillespie, not knowing when to throw his hand, leaned across the table to his poker-playing comrade. "That a threat?"

"Yes, Jimmy my boy, that *is* a threat."

Jim Gillespie asked no more questions. He sized the Elder up and hesitated, a darkly sparkling gleam in his eyes, and then sat back in his chair once more. "The sooner this planet's screwed, the better. Lessens the competition."

"The storm is on the rise again," the Elder said again in that calculating tone. "Temperatures are steadily increasing. Disappearances are escalating. Such things may have reasonable explanations which work in our favor. Whilst chronological disturbances have yet to be detected, communication networks globally have begun experiencing interference. This is merely the beginning of a resurgence. We must ensure success—unlike before."

What these beings didn't know of Black Eternity couldn't be corrected. What they knew, no other did. They had been around a bit, and then a bit longer than that.

However—and as often occurs in cases of unrestrained passion—there had been a great many losses amongst the Dark Suits, corresponding with past Earths lost to Black Eternity. But enough had survived throughout the millennia. A band of renegades, their knowledge had gradually accumulated from information communicated back and forth to their supporters on Anphilian 4, but it had been over a decade since this group had last received an update. Seemed they had been playing solitaire, even though the game suggested poker.

Amplified by the proximity to the magma core, attempts to communicate continued unabated nonetheless. Did it matter that they seemed to have been excommunicated, left in the dark, even by those who shared their cause? No.

Stranded, strength came via trust in themselves and each other. Besides, Anphilian 4 had long renounced the Dark Suits' ambition; this group knew as much. But the cause would never be allowed to die, unlike those in this buried room. They were expendable, as they had always been.

And so, like a captain and his crew on a sinking vessel, this group of happy assholes were all prepared to go down for their glorious—if ultimately ill-conceived—cause.

Jim Gillespie's breathing had quickened. "The problem should have been eliminated years ago. The likes of Raoul would not have mattered."

"To what cause?" the Elder asked, his tone winter ice.

This seemed to flummox Jim Gillespie for a moment. "Avoid this… this mess."

"You have a short memory, Jimmy my boy. So let me remind you, as you seem to need such, due to that dull wit of a brain. We are few amongst an entire race, and quite impotent if discovered. We act *only* when it serves to strengthen the end result."

"We should eliminate *all* possibilities *now*, not just that fucker Raoul."

"He was never part of the core group," another spoke up, flashing a look at the Elder.

"I knew Raoul." The Elder's hands remained clasped on the table, his cards lying face-down beneath them. "He possessed all the characteristics to make it into the core. His heart was in the right place."

"Like the infidel Reynell," Jim said with unbridled sarcasm.

"That may have been so in the beginning."

The Elder shot him a glare, a disdainful twist to his mouth.

"You just can't tell who to trust." Jim was pushing his luck again, feigning remorse. "It's a pity when it comes to this."

The Elder continued glaring.

"Raoul *must* be taken out of the picture—the sooner, the better. And while I'm at it, I can see to the others."

"You, Jimmy my boy, will do *no* such thing!" The Elder stood, his body a rigid silhouette amongst the fluoro light. "I strongly suggest you do *only* what *I* have ordered."

Jim rose from his seat, wearing a shit-eating smirk. His teeth gleamed in the light from overhead. He went to leave.

"But..." The Elder's cold calculating tone was as dire as the approaching storm. "You'll be accompanied by Raditch."

"Under the circumstances, I thought I'd be working alone."

"You know our policy."

"I'm more than capable of accomplishing this alone."

"I don't trust you."

Jim lost his smirk.

"Raditch, you *will* oversee this mission," the Elder said without taking his eyes from Gillespie. "You *will* do only what I have ordered. Nothing more."

Deciding whether to advise the Elder how best to fuck himself, Jim Gillespie quietly exited the room, leaving a decidedly malevolent air in his wake.

∽

Whilst the hour struck 10:00 P.M. across Surrey Downs, England, and madness came to play, such matters went unknown, here or anywhere else.

Some eleven hours earlier, halfway across the world ...

A young boy sizzled along the sidewalk of Chasing Boulevard, California, over the wheels of his *Astra-Links*, the finest skateboard and the one to own since 2020. He was 'in the zone' and blissfully unaware that life as he knew it was protected by the cosmological equivalent of Cling Wrap: *It seals in the freshness… keeps consumables fresher for longer…*

His shoulder-length blonde hair, having turned a light-brown with sweat, agitated against his scalp. He was no longer a kid on wheels, but an eagle effortlessly gliding above the sunbathed network of Corona's sidewalks.

Though on his way to Leon's, who lived no more than a hop down Chasing Boulevard, he'd opted for an extremely convoluted route by heading south rather than north.

The nightmare, the same that had plagued him for months, had been successfully relegated to a manageable thread in the usual fabric of life. No biggie. He had a handle on it.

Until next time. No—scrub that thought. There was no room for the blues. Not now.

His feet had left the ground, the eastern sun was bright, and the air sat at 36^0 C (97^0 F). It was slightly hotter than usual; but California, in his qualified opinion, was the best place in the world to live.

There was one other ray of brightness: it was 'Staff Development Day' at Citrus Hills Elementary. Frankly, Joshua didn't give a damn about staff development. Except, had anyone bothered asking for his suggestion, he'd have openly confessed that Citrus Hills staff required a lot of development; say—and this was just a guess—once every second day.

Giggling, he stuck his arms out to either side. The air against his body was bliss. His senses were tingling, making him giddy with excitement.

Today was a 'Joshua Triplow Special,' and he was determined not to let it slip through his fingers.

Being your typical morning person, he'd wasted not a second in hoisting his legs from under the sheets and getting the day's proceedings underway. Besides, anything to do with bed just of late struck an unpleasant chord within.

Secretively, because he'd never admit this to his folks, fearing they'd think him utterly loopy, he'd become scared of going to bed. It had started months ago with an odd sensation deep in his stomach, the kind of thing that had made him feel squeamish, yet with little effort had been packaged up and readily discarded. However, this was no common garden-variety McDonald's wrapper, as it came with festering spite. And it was this spite that'd gradually become harder to remove as the weeks had passed by.

The simple act of saying 'goodnight' had become a difficult challenge, one that had built with dark intent. His stomach would begin to churn with a pit of rattlers writhing and hissing on his way upstairs. The nearer he got to his room, the angrier they would become, ready to strike and inject their fangs deep into his flesh or whatever plump and juicy organ might get in their way… often his testicles. They'd begin to ache and go north, despite the rattlers residing there.

Sometimes—not always, but sometimes—the ache would be so bad, he'd perform a self-examination in the bathroom, fearing but not believing for a moment he had the dreaded C.

Having heard all there was to know on the subject of cancer in the schoolyard, he'd arrived at the firm conclusion that any strange lump in the body signalled *DEATH*. But what scared him the most when forced to self-examine was what he'd do *if* a lump was found. Would he do the smart thing and tell his folks? Would he wait a while and see if the lump went away? Would he stew in fear but say nothing, because the sheer embarrassment of telling his folks of a lump on one of his balls had the potential to kill him instead?

Joshua shook his head to rid himself of these unpleasantries, muttering, "Joshua, this is *your* day. Don't be an *asshole*."

He sizzled into Cresta Verde Drive, the little wheels of his *Astra-Links* biting merrily away at the cement sidewalk. It had a steep descent. At its summit, he took a moment, as he always did, before taking it at breakneck speed for that sensation of total liberation. He was once more yearning that adrenalin rush... wanting to soar even higher against the sky's sea of blue, sending his tingling nerves to the moon.

Regardless of his addiction, or maybe in honor of it, Joshua Triplow was a sensible boy, perhaps best described as 'the kid next door.' Besides having a natural flare for strategies, he wasn't particularly outstanding at anything. He was no mathematical whiz kid. He didn't read ten books a day and then recite them verbatim at will. He didn't play a musical instrument with the genius flare of a modern-day Beethoven—though who the fuck would want to?—while dancing on one leg. Though vulnerable to neither the persuasions nor dissuasions of his peers, he fit in with groups of all ages and was well-liked. If his friends had been asked to recall an incident of him having become involved in a fight, they'd have been left scratching their temples before the inevitable shrug of the shoulders and blank expressions.

His mother, Susan Triplow, however, would've confessed— without the hysterics of a mother wishing her son to aspire to higher standards—that he lived in Adidas and New Balance sportswear, while rarely out of his Nike trainers.

Occasionally, she would remark on this. But a remark was all it had ever been. Nothing else.

Standing at Cresta Verde Drive's summit, crash helmet swinging gently in his right hand in a mild breeze, Joshua prepared for the ride of his life. And, of course, it paid to protect your assets when planning to travel at hyper-speed. Well, at least one of them, anyway.

Joshua shoved the helmet on. He took a few deep breaths, steadied himself, and then kicked off.

What a rush!

⌒◦

At about twenty past ten, some twenty minutes after leaving home, he finally arrived at Leon's, just six houses down Chasing Boulevard.

Leon's mom, Marlene Mendoza, answered the door and said, "Hello, Josh."

"Hi, Mrs. Mendoza." Joshua's helmet had been relegated to his right hand once more.

"Already been on the board?" she commented with a pleasant grin. She called upstairs and her son immediately took to them, trampling down like he'd been called to his first meal in days.

"Howdy, Josh! Whatcha up to?" Leonardo Mendoza asked brightly, coming up to his mom's side. Although, at once, it was quite evident what he'd been up to.

His friend was slightly red in the cheeks, excitedly bright-eyed and presenting the suggestion that he had built up a sweat that had recently evaporated like the last drops from a salt lake. His arms, legs and face glowed with a slight sheen.

"Cresta Verde Drive, huh?" Leon remarked before Joshua could open his mouth. "Why didn't you come and get me? We could've gone hyper together!"

"Well, I'll leave you two boys to it," Marlene said, walking off.

"Okay, mom."

Both boys' parents had long held the conviction of them being joined at the hip, though Joshua's folks were one hundred percent Australian and Leon's a mix of both French (albeit distant) and Hispanic (or so it was unquestioningly believed).

Being the descendant of an ethnically diverse background had its distinct advantages: Leonardo, better known as Leon, sported the jet black silky hair of his father, upon a refined framework compliments of his mother. His large dark brown eyes, parted by a slender nose, shone from an unmistakably European complexion of light milk chocolate. His love for outdoor activities supplemented this natural color with a daily dose of Vitamin D.

Joshua stared apologetically at his friend. "Sorry."

Leon shrugged. "Don't sweat it."

"I needed to get my head right, so I kinda wanted to be by myself this morning. Promise I'll come and get you next time."

"Bullshit."

"I heard that!" Leon's mom sung out in the background.

Leon pretended not to hear.

"Bad dream again?" he asked under his breath.

"Uh-huh," Joshua nodded.

"Me, too."

Joshua took in a long deep breath. *This was his day, goddamnit!* "Come on!"

"Where to?"

"Chasing. Or the park?"

"Park!" Leon burst forth, rushing back upstairs to get his board. "Shall we give Sammy a buzz? What about Ethan and Craig?" he yelled as he went.

"Why not?" Joshua said with some reluctance.

"What's up?" Leon frowned down the stairwell.

"Just make it Sammy. It'll take too long to hustle the other guys… by the time we do, the day'll be over. I want to get out there." He pointed behind him, leaving nothing to doubt. "It's a really great day, Leon—we don't have school!"

With a laugh and a smile, Leon conceded, "Alright. Sammy it is."

Having gathered his board, and now at the foot of the stairwell, he turned solemnly to his friend, mobile to ear, waiting for the line on the other end to engage, and uttered: "So, how bad was last night?"

Joshua shrugged.

"Same here," Leon had time to say before Sammy answered.

Saturday, April 16, 2022 (five weeks later)

A jet dreamily cruised high overhead, laying a solid fluffy-white contrail against an endless sea of blue, a boat with wings instead of a rudder and flipped upside down, passing stars instead of starfish. Only, Joshua couldn't see the stars because it was daylight, just as you couldn't see starfish when they did whatever it was that they did in the depths.

Maybe they goofed about like the one in SpongeBob SquarePants. It might've been 2022, but some things were amazingly enduring.

Heading for lands unknown, the jet continued on its way, oblivious to Joshua's gaze and the wonderment it filled him with.

Except for the holiday in Malaysia a couple of years ago, he'd never been outside California his entire eleven years. Well, almost eleven; his big day was five months off and approaching fast. He could only imagine what kind of clouds would sketch across the sky wherever that jet was going. Would they represent puppies wagging their tails and hunched down on their forelimbs, ready to play? Or would they represent faces of witches and warlocks and God only knows who or what else? Maybe a man—a strange looking man. A man, dressed all in black, determined to make life a misery.

Joshua had learnt through his sixth-grade teacher, Mrs. Bruckheimer, that people had a habit of wanting to see faces in things when faces were never really there. "It's a human trait to find our own representation in all matter of things," she had said, "from rocks to accidental spills, and particularly clouds. Look up and, at any stage there are clouds in the sky, you'll see faces soon enough. Sometimes not at first, but a slight shift in a certain cloud will reveal all. Of course, we know it's impossible for people to be merrily floating about up there, but our brains will interpret people up there just the same."

A kindly breeze whiffled through his blonde hair on yet another exquisite spring morning. It playfully caressed the fine hairs on his face, arms and legs. Although he didn't quite know what the word "seductive" implied, he sure understood the churn it caused within.

Take your clothes off, Josh. Go on, no one's looking!

Sure thing. And not likely.

In an instant, he put his right foot to the ground and pushed off, the wheels of his *Astra-Links* trundling beneath him. It seemed his skateboard knew where they were going and how to go about getting there, which was a mighty good thing since his head was rather fuzzy. 'In the clouds' was what his mom was apt to say on occasions when he found himself travelling slightly off-kilter with the rest of the world. Like now.

The slow wearing down of his inhibitions was the by-product of a lack of sleep. These days, thanks to the man in black, a full night's sleep with no thrills attached was a rare thing. There was something else, too. Along with the fluttery churn in the pit of his stomach, and the buzzing sensation it had set up in his fingers and other appendages—especially the rude one—was that of 'thick'. It was the best description he could apply to the heavy stuffing that filled his head and ran through his veins like polluted rivers. This morning was no different and since he had arisen, everything had passed by as if he were peering through a sullied window at the changing of tired props in a dingy theatre.

Having hooked up earlier, his best friend in the world was by his side. He had patiently waited while Joshua had taken time out to immerse himself in the jet. He had also got himself moving when Joshua had decided time-out was finished and to continue onto Ethan's. A glance to his right reminded Joshua that he wasn't the only one affected this morning. By the expression hanging on Leon's face, like a wet sheet in still air, he too felt 'thick.'

In fact, upon reflection, most kids he bumped into these days were 'thick.' And what had brought about this plague, like a cold virus doing its annual rounds? The dream, of course. Unlike a cold, however, this epidemic had been gearing up for months; and rather than showing signs of abating, it was gaining momentum.

There was just the one dream... and every kid he knew had patched into it.

The idea this morning was to gather the group at Citrus Community Park and practice the latest and greatest brainchild from one Joshua Triplow.

The *Cha Cha*. This involved the full use of the park's skating ramps, and demanded a complex set of skateboarding manoeuvres: three 360s to the left, followed by three 360s to the right, which was then followed by one jump and three airborne swivels. This required a deep breath and no shortage of bravery, as near-lethal speed was a binding catalyst in the maintenance of a foothold on the board. Not to be outdone, the series was repeated before bringing the show to a close with a sharp 180 slew before an abrupt kick stand.

Adults wouldn't have understood, branding it an act of stupidity. But its gritty edginess was just the way the boys liked it.

The *Cha Cha* was, without exception, the greatest series of skateboarding aerobatics ever to be conceived by mankind. And since it remained unbeatable amongst the boys, it was a sure bet that no one else would ever master it. They had even considered taking the invention to the Guinness Book of Records.

"It runs in the blood," Craig had once said, initiating questioning looks from the rest. "Your dad, Josh: *he's* an inventor," he explained, as if this should've been clearly acknowledged by even the dullest of dopes.

Today, though, there were more spills than jumps, as well as a few bruised egos. The group often resorted to a sudden interest in things totally removed from their fallen friend: an imaginary flying insect, a fascinating fat-assed bee, or something they had spotted stuck to their clothes from the endless bits of fluff people had a habit of finding on such occasions. At one stage,

Craig was struck down by a sudden coughing fit—only he had no need to cough—which necessitated several others patting him on the back, drawing their complete attention.

Somewhere amongst the proceedings, Joshua remarked under his breath that, from a bystander's point of view, the park might've appeared a carpet of green grass and a stand of trees, around which kids meandered like victims in a B-grade zombie flick.

Leon gave him a curious look and remarked, "Sorry, what was that?" Joshua simply shook his head and Leon guessed it wasn't that important.

No one had that Saturday pizzazz. For that matter, no one had that *any* day pizzazz. Everybody seemed drained of zeal, and things seemed to be unfolding in forced fashion. Even the sporadic sounds of laughter appeared forced, like everyone was telling bad jokes to which the audience politely acknowledged.

The 'thick' was rife.

It came to Ethan's turn. He struggled through the first two 360s before losing the plot entirely. He came down with a sickening *umph*, and rather than having the wind knocked from his lungs, it was resoundingly belted from them. He lay on the ground, gasping to catch his next breath for some time, and going horribly red in the face.

This was a serious fall and the boys immediately rushed to his aid. His skateboard hit the cement scoop with a loud *crack* and continued its own unique performance, wheeling and tumbling off towards the grass. He was, arguably, the best skateboarder amongst them, Joshua a close second. But he, like the rest, had a bad case of 'thick.'

And the 'thick' had had its way.

It had been one of those days where nothing had gone to plan and where nothing was obviously going to. The boys considered this bad. Their skateboarding prowess had been considerably affected, so it was only appropriate to call it a day.

$\mathcal{C}\!\!\sim\!\!\mathcal{D}$

The late afternoon's sunlight while heading home was like a fake suntan from a tube. Yet everything amongst it was real enough: the birdsong from surrounding trees and overhead streetlights; the wash of a far-off radio; some dude splashing water over his metallic lover to rinse it of suds; a dog barking, more dogs joining its chorus; a couple of kids Joshua recognized, but didn't personally know, involved in an age-old argument on the opposite sidewalk as to whose turn it was to mow the lawn.

"I did it last weekend, Brody!"

"Uh-uh!"

"Did too!"

"Couldn't have, 'cause I ran over mom's fuchsias, remember?"

Don't do it, kid. You'll run over your foot and chop it off! Joshua was near to delivering this wise admonishment when he shut his mouth. They'd only think him weird if he yelled this out, like an old man sticking his beak in where it didn't belong.

"*Tyson!* It was *you!*" His mother joined the act.

Listening to the skateboard's wheels, and that of Leon's, gnashing at the cement sidewalk and *clacking* rhythmically over the expansion grooves in them, seemed crazily like one continuous extension upon this morning.

But they had arrived at Citrus Community Park, hadn't they? He had gotten off at some point, hadn't he? He had tried on the *Cha Cha* and had helped Ethan up from the ground, hadn't he?

Yes, and—

It was easy to overlook all those things. It was easy to think that none of it had happened, that he had been cruising Corona's streets with Leon all Saturday long, and was only now realizing the fact.

Like those mystical lands wherever the jet had been on its way to, under the faces in the sky, this eclectic arrangement merged into an exotic and near psychedelic mix.

Joshua was too young—and too sensible—to appreciate the cognitive amplification experienced during crazy psychedelic episodes. But like the fashionably rejuvenated hippies of the day (that's right, they made a comeback in 2022, along with beads and long, long hair), he could've described what it was like to be bordering on one. What was more, he could've done so and laid claim to being under the influence of no self-induced substance.

The boys were leaving long shadows on the ground. The sun was even brassier than before.

With the day's all too rapid closing, Joshua began to remember last night. He didn't want to: hours remained before he had to turn in for bed and say goodnight. And it was Saturday, for crying out loud! But there was no stopping the process; this had been a day where everything had been caught in the soupy swill of 'thick.' The overcast of surrealism was tenacious, beginning with a ride on the skateboard, around which things might well have transpired without him ever getting off. He was being driven helplessly to remembering last night and the man in black.

It had been the worst yet, and one of the rare misses of him yelling out in abject night terror. Or maybe he had, but it had somehow gone unheard by his mom and dad.

All the man in black had done—all he had ever done—was sit in his chair, his face in semi-shadow beneath a hood. And besides his furious writing, with equal furious concentration he'd done nothing else, just sitting there surrounded by darkness beneath a single swatch of muted green light. He had somehow lured Joshua in when he had been most vulnerable. Why? Why, when all he did was sit, write and ignore him?

There was one other thing: since the man in black's arrival, everyone's parents had been acting weird. They weren't acting 'thick,' they were just acting stranger than usual for grown-ups. Their behavior suggested a belief system which insisted the man in black stalked the streets of the fantasies that ran between the mouths and minds of their children.

Like a Chinese whisper, the story passed from one to another, its influence gaining strength as it progressed, until they were all jabbering... and imagining... all sorts of wild folklore.

A strange sort of exhaustion now came over Joshua; the 'thick' had taken its toll, the memory only adding to its weight. His limbs moved but he didn't know how. And it seemed the closer he got to home, the harder it was. He shivered despite the balmy spring afternoon, already dreading the word 'goodnight'... dreading sleep.

Both he and Leon trundled along Valencia Road; Chasing Boulevard was just one corner away. Consumed by thoughts of the coming night, and having stopped taking notice of the surrounding suburb, Joshua knew the man in black wasn't done with him yet—not by a long shot. But what he could never have known was the intimacy that he and the man in black would eventually share.

❦

March 2022
Eighty kilometres (fifty miles) south of Los Angeles

Two current truths surrounded Corona's comparatively small community of some one hundred and thirty thousand.

These were recent developments, and had changed the leisurely spirit that had only too recently prevailed.

For starters, those between the age of six and sixteen, therefore implicating some forty percent of the population, had begun acting 'strange.' Many carried their newly-discovered stress as a kind of statement about the new age. Like the resurgence of long hair from the late 1960s, the invention of rock and roll in the late 1950s, and the bikini in the late 1940s, the growing dark crescent moons under the red-rimmed eyes of 2020s youth was cause for mounting consternation.

And damn if those dark moons and red rims didn't alter from one day to the next, from barely visible to a ghastly knock-out shade of purple below bright scrawls of red.

As for seconds, lengthy appointment schedules across every available medical practice had also become a statement of the new age. And the longer this endured, the harder it was to get little Johnny in to see the family doc, which didn't improve the situation. In fact, in some circumstances it was downright belligerent.

Adults had attempted to reason away the cause as nothing more than fanciful thoughts and suggestions. Blame social media for allowing such things to manifest. Once it starts, it's a runaway train. It couldn't be a virus that targeted only the younger ones in the community. Though, viruses could do that, couldn't they? Like the Covid-19 of 2020, and SARS some years before that, pathogens that sought out the feeble, the elderly, those with medical issues, as well as the somewhat rotund. What was more, mainstream media hadn't picked up on this, and usually if there was ever a story, they were on it like hounds. So, it was just a silly little thing that would go away as fast as it had come.

Right?

"Listen, here, missy, I've been seeing Doctor Marcus since before you started using meds, so unless Doctor Marcus would prefer he fuck himself with a ten-foot ramrod, I demand to see him!"

Little Johnny wasn't doing so swell in the greater pastures of life. In fact, little Johnny appeared to have gone Goth… and on the worst days, this reinforced his folks' desperation. The rock-solid shell of parental rationale had started showing signs of fatigue. Such affects were, as always, handled with varying degrees of dexterity. The more colorfully agitated frequently disposed themselves of civilized control, often centred on suggestions of masochistic if not physically impossible actions.

Receptionists in the frontline of battle could have testified to this. And the worth of their position was never more greatly appreciated. However, not all incursions were successfully opposed at the surgery's desk.

Pushed to the precipice of a very dark place on the vitriol from once grateful patients, one doctor had reached his limit.

At 6 P.M. on March 6, 2022, Dr. Marcus left his surgery, never to return to it again. Sixty-seven had come around all too quickly months before, and by rights he should've retired years ago. It wasn't as if finances were the problem. Oh no—it was his seductive mistress, the love affair he had with helping others, which had kept drawing him back year after year. But now it seemed that seductive mistress was bringing litigation against him. She wanted his balls on a plate.

A growing pressure had built inside his head. It had started as a passing headache that a few Tylenol easily dispatched. But over the months, despite anti-inflammatories being swallowed before, during and after work, the pressure had persisted. Worse still, it had started growing fat, its malignant fumes pressing ever harder against his skull, threatening to lift its lid like a Toby jug. On March 6, quite out of the blue, the flare of a match had opened up amongst those fattened fumes.

And so he had stepped from the doors of his surgery and closed them tightly behind him. He had had his secretary close shop earlier than usual, telling patients either that there was a dire emergency elsewhere or, for the less abusive, that the appointment book was overloaded. Sorry, please call back tomorrow, or if this is an emergency call 911. Whatever excuse fitted.

Of course, the situation at the frontlines didn't improve with this, and by the time Dr Marcus' secretary had completed her day's work, she was grateful to be going home herself and leaving the phone well and truly behind. A stiff drink—or perhaps a whole bottle—until the day dissolved into the swills of intoxication.

The good doctor tested the doors' resistance by vigorously jigging them to and fro; not for a few seconds, or a minute, not even three, but for some five minutes. While he had done this, his eyes had taken on a glaze, not unlike that of a dead fish. The doors' rattling protests caught the glances of a couple passing by. They turned, frowned; one paused before noticing she was being left behind. She quickstepped to catch up to her partner, and they continued on their way.

Finally, Doctor Marcus had gone home, where he kissed his wife who barely noticed, engrossed in her favorite TV show, *Deal or No Deal*. He had then turned to a bottle of Kentucky's famous mash, in similar fashion to that of his secretary that same evening.

Sneaking into the quiet solitude of the garage, away from the blare of '*So, with fifty thousand in the bank, what's it going to be? Deal or no deal?*'—Beth was deaf as a post, though she staunchly claimed the contrary—he had proceeded to chug down the bottle's entire contents, spilling not a drop.

This hadn't been conducted in one continuous act, though; rather, one mouthful of warming liquid followed by a couple of sedatives. The dead fish glaze in his eyes, if anything, had become milkier.

With the task completed, and feeling mighty chipper, all things considered, he had picked up a revolver and brought it to his head. With its muzzle pressed firmly to his right temple, making a little dent in the flesh, and squeezing back on the trigger, Doctor Marcus had broken out into a head-splitting smile. *Relief was close at hand!*

The silly bitch didn't take the deal and so lost *ALL* her money. Rather miffed about the stupidity of people, the good doctor's wife had gone in search of him, wanting to tell him that Margery had the flu and there was Beef Stroganoff for dinner. She was also rather curious as to why he had come home early. She wasn't complaining. Just curious. When she finally sauntered into the garage, she noticed all was not as it should've been. For starters, there was a bit of a mess on one of the walls. And for seconds, Marcus was dead to the world in his chair.

She had moved in closer. Why in the hell Marcus was in the garage, gobbling down strawberry jam when he knew dinner would not be long, and making a right mess, she'd never know.

The closer she had gotten, the more evident it became just what a mess Marcus had made. The missing half of his skull was misinterpreted as some kind of Halloween costume, even though Marcus had always resisted the celebration. Furthermore, Halloween was months off!

Then, just when she had been about to wake him, realization promptly came up and landed one meaty fist in the centre of her head.

With every nerve fibre totally jangled, the good doctor's wife had shambled to the phone that sat on a bench across the way. Something entangled around her feet. She lost her balance and went sprawling, her pants pulling up into the crack of her butt. Clutching her chest, she'd tried getting up. And had *almost* succeeded.

Marcus wasn't in celebration mode, was he? Quite the opposite.

Lying on the floor, sucking in one harsh breath after another, the woman to whom the good doctor had been married for some forty-five years had stretched one arm forward to take hold of the phone's base station cord. Her arm was shaking badly. She went to yank on the cord—the blasted thing was slipping right through her hands—when that spiteful pain in her chest ripped across her in one massive swipe of brilliant chrome. Her hand had spasmed while her fingers splayed, jerked and snagged the cord. The base station flew off the bench and smacked her square between the eyes. The phone itself skittered across the floor like a model car without wheels.

From the handset had come a little radio voice, squeaky but precise: *At the third stroke, the time will be twelve... twelve o-one A.M.*

Beep! Beep! Beep!

As events had it: two days transpired before the good doctor and his wife were found. The rest, as is so often the case, was history.

Despite such tragedy, it was fair to say that these were boom times for both psychologists and psychiatrists. Practices throughout Riverside County had been forced to close their books from upwards of three to ten months. This, of course, further inflamed little Johnny's parents. With options coming under increasing pressure, family doctors—those still with the capacity to think, let alone breathe—were scrambling to refer further afield, some suggesting possibilities as far away as Seattle and New York. What about a trip overseas? Finland? They're doing an amazing job in reducing the suicide rate, so why not?

Besides dark eye shadow and red-rimmed eyes, the children of Corona were exhibiting other symptoms Joshua Triplow had so aptly termed 'thick.' The combination was in one way or another derailing the once self-assured community.

"I like to hold discussions on what I call a 'formerly casual basis,'" psychologist Betty Mae was saying. She had the haughty tones of one who had just swallowed a plum that had gone all the way down to her ass.

Sue was less than impressed.

"I realize the oxymoron conveyed," Betty went on, "but the message is clear: *I keep things friendly.* Therefore, within these walls, Christian salutations are muchly preferred." She performed the cardinal sin of any worthy psychologist: breaking eye contact and speaking to the ceiling. When she lowered them, she carried a smile that Sue regarded as pompous, which suited her since it was in keeping with the woman's overall 'plum up the ass' decorum. "As you know, I am Betty Mae and you are Sue and Bob Triplow."

Christ, the woman's a genius, Sue thought, fighting hard to repress a snorting laugh. *Next she'll figure that we are man and woman and that maybe we are not siblings but a couple. Bring out the cheerleaders!*

The woman reached forward and shook their hands. Sue smothered a grimace; her hand felt fat and slimy, similar to handling a freshly caught fish. Whether imagined or not, the urge to wipe her hand down her front was damn near irresistible. "I choose not to have a desk because it is in poor taste to place such barriers between me, the specialist, and you, the unfortunate clients. A coffee table will suffice."

"Are we paying by the minute?" Sue asked.

"Oh, no no. Surely all that kerfuffle was dealt with by Janice, my secretary?"

"It was, but it never hurts to double-check."

Bob shot his wife a vaguely reproachful glance. "I think what my wife—"

"Sue," Betty interjected.

"Sorry?"

"Remember, Christian names only."

"Mm-hmm." Sue offered him an expression of 'that's what you get for kissing ass.'

"We're both concerned for our son, *Joshua*," Bob hastened, fearing another reprimand from Betty Mae. "He began having nightmares... when was it, honey?"

"Sue," Betty interjected once more.

Sue immediately raised her eyebrows and muttered, "Jesus."

"I am sure Bob wasn't referring to one of such immanency." Betty smiled her sweet, utterly infuriating smile.

The conversation stalled momentarily, while Sue decided what she should do about this hopeless situation: Cut their losses and run? Inform the woman that she was a Class A Pompous Bitch... *and* at their expense? But for the sake of diplomacy, Sue picked up the thread. "*Joshua* began having his nightmare late last year, around November."

"That's right." Bob nodded furiously, like a child in class who desperately needs to go to the bathroom. "It started as nothing more than the occasional nightmare, perhaps occurring once a week, and it sort of remained like that until Christmas."

"Sort of?"

"Yeah, you know, if not once a week, perhaps twice, but never twice a week in a row."

"I see." Betty was nodding and Sue doubted whether she saw anything beyond her own self-importance.

Now that they were sitting before the woman, she understood her seemingly miraculous availability and still debated cutting their losses.

"And what did these nightmares involve?"

"No, Betty, we are *telling* you that it is *one* nightmare—Joshua has the same nightmare night after night."

"Okay, Sue, thanks for that. Now, can you tell me what the nightmare consists of?"

"He always wakes in terror, screaming and thrashing about. I mean, he's *truly* terrorized by what he sees."

"Christian names, Sue—else I might become confused as to whom you are speaking of. Using the 'keeping it simple' rule overcomes errors through misinterpretation."

Sue held her forehead. "Oh, Jesus Christ. This isn't helping."

"I speak for us both, Sue and myself," Bob quickly interjected, "when I say we're feeling guilty—as if *we* are somehow responsible for Joshua's nightmare. It's such a hopeless feeling watching someone you love—your child, your *only* child— terrorized by something you can neither see nor do anything about. We awaken in the dead of night and go running to Joshua. It's become something of a routine: consoling him, telling him that everything's going to be all right, when we can't begin to imagine what chases him when alone."

"Then why say things you cannot honor?"

"Because," Sue spat out, her eyes blazing jewel blue, "it's better than saying, 'Gee whiz, honey, too bad for you. How about a hot cocoa?' while your heart's about to leap through your chest." *Stupid bitch!*

Bob thought, *God, what a turn-on!* He had never grown tired of the way her eyes could fire up. He smiled a little, despite the tension in the air.

"I see." Betty Mae's overweight hands were folded together and lounging about in her lap like dead squid.

"What do you see?" Sue asked with exasperation.

"What *do* you understand of Joshua's nightmare?" Betty Mae ignored Sue's heated emotion. "What has Joshua told you of them?"

"It's a man." Bob was quick to intercede again. "That's all Josh can tell us—it's a man in black. And that's the thing, Betty. How do you begin to combat something like that? Something that... vague?"

Betty was searching his face, scrutinizing every inch. Bob shifted in his seat—Christ, he really *did* need the bathroom! "I understand from what you are saying that the repetition has increased. Can you and Sue tell me if anything has changed in your lives?"

They turned to one another and stared into each other's faces, trying to figure if anything had possibly altered in the usual lilt of the Triplow household.

Bob returned his attention to Betty, shaking his head. "Home life is just the same, and Joshua still enjoys the company of his friends and his passion for skateboarding."

"He has *lots* of friends," Sue added, because it seemed somehow necessary. "He's not hiding himself away, not wanting to see others. I mean, when morning comes about, you'd swear everything was normal."

Again Betty ignored her, which really pissed Sue off. "Is Joshua spending increasingly more time out of the house, then?"

"No more than usual," Bob said.

"You regularly attend the PTA?"

"Do you mean the Parent Teacher Association?" Sue inquired. "I'm trying to keep it simple here, Betty. You know, sans the acronyms?"

"Sue and I try to attend every PTA meeting." Bob squirmed again in his seat, thinking, *Shut up, Sue, we need this woman.* "Sometimes I can't because of work commitments. Why do you ask?"

"You can often learn much about what is going on in a child's life through the eyes of a third party. And who better than the child's teacher? After all, it is where they spend a great deal of their time during the week. The teacher, if you like, becomes the surrogate parent."

"I doubt that," Sue said coldly, measuring the woman with a stony gaze.

A smile flickered over Betty's face. "I understand," was all she said before taking a brief pause and shifting her attention to Bob once more. "You mention work commitments, Bob; what are they?"

"I invent things."

"Bob means he's an inventor," Sue interjected sharply. "And sometimes his projects go full steam ahead and become quite consuming with hectic suddenness."

"So things are spasmodic work-wise? How are your reactions when there is a lull?"

Bob shrugged and flashed Sue a look. "I don't think there are too many lulls. But even when there are, I guess I'm the same, aren't I, honey?" He turned to Sue, but before she could answer, Betty said, "These peaks and valleys, do they impact on your attention toward Joshua?"

"No. Not really." Bob was shaking his head. "At least I don't think so."

"I see."

Sue's bright blue jewels became narrow bands behind pinched lids. "Betty, home life is wonderful and the relationship we share with our son"—she purposely left off his name —"is one of love and nurturing and protection. Bob has made us comfortable financially, and his work remains a constant affair."

"What about school grades?"

"That would be Joshua's school grades, would it, Betty?" Sue was unrelenting in her dislike for this Class A Pompous Bitch with a plum up her ass.

"Yes." It was the psychologist's turn to shift in her seat uncomfortably, and Sue took delight in noticing.

"Like home life, his schooling hasn't altered. Joshua still has average to high grades. He's no genius, but then most of us aren't. He's in sixth grade at Citrus Hills Elementary and his teacher, Judy Bruckheimer, reports what teachers in the past have said about Joshua's attitude within the class and regarding his relationships with his classmates: he's well-liked, respectful and a studious worker. One point in particular always shines through, and that's Joshua's ability to think things through. I don't mean in a mathematical sense, more in an intuitive sense." Sue thought through her words for a moment before continuing, "He's an average math student, whereas his problem-solving is a natural talent."

Betty was nodding.

"If there was a problem at school, this would be the first casualty."

Betty was still nodding. "I see."

Sue's eyes had pinched down to slits once again; and while she refrained from verbalizing her dislike for Betty Mae, her mind had less of a concern with diplomacy. *They drilled that* *line into you, didn't they, honey, while you were getting your piece of paper that said you were a qualified Class A Bitch? Remember, if all else fails, use your standard back-up 'I see.' Hasn't failed yet. It doesn't say anything, including the fact that you're stumped and, like a beached whale, you're stranded and fully exposed with nowhere to hide. Yep, **I fucking well see** will be etched into your gravestone, honey.*

"Furthermore, Betty, it'd seem Joshua is amongst a good many children within the Corona district afflicted by this nightmare. The very same nightmare. So unless Bob's work ethic is somehow affecting the entire county, I'd be looking elsewhere, away from home base."

The healthcare professional shrugged this off; but her overall hoity-toity posture, having taken a bit of a battering, slumped satisfyingly further. Next minute, she'd be no more than a blob of fat in her seat. Sue smiled at the image, still bitterly aware they were meant to be here for Josh. Although she didn't hold out much hope.

Bob looked at Sue. Her forehead was in her hands again. "It seems every kid in the area is having the same nightmare," he reiterated, still astounded by the magnitude of the problem and the fact that Betty didn't seem to have a clue. "It seems to be getting worse, Betty. Not *just* with Josh. The adults are being left behind in despair."

"And it is only happening among the children," Betty said rather than asked.

"Yeah..." Bob's tone conveyed his sense of bewilderment.

Betty reached over and pressed the open channel on her intercom.

At the third stroke the time will be—

"Janice?"

—*twelve... twelve o-one A.M.*

"Janice?"

"Sorry, Betty."

"What's going on?"

"Interference..."

"Oh," Betty frowned. *Strange... interference over the intercom. Oh well...* "Would you please bring in three coffees with the usual accoutrements?"

"Be ready in just one minute," came the perfectly miniaturized voice of the secretary, sounding nothing like the interference.

"I take it you both drink coffee?"

The Triplows nodded and said 'yes' concurrently.

Betty folded her pudgy hands in her lap. Her posture opened up, becoming friendlier. "Life has become full of stressors. It is said that today we have never had it so good, but I wonder about those saying this and if they are truly in touch with the vast majority. We are toiling over work commitments, not as our grandfathers and their grandfathers did in the field, but from behind desks under artificial lighting. And we are doing this at a breathtaking pace that our forefathers would have considered insane. For this, we have our fancy cars and our luxurious homes, material objects our grandfathers would have ogled at, amazed at how such things could be afforded. But *everything* comes at a price. With ever-rising expenses and bills, it is a fight to keep these lofty standards that we have set ourselves. Work commitments have to keep up with the ever-increasing pace, and so the first sacrifice is time with the family. After all, the bills will not simply go away; and that latest gizmo, assaulting us from every form of advertising, becomes a must-have on the shopping list. Our ego must be satisfied materialistically, and to hell with family—*human*—values.

"This creates a pressure-cooker environment: increasing hours at work, fewer hours at home, poor sleeping habits, more tablets to keep ourselves going at such a pace. True enough, we each handle these modern stressors in different ways, but often physical abuse, or conversely physical detachment, becomes an insidious mainstay." Betty held up one hand, noticing Sue was on the verge of speaking her mind. And that wouldn't do. Not at all!

"I am not saying the Triplow household experiences either, *but* the wash-off effect of increasing pressures external to the home environment *does* begin to show strains; and cracks begin to appear where solidarity once stood firm."

"That's not fair," Sue managed to interject, her tone ice-brittle and defensive.

"These stress fractures happen, Sue, with such surreptitious cadence, they are often overlooked and therefore extremely difficult for the unaccustomed to notice. Think about it this way. How is it that most of us are better at describing a place we have visited on vacation than we are at describing what resides down the end of the very street in which we live?"

"It's new and we look at things closer when they're new," Sue said off-the-cuff.

"Yes," Betty returned brightly. "When pressed, we can usually cobble together some sort of glancing description of those things constantly around us. But when asked to describe them in detail, things become full of 'ums' and 'ers'... a bit of color here, some detail there, but nothing of complete structure."

Sue lowered her defences. Betty had undergone a sudden transformation: from a hoity-toity Class A Pompous Bitch, full of her own importance and complete with ass plum, to someone actually making sense. The type of sense that sent butterflies aflutter within her stomach, and created an open chest-freezer in her heart.

Bob looked at her, and she at him. They each saw the other's guilt. Were they the kind of people who had become victims of lifestyle? Surely not! Considering their humble background, this seemed outrageously inconceivable.

"There is nothing to be ashamed of here, for either one of you. The trick is in turning around the reactive situation we see in our children. Of course, it will be up to individual families to do this, and the same vicarious options will be available to all. *Replacing* those egotistical behaviors that have slowly invaded our lives will not come easy. It will require positive reinforcement again and again. But the payoff will be a better, more balanced lifestyle. Ask yourself this: Is it really necessary to have a computer and a television set in every room of the house, so the family can do and watch what they want when they want?"

"We don't," Sue corrected.

Betty opened her hands and drew them apart. "An example," she said, "but I think you get the picture. We can easily retain our lifestyle—we have worked hard for it, after all. But must we keep raising the ante? Is that really making us happy, or have we fallen into a trap of having to have for the sake of having to have?"

"What you're saying is that *all* the children are affected by the strains of today's commitments?" Sue asked reasonably, yet not convinced that this was the answer.

"Yes."

"And this is causing them to have this nightmare of a man in black?"

"Sue, when stressed, and maybe even depressed, we almost inevitably carry our disturbances into our hours of sleep. We can pretend to switch off, but the mechanisms inside us have their own will, and they will not be dictated to. This leads to all sorts of behavioral turmoil: withdrawing from the world and going deeper within ourselves, tossing and turning and calling out in our sleep. And, of course, nightmares are merely common symptoms."

Bob and Sue exchanged a painful glance—memories had opened within them of a past which thrived on such a beast. When torment and torture had twisted and torn through Bob night after predictable night, cutting and pulling at the fabric of his mind with its endless thorns. Thankfully they were long in the past, and sleep had been a relatively contented affair ever since. But the memories were still all too vivid when resurrected.

"As adults, we have the ability to *think* through the stressors and apply our knowledge of worldly experiences, whatever is necessary, to eliminate or modify them, so that at least we can live with them." Betty laughed a little. "This, however, even for us, does not always succeed. Children, on the other hand, have little of this at their disposal. They're raw and vulnerable to such incursions, relying on adults to provide the greater part of their world, to make it safe and predictable. Parents are crucial in this role. When they see their world as not being safe or predictable, they begin to experience the *rawness* of their vulnerability.

"While lacking worldly experiences, they do have one weapon with which they can wield with ruthless efficiency."

There was a knock at the door.

"Cosme in, Janice," Betty said.

A tray with three mugs of coffee, accompanied by a small bowl of sugar and another of cream, was laid on the low table in the middle of the group.

"Thank you, Janice."

Janice smiled and exited the room without exchanging a word.

"Please, help yourselves."

There was a slight pause in proceedings, then: "Bob, what do you enjoy, as in hobbies?"

Immediately and with a grin, he replied, "Fishing."

"I see. And how do you go fishing: on the shore or in a boat?"

"Boat." He felt the urge to add 'with a rod and reel,' but thought better of it.

"I see. You obviously derive a lot of satisfaction from fishing?"

It was Sue's turn to grin. "Half our garage is full of the latest and greatest stuff meant to catch the biggest fish of this or that kind. I can tell you, none of it works."

Betty laughed. "Does Joshua enjoy fishing, too?"

"Try keeping him away," Sue said.

"And you?"

"Sure—it's a great getaway from it all."

Betty nodded and took a sip from her mug. "When was the last time you all went fishing as a family?"

Bob and Sue exchanged yet another glance. Bob wore a distinct expression of guilt and went a shade of red.

"You understand that Joshua has not been fishing as much as he is now," Betty said. "His intended catch, however, is not some pelagic denizen of blue waters. This sudden exploitation applies to almost all the children we see afflicted with this nightmare of the mysterious 'man in black.'

"I have seen my share of parents and children because of this nightmare. If I remember correctly, it began roughly halfway through last year; before then, not a single case of the like had presented itself. Regardless of when it started, it did so with the sudden rush of a dam wall exploding apart. This nightmare has run rampant among the younger generation, sweeping up all who stood in its path and carrying them away.

"Mass hysteria, perhaps. What one sees or feels, what one experiences, gradually leaks out amongst their peers… starting as a trickle and fast gaining momentum, until it becomes an explosive tide." Betty laughed softly, knowingly. "Look to the sky and point excitedly, *wildly*, at what you conceive to be a UFO. Sure enough, others will start doing the same. In some factual accounts, this becomes overwhelming within small clustered areas, and before anyone knows the difference, there are UFOs stalking the skies. In this case, it is not due to UFOs, but a mysterious 'man in black.'

"If the marketing machine ever figured out that one specific catalyst, we would all be in trouble. They try and often succeed, but not to such a blanketing effect. What is being advertised here in Corona cannot be found between the glossy pages of a magazine, but rather from word of mouth. Maybe there are visible trails of what led to the outbreak in email inboxes and Sent Items folders. This would be something worth exploring. But the culprit—the cause behind that great explosion—is a lack of attention from the adults who are meant to ensure that their children's lives are safe and predictable."

Sue took a sip of her black coffee, having foregone both sugar and cream in her usual manner. "But we don't ignore Joshua," she said, shaking her head.

"Not intentionally," Betty returned. "But one of the most important family activities, one which you all enjoy, has suffered. The sudden outbreak of this nightmare is no mystery. As one child began performing their 'man in black' nightmare, with success came notoriety. And so the habit grew. Shrewd viral marketing at its best."

"So what you're saying, Betty, is that this is nothing more than a phase? That the children will eventually lose interest in the man in black?" Sue was genuinely intrigued, if still not convinced.

"Attention-seeking is an old trick, Sue. We all know it well, for we used to employ it to manipulate *our* parents. In fact, some pretentious adults still do. Why is it that this nightmare seems contained within the demographics of Corona? We hear of it nowhere else. Had this been a phenomenon of a larger scale, media empires would have sent their scouts swarming all over it.

"But we do not need them to tell us that this *is* serious business. It has identified us adults as failing in our duties. Joshua is desperately reaching out to you both for your attention... or more of it. Should you give him this, the 'man in black' will fade into the background and soon become unnecessary, a thing of the past."

"So we need to go fishing more often?" Bob asked brightly.

"Not necessarily." Betty took a sip of coffee. "Most likely all that is required is more family time, sitting down with each other and simply enjoying each other's company."

"We watch *The Twilight Zone* together," Bob returned.

Betty frowned. "Preferably *not* in front of the television."

Sue dug amongst her thoughts and was embarrassed to find that excepting mealtimes, Joshua was usually off doing his thing while she and Bob were off doing theirs. Her lowered gaze said more than words could have.

Betty nodded. "For the greater majority, these children do not outrightly recognize the causes behind their distress. When asked, they give all sorts of vague explanations and invariably return to the mysterious 'man in black' of their nightmares. For all I have sat with over the past months, there seems no common thread in their answers, except for the 'man in black'. It is exactly the same as saying 'The boogieman is after them at night. Watch out for the boogieman because if you don't *he'll* get you'. They know this will get them the attention they so desperately seek… and it is something they know cannot be proven or dealt with directly on a physical level. They know this, but do not recognize it for what it is."

Betty took another sip of coffee. "A man in black is *not* stalking the subconscious minds of our children. Such an event would not merely border on the supernatural, but truly enter deep into its realm. Reality—and, more to the point, human predispositions—dictates that once a child has tasted success, others will follow suit. It may sound ham-fisted, but Corona's children are making purchases on love. Show your son a little extra attention over the following weeks, and see how that impacts on his nocturnal state of mind. I think you will be pleasantly surprised."

That night, with both bedside lamps burning, Bob and Sue sat beneath their comforter and discussed Betty's theory. Of course, it might've been expected that they did this on the way home from her practice, or before Josh came home from school. They hadn't; each lost in their own thoughts… some of them not altogether flattering. Amongst this species was their status as 'Worthy Parents.' How good were they on the job?

"I don't believe for one second we ignore Josh, Sue," Bob was now saying, "but I *do* break my promise of fishing more often than I care to admit."

"Honey." Sue propped herself over on one elbow and started stroking his arm. "You've got your work, and if a prospective buyer is interested in what you have to offer, it'd be pretty unprofessional to make them wait."

"Yes, but I think that's what Betty was trying to convey."

"Good for Betty; but, not to put too fine a point on it, I *like* eating. And who's Betty to talk, sitting on five hundred dollars an hour? It's easy for her to say not to worry about having for the sake of having."

"We *could* do with less."

"We *have* done with less, Bob. We've done it bloody tough! And I'm not sure about you, but I for one don't want to return to those dark times, and neither would Josh."

"*Denizens of the deep.*" Bob put on a grave Betty Mae inflection and shook a fishing encyclopaedia in his hands.

Sue laughed. "What? *You?* Try undersized whitebait!"

"Hey, not fair! Last time we came home with a haul of—" He thumbed through several pages within the index section, stopped and proclaimed, "A haul of *Sphyraena argentea*, or what you plebes refer to as 'barracuda.'" Having assumed the rarefied air of Betty Mae, he went on to say, "I feel confident of a large haul of—" He thumbed some more. "—*Paralichthys californicus*, or what you mouthbreathers might know as—"

Sue snatched the *Popular Fishes and Destinations of California* from him.

"I was reading that!"

"Halibut! Huh!" she scoffed, giggling. "How about a tiny haul of *Engraulis mordax*? Being the expert you are, I have no doubt that informing you of this scientific reference's common name is entirely irrelevant. Diddums won't have an ounce of trouble correctly identifying de wittle fishy-wishy."

"Hammerhead shark," Bob uttered with a sideways glance.

Sue shook her head, giggling harder.

"Plesiosaurus?"

"Try anchovy, Einstein." Her giggling burst into laughter, the type that made the bed jiggle.

This got Bob going, and, for a while they were both laughing hard. They needed some medicine, and this was good medicine. A kind of release valve.

Eventually, the laughter ebbed and talk between them seemed to have dried up.

The night was almost unnaturally still; not a sound could be heard. Listening to this nothingness set up a miniature orchestra in their ears, and the ringing could've almost been maddening if concentrated on.

Having reclaimed his encyclopaedia, Bob flicked through the pages with no real intention of reading its contents.

Sue shifted her eyes to the expansive bedroom window. Though streetlights burned along Chasing Boulevard, the darkness seemed to swallow it, leaving the window a square patch despondency. A wave of gooseflesh passed over her, and she shivered.

"Josh loves his fishing, Sue," Bob said finally, giving her a start.

"Sorry, honey?"

"I haven't allowed that to happen as much as I should've. And, honestly, what would the harm be in telling my clients that I'm taking my family out for a day or two, and that they'll have to wait until I return? I'm sure the Malcolm Edwards CEOs of the world could wait forty-eight hours. And if they can't, then there really is something wrong in the way we regard family bonds. It's how Betty said: we're losing our perspective on a balanced life in the chase for living standards. Everybody wants; nobody wants to give."

"So we need a plan."

They began figuring out how best to divide their days, so the Triplow family could enjoy extra quality togetherness. Much to Bob's disappointment, though, it was soon evident that making fishing a priority was fine in theory but a pain in the ass otherwise. "Not much point having a boat, is there?" he said dejectedly at one point.

"Oh, stuff it!" Sue said with a cheeky grin. "Let's buy a bigger boat and live on the high seas. You can be Captain Bligh and I your Girl Friday, and together we can navigate the world."

"I think you're mixing your tales." Bob lowered his eyes.

"Party pooper."

The biggest culprit against the planning was that the Triplow family *did* enjoy possibly more time together than either Sue or Bob had given credit to. Into the mix was their so-called attention-seeking son. Whilst a loving boy, Joshua's unflagging desire to meet with friends at any given opportunity for skateboarding took precedence over almost all other matter of things, either along Chasing Boulevard (when time was squeezed and a fast solution mandatory) or at the Citrus Community Park (when a sense of indulgence held sway).

The bedside lamps burned into the wee hours of morning. The only conclusion drawn from their endeavors was that there probably wasn't much to be salvaged from Betty Mae's suggestion.

Then Sue said, "Bob, does this remind you of 'before?'"

"What?"

"Adelaide... the heatwave... people losing the plot. I mean, there are similarities that seem to be getting stronger."

Bob fiddled with his glasses, saying, "Oh, hon, no, this is *nothing* like 'that' time. Besides, you're forgetting that Covid has left people a little raw. Is it any wonder people are acting the way they are, what with the kids behaving a little... odd?"

Sue was unnerved not by what Bob said but what he had done. He hadn't fiddled with his glasses in a very long while. How long? Well, she honestly couldn't remember. He was anxious and that was evident. So whilst he was saying one thing, he was thinking something very different, and the connotation she had raised was certainly not lost on him.

Long after Sue had turned her light out, Bob lay awake, still mulling over what had been spoken about that day, and if there was something—*anything*—in the idea of Corona having produced a generation of emotionally stricken and deprived children. Whilst he believed Betty Mae's theory had credit, there was something that didn't sit right in him.

And what about what Sue had thrust upon him?

Surely it can't be happening again.

He stared down at his best friend in the world. The woman who had gone to hell and back with him. Her long shiny brunette hair swam seductively around her shoulders, even in her hours of sleep.

He pushed his glasses around the bridge of his nose, then stuck a finger behind them to rub his right eye.

He sighed deeply, ruefully, turned over, placed his glasses on the side table, and switched his bedside lamp off, although sleep was hard to track down. He stared into the streetlit darkness of their bedroom, wondering… dismissing… desperate not to allow such thoughts the impetus to grow and become more than an offhanded suggestion.

But what Sue had instigated—my, it was tantalizing. Like how picking at a sore and digging ever deeper, until it became an abscess, might start out as tantalizing.

So Bob crept about, looking for that cloister hidden far, far away from the usual trappings of life.

Oh, and there it was.

He reached forward, turned the dull brass knob. No locks here. The door swung open and revealed the gruesome details and indecencies from that apocalyptic past of 2011. They remained in full swing within the confines of this room.

Once normal people, living their normal lives, going about their normal business, had deteriorated into the swills of madness, the heatwave soaking amongst the dendrites of their minds and destroying all rationale.

Funny thing was—although there was nothing funny about it—this had taken place only within the borders of South Australia, Australia.

The state had become an asylum for the insane.

Terrible acts had been committed. Emergency services were stretched until they disintegrated. Even those who had supposedly been there to help you, might have just slit your throat in a fit of lunacy.

The lucky ones had escaped or died. And when you boiled it all the way down, it was just the same.

What a time. What a time to forget.

Bob pulled away from these visions.

The door closed.

Best not to venture here again. There was no prospering to be found in such travels.

Deep into REM sleep, Sue's mind was ablaze with both vivid and psychedelic animations of her own, although it had nothing to do with the realities of the past. Whether it was her background in law coming to the fore or not, she couldn't quite tell. However, she was beginning to think that perhaps something had polluted the air or water of Corona. Okay, so it wasn't a heatwave, but the smaller bodies of the children were unable to cope with whatever the contagion was. This would explain why the adults were unaffected by visions of a man in black.

She unconsciously pulled the comforter around her chin, though the night was mild.

Her subconscious was playing with the facts, as the subconscious was prone to do. Taking a movie she'd once seen and meddling with it, so whilst recognizable, it was different. In this version was a kid called Joshua Triplow, and he was surrounded by townsfolks. And they were all becoming gravely ill except for him. Their bodies distorted with huge festering pustules, blood erupting from their mouths and noses in the latter stages of the disease.

People were losing their humanity, turning into raving lunatics, making them mutilate themselves and others.

The cause was in the water… in the water…!

DON'T DRINK THE WATER, JOSH! Sue heard herself shout, her voice coming from a very long way down some unforeseen tunnel. *DON'T DRINK THE WATER...* The more she shouted, the coarser her voice became. Now it wasn't just sickeningly echoey; it had the timbre of gravel, pulverized deep underground.

Her son, who'd once loved skateboarding with his friends, was increasingly swamped by the gross acts of insanity and disfigurement.

His friends were either dead or dying. His parents had gone insane with the disease, their faces distorted beneath the volcanic ruptures squirting unmentionable fluids.

DRINK THE WATER, HONEY! Her voice was now inhuman. *BECOME ONE OF US! DRINK THE WATER, YOU LITTLE BASTARD, OR MUMMY WILL RAM IT DOWN YA THROAT!*

Sue awoke with a start. Pulling in a harsh breath, she felt both giddy and somewhat nauseous.

Slipping from under the comforter, she went to check on her son.

In the light of morning, while mashing over toast and Vegemite, she remembered the nightmare and finally identified the movie from which it had been constructed.

The Curse must have hit the screens some four decades before. Perhaps earlier. Of course, she wasn't *that* old, having seen it some years after its release. A kid called Wil Wheaton had played the part her mind had bestowed upon her son, remaining sane when everyone else was losing their minds.

God, it seemed real—so disturbingly real.

But it was the kids acting strange in this case, not the adults in these here parts of ole Corona, wasn't it, ma'am?

She stared across the breakfast table at her son and wondered where the hell this was all heading.

⌣〜

Rather than abating, Joshua's nightmares had gotten worse. More consistent.

Sue gave up the idea that there was a contagion in the water. Nonetheless, no amount of dividing the days so they could squeeze in extra family quality time was going to overcome whatever was stalking their son in the dark hours of night.

The thrashing and crying out was so disturbingly similar to Bob's past. And, of course, there was the repetition. A near nightly event saw them leaping from bed, running along the upstairs hallway and bursting into Joshua's room to console him; to chase away, the best they could, the terrors of yet another visitation.

Neither Sue nor Bob felt Betty Mae's expertise could provide further assistance. They never contacted her again.

⌣〜

Friday, April 22, 2022

The week ended on as fine a note as it could. Friday afternoon had forced its way through the 'thick.' It had taken some effort, though, like watching each minute amble by, second by ponderous second.

Joshua had had his sights on this day since last Sunday evening, and that seemed an impossibly long time ago…

seemingly forever. School had let out for another week and he and his folks were on their way to see a movie. No reruns of *The Twilight Zone* tonight, as was the usual fare for a Friday evening in the Triplow household.

He and his dad revelled in the mysteries of the unknown. *What was behind that door?* Recorded from earlier episodes screened on Wednesday late evening, they'd sit glued to the TV, their intrigue and fascination never flagging. Sometimes, if it was a really good one, they'd watch the same episode twice in the one night. And if it was really, *really* good, three times!

Sue had mused over this as a potential cause for Josh's nightmares, but swiped it aside as that made no sense, either. Reruns of *The Twilight Zone* could hardly explain how other kids were being affected, unless the entire county of Corona was addicted to the series. If it was some kind of new fad, maybe. But the series was about as old as granny's linen drawer and, therefore, a minor miracle that it still aired.

The sky had toned down to a mellow interlace of grays, oranges and yellows. A few wispy clouds jollied about, adding their white flicks to the evening portrait.

Joshua was staring up from the back seat, his eyes droopy. If he kept busy, he wouldn't fall asleep before they got to the movie. Despite his desperate bid to see a face up there, the clouds were just too tenuous. But somewhere up there *was* a face.

He lurks in the sky. Like Father Christmas, he knows what the children do! He knows if you've been good or bad… and if you've been bad, the jolly fat man would present you with a pencil with which to write!

Joshua blinked rapidly, wondering where such a thought came from.

The man in black!

Bob glanced in his rearview mirror. "Something up, mate?"

It was the nightmare, of course, didn't he know?

No face up there, but surely the man in black blazed down at him, his stare greedy, dark and threatening. In the entire city of Corona, within the entire county of Riverside, he was bothered with none of the other kids this evening but one: a kid currently sitting in the back of his parents' Ford Ranger.

His face was masked, as always, in shadow, the hood flopping around it, but somewhere… in there… from amongst the darkness… *his* stare drilled into Joshua.

Hello, son, watcha doing? Joshua heard as he imagined the face he couldn't see. *Here—take a pencil!*

"Earth to Joshua Triplow!" Bob sung out.

Sue turned around to see her son staring bug-eyed through his window, before gasping at the sound of his father.

His skin had grown cold, as if he had been immersed in ice. His excitement of seeing the latest *Get Smart* movie fell away from him in much the same way ice sheets peeled from the sides of mountainous glaciers.

She frowned. "You okay, honey? You look like you've seen a ghost."

"I'm okay," Joshua mouthed. His lips were numb. *If only you knew, mom,* he thought with bitter sarcasm.

The Ranger's sheet metal had become tissue thin and then some; he was exposed. Worse still: he was *trapped.* He couldn't exactly fling the door open and make a run for it. He could ask his dad to stop, but then what? And if he ducked down below the window seal, it'd make no difference. Those dark bottomless eyes from above could penetrate through things.

Ford's latest breed of off-road vehicles, claiming to return near forty miles to the gallon, growled softly through the intersection of South Main Street and East Grand Boulevard.

Sue gave the sort of laugh that forecast her doubt.

"*Really,* I'm okay!"

Joshua's tiredness was beginning to affect every nuance of his life, and now he was being stalked by his own imagination—the weirdest stalking ever. People went *mad* when that happened, didn't they?

Exhaustion washed backwards and forth like water slopping around in a bucket. He slumped against the seat, wishing his mom would turn around and forget about him. But of course, she was his mother, and it was her duty to be concerned even when it wasn't wanted.

Joshua struggled to keep his eyes open. It was barely seven in the evening and he was ready for bed.

Or not, having come to dread 'goodnight.'

But the pull of sleep was drawing him down into a place where resistance's wall was disassembled brick by brick.

"How's it going back there, mate?" Bob asked, turning the wheel through another intersection.

"I'm not sure whether we should give the movie a miss," Sue said.

"Mom, I *really* want to see Get Smart."

"What do you think?" Bob asked his wife, as if he hadn't heard a word Joshua had said.

"I *want* to see the movie!"

Bob had his own doubts. A glancing appraisal of his son's reflection in the rearview mirror told him Josh could barely keep his peepers open.

"What do *you* think?" Sue rolled the question back to him.

"I don't know—guess it could be good," Bob said, as if on automatic. "It should be funny," he quickly added.

"It'll go till late."

"Yeah, but funny is good."

"What happens if he falls asleep?" Sue asked with a certain amount of gravity.

Joshua's parents stared at each other, thinking roughly the same: *Joshua might very well fall asleep. Then what? Awake, filling the cinema with his screams, gaining looks of horror from those within its walls and wondering what kind of parents they were?*

Joshua stared ahead, rather pissed off at the way his folks had commandeered the conversation. After all, they had started out wanting his opinion, only to suddenly relegate him to some fart in the back seat. His mouth agape, rolling his eyes, he stated very deliberately, "I-want-to-see-the-movie," as if explaining to a couple of imbeciles. *I am NOT a fart!*

"You're *really* up for it?" Bob glanced in the mirror again.

"Jeez, Dad." Ultimate frustration.

I'm okay, you're okay. We're all okay!

Problem was: nothing was okay. In fact, it was getting a whole lot worse.

Get Smart: Controlled Chaos was side-splittingly funny, and Joshua's tiredness and fear of saying 'goodnight' had been rapidly, albeit temporarily, placed on hold. He had, for a while, escaped the trauma of the man in black, laughing on occasions until tears were shed. Agent Maxwell Smart's antics had typically led to victory at day's end. Bumbling secret agent or not, he was the right man for the job. C.H.A.O.S. never stood a chance.

Upon the return trip, amongst heightened emotions and chatter, in which the funnier moments were recalled, the laughter continued but it wasn't the same. Having to be generated between his mom, dad and himself, it demanded more than a passive input.

Joshua's eyelids had returned to drawing down, before he snapped them open with increasing difficulty and often a little jerk of his head.

He had avoided the lure of sleep until now. But the Ranger's momentum was gently rocking him further into the realm of the sandman. His head wobbled upon his shoulders, arms lying dead in his lap.

Joshua looked up blearily and caught his dad spying in the rearview mirror. He snapped alert, pretending there was something in his eyes.

Cars always felt safe: they were fast and powerful, and they could get out of tricky situations. But that feeling of exposure, sitting here in the back seat—*trapped*—had also returned. And he wished he'd been wearing long pants and a long-sleeved shirt to cover up the flesh left visible.

While waiting at traffic lights, Joshua gazed from his window. His neck felt as if it had seized up and was in dire need of lubrication.

A semi-trailer, growling up through its gears, rumbled past in the opposite direction. Scrawled across the aerofoil on its long snout, almost iridescent amongst the bright orange streetlights, was the phrase 'Too much pussy.' 'Too much' was on the passenger's half of the aerofoil, whilst 'pussy' sat before the elevated driver. Joshua could barely make out the man's face in the momentary wash of traffic lights that filled his cabin.

"Too much pussy," he repeated vaguely, casually.

"What?" Sue asked, her voice carrying the blush that had risen in her cheeks.

At ten and a half, Joshua mightn't know all the connotations conveyed by adult talk, but he was far from naive. The message on the aerofoil wasn't the type to be reading aloud in front of one's parents. His eyes ballooned—he was fully awake again—and he bit his bottom lip whilst holding his breath. He didn't say what he thought he had said, did he?

"What's going on there, mate?" Bob peered in the mirror; the stoplight's red splash dusting his face an Indian totem pole.

"That truck—" Joshua honestly didn't have a clue where he was taking this, fully awake but with a head full of 'thick.'

"What about it?"

"I don't know."

Bob began laughing so hard, it took the sound of a frustrated driver's horn behind to alert him to the fact that the light had turned green.

At roughly five past ten, the Ranger pulled into 22 Chasing Boulevard.

Joshua was out less than seven minutes after.

And at 3:30 A.M., another night terror shattered the darkness.

The following Sunday morning

As within the Triplow household, the situation was disintegrating across Corona.

It was in the grip of something bad. Something intangible… something '*out there.*' And worse still, it taunted the adults like a malicious clown might taunt a child. They couldn't allay what they couldn't see, regardless of umpteen trips to doctors and mental/behavioral specialists. Like Betty Mae, none had the answer. But this didn't stop desperate parents from *thinking* they did and flocking to their doors. When it was discovered they didn't, this served to inflame the angst in a population already poised at the fine thread of a tripwire.

Sue and Bob had decided to act on Betty Mae's suggestion, whether it would do much good or not.

And, maybe, it wasn't in the water but in the air. Christ, who knew? But a day's fishing couldn't hurt, could it? Besides, removing themselves from the hotspot gave them solace, a ray of sunshine in an otherwise storm-laden sky.

"Now, mate, what d'ya think ya gonna catch?" Bob asked brightly. The boat was fully loaded and in tow.

"The one that didn't get away," Joshua came back in a flash.

The sun peeking over the horizon was a warming sight, pushing the gray overhang further to the west. Though no more than a twenty-eight, maybe thirty, kilometre trip to Newport Marina, which roughly equated to eighteen miles, Bob had organized an early start to the day, despite miles sounding a lot less arduous than kilometres. Like a true fisherman with the scent of victory in his veins, there was to be no loitering. He meant to be removed from terra firma for most of the day. This didn't pose a problem for Joshua since he was an early riser. Besides, these days, if sleep wasn't a requirement, he'd have cheerfully given it a miss.

As Bob pulled into Newport Marina, the smell of the sea instantly filled their nostrils. The fresh salty odor renewed

Joshua's senses, as it did whenever around the sea. This disinhibiting—if there was such a word—effect filled him with a sense of *que sera sera*. A true unaffected sense of 'I'm okay, you're okay—everything's okay.'

So the man in black popped up unannounced more often than he cared for. Had he ever done anything to him that he could've interpreted as threatening?

No! Not exactly.

Had he spoken to him, using words that carried far more of a message than mere words alone?

No! To be frank, he didn't talk!

Had he ever pulled a knife, a gun, or a nuclear bomb on him? No, *sirree*!

So what's your problem, Joshy-Washy?

Roaring through an intersection in Joshua's mind, changing up gears and leaving the smell of diesel in its wake, was that Kenworth with the risqué caption: *Too much pussy*. From behind the wheel, the driver leered. "*Read it, son. Go on, then, read the fucker 'cause you're it: one big pussy-mister!*"

Joshua helped his folks prepare the boat for launch. His skin tingled as the early morning sun danced upon it, the velvet touch of the sea air reinforcing the sensation. His nerves were running on high, much the same as when challenging Cresta Verde Drive. He felt himself getting aroused, and embarrassment lingered just below the surface of his cheeks.

Sea gulls squawked here and there.

The sun bounced off the rippled water.

Bob and Sue exchanged a look. He approached his son and rubbed his shoulder firmly. "Feeling alright?"

"Feeling alright, Dad," Joshua returned with a cheeky grin, standing as close as he could to the boat. His sparkling blue eyes; so like his mother's.

Actually, Joshua felt better than alright. The man in black had been easily dispatched. Yeah, that's right! Dispatched! And when he faced facts, he realized that though he had no way of controlling the guy's visitation rights, he didn't have to do much when he arrived. Actually, he reckoned if he ignored him, he might slowly lose interest and piss off altogether.

He couldn't wait to see Leon and tell him of this new and entirely liberating revelation.

Though his other friends had been plagued by the man in black, only Leon could he open up to. If he tried this on the other guys, they'd only turn the subject into schoolyard trash, as if choosing to ignore what was happening and the effect—the 'thick'—it was having on them all.

Maybe they'd be right to do so.

Yeah, they might well be, pussy-mister.

Whilst a little confronting—nobody wanted to own up being that screwy!—relief took hold and he found himself amongst the boundless blue of another sky. From horizon to horizon, he soared upon warm updraughts, his eagle wings carrying him effortlessly to somewhere and nowhere in particular. His exaltation was somewhat offset by his rising embarrassment; he'd have to calm down, else he'd never be able to leave the side of the boat.

There was the blast of a boat horn accompanied by a burst of cheerful shouting. A group was frantically waving from the rear deck of a cabin cruiser leaving the marina. Onshore, another group was waving in return, and yelling things Joshua couldn't quite decipher through the distance and hum of background noise.

He watched the cruiser slowly burble towards the entrance that spilled into the Pacific Ocean.

"Hey, mate!" Bob called from the front of the boat.

Joshua came to with a little start.

"You wanna finish hooking up that guide rope so we can launch this thing?" He gave a nod toward the boat as he spoke.

Joshua smiled and blushed. "Sorry, Dad."

"You were miles away, I know, but I really want to get amongst the fish sometime today, and the sooner the better."

"Me, too."

⌒

Early May, 2022

Despite Joshua's optimism, the man in black was not so easily dissuaded.

That Saturday morning was followed by another night of wrecked sleep. Now here on Sunday morning, the Triplow family had perched themselves around the breakfast table. Sue was staring at her son. Bob was staring at his son. Joshua, for his part, was avoiding eye contact with both. Instead, he stared at the piece of toast on his plate, as if it wasn't covered in a thin film of butter and orange marmalade, but perhaps gold dust or maybe something never before discovered by mankind.

His folks had risen early today too. And now they were attempting to hold some sort of conversation, the type grown-ups held when they were pretending not to be intrigued or baffled, if not more than a little frightened. Trivialities were usually the order of the day, and this was no exception. The weather, for example, was a popular favorite. Right up there with how a patch on the front lawn was yellowing... perhaps a new chip in a cup had been discovered, or a scratch on the boat. When what they really wanted to do was probe Joshua for things he couldn't explain, but things they'd want to know about nonetheless.

His feet wriggled beneath the table. It had begun as a mild jiggle, but soon evolved into a full-blown bouncing on the balls of his feet. "Mom," he said out of the blue.

Sue almost choked on her mouthful of toast and Australia's iconic table-spread, Vegemite.

"Yes, honey," she spluttered.

"Were you wearing jewellery last night?"

They stared at each other.

"When you came into my room?" Joshua continued on.

After some pause to digest this intriguing line of inquiry, as well as her last mouthful, Sue replied, "No."

"You did have your pendant on," Bob said a little too thoughtfully.

"I took it off just before we went to bed."

"You're wearing it now."

"I put it back on this morning," Sue returned somewhat irritably. "Why do you ask, anyway, honey?"

Joshua shrugged his shoulders.

"Well, you must have a reason."

"I just thought that you might have worn it through the night."

Joshua's unusual curiosity in Sue's jewellery seemed to fuel the breakfast table's awkward lilt.

Having finished his toast and last scoop of Cheerios, he immediately excused himself to visit his soulmate down the road.

"Leon, when you dream of the man in black, do you... do you hear something that sounds like... like bells... like faint tinkling?" he stammered a little.

Leon took on the appearance of total bemusement. "Yeah, I think I do, but if you hadn't asked, I don't think I would've thought of it, because it's not something that big. The man in black, he's all I seem to remember."

There was a pause between them.

"What d'ya think it means?"

"That we're certifiably nuts," Joshua returned in such a way that both boys broke up in a gale of laughter, not entirely without nerves.

LOUIS ARMSTRONG

~~

Friday, August 26, 2022
End of the first school week

It was high summer in Corona.

The bell blared for the commencement of another school day. Shadows stretched like daggers across the ground. Trees were alive with the chirruping of birds, and Joshua felt a strong pang of repression, wishing *he* was also able to play without being told what to do and what not to do, when to do it and when not to.

At the foot of the school building's steps, he stared over his shoulder. His eyes, longing and envious, fixed on the birdbath set below a sycamore some thirty yards from where he stood. Below it, a large group of sparrows squabbled amongst themselves, darting in and out of the water and fluffing their feathers. Large droplets sprayed hither and thither into the heat, looking like miniature spaceships, flashing colors as they caught the rising easterly sun.

Lost in thought, Joshua was creating a bit of a roadblock halfway up the stairs. Kids were backing up behind, while others bustled to move around him. Most were obvious victims of the 'thick', and therefore not in the mood to give him lip on the etiquettes of ascending a staircase.

If Joshua was able to be reincarnated, he reckoned on coming back as a bird. He wasn't convinced such a thing was possible; on the other hand, it seemed like it'd make death kinda acceptable... a statement on life simply carrying on. He did, however, see one glaring fault: birds weren't renowned for their prowess upon a skateboard. And where would the fun in that be?

He looked past the school's doors, into its interior. "And where's the fun in this?" he muttered.

Leon was a little annoyed at being bumped and shoved by an army of kids and their schoolbags. "What?" he asked without any real interest in what had been said, only on getting out of the other kids' way.

Joshua looked at him as if he had forgotten he was there, then at Sammy standing further behind, leaning against the metal balustrade, when a sudden sense of dread had him fumbling for the handrail.

"You alright?" Leon asked, concerned, as yet another wayward schoolbag found its target.

"Yeah," Joshua returned distantly.

"Come on, then, or else we'll be late."

Sammy continued standing where he was, pretty relaxed, with an impish smile.

Leon didn't see this at first, but he caught Joshua's look of bemusement and turned around. "What?" he asked, now getting *really* irritated.

"I'm feeling randy," Sammy said without any attempt of lowering his voice.

Leon looked down. "Oh, jeez, Sammy, keep it down!"

The glaze melted from Joshua's eyes and the boys continued on.

Once in the building, Sammy broke away, heading for his sixth-grade class further along the corridor. "I'll see you guys a bit later," he said, that impish smile holding fast.

"Yeah. In the meantime, take a cold shower," Leon suggested.

"More like jump in a cold lake," Sammy quipped before submerging into the incoming tide of students and getting swept away.

It had yet to go 9:00 A.M.

Partly due to the other kids and partly due to the wobble in his legs, Joshua couldn't quite walk a straight line. He headed for the stairs, unusually annoyed by the fact that Sammy's classroom was on the first and theirs was on the second. Worst still: it was located at the far end of the corridor and seemed an awful long way to go, when every footfall was his Mount Everest. He'd entered the Dead Zone, where oxygen was so thin that each movement was to be exploited with absolute human endurance.

One... two... three...

His Nikes trudged by the school's motto:

CITRUS HILLS ELEMENTARY

**I respect all others
Whatever their race, culture or beliefs
We are united
And together we will excel in protecting our planet
and all living creatures.**

"I don't know," he said to Leon, ignoring the declaration on the wall adjacent, "I think my chances of arrival are slim."

As they headed for Room 612, Leon had to constantly hitch his school satchel over his shoulder. The thing had a mind of its own.

Again, Joshua got that sense of all the kids being extras in a B-grade zombie flick, just slumming about until whatever triggered their bloodthirsty instincts into hyperdrive.

What did you learn today, Joshy-washy? The pert voice didn't sound dissimilar to his mom's, although it was a little tinny, as if she had swallowed a case of wind instruments, not to mention a little childish.

Oh, I learned heaps from the teacher, Ma, sure did! I really and truly picked her brains and so did the other kids. It was murder.

That's my boy, Joshy-washy. That's what schooling's all about: to learn and become better armed with knowledge.

Yeah, Ma, I'm sure better armed. You'd be surprised just how so! Why don't you come here and I'll show you?

Joshua shivered at the awful images of kids slobbering down the brains of their adult prey, chunks of it tumbling down their chins like pulp from well-ripened peaches. The images danced across his exhaustion, seemingly hellbent on going the distance until the lights went out and the audience filed into the aisles.

"Now what?" Leon asked belatedly, having bumped into his friend's shoulder, acknowledging that 'what' seemed to have become his favorite word for the morning.

"Does everyone seem more out of it than usual to you?"

"Josh, man, that's hilarious coming from *el grando queso!*" Leon snorted wearily.

"Yeah, well, I just need a good night's sleep."

"No, man, face facts; you'd be real perky if it wasn't for this place." Leon swept his right arm around in a large arc, almost hitting a kid as he passed by, who burst forth with: "Watch it!"

Unlike Rob Hall and Scott Fisher of the ill-fated 1996 Mount Everest expedition, Joshua Triplow and his friend Leon Mendoza made it all the way to their summit: Citrus Elementary's Room 612.

They slumped into their seats and endured the tedious task of roll call. Mrs. Bruckheimer was way too chirpy and bright for the occasion.

After that, the rest of the day was a bit of a blur. By the time the bell rang for school to let out, Joshua was running on fumes. He had chugged down a sports drink from the cafeteria at lunch time, with a Red Bull chaser he'd bought as a six-pack from the 7-Eleven the weekend before.

His mom was not in favor of him consuming things like Red Bull, stating that it juiced people up on an overdose of caffeine, and that he was going to get addicted to the stuff.

Therefore he'd squirreled it away in his wardrobe, taking a can from the pack each night and burying it in the depths of the refrigerator until the next morning.

Beating his folks to the kitchen before school was usually a cinch. But, of late, he planned his mornings specifically so he could safely retrieve his goods before they arose. He would wrap each in several sheets of yesterday's edition of *The Sentinel Weekly News* before burying it in the depths of his school bag.

Whether or not one could get addicted to such stuff, Joshua could've told his mom that it simply didn't apply to him. In fact, he reckoned that it pretty much wouldn't apply to any kid in Corona. Thanks to the man in black, staying awake on an overdose of caffeine was damn near impossible.

"Thank God it's Friday," Leon Mendoza uttered as he, Joshua, Sammy, Ethan and Craig trundled from the school building into the bright light of afternoon.

"I'm glad it's over, but it wasn't half as bad as I thought it was going to be," Joshua said idly, just pleased that he was still sane and the school week was over.

"Why?" Ethan asked.

"Huh?"

"Why?" Ethan shrugged, raising his eyebrows.

"Oh…"

But before he could come up with a line, Sammy snuck in. "He thought the boogieman was gonna get him."

"Yeah, and your boner," Joshua returned.

"Oh Christ, you're not going on again about '*the man*'?" Ethan had a healthy amount of scepticism in his voice.

Cars and kids were choking South Main Street, as the boys spilled onto the sidewalk along with hundreds of others.

"Well, it's pretty weird that we're *all* having the same dream, don't you think?"

Ethan rolled his eyes. "Mom and Dad reckon it's got to do with suggestive behavior."

"Suggestive behavior?"

"Yeah! Once one kid blabs about what they dreamt, other kids dream the same thing."

"You reckon that holds?" Joshua asked incredulously.

"What do you think?"

But, again, before Joshua could answer, Sammy broke into laughter, saying, "It's all got to do with alien probing!"

"And we all know probing's top of your list," Joshua returned.

"I protest!"

"So we saw this morning," Leon said, joining the banter.

Again, Ethan rolled his eyes. "Jeez, Sam the Man, you've no control!"

"It's a male thing. You wouldn't understand."

The others cracked up, except Joshua, suddenly overcome with that powerful sense of unfounded dread for his friend. But so *real*. So… *tangible*.

"Bullshit!" Ethan spluttered. "It's a Sam the Man thing. One day you'll get that thing stuck somewhere it shouldn't be. The TV cameras will come along and start rolling and you'll have your gonads richly displayed on CNN. Your folks'll get to know your most intimate parts all over again."

A passing group of older students from another school, sporting tops which stated 'Home of the Jaguar,' began smirking. A parent waiting for her child at the side of her car caught drift of their conversation and felt slightly amused, slightly embarrassed.

The boys weren't making a spectacle of themselves, nor were they ostentatiously rude or lewd, but their chosen topic of conversation wasn't exactly transpiring in whispers, either.

"Your folks got an answer for that?" Leon managed to ask Ethan between breaths. His school satchel fell from his shoulder for the billionth time that day. He hitched it up without a thought—for the billionth time that day.

"Yeah, cut it off," Ethan quipped.

Joshua hadn't a clue for his feelings of disquiet. But if he had to sum it up, he'd have said it was as if Sammy had suddenly caught some dreadful disease, for which there was no cure. *Daft, right?*

Somewhere along the street, a couple of cars were engaged in a tooting of horns, none of them heard.

Sue Triplow pulled into the curb, the front windows down. "Who's up for a ride?" she asked, but the boys didn't notice her. The afternoon sun was a breezy 32^0 C (90^0 F). The air was bright and abuzz with a 'sort of' summer cheer. 'Sort of' because that good old 'thick' was ever present, just hanging about to mess things up a bit.

Once the group managed to bring themselves under control, the boys huddled together. An impromptu plan for the weekend schedule was mandatory. This was of such serious business that not a single snort of laughter broke their brainstorming. Suggestions and counter-suggestions came thick and fast until a plan was hatched. Catching up this afternoon was a given. Then at ten o'clock Saturday morning, meet up for skateboarding, try their hand at the *Cha Cha* again, and hopefully not screw it up this time.

"Right, Sam the Man?" Ethan taunted.

"I wasn't the one who took the worst header ever, so up yours," Sammy promptly replied, loudly.

Joshua raised his head from the group, hoping no one had heard that. It was then he noticed his mom. He waved. "Hi, Mom!"

"Do any of you boys want a lift, or should I have saved myself the effort?"

"In a tick, Mom."

Sunday: catch up at ten o'clock for skateboarding, Sammy an hour or so after, as he had Sunday School—what a drag!—practice the *Cha Cha* some more, and hopefully not fuck it up.

"Jeez, Sammy, keep it down," Craig admonished, blushing somewhat. Joshua's mom was in earshot.

"Sam the Man doesn't know the meaning of 'keeping it down,'" Ethan snorted.

"Shut up," Craig hissed through gritted teeth.

With the schedule completed, they each said their goodbyes and went their separate ways, except for Leon and Joshua.

"Sam the Man, now remember, be careful or you'll get yourself on CNN or, better yet, TMZ," came Ethan's sarcastic parting shot, and Craig giggled nervously as the boys cross the road.

"Thanks, Mrs. Triplow, we're all good," Sammy called out brightly, already heading away.

"Always has to have the last word, doesn't he?" Leon muttered, wondering if Mrs. Triplow understood what flowed from Ethan's impulsive mouth.

"Yeah," Joshua muttered in return, sensing that feeling of dread steal into him once more, now that the euphoria of the weekend schedule had ebbed like a sudden low tide. "So long as Sammy's alright."

"Why wouldn't he be?"

Joshua shrugged. He was going to confide in his best friend, but ended saying nothing more intellectual than, "I don't know." Then, "Sammy, you sure you don't want a ride home?"

"Nah, Josh, it's a great afternoon for a walk," he returned, some ways down the sidewalk already. "Besides, I'll be warmed up for the board when we catch up a little later."

The boys hesitated a little longer at the side of the Triplows' Ranger as Joshua watched Sammy Debnar slowly disappear along South Main Street.

꩜

That evening, a spectacular sunset painted its spellbinding artistry across a cloudless sky. All too soon, however, it faded from sight. Dulling by degrees, its layers of crimson, orange and yellow dissolved until nothing was left but a fragile after-light of chromatic blue on the edge of the western horizon.

Night's first star chips poked through the graying canopy, sending their Morse-code twinkling down to planet Earth, from which at least one small boy gazed up, watching their silent rhetoric.

Having returned from an end-of-the-day catch-up with Leon, Ethan and Sammy—Craig having gone out with his folks— for a bit of Chasing Boulevard skateboarding, and of course Joshua's personal favorite, Cresta Verde Drive, Joshua now sat in his backyard. Well, he wasn't precisely sitting, but rather lying with his knees bent and legs spread.

Doing a Sammy, his mind quipped in the growing darkness. Though there was no humor to be savored from it, since his earlier misgivings continued to give him bother.

What is it about Sammy? Why does it feel as if Sammy's got some kind of ticking time bomb attached to him? Or inside *of him?*

It seemed he'd returned to testicular cancer. But surely not! It was just his overwrought mind screwing with him. *Right?* He sighed heavily.

That afternoon they'd used the sidewalks, curbs and driveways in the usual manner, doing the Ollie up and the Ollie down, simple stuff, really, nothing as sophisticated as the *Cha Cha.* That was for the weekend proper. In addition, they had run Cresta Verde... to go hyperdrive. And while absorbed in the moment, they'd overcome their lethargy. Somehow. It was as if the stale cobwebs of the day... the weeks... the *months...*

had broken like fine strands of gossamer and, until the wheels stopped rolling beneath them, they had forgotten how faded they were feeling.

But now, with his stomach satisfyingly full of his mom's speciality, lasagne with extra white sauce and cheese, those strands had reconnected to become one big fuzzy, if not gooey, ball of 'thick,' as if part of mom's specialty had decided to transit to a plinth strung between his ears.

He tried hard to listen to the night sounds, which helped to keep his eyes wide open and his mind focused on other things than those internal misgivings. But man, watching those constellations take shape from their lofty perches wasn't easy. They kept drifting in and out of the here and now.

Dogs were barking here and there and on and off, talking to each other from their backyards. This was intermingled with the sound of a couple of kids somewhere nearby, making the most of the last vestiges of light. He didn't think it was the Dallases across the road... perhaps the Rileys further along Chasing.

"*Hey! That's not fair, I couldn't see the ball!*"

"*You're It!*"

"*That's not fair, Christopher!*"

Moments later: "*Come on you two—inside! It's getting way too dark to still be out there!*"

Yep—it was the Rileys.

Kids. Joshua shook his head at the ripe old age of eleven. Well – almost eleven if one was to be so pedantic. *They never learn.* An idiom that was surely indisputable. Now, had it been him and had he had a brother or sister to argue with, the strategist within would've figured that arguing was counterproductive. He was certain that arguments had their place within the world, and that much had been achieved through arguments. Good things. As well as bad.

But there was a right place and time to argue, and then there was a wrong place and time. Shouting at each other on the justices of fair play beneath the stars was certainly not going to win the day for kids in the 21st century front yard.

The constellations drifted badly.

Joshua was struggling. His limbs were getting heavy and going limp: arms flopping to either side, his legs splaying further, so his knees almost touched the ground.

Finally, those constellations broke apart and disappeared and Joshua's breathing became very relaxed. The first adventurous steps into sleep were smooth and effortless. His feet having turned to liquid which had begun gliding along a descent surely as steep and long as that of Cresta Verde Drive. A little ways further and he would have delved into the depths of his subconsciousness, if not for a sudden ruckus off to his side.

Joshua's eyes fluttered open. Disorientation washed over him like a suffocating flow. He was still gliding along the pathway into sleep, whilst somehow also lying in his backyard under the stars. He was tired—very tired—and would not have been in the least surprised if he were trundled off to Dr. Keon and diagnosed with a moderate case of sleep deprivation. Of course, this would not have happened without the mandatory ritual of having a thermometer shoved into his mouth and then asked to do the impossible by saying 'Ar.'

Inch by laborious inch, disorientation slowly exposed him to the realities of his backyard and he determined the intruder upon his sleep was the sound of a bird squawking and flapping about in the photinia bush to his right.

Did mom or dad hang a wind chime in it to stop birds from…?
From what?
  Picking the fruit?
  But there is no fruit!
And so there wasn't. Just the bright fragrance of the photinia's white flowers.
  And what self-respecting bird nibbles at night?
Something sniggered through the fence, accompanied by that soft touch of a wind chime.
  No—not a wind chime. Bells—which sound eerily like a baby's rattle.
Joshua sat bolt upright, heart pounding in his ears, a fine mist of sweat shimmering on his forehead.
Dylan O'Casey lived next door. He even went to the same school: Citrus Hills Elementary. He seemed a good kid. Strangely though, Joshua never seemed to have had the opportunity to strike up a friendship, which was kind of odd now that it crossed his mind. But the O'Caseys didn't have a baby and, even if they did, why would they have left their precious bundle in the backyard after dark to play with its rattle?
"That you, Dylan?" he sung out. The sound of his own voice was alien to his ears, like a character caught within the fictitious fabric of a nightmare. But he was fully awake, and the bird was reacting to something.
The sniggering—or was it singing?—intensified, as if one had been joined by many in a somewhat risqué joke—or song. The only one not getting it was Joshua Triplow.
The bells then rattled vigorously and the bird crashed through the bush, taking to the night on terrified squawks as leaves fluttered to the ground.

Maybe there is *a deterrent hanging in the tree. Maybe. But that's the sound of something* really *scared,* Joshua thought, sitting on the verge of the paved area beneath the veranda of his house. His skin prickling with nerves. The squawks fading into the long tunnel of the bird's flight path across the darkness.

Warm light softly spilled through several expansive windows behind, including the sliding door to the main sofa room. Safety was but a mere arm's length away, despite the sliding door being locked nice and tight, to stop potential intruders helping themselves to their belongings.

He could see his mom, sitting with her legs scooped up underneath her on the sofa. She had her head in a magazine. If anything untoward happened—*anything at all*, like something shaking or wearing bells and stalking him under darkness while laughing at his pain—he could yell to her. She was right there!

So why did everything, including his mom, feel impossibly out of reach, as if he were marooned on a faraway island?

There was a loud *BANG!!*

A sudden snap into the yard once more had his neck protesting with a series of bone-jarring cracks.

More sniggering, which seemed to carry indecipherable words, and more bells.

Joshua scrambled from the soft grass. His feet were nowhere to be found, as if he'd carelessly left them on their unctuous descent into sleep, but somehow he managed to get to the back door. Only after he had slammed it tightly shut, did he chance a look into the yard.

There was nothing there.

Nothing!

He was scaring himself, that was all. He was being one big pussy-mister.

With a quick turn of the door's lock, and its satisfying *click*, the warm cascade of relief restored Joshua's feet to their rightful place. He turned his back to the night and begun along the downstairs hallway as his dad emerged from the basement. "Whatcha been up to, mate?"

"I fell asleep in the backyard." Joshua knew his dad had detected the nervous twang across his vocal cords.

"Did something happen out there?"

"No." Another perfect example of Joshua's poor execution when it came to lying.

Bob stepped toward him. "I'm quite aware that my eyes are square behind these glasses. It happens," he said, putting on a face. "Been in the basement pouring over stuff for Crystal Bell... but you look spaced out. You sure everything's alright?"

"What's going on, you two?" Sue followed her voice into the hallway, wearing the same curious expression as his dad.

"Nothing." Joshua insisted, and found himself slightly amused by the impromptu family rendezvous when, on a glance to the left, a perfectly good yet empty sofa room was up for grabs. Perhaps they could choose the toilet for their next such gathering. "I feel rather stupid at giving myself a fright when a bird became startled. That's all." Due to the fact that an ounce of truth was woven into his explanation, it was a reasonable effort and one that Mrs. Bruckheimer might have even given him 75 on a points system of 100.

Bob removed his glasses and dragged a hand down his face, before popping them back on. After hours committed to finalizing loose ends, his face felt rubbery and swollen, as if he had taken to self-administering a shot of Lidocaine just to keep things from getting too monotonous and boring. Malcolm Edwards of Crystal Bell Corporation was on his back to get those ends of his latest brainchild neatly tidied away. But he was over it for one night. Besides, it was Friday and it was 'family time.' TV or not. So he suggested their usual 'Friday thing' of watching recorded episodes of *The Twilight Zone.*

"Great!" Joshua gushed. "Except…"

"*Except?*" his parents said in unison.

"Since when do you place exceptions on *The Twilight Zone?*" Bob asked.

"I just don't want to see the episode where that man is walking down that long corridor and those bells are playing somewhere in the background."

"Oh, I like that one," Bob remarked with cheery introspection, thumb and index finger rubbing his fat and rubbery chin like a professor, perhaps sporting a beard, and who had just exited a dentist's appointment less one tooth.

"I do, too. Just… not tonight."

"Okay, whatever the master says."

If only, Joshua thought.

"Honey, you asked me about bells the other morning. What is it with you and bells?"

Joshua shrugged and Sue reluctantly placed the subject on ice. Again. But if this theme continued, she would need to know.

Later that night, after three episodes of *The Twilight Zone* back to back, and with Joshua having nervously turned in, he was haunted by what had transpired in the backyard. And though he had joked to Leon about being certifiably insane, he feared that might become a distinct possibility more than he feared yet another visitation by the man in black. Because, for the first time, it seemed that something had followed him as he had slipped in and out of Joshua Triplow's twilight zone. No less terrifying than if he had gone in there and grabbed onto the man himself to drag him into the real world. And who was to say that wasn't what he had done?

It wasn't healthy, that much he knew. And, for that, he didn't need Dr. Keon's input nor his medical eccentricities.

If the man in black had followed him into the backyard, he had just as suddenly vanished to wherever he had come from, shaking his baby rattle as he went.

Sammy's house... he receded to Sammy's, once more, because Sammy's in trouble and needs the helping hand of a friend.

Joshua rolled over in bed. His limbs were the weight of lead and seemed near impossible to move, having poured their energy into the most vital organs: his heart and brain. The night was chilly, but his bed was uncomfortably damp with the sweat that came from his seething panic.

Am I for real? Is this shit for real or am I already certifiable only I don't know it?

"Now, say 'Ar' and lets see just what's going on in that there brain of yours."

⌒

Saturday, September 3, 2022

Humans are given to both ingenuity and adaptation. This is what gave them the edge to dominate over those predators that munched on their ancestor's bones in the first days of exploring from beyond the trees. And so it was with the entire community of Corona, including Joshua Triplow, who, after consulting the abridged version of self-conviction with set determination before rising in the morning and after retiring at night, found some level of peace.

Weeks had passed and Sammy was still his usual self. He wasn't dying of cancer and his house wasn't overrun except for his mom's compulsive, excessive passion for cleaning. If it wasn't the vacuum whirring away, she would find some figurine in need of a vigorous clean with the microfibre cloth that seemed to be forever clutched in her hand. Today yellow. The next blue or pink or gray.

But for Joshua, it was an uneasy truce. One that was exemplified by his jumping whenever a bird flapped frantically amongst a tree.

Having caught him in action one day, Ethan cackled. "They're making sweet, sweet love, Josh, just like that time you walked in on your folks. Never been the same since, have you? The image is now burned into your brain forever."

The other boys, including Sammy, scolded him for his usual inclination of talking not so much from his mouth as from his butt.

The children's nightmares of a man in black continued, but they hadn't escalated. And nothing had *really* happened. Nothing *bad,* at least. And there was a noticeable improvement in the demeanor of Corona's young.

The Riverside County's population had *adapted.*

The kids were still 'thick.' But then, they were *kids.* And the 'thick' was by no means as extreme. Gone were the days in which they coursed their way through each hour like extras in a zombie flick. School grades had increased with their general rejuvenation.

The man in black had lost his potency.

A balance of life had re-established itself and talk on the street about little Johnny not doing so swell had given way to normal daily issues. These mostly centred around politics and work or business, which was hardly surprising since the post-era of the 2020 recession brought on by the coronavirus had yet to completely run its course. The vicious cycle of politics affecting business and business affecting the economy had begun pulling out of the mire, but there still remained those niggling patches of 'collateral fallout.'

2020's market correction—because politics staunchly denied it being a 'crash'—was minor compared to that of 2007 - 2010. But it had left its mark on the strength of a multitude of sectors. Small businesses and, in particular, those associated with or directly involved in hospitality had suffered the brunt of that fallout. However, after months of cutbacks, reduced hours and a tightening of the purse strings, things had begun looking up here, too. In fact, the true barometer of financial strength and well-being sat in the unemployment figures and these had started their journey downwards from 8.5% to 7.9%.

Things were, indeed, looking up...

Until the small hours of that Saturday morning.

For the 'storm' had continued gaining strength.

And sequestered somewhere within its infinite bounds, toiling away endlessly, furiously, a young girl sang. Her voice both soft and eerie, the abject pinnacle of torture and loss:

> *In a place far over the rainbow*
> *The Boogaloo is out of sight*
> *In a place far over the rainbow*
> *Everyone's lost in a lullaby...*

It echoed into that infinity. Slowly teasing into ever thinner threads until snuffing out like a tiny speck of a flame in the heart of a cold dark universe.

This had nothing to do with what Joshua Triplow heard, though it was very much projected toward him.

Rather than a girl's haunting tones, what came to his attention was old-fashioned, and it filled the air with a kind of dusty nostalgia—if a trumpet blowing an old 1930s big-band tune was the kind of thing that got one's rocks off. Joshua was hardly excited, but he had heard this kind of music before, maybe in a pawnshop in which all matter of yesteryear seemed to accumulate.

He could see the trumpet and the puffed cheeks surrounding its mouthpiece. He could see the man behind the trumpet and, for one shocking moment, he thought it was the man in black. But no. It was a dark-skinned man, that was all.

Women in big flouncy skirts and men with hair greased to the scalp must have once 'cut a rug' to this tune. And, again, in his mind's eye he could see them, like faded pictures almost lost to history, dazzled by the sights and sounds surrounding them... lost in their world of dancing... dancing to the dusty sounds of a Black man's trumpet.

Joshua had come to a halt, even though the trumpet made him feel funny inside, almost queasy.

Leon walked into his right side, bumping heavily into his arm. "What are you...?" he started asking, when he followed his friend's gaze.

Standing on the sidewalk, they stared at the house from which the tunes flowed.

Its architecture seemed to straddle the present and the past. There was something not quite right with its design; whilst the pretence of it fitting into this world was reasonable, it just didn't quite work. The world had long moved on from when its first bricks had been laid. And the tune flowing from within seemed to stand as strong testimony to this.

"That's Satchmo, my friends," a dry voice cut across the music.

Joshua and Leon both turned abruptly in the direction from which it came. Neither had seen the old man standing there, in his bib-and-brace overalls, at the front of his house.

The man was amused by the boys' stunned expressions, his wiry hair shifting across his balding scalp on a lacklustre breeze. "Best playin' jazz trumpeter ever, and I'll jump if that ain't so."

"Who?" Joshua asked the question on Leon's lips.

"*Satchmo!*" The old man tugged at the straps of his overalls. "Got every record he ever cut, I have," he said proudly.

"Who's Satchmo?" Leon couldn't contain his curiosity.

"Ya ain't joshin' me, now, are ya?"

Leon shook his head. Joshua had some idea.

"Well, I'll jump if that ain't so!" he said, almost delighted at the prospect of their ignorance. "Ya young 'uns have a lot to learn. School's too soft these days."

The boys looked at each other, then back at the old man.

"Best damned horn player before, durin' and after his time." He stepped over to the fence.

"Sad—really sad," he said, shaking his head morosely. The fine strands of his hair wisped about his scalp again. "Poor son of a bitch went and kicked the eternal bucket, didn't he?"

Joshua again cast a look at his friend. "Um." He didn't know quite what to say. Perhaps 'sorry.' But neither did he want to give this old man a reason to prolong the conversation.

"That he did. Oh, yes sirree. Died of a heart attack before his time was up. By Christ, he was only sixty-nine." The old man paused, lost in his thoughts, then shouted: "*Sixty-nine!* Ain't that a son of a bitch?"

The boys remained quiet. Joshua was now thinking it had been a bad idea stopping here in the first place.

"They say the music died when Buddy Holly took a dive in '59, but I says it really died when Satchmo took his horn from this world. Reckon they'll be cuttin' up a rug in ol' Heaven, what d'ya think?"

Neither boy knew what to think besides hightailing it away. The old man had started exuding an aura, like an unstable explosive that shouldn't be handled.

"Well, of course ya can't, since ya don't *know* the great Satchmo!"

Joshua and Leon took a step away from the man. He now approached too close for comfort and his voice had gone from conversational to querulous. He stooped his tall lanky body so that he was face-to-face with them. "Hear that?" he asked in a crooning voice. "That's sweet New Orleans ragtime, boys… straight from the heart of the Mississippi. He rubbed shoulders with the greats of the time, but I reckon he had a bit of a thing for Doris Day and liked the idea of… *dreamin'*."

Joshua and Leon furtively glanced at the house, the air now cloyed with those tunes of yesteryear.

The old man saw their nervousness and started laughing, like he had a cracker stuck halfway down his throat. "Muggles," he squawked, and Leon found himself nodding.

"Liked a bit of reefer, did ol' Satchmo," he said, then dragged back hard and deep on a pretend joint. "Probably what gave the poor SOB his heart attack. Guess he's doin' quite a bit of dreamin' now… might even be with that sassy Doris right this minute. Maybe they're dreamin' together."

He eyed the boys closely. "Reckon ya'd like a bit of reefer, too?" And there was something offensive in his tone.

Joshua took another step away, saying 'no,' while Leon nodded again, muttering 'yes.'

Joshua grabbed him by the arm. "No, you don't!"

The old man stood fully erect, leering over the top of Leon to get a good look at the other boy on his far side. Again his brittle laughter mixed with the dusty tunes of Louis Armstrong, with a new accompaniment of distant bells. Their dainty ringing seemed connected to both the house and the man. "Ya need to let your friend speak for himself, sonny; he's got a mouth."

Joshua ignored him. "No, you don't, Leon," he repeated in a firm whisper.

Leon blinked a couple of times, and then admitted, "I don't even know what it is."

"I think he's talking about…"

"*Mary Jane!*" the old man cackled, but he was obviously pissed with Joshua, the cackle more a ruse than the real thing. "Mary Jane's a *real* smooth talker. Reckon ya young 'uns would like the taste of her, and ya'd be all ready to have some fun. We could have some fun together." His croon returned again, thick and threatening. "Bet ya never had *that* sort of fun, hey? I could make ya feel real tingly while Mary Jane spins ya head and ya go into a dream."

Both boys had started backing down the sidewalk. The fence, standing between them and the old man, was an extremely weak barrier.

"Been a *real* long time since I had some fun like that myself!" The old man's tone was so deliberately offensive at this point, it could've been interpreted as nothing else but.

Joshua and Leon turned and began running, but the old man jumped the fence, the dainty ringing of bells rising to a crescendo: "*Y'all come back now, ya hear! We can have some fun—reckon ya'd like that! We'll make our acquaintance to Mary Jane and have some fun!*"

After several streets, in which his cracker-barrel laughter stalked them in hot pursuit, the boys finally had the lung capacity to leave him wheezing in the distance.

With his laughter and bells still ringing in their ears, they pulled up. Leon leaned over and placed his hands on his knees, sucking in hard breaths.

Joshua reached down and pulled him up straight. "Leon, do you… do you *ever* remember seeing that house before?" He was panting heavily, but the strain in his voice was distinct.

Without hesitation, Leon was shaking his head.

"Do you ever remember seeing that old man *anywhere?*"

"He was talking about dope, wasn't he?" Leon asked.

Joshua looked most unimpressed. "Leon, that's *not* the issue here. That house, the old man—*where did they come from?*"

"You… wanna go back and see?"

Joshua thought it through. "Do you?"

Leon shrugged, the fire in his chest now mellowing to a simmer.

"Come on." Joshua flicked his head in the direction from which they had run, and they all headed off.

Leon soon fell in by his side.

They searched the streets, but could not find the address upon which the old man and his lost-in-time house had stood. Nor could they hear anything like the tunes that had drifted from it.

"This is bullshit!" Joshua finally said.

"We must've taken a wrong turn, that's all," Leon reasoned.

"Listen!"

"What?"

"Just listen. Let's see if we can *hear* where the house is."

"The music wasn't that loud."

"Just listen, anyhow," Joshua said, holding up one hand in fierce determination.

Nothing. Not a sound besides that of the breeze through trees and the odd leaf skittering along the ground, which in itself was odd. Where were the sounds of birds? Where were the sounds of other kids? Where were the sounds of normal everyday things, like traffic? Where the hell was the traffic? Any traffic? Joshua would've been thrilled just to see some grandma on a gopher, or Lucille Goldman nosing about for her latest piece of thrilling gossip. Hell, he could even regale her with some neighborhood mystery that would keep her busy for months!

"We took the wrong street," Leon repeated. "That's all."

"Leon, we're not stupid. We both *know* these streets. Jeez, we skate the things enough! We didn't take a wrong turn… the house with *Satchmo* and the old man no longer exist."

"Now, that *is* bullshit," Leon said with a nervous laugh.

"So you explain what happened to them."

"Wrong st—"

"And don't give me crap about the wrong street." Joshua was annoyed and frightened. "Besides, what can you hear? *Who* can you see?"

Leon simply stared, saying nothing.

"Exactly, Leon." Joshua didn't know what else to say; everything was wrong. He looked up the street, then down it, before laying a hard stare upon his friend. "You heard those bells?" The breeze picking up his hair.

Leon nodded, unable to speak.

He grabbed his friend by the arm, pleased to feel his flesh—his *reality*. "Come on, Sammy will be waiting." But he had serious doubts. The dread he'd felt for his friend weeks before had returned, full and ripe, fingering through him like rampant bamboo shoots.

They walked pretty much the rest of the way in silence, each lost in their own thoughts, none of which were the slightest bit helpful in dampening their nerves. They took Alpine Avenue before finally arriving at South Lincoln Drive. The journey was ponderous, as if they had waded through knee-deep water.

They approached the front door and rung the bell, below which was a small slip of paper held beneath a plastic cover, reading **DEBNAR**.

The boys waited.

Joshua took the time to look out across Sammy's front yard. He guessed he'd noticed it before, but now it struck him as very odd. Everything *seemed* alright. But the sun... it was like something someone had conjured up on a whim of what

sunlight should be like and not the real thing at all. It was…
well, it was syrupy. Together with the lack of sounds, it made for
a surreal hotchpotch, and the type of stuff upon which Joshua's
dread strengthened.

He couldn't wait to get inside; yet on the other hand, he
couldn't wait to get back home. It seemed he needed further
affirmations of reality. He trusted Leon's reality, and was
profoundly grateful for that, but everything else was from
Weirdoland.

The idea of playing video games with Sammy had lost all
appeal; a good idea gone rotten, leaving a rancid taste at the
back of his mouth.

Leon reached out and rung the bell again.

"Sammy knew we were coming, right?" Joshua asked nervously.

Leon looked at him in a quizzical fashion. "Well, you called
him."

"Uh-uh. You did, didn't you?"

"Nah."

"So whose grand scheme was this, then?"

Leon shrugged. "We're here now."

"I guess. But why?"

"Um…"

"Do you know what you came here for?"

"The same thing as you."

"Right. So what was that?"

Leon frowned. "You first."

"You *really* don't know, do you?" Joshua's dread was now
ready to explode. *And why won't Sammy answer the door?* "We're
both here to play video games, right?"

Again, Leon shrugged. "Yeah, right."

"No, Leon. Nothing's right. *Nothing.*" With a stab of the finger, Joshua rang the doorbell for the third time.

"What are you saying, Josh?"

Joshua looked over the immediate neighborhood. "What do you make of the sun?" The worry coursing through Leon had etched deep horizontal furrows across his forehead. "I give up. What *do* I make of the sun?"

Joshua shook his head. "It isn't just not right—it's *all wrong.* It was *all wrong* when we couldn't find the dirty old man and his shitty music. It was *all wrong* when we couldn't hear any noise but the wind. And this is *all wrong.* You don't even know why we're here. I do; you don't."

"I forgot, that's all."

"That's *not* all, Leon. You didn't *just* forget. You didn't *know.* You were following me!"

"You wanna go home?"

Joshua had a sneaking suspicion that perhaps they were already home, they just didn't know it. But he couldn't leave without looking behind Door Number 17.

"Jesus, Sammy, open up!" Joshua rapped on the door and, to the boys' amazement, it whispered ajar.

They gave one another a nervous glance and stepped back.

"Sammy, you there?" Joshua yelled out, producing a strange cavernous echo inside the front hall.

You there? You there? You there? You there?

"Jeez, Josh, don't—"

"*Shhh!* I can hear something," Joshua whispered close to Leon's ear. "Something's moving about inside."

He reached forward and, as he pushed the door fully open, Leon warned in a nervous whisper once more, "No, don't!" But it was too late.

They peered past the door's leading edge, their eyes big as moons.

It was dark inside. Impossibly dark, as if all the windows had been either boarded up or painted over. The hallway extended so far from the front door that it defied the house's outer dimensions.

Instead of taking a step back into the yard, Joshua took one forward.

Leon stabbed a hand out to stop him. "Josh, I can't go in there."

Joshua found himself mixed with both high anxiety and empathy. "You stay here, then. If I don't come out, send in the caviar."

"The caviar?"

"Yeah." Joshua tried for conviction but came up with doubt. "Isn't that what they say in cowboy movies?"

"I don't know. I really haven't seen any."

"Me, either."

"Isn't caviar fish eggs?" Leon kept staring into the darkness of the hallway. He needed to escape it before it swallowed him whole. "You want me to call in the fish eggs?"

"Yeah," Joshua said, crossing the threshold.

"What are you going to do with fish eggs?"

"Eat them," Joshua replied before slipping into the darkness beyond.

"Please," Leon begged. "*Don't!*"

But Joshua was now compelled to move forward, to investigate that sound coming from within Sammy's house. He could still hear that *shifting*, like mice skittering over bare floorboards. Did Sammy have bare floorboards?

For all the times Joshua had visited him, he now couldn't remember. Like his dread, Weirdoland had grown full and ripe. *And where was Sammy? Where were the Debnars?*

He continued into the darkness toward that sound, heart pounding against his eardrums.

Amongst the syrupy sunlight fingering down the hallway, like old curtains that had hung in a window for eons and had gone brittle and faded, Joshua was struggling to see an inch in front of him.

The darkness oozed around him like liquorice mousse, the skittering haunting him from every angle. The doorways to pitch-black rooms off to either side seemed to yaw, large and hungry.

Joshua's skin firmed with a severe case of gooseflesh. Not for the first time in his life was he reminded of the exposure he presented in shorts and T-shirt. *Send in the caviar, 'cause I shouldn't be doing this.*

Step by tentative step, he went deeper into Sammy Debnar's house, leaving the front door far behind. It was now little more than a tiny peephole.

He chanced a snap look behind. Leon's figure seemed to move in spastic jerks, and appeared alien and emaciated. Here the syrupy sunlight broke into a fine ethereal mist and, a mere few more steps on, it disappeared altogether.

It took an age to reach the entrance of the main sofa room.

It was unrecognizable in the aftermath of the worst case ever of spring-cleaning. *Maybe Sammy's mom* had *gone berserk! Her cleaning habits having gotten the better of her!* Everything had been removed, leaving nothing but bare floor space. The floorboards were exquisitely polished and seemed... *liquefied*, as if they had turned to water.

And who says they haven't, Joshy-Washy, came a taunting inner voice.

The skittering was not loud, but it was stronger here.

Joshua licked his lips, then sucked his lower lip in and bit down. He stuck one leg out and dabbed his right foot against the floorboards, honestly expecting his shoe to come away wet, his toes to penetrate the surface.

They didn't.

The floor was firm.

The sofa room was designed in an L-shape and so the other half was hidden. In this hidden part, a light emanated of the sort that bathed your eyes when pressing a sheet of green cellophane into your face and marvelling at how it distorted the world. The skittering continued to get louder, only "louder" in this case meant a mere shade above something there... or maybe not...

As he rounded the corner in the middle of the room, he pulled up sharp, gasping at what confronted him, his breaths coming in short rapid stabs.

But part of him had known all along what this would be.

Any minute now he'd start screaming out of his mind.

Because there he sat. The man in black. A fall of soft green light pooled around him.

Skittery-scratch scratchy-scratch...

Joshua stood transfixed by the frenetic actions of the man in black. The man who had haunted the kids of Corona while they slept. The skittering sound emanated from his actions and crept out in fine tendrils to fill the darkness, like sparklers that burned without illumination.

In his typical manner, his head was bowed, never looking up, too busy with the task at hand, scratching away at some unknown story.

And it must have been a belter at that.

Skittery-scratch scratchy-scratch...

His hand worked feverishly, not like a man's at all, more like that of a robot plugged into a million volts.

"Joshua!" Joshua! Joshua! Joshua! came Leon's distant call.

"Come on, man, get out of there!" Come on man, get out of there! Come on man, get out of there! Come on man, get out of there! Come on man, get out of there!

Skittery-scratch scratchy-scratch...

Joshua withdrew from the man, but felt some fantastically powerful compulsion to stay put, and, after two or three hesitant steps backwards, held up on the spot. Sweat stood out on his skin in shimmering fish scales. Comprehension was having a tough time amongst the well-spring of fear. He couldn't see what was being written. He didn't want to. He didn't want to get any closer. He had gotten too close already.

Skittery-scratch scratchy-scratch...

"JOSHUA!" JOSHUA! JOSHUA! JOSHUA!

Recognition finally hit its mark. Joshua seemed to be drifting further from his friend. And where was he drifting to? Further from the front door. Further from the light and deeper into the darkness. *I could make you feel real tingly...*

Skittery-scratch scratchy-scratch...

Joshua seemed entirely disconnected from everything of the normal world. It was as if he was on a fast track to someplace else, reality slipping like burning rope through his fingers.

Something caught his eye off to the side.

"Sammy!"

The man in black raised his hooded head, just as something seemed to drift up from between his hands. Whatever it was, if anything at all, had slipped into the darkness.

His eyes were gone, replaced by stagnant black pools that drilled into Joshua and squeezed his heart, closing down his throat.

"Joshua, come on, man!" Joshua, come on, man! Joshua, come on man! Joshua, come on man!

Leon's pleas were becoming less intense, the distance between him and Joshua growing rapidly, as if they were each on separate travelators speeding in opposite directions.

Joshua stumbled and fell with a hard thump on his ass. Under normal circumstances it would have knocked the wind from him, but since he had none to give, it managed to instead knock some sense into him.

A door slammed upstairs, somewhere in the pitch-black darkness of Mrs. Debnar's cleaning extravaganza.

Joshua catapulted to his feet.

The man in black's eyeless sockets never broke their stare. As endless as the bounds of this house, each socket was brutally intensified by the hood enshrouding his head.

RUN!

Good advice, only his legs didn't seem to want to obey, seemingly glued to the floor. Or was it that he was running, but he simply wasn't going anywhere?

He spun about, managing to slip on the floor's unctuous surface, and upon a rather indelicate belly-flop went sliding into the hallway like a human-sized hockey puck.

At this rate, he might as well give up. Either that or slide out of this madhouse, counting the floorboards as he went.

Oh, Mrs. Debnar, you missed a spot! And while on the subject of missing: What have you done with Sammy?

Skittery-scratch scratchy-scratch...

Again, in a flurry of actions, he found his feet. Almost went for another spill.

The oblong patch of sunlight an impossible distance ahead of him.

"JOSHUA!" Joshua! Joshua! Joshua!

He ran for his life, each breath rasping through his throat. The menacing doors to either side of the hallway flew past as he bolted for the patch at its extreme end. His lungs burned as if he had inhaled acidic vapors, his throat both warm and frigid at the same time. There was also the faint taste of blood at the back of it.

In his panic, he could no longer hear the scratching of the man in black, but he knew it was there, filling the darkness all around him.

That syrupy sunlight, falling between the front door's frame, was getting closer at an excruciatingly slow rate.

Amongst it, his friend was willing him on, bending at the knees and waist, screaming into the darkness.

Joshua reached out desperately and, with one last herculean burst of effort, took an enormous lunge forward, spilling onto Sammy's front lawn. He went down solidly on his knees before belly-flopping once more. The well-manicured lawn surrounded him in a sea of green.

∽

No time to think—just act or be acted upon.

It was as if the lawn had turned to water. It was all around him, over his face, around his arms, around his legs, binding him up like an Egyptian mummy. The more he thrashed, the tighter the bindings of seaweed became.

He gasped for air, took one huge gulp and snapped his eyes open.

He whined and thrashed at the thing over his face. When he discovered it was nothing more than his comforter, he was left feeling nonplussed and mighty stupid.

His arms and legs poked out from the dudes on skateboards printed over its fabric. His head wobbled groggily. His former feelings were muscled over, but not completely eradicated, by a sense of profound disorientation. He couldn't decipher whether he was upside down or inside out. One second he had feared drowning in Sammy's lawn, which had somehow turned to water, the next he feared he was running late for school and wondering why his mom or dad hadn't woken him.

Slowly and with the weight of heavy thuds, things fell into place, leaving Joshua uneasy and exhausted. So acute were these sensations that neither had been experienced before this moment.

Disentangling himself from his comforter, the dudes on skateboards concertinaing, he managed to sit on the edge of his bed. There he waited until the last vestiges of disorientation vaporized.

It took an awfully long time.

And he still did not feel entirely without a nauseating hot bitterness that rose from his stomach and into his throat.

Joshua didn't have a clock in his bedroom; he'd never cared for one, since his internal body clock usually ticked away without fault. Also, he was a pretty good judge of time. By the light gray outside his window, he guessed it was about 6:00 A.M.

When he got down to the kitchen to cobble together something resemblant of breakfast, sure enough the kitchen clock declared it was five minutes past the hour.

There it was, ticking away without a care in the world. High on the kitchen wall, constantly looking down on life, knowing what the next second would bring, making sure that all under its power obeyed without question.

At the moment, Joshua had a sudden hate for the thing. Maybe if it shut up, it wouldn't be so bad. But the *tick... tock... tick... tock* sent a strange feeling through him. Was it fear? And if it was, what was he supposed to be frightened of? He knew what jangled his nerves, and he didn't think it had anything to do with the rhetoric of time.

Having remembered it was the weekend and not a school day, he kept eyeing the phone on the wall near the refrigerator and damn near spilled the orange juice over the floor instead of over his cereal. Orange juice? That's right, since the taste of milk was equivalent to vomit in Joshua's opinion. And considering his somewhat fragile condition, he was forcing himself to eat something, so maybe that hot bitterness would finally be extinguished.

He placed the juice down and then dropped the box of muesli. "Christ, Joshua, you've turned into an uncoordinated asshole," he berated under his breath, but started giggling, nonetheless, at the image of what an uncoordinated asshole would look like.

As he went to pick the box up, he muttered, "Nice one, Mom." She'd bought blueberry muesli. His equal favorite to Cheerios.

When he stood, his eyes returned to the phone.

It hung there begging to be picked up, while overhead came the *tick... tock... tick... tock...*

He resisted. It was too early to be calling anyone, and it wasn't anyone he wanted to call, to wake up, to speak with... to *warn*. And what would the Debnars think if he did: that Joshua Triplow had lost his marbles at the tender young age of ten?

But, Mrs. Debnar, soon I'll turn eleven just like Sammy!

Firstly, though, he had to speak with Leon because... because of what?

He chomped away at a mouthful of blueberry muesli. Had his parents walked in on him at that moment, they'd have seen the face of profound thought and of, perhaps, one soon to turn fifty rather than eleven.

He had been *there with me, hadn't he? He had* actually *been in my dream?*

Sure, Joshy-Washy, and Santa Claus wants to give you a pencil with which to write... 'cause you've been a bad boy!

He tried for humor and all he got was a determined resolve to speak with his best friend, and a severe case of the heebie-jeebies. Then after that, he needed to confront Sammy.

Why?

Because Sammy was in trouble. He was as sure of that as he had ever been about anything.

⌒

"I don't know," Leon was saying uncomfortably, rubbing his forehead with furious intent.

It had just gone 8:30 a.m. and practising the *Cha Cha* was the last thing on their minds.

"Leon, don't you think it's a bit weird we were in each other's dream?"

"Yeah… but now you want to warn Sammy that the man in black is somehow going to invade his home? And when he does, Sammy and his folks are no more? Josh, I…" Leon stumbled badly.

"You what?"

Leon went red in the face, his dark brown eyes beaming like marbles. "I—I love you more than I could love a brother."

Now it was Joshua's turn to crank up the rheostat on facial color.

"But walking up to Sammy and saying that we think he's in real danger from the man in black 'cause of something we dreamt…" Leon winced. "He'll think we're frigging crazy. And in case you haven't noticed, things have quieted down at school. No one gives a shit about the man in black." He leaned forward in a conspiratorial fashion. "We're back to being kids—doing kids' stuff. And I like it that way. Besides, Ethan would have a field day if he caught wind of what we were thinking. And, something else if you haven't noticed, Sammy's a great guy, but he doesn't always think of what he's saying and the consequences. He's just as likely to blurt to Ethan what we told him. Then what?"

Joshua agreed, but remained steadfast. "We can't ignore last night."

"Why?" Leon was back to rubbing his forehead and going a shade of alabaster.

"Because it was a major warning, Leon." At least, that was what Joshua was hoping for, that it was not too late. He was being a right royal worry-wrought, wasn't he? "I think it was some type of… premonition. You know, seeing something before it happens. And what I saw was Sammy's house in complete darkness and the man in black sitting under his barfy green light in the middle of it. *Right* in the middle," Joshua emphasized. "At the very least we need to tell him to take precautions."

"O… okay, then," Leon stammered, turning completely alabaster.

He bolted from his bedroom to the upstairs toilet, slammed open the door and began dry-retching. It certainly wasn't a quiet affair.

"Honey?" came Mrs. Mendoza's concerned voice up the stairwell, followed by her rapid footsteps.

She hurried onto the upstairs hallway. "Honey, aren't you feeling well?"

Leon pulled out of the toilet, still looking under the weather but embarrassed, as well. "I—I got excited."

"And threw up?" Mrs. Mendoza said in disbelief. "That's some excitement, Hon."

Joshua could see his friend was going to dig himself a hole which, as much as he'd fumble to save himself from, would be futile. "Spit went down the wrong way, Mrs. Mendoza," Joshua lied real good. A miracle, but he pulled it off. Nonetheless, he thought he'd be sprung any second as her gaze drilled into him inquisitively. But after his ordeal last night, her eyes were at least human, and he could manage to hold his nerve.

She finally turned to her son. "Spit?"

Leon was nodding, his face deadpan.

"What are you boys up to today?" she asked, knowing full well what they were up to, but slightly anxious with these turn of events.

Reliving our collective nightmare, Mrs. Mendoza. Oh, it'll be so much fun! Bags of laughter. We're going over to Sammy's to tell him so. Want to join us?

Neither boy said a word.

⌒◦

Somewhat bashfully, they approached the doorstep of 17 South Lincoln Drive, rung the bell, and stepped back a little, not really knowing what to expect: a hallway that stretched impossibly far to where the man in black sat writing...

Skittery-scratch scratchy-scratch...

Instead, Sammy's mom opened the front door with a pleasant smile and a cleaning rag in one hand. Today's color of choice: orange. "Hello, boys." And without further salutations, "Sammy's upstairs—playing a video game, I expect."

"Jesus," Leon muttered.

"Sorry?" Mrs. Debnar asked.

Leon shook his head. "Nothing." But he avoided eye contact with her.

With relief came an unhealthy dose of dizziness. Joshua's vision was going in and out of focus, like a camera having trouble getting a fix on things. But, as with Mrs. Mendoza in the upstairs hallway, he managed to keep things together.

"I expect you boys will be on your skateboards before long," she said brightly.

"Sure will," Joshua returned the brightness, however false.

"I've got a handful of Ziploc bags, a pile of chicken-salad sandwiches, and a six-pack of Mountain Dew. I'll divvy them up so you three can take them with you when you go to the park." Jenny Debnar started walking from the front door before pausing. "Because I'm assuming that's where you'll be headed, right?"

"Right," Joshua said. "Thanks heaps, Mrs. Debnar." More false cheer.

"You're welcome heaps, Master Triplow," she said with genuine fondness. "And being a Saturday morning, there's no time to waste, is there?"

Joshua walked into the hallway of the Debnar household. Things certainly looked different in the bright light of day. Why, there was even carpet on the floors.

Leon followed, still thinking, *He's playing video games.*

Both got the weirdest sensation, expecting the interior to mutate into something abnormal at any second. Worse still, they had yet to enter the sofa room to take the staircase to the second floor—*where Sammy was playing video games.* Of course, they could've taken the alternate route which came in from the top of the sofa room, but that would have been pandering to unreasonable fears.

Leon's stomach was back to performing some impressive acrobatics, as if he had accidentally eaten his share of nasty microbes and then some. Whatever was in his mom's quesadillas the night before was doing a bit of a cha-cha all of its own.

Once in the sofa room, Joshua took full notice of the floor. That too had returned to its usual self. Gone were the impossibly shiny floorboards that fooled the eye into believing they were the surface of deep water, replaced by a pale pinkish carpet.

On rounding the corner into the second half of the L-shaped room came

Skittery-scratch scratchy-scratch...

Joshua sucked in a harsh breath.

"Hi, boys!" Lachlan Debnar said cheerfully. He then changed his tune. "Is anything the matter?" He placed his pen down, attempting to stretch his neck around the corner to get a better look of the boys.

Stepping further into the room, they laughed, red-faced.

"Everything's fine; we thought we'd disturbed you, that's all." Again, Joshua's lie was a fair attempt for a kid who couldn't lie for shit.

Lachlan sort of bought it because there wasn't much else that made any sense. "Tax returns, kids. They give me the—"

"Language," Jenny warned, coming into the room; she was smiling nonetheless, and wafting that cleaning rag about like some sort of cheerleader rehearsing her moves. In fact, it occurred to Joshua that Mrs. Debnar did a good deal of smiling, and he liked her for that. He *remembered* her for that. A nice lady whose smile often popped into his head when thinking about nothing in particular. Yet he was suddenly struck by the brilliance of her teeth, and the comparison they made to the image of her floorboards from last night. In the same manic style, he nonsensically reckoned it was possible she'd popped an Angry Mama into her mouth instead of the microwave where it was supposed to go, and after Mama had done some bitching de-scaling, it was Mrs. Debnar's turn to finish with a bitching scrub.

Lachlan raised his eyebrows. "Well, you get the idea, boys."

"Yeah, taxes are scary stuff." Another nervous laugh accompanied Joshua's reply.

When they entered Sammy's room upstairs, they pulled up on the spot, staring. There he was, sitting cross-legged in front of a widescreen monitor set up on the floor. Sammy preferred that to using a perfectly good desk nearby—and whether that made any sense or not, neither boy could have cared less. Fact was, Sammy was engrossed in a *video game*.

Both were having second thoughts about discussing last night's exciting adventures of the Incredible Duo at Sammy's. They hedged around the subject, sensing it sitting in the midst of their incidental jabber, like some wayward piece of junk, until Joshua broached what in Leon's opinion really should've been left aside.

Sammy listened attentively, his game on pause.

He then rolled over on his back, cackling.

Leon stabbed a look towards Joshua, and in it were the reproachful words of '*I told you so!*'

"That's a good one, Josh," Sammy said when he finally gathered himself. Without further regard for the Incredible Duo's adventures, he said, "You want to get out of here? Do the park?"

"Please don't say anything to Ethan," Leon said, feeling like a complete ass.

"What makes you think I would?" Sammy was a little offended.

The expression on his friends' faces told him that they considered him apt to such indiscretions. "Well, of course I won't, guys." His face then firmed into a serious mould. "I won't 'cause I had a dream last night, too."

Neither Joshua nor Leon spoke. Joshua could hear the blood rushing through his veins. *That's the sea, honey,* he could hear his mom say. And, in return: *No, mom, that's the sound of me crapping myself.*

"I didn't dream of the man in black, but I dreamt of being someplace dark. It was as if I was surrounded by moonlight that came out of nowhere. Everything was outlined in silver and the street was deserted, even though stores fronted it on both sides."

"What do you think it was?" Joshua asked in a hushed tone.

"I don't know, Josh."

"Where do you think you were?"

"I really don't know," Sammy replied in alike tones. It was as if the boys had suddenly become fearful of what the walls might do if they were overheard. "But I wasn't alone; at least, not to begin with. Some stranger was with me who wanted to ride my skateboard. I can't remember it all that well, only that it was worse than the nightmare of the man in black. A thousand times worse. And," he paused, fidgeting, "I'm a little scared." His hands were trembling.

"Did—did you hear… anything else?" Joshua asked softly.

"What makes you ask?"

Joshua shrugged, thinking of *that* sound skittery-scratch scratchy-scratch...

Sammy frowned, deep in thought, his eyes introspective. "I did. I think I did."

"A trumpet?" Leon recalled some fellow who'd died of a heart attack because of Mary Jane, yet still played the trumpet.

"No." Sammy shook his head, giving it some thought. "I heard… bells, but… they weren't loud like church bells, just kinda babyish. You know how nightmares are?" Sammy smiled nervously.

The boys were silent. Yes—they could all say with their hands on their hearts that they knew exactly what nightmares were like.

"I heard other things, too."

The boys remained deathly silent, fearing that their breath might be too loud... but for whom?

"I heard singing. It was out of tune with the bells."

Leon was shaking his head. "That doesn't sound like the man playing his trumpet."

Joshua felt that wave of dizziness flow through him once more. He rocked unsteadily on his feet.

Sammy's bedroom door cracked open.

None of them saw.

Then: "*BOO!*" Ethan shouted and burst into the room.

All three boys jumped and yelled with fright.

"Ethan!" Joshua snarled. "You're an asshole!"

"Language," Jenny called from downstairs.

"Sorry, Mrs. Debnar."

"That's okay, Josh."

"I almost *shit* myself!" Sammy griped quietly. "You could give someone a heart attack doing that."

"Sam the Man, you'll give yourself one long before anyone could even think of doing that to you, the way you play with that thing."

"Give it a rest," both Joshua and Leon chimed together.

"Sorry, guys. I just... I had a *really* bad night." And by the look of Ethan, he wasn't kidding.

"Huh, join the club," Sammy said in a forgiving tone. "So what's your story?"

Ethan looked at them sideways. "It's like mom and dad say: suggestions are made and then you dream them."

The others nodded like the three wise men. Though the man in black hadn't been on the top ten list of dreams for some time, things seemed to be ramping up once more.

Having met up with Craig and arriving at Citrus Community Park just after 10:00 A.M., it was obvious that despite the rough night had by most, if not all—they didn't speak of the subject for the rest of the day—they were on fire. And though it was usual for Ethan to claim the best moves, today's accolades went to Sammy Debnar.

Being the oldest at eleven, and with a little more leg power, he was the star attraction on the day: pulling strongly through the Cha Cha's three left 360s, then following this up with three impressive reverse turns before hitting the ramp. He was getting massive air, and was able to swivel the board at the very top of each jump with a quality of power and precision the other boys couldn't match, try as they might.

At one point, Sammy launched higher than ever and Ethan followed him up, up, up, shielding his eyes against the glare with one hand, even though the sun was behind him, and exclaimed, "Damn, he almost touched the clouds!"

The others laughed. Leon danced from foot to foot as if he had a full bladder and Joshua soaked up the moment, enjoying his time with his friends and his passion.

Things at the park hadn't started well for either Joshua or Leon, but they too eventually found their form. It seemed Sammy's gusto and brilliance was contagious. And it was a damned good bug to catch. Last night's disturbing dream, and the upside-down inside-out residue it had left them all with, had evaporated completely by late morning.

When things wrapped up about five that evening, as exciting, fun-filled and action-packed as it was, they were exhausted. No thanks to the impact of a bad night's sleep.

Tomorrow was Sunday and some had other commitments, or their parents did, which meant some could catch up and others couldn't. The Debnars always went to church. This was a total drag for Sammy, who believed he spent enough time just in regular school, making the further studying at Sunday school about as popular as haemorrhoids on a bad day. And Ethan's folks were having a barbeque with several of his cousins. Ethan didn't rate this affair quite as poorly as Sammy's, but still regretted the commitment. His cousins were several years older and they seemed to be somewhat full of themselves, as if by turning mid-teens was a right of passage to treat anyone younger as insignificant castaways not worth the bother of saving.

All was not lost, however: there was the upcoming pupil free day and so they hatched a plan for that coming Wednesday. As usual, they'd meet early in the morning, spend the day *Cha Cha*ing, then go home to finish the last two days of the week before another weekend.

This truly was shaping up to be a very good week.

Unfortunately, that Wednesday would be punctuated by Craig's absence. It was entirely unintentional, yet entirely avoidable.

Craig should've known better; he'd had past experiences with too much ice cream and cashews. Tuesday night, though, saw him hoeing into a second helping behind his parents' casual eyes... and these helpings had the added extra of choc-chip cookies. No problem there.

By the following morning, however, his stomach was having a few objections. He was careful not to let on to his folks, and tried to dismiss the griping pain. Deep and thoughtful breaths seemed to be doing the trick. The pain began to relinquish, and so he decided to make his way to Citrus Park. With a forced smile, because that also helped keep those nasty cashews (which hated his guts) at bay, he managed to get the entire way to the end of his driveway. Almost home free and out on the sidewalk, as if by magic that strip of cement would cure everything, the pain hit hard, rendering any idea of the *Cha Cha* about as appetizing as Sammy's haemorrhoids. Subsequently, the remaining members of the group would change their plans, opting for civil mayhem along Cresta Verde Drive and jumping the curbs of the local streets.

Regardless of the venue, Saturday the 3rd of September 2022 marked a significant change for these friends. Never again, in the passing of years, would they gather together at Citrus Community Park or Cresta Verde Drive.

Or anywhere else, for that matter.

THE DARK SUITS

~~~

Wednesday, September 7, 2022

It had begun as a delicious day, crisp and invitingly warm like clean cotton bed sheets, but would turn into a scorcher by mid-afternoon. The air crackling in the evaporation of its humidity like logs casting miniature explosions within an open fireplace.

The doorbell rang once; the chime relayed into the garage.

Bob swore under his breath, not relishing the idea of being disturbed.

He sauntered down the driveway to the front of the house, in no mood to rush. In fact, he and Josh had been sorting through the fishing tackle for the trip he'd promised him to Lake Welland, some 160 kilometres south of Corona, the following Saturday. Having joined Joshua in rising early that morning, they'd made the best of it.

Keen to see as many rigs were made or in order, Joshua had staunchly maintained his opinion that each fish required a certain rig.

"Mate, do you think the fish are going to know that the hook is above or below the sinker?"

"Dad, it's *what's* been proven to catch sea bass," Joshua had returned, frustrated.

"Oh, well, we shouldn't mess with the powers that be, so long as the fish are just as aware." Then, slightly mischievously: "Bait."

"Sorry, Dad?"

"It's pointless snagging an old sock on a hook to catch the sea bass of the century. What to do with bait." Bob had begun fishing earlier than anticipated, knowing this'd get his son fired up.

It'd been a good morning. A cheerful morning. One of those 'special' moments in time. An occasion to cherish. And, to be frank, there hadn't been a great deal to sort through, but that hadn't stopped them from indulging in their passion and prolonging that moment together.

When it was obvious there really was nothing else to do, Joshua had left to meet up with his friends and not without with some pangs of regret.

The night before, they'd sorted the boat, chatting incessantly about 'the spot' reputed by Zachary Mendoza to damn-near guarantee humongous catches of line-busting sea bass and halibut. It was a claim backed by several others, though perhaps not as biased as Zach. The thought was intoxicating and, walking along the driveway, Bob was still giddy with boyish excitement and annoyed at being disturbed. Unless it was Zach with more Lake Welland line-busting stories.

The Mendozas had a wedding commitment that they couldn't break the following Saturday, much to Zachary's irritation; otherwise they'd be joining the Triplows as they'd done in the past. It wouldn't quite be the same without them, but Bob was determined to spend quality time with his son, and not make another addition to the shameful trail of broken promises. Since Betty Mae's consultation, he'd made good on his word, irrespective of whether he was the type of father to break more promises than he kept. And, as far as he knew, Joshua's nightmare of the man in black had quietened considerably.

Maybe Zach had come over to say that he'd changed his mind on the wedding. Smart man, indeed.

But it wasn't Zachary standing at the front door. It was a tall, slender, dark-haired man, broad at the shoulders. Not entirely dissimilar to his friend, and for a moment Bob had to do a double-take. Though dressed in a short-sleeve cotton shirt and denim pants, something about this man's aura made Bob feel decidedly uneasy.

He'd begun raising his hand in recognition before realization settled in. His hand fell to his side once more.

The stranger turned toward him. "Bob Triplow?"

"Yes," Bob replied in perfect synchronization with Sue opening the front door.

"We need to talk."

"What about?" Sue asked from within the house, but the stranger's attention remained fixed on Bob.

"Important affairs relative to you."

"What important affairs?" Bob asked. The faint spectre of anxiety fluttered somewhere between the back of his throat and stomach, pushing aside his boyish giddiness. Immediately, he wanted nothing to do with this stranger whom he judged as being the bearer of bad news.

"There is much to tell you, much you have to know, and I'd rather talk inside, if that's alright with you?"

"Do I know you?" Bob inquired.

"No."

"Then why should we let you in?" Sue had picked up similar vibes to her husband.

Without a single note of hesitation, the dark-haired stranger said, "Your family has something very important to offer all."

"Really? And because of this you want to discuss matters in private?" Sue remained entrenched in the doorway.

"Yes," the stranger returned pleasantly, never taking his eyes from Bob.

The anxiety fluttering near the back of Bob's throat had gotten a whole lot worse, so much that it had started unplugging his thought processes, scrambling them so the red wire went where the green wire was meant to go, and the green wire went where the purple wire had come adrift.

Congratulations, Mr. Triplow, you're our winner for the day! How would you like it: in the head or the stomach? I have to tell you, stomach wounds are awfully painful. If you're going to die, might as well make it quick!

"So what's your story?" Sue flashed Bob a look that suggested this fellow wasn't going to take one step beyond the threshold.

"Please, I'd rather not be discussing matters at your front door," the stranger reaffirmed. "I can assure you I mean you no harm, nor do I intend to cause you trouble." That would turn out to be an out-and-out lie, but it was one the man had no choice but to use.

Bob hesitated before sliding between this bringer of bad tidings and Sue. "You're not selling religious goods or encyclopaedias, are you?"

The stranger smiled. "I can assure you I am not here to sell you anything." *Oh, but he was!*

"Oh, good," Bob said flatly, poking a finger beneath his glasses and rubbing his right eye, "'cause I'm not the religious type."

Sue laid a firm hand on his right arm that conveyed, *Honey, don't!*

In that same flat style, Bob said, "Just a concerned citizen, right?" and beckoned the man in. And he did this because, as the winner of bad news, it'd be poor sportsmanship to turn it down.

The stranger smiled and nodded to Sue on his way through. With deft surveillance of the house's interior, he crossed the sofa room and peeked in through to the dining area. "Mind if we sit here?"

"Is this going to take long?" Bob's voice retained that flat resonance. He was suddenly sounding extremely tired.

Winner! Winner! Winner! Take a seat and we'll blow your brains out!

"Matters need to be discussed," was all the stranger said.

"You have me at a rather uncomfortable disadvantage; do I know you?"

"Forgive me. My name is Raoul."

"So how is it that you know my name when I didn't know yours?"

Sue stood slightly behind the men, her eyes blazing jewels of near iridescent blue, her arms folded hard across her chest and her lips pressed flat together.

"Twelve years ago, Bob Triplow, you had an experience. One that no other, as far as it's known, has survived." Raoul invited himself to a seat at the dining table.

Bob's blood had begun to freeze in his veins. It was a case of either stumbling to the dining table and taking a seat next to his new bosom buddy, or collapsing on the floor. He opted for the chair and sat with a thump, saying, "I don't wish to reopen those wounds."

"You have no choice."

"Oh? And who's making such demands?" His voice warbled past a lead lump. *Five minutes ago I was sorting fishing tackle. I want to go back to sorting fishing tackle, if you don't mind. I want to show this fellow the door who says the wounds haven't closed.*

But they haven't, have they?

Winner! Winner! Winner!

"Your son."

"Joshua?" Sue immediately interjected, approaching the table but refusing to sit, an acute prickling sensation taking revenge on the back of her neck.

"Your son's been afflicted by a reoccurring dream these past eight months or so. They are intensifying, and you've been concerned enough to visit a psychologist to see if something's amiss."

"They've actually gotten a lot better," Sue said with distinct dislike for this stranger, her arms white across her chest. "I don't mean sounding defensive, but you barge into our house, begin assaulting my family, and then state you've been stalking us."

"*Every* kid in the area's been having the same dream," Bob reasoned.

"Of all the children in Corona, you'll find Joshua was the first to dream the dream." Raoul remained fixed on Bob. "It's possible all the other incidents have been merely a ploy for maximizing your son's attention. It's highly probable that, ultimately, none of the other children were ever the intended target."

"I've somehow brought this upon Joshua? Because of my past?" Bob's mouth had gone as dry as desert sands. His words chafed across his tongue, sounding *clacky*, as if he were giving a botched attempt of the African Bushmen's phonetic language.

"Einstein believed both time and space were integrally locked, like the cross-weaves in a fabric, and that there were levels in this fabric which made travelling from one point to another as easy as walking from your sofa room into this dining room. Twelve years ago, you, Bob Triplow, travelled into another dimension—and returned. In the existence of everything that has ever been, you would seem, beyond question, one remarkable being. This is a special gift, most likely one in an entire universe—or universes, if you will—and it seems to be a gift you have passed on to your son. It is this that you will use to guide your son through this other dimension, because you *will* need to make this journey yet again."

Bob's anxiety had increased tenfold. The very thought of reliving the past horrors of Adelaide in 2011 caused a narcotic swill at his physical centre. Here it whirled in a giant eddy and as hard as he fought its currents, it seemed a losing battle. He could feel himself going under. He had to stay afloat.

The quietness that oozed through the room was deafening, setting up a choir of mosquitoes in the ears of those within it.

It was a pupil free day at Citrus Hills Elementary, and since most kids in the area under the age of twelve attended the school, the distant sound of child's play was no surprise. However, in the fey quietness, the sound seemed almost intoxicatingly odd.

"My son's going nowhere." Sue's words were chips from an Arctic blizzard, that prickling sensation now painful.

Raoul finally directed himself to Sue. "Your son needs to return to the other dimension, which your husband has travelled, in order to avert the ultimate catastrophe." His face bespoke a man who was not fooling around. A man who didn't enjoy the situation it placed these people in, but was resolved to finish what he had come to do. His face was that of a stone carving.

More silence hung in the air, in which far-off child's play mingled with the surrealistic sound of fictitious mosquitoes, both riding the balmy spring morning within the Triplows' dining room.

"I've heard enough." Sue was feeling somewhat light-headed herself. It was Raoul's steely determination that she found completely disconcerting. "Leave, *now!*"

But it was more. Much more. She'd been by Bob's side in 2011 and she'd seen things, fantastical things, that she'd never have believed if she hadn't seen them herself.

Mad dogs and Englishmen, Suzy. She heard the voice of her mother. A voice she hadn't heard since that hellish journey, one in which her mother had succumbed.

As if reading her mind, Raoul spoke with quiet affirmation. "He must undertake this journey."

"The only reason I don't pick up the phone right this minute and call the cops is because…"

I believe you

"…I'm desperately trying to be reasonable. You, however, are a very sad man. You're intruding on *our* morning. And you're making it very difficult for me to remain reasonable."

"Either your husband and son act, or the fate of the human race will yet again suffer obliteration. Illogical as this seems to you, the consequences of not returning to this other dimension will be global annihilation. By ignoring what should not be ignored, you will put in peril every living being on the face of this Earth."

"Yet *again?!*"

"It's happened before." Raoul's eyes returned to Bob's. "On other Earths. To other human civilizations."

"I'm in no mood for… fairy-tales of little goblins down in the backyard, conceived by the mind of a raving lunatic," Sue said in the wake of her storm through the sofa room towards the front door.

Mad dogs and Englishmen, Suzy!

"Now, fuck off!" Any attempt at social politeness had gone by the wayside. Christ, she was now using the kind of language her mother had been somewhat renowned, or infamous, for. She opened the front door to demonstrate to Raoul how he could do just that.

He made a move as if he were about to get up, before calmly stating, "You've known for an awfully long while that something hasn't been right, Bob Triplow. The night you first went to your son's bedside to calm him from his screaming night terrors, you knew. Try as you might to repress those uncomfortable wounds, there's no denying Joshua's dream has set much consternation within you."

Instead of siding with his wife, Bob leaned forward, elbows resting on the table, hands clamped together, and replied, "We deserve an explanation, far more than what you're giving us. Sue's right: you *do* sound utterly crazy. Here you sit, calm as can be, implicating us in some sort of magical tale that no one could be expected to believe." He delivered this with a calmness that defied the turmoil that had built within. "I mean," he started, before dragging his hands down his face and laughing, "I've watched *One Flew Over the Cuckoo's Nest.*"

"Bob, enough bullshit!" Sue's anger was tainted by trepidation. Maybe if Raoul "fucked off" as she had so eloquently suggested, what he was saying would… what? Be reversed? Undone? The lilt of the morning picking up just prior to the doorbell ringing? The past horrors of Adelaide would, once more, disappear into the ether of all things that have come and gone. And maybe she'd stop using such language.

"I'm at a loss to give you what I do not have—that *no one* has," Raoul was saying. "However, you *do* know that you ventured into this other dimension."

Bob shook his head.

"What did you see?" Raoul eyed him closely.

Continuing to lean heavily on his elbows, and peering glassy-eyed over a bunch of clasped fingers, Bob desperately did not want to remember. His face had drained of all color. His own nightmare of yesteryear, however, was bubbling up through the eddy of those emotions threatening to drag him under. The Terminus of Death… the dead people… the wee-whaaing buses… the sliding glass doors… the enormity of it all, floating amongst an endless sea of gray. Mostly he was recalling her— the *bitch*!

*COME HERE, YOU WORTHLESS LITTLE SHIT, AND
TAKE YOUR COMEUPPANCE!!*
"Most of what I might've known has been lost," Bob finally
managed to pry from his mouth.

"Repressed?"

Sitting motionless, Bob mumbled, "I guess," sweat coursing
over his body.

Raoul wasn't convinced, but there was no point getting
bogged down. "What I can tell you is that we believe that this
other dimension could be another universe co-existing aside
this one. We refer to this universe as 'Black Eternity.' We believe
it's an asylum for the mad; at least, madness projects from it.
The very tether that compels Black Eternity to devour Earths,
we *think* we understand. *Had* anyone escaped, as you did, Bob
Triplow, it's reasonable to believe that the progressive devouring
of Earths would have ceased, or at least been disrupted in the
long ago past. Just as it has been here since 2011. This Earth
should've met its catastrophic end. By rights, it should not exist.
And you would seem to have somehow allowed this to happen."

Raoul paused briefly. Then, "However, this Earth would
seem to remain in the grip of its event horizon."

"It's a black hole?"

"We do not know—not for certain. However, there is one
profound distinction: Black holes consume regardless. If caught
in a true event horizon, life would take on a vastly different
slant; you wouldn't simply take a stroll along a road, because
that road would be coming adrift, as would you and everything
you'd come to know. I'm afraid Black Eternity, whatever it is,
has merely regressed… It has been waiting for twelve years. This
tenuous cessation," Raoul's voice took on a deeper resonance,

"is bombarded, *threatened*, by a constant enticement that lures it to Earths, like fish to bait."

"You keep saying 'we;' there are others who know of this... this Black Eternity?" Bob was going under. That eddy was devouring him from inside out.

"Yes."

"Like a secret society?"

"Yes."

"For what purpose?"

Raoul contemplated the worth of such a revelation. Then conceded. "We are from the stars." He held up a hand before Sue could start; she'd crossed the sofa room to take position at the dining room entrance. "As preposterous as this sounds amongst all else, I'd have an educated guess that we are not the only ones walking amongst the human race from the stars. Your own historical records tell of interactions between other beings and yourselves. SETI would have you all believe that your technology is sophisticated enough to foil any would-be star traveller. Both a brazen and foolish assertion."

"And your purpose?"

"Not mine. But those of whom I'm a part do not wish to compete for planet colonization with the human race. Their objective is to ensure this other dimension succeeds in devouring one Earth after another, as it has been for, perhaps, millennia."

Bob was shaking his head. It hurt and he was drowning within. "I don't... understand."

"There are other Earths scattered throughout the universe, and I dare say throughout others. At least, it's possible. But there's only one other species that shares many common traits to *Homo sapiens*—us."

Sue laughed disparagingly. If she opted for sarcastic ridicule, she might come to her senses.

But those things she'd seen... that hellish blight in South Australia's history... had no scientific explanation, and remained a conundrum. Unresolved, regardless of the scientific community's declarations to the contrary.

"And that places your species in direct conflict with *some* of my kind. Whilst nothing more than a small band of renegades, and a dying breed of their own, their intention to steer this Earth to an early demise is no less diminished. No less lethal." Raoul didn't waver. He didn't blink. "And such groups have populated other Earths, no doubt."

He allowed this to be absorbed before continuing. "They're able to see signs of impending disaster, and assist in ensuring that that disaster is successful. The signs have been strengthening over the past year."

"Joshua and myself—are we in danger from these renegades?"

Raoul lied yet again. "I believe they are more interested in the grander picture and, whilst you and Joshua are part of that, their arrogance overlooks your potential, despite the past."

"But you're here."

"I do not wish to see this Earth's demise. I am convinced both you and Joshua can stop this from happening. I also believe if you stop this from happening here, it may positively affect the future for all Earths."

The surreal mosquitoes buzzed in the silence.

Children played in a far-off land.

Bob placed a finger under his glasses and rubbed an eye with some force. "What was I supposed to have done?" His mind was racing. "You say this implicates Joshua. Jesus, he wasn't even *born* in 2011!"

Raoul unnerved what was left of Sue's resistance in an instant, by abruptly turning to her and saying, "Your son, too, has entered the other dimension."

Her back didn't quite slam into the kitchen wall, but it hit with enough force to jiggle the clock above her.

"And he has done so through the man in black's supplications."

Bob removed his glasses, placed them on the table, and pressed his fingers into his eyes. *May I say that the 12-gauge is the best option? It blows your head clean off your shoulders in an instant!*

Winner! Winner! Winner!

The children playing down Chasing Boulevard continued screaming and living it up. Goosebumps garlanded Sue's arms, spine and legs. She shivered, her mind abuzz.

The kitchen clock ticked in its tireless fashion overhead.

Her mother had paid the ultimate price for her love. She could've simply packed her belongings and left the state. But then, what mother would abandon her child? An only child at that?

Deranged dogs and Englishmen—the leashes have broken… the dogs have escaped. Worse still, their deranged owners are running amok, ranting stories of Armageddon and threatening to take my family, my oven and my baking trays. And I've had enough of the things I love being taken away!

She sidled across to the wall phone and quietly lifted the handpiece from its cradle. There she stood, just hanging onto it, in a daze. Her finger unintentionally hovered over the phone's keypad. Just who she was going to call, she had no idea.

"The man in black was once just a man. But at some point in the history of this universe, something must have gone tragically wrong. We believe he remains forever incarcerated deep within Black Eternity, and it is from here that he fulfils his poisonous invites by writing the numbers zero-zero, zero-one. An irresistible incitement to which Black Eternity seems compelled to respond. Whilst conjecture, our confidence in the probability is high. The information so far gathered has this as a constant marker."

"You haven't answered my question." Bob was numb all over.

Raoul nodded. "For as many Earths, there are and has been as many Patrick Nesmiths—the man in black. At the moment he's born, his fate is to one day begin writing zero-zero, zero-one."

"So if this is inherited," Sue asked, "why hasn't someone taken care of the next Patrick Nesmith before he… transgresses? He's one person compared to a global population." She'd rather avoid Bob getting his answer. Perhaps there was a way to defeat Patrick Nesmith, to thwart this Black Eternity's desire. That being so, her family could be left alone.

"Populations," Raoul corrected. "Killing a man who's already dead? Tricky."

"You said—"

Raoul laid a firm gaze upon Sue. "I said that for as many Earths, there are as many Patrick Nesmiths. I didn't say that taking care of the next Patrick Nesmith's life would disrupt the invitation. Just that each such man would seem predisposed to follow the last. In a desperate bid for atonement, each eventually takes a position in the church."

"He's a man of religion?" Bob asked, his vocal cords rasping against each other like useless bellows.

Again, Raoul nodded. "Redemption remains forever elusive for the living, and effectively dealing with a dead man that is somewhere—"

Over the rainbow, Raoul hesitated at the sudden intrusion.

"—that no other, but you, has returned from. Problematic. Like a record, or as paranormal investigators call a 'residual haunting,' the invitation may be caught in its own loop. Perhaps augmented by each subsequent Patrick Nesmith's absorption. The originating source *has* to be broken—the loop severed, not merely disrupted, as you managed to do twelve years before."

"You keep avoiding my question of how I achieved this, because it's completely lost on me."

"Bob, I cannot provide answers that are simply not known. You are looking for a solution that only you can discover. Or rediscover." Raoul felt for the man and, eyeing him closely, in the quietness that ensued, he asked, "Did you ever have a recurring nightmare, like your son's, before 2011?"

"No," Bob said, then changed his mind. "I might've, but it wasn't of a man in black, just a product of a tortured childhood."

Sue looked on in wonder and silence. Could there be a connection? Could this be something passed down from father to son? A Triplow predisposition? "Bob," she warned, fearing for her husband, hysterical though that might be.

Bob laughed mirthlessly. "It's okay, hon. Such things are long in the past and, until moments ago, long forgotten."

"What was *your* nightmare?" Raoul pressed.

"The *bitch,*" Bob spat forth, "tormented the children under her care. She was as evil a person that could walk this earth. She was a living nightmare and she chased me long after I escaped the orphanage." He glared at Raoul. "That doesn't sound at all like this Patrick fellow, does it?"

"Could you be mistaken?"

"There's no mistaking the *bitch*!" Bob seethed.

"Is she the one who lead you to Black Eternity?"

Bob shook his head slowly. "No… maybe… I really can't remember," he said through numbed lips. "If you think I hold the all-conquering key, I do not."

Raoul continued without further digressions. He feared he'd given over more information than anyone could possibly be expected to grapple with in a single lifetime, let alone a single morning. "You've no choice. Doing nothing guarantees this world's eventual loss to Black Eternity." Raoul's stony expression firmed even harder, if that was possible. "Patrick Nesmith remains, even in death, desperate to make atonement, desperate for someone to step in and break the loop which has been perpetuated for millennia. If he did not lead you into Black Eternity twelve years ago, then it could be due to your ability to escape Black Eternity that he has chosen Joshua for this purpose. For a child's mind is open, accepting, and therefore ready to believe what adults dismiss."

Bob was shaking his head slowly in disbelief. If the whirlpool at the centre of his soul strengthened further, he'd disappear into his very own event horizon.

Click!

Fuck—a misfire!

"You conveniently fall back onto suppositions, and yet are so confident with regards to my family's involvement," Sue said with some suspicion, phone still in hand.

"Take a telescope and point it to the stars. What do you see?"

"What the hell has that got to do with it?"

"You see galaxies and stars and planets and asteroids. All kinds of objects and phenomena. For at least twelve years—perhaps much, much longer—Black Eternity has resided beside this world, but nobody knows. Nobody sees. Not even we, but we know the signs to look for. And should any other happen to stumble upon a mote of evidence, they assume it's the result of technical malfunctions or the weather changing due to global warming, and so discard such findings. We have been looking for a very long time and have caught the odd glimpse here and there. And with each subsequent glimpse, our pool of knowledge grows just that little bit stronger. Black Eternity does not want to be known. It does not want to give up its secrets. Suppositions and confidence are the only tools we have."

"There's no point, then, is there?" Sue uttered in a dreamlike state.

"Bob came close twelve years ago," Raoul reiterated.

"But no cigar."

"Not then," Raoul said simply, leaving the doorway well ajar on possibilities.

Mad dogs and Englishmen...

Bob swallowed an enormous lump, which momentarily threatened to suffocate him. "How do you propose we go about this sordid adventure?"

"Whilst this Earth's Patrick Nesmith has long been gone, his last known whereabouts was in the church parsonage. Located in the suburb of Lower Mitcham, Adelaide, South Australia, you'll be best to begin on Nesmith Drive."

"Can't be," Bob choked.

Raoul raised his eyebrows.

"When I slipped into this... Black Eternity, I was in Noarlunga, Adelaide, South Australia, which is a helluva long way from Lower Mitcham."

Unwaveringly, Raoul reinforced, "Though the parsonage no longer exists, it remains a strong starting point of reference. Possibly a portal exists between dimensions."

"I was in *Noarlunga*," Bob repeated as if it meant something.

"That might be so, but it's neither your, nor your son's, first destination. If Lower Mitcham proves fruitless, perhaps..."

Bob heaved in a shuddering breath.

"Bob," Raoul said gently. "Patrick Nesmith has chosen Joshua for a reason; he'll be the one to identify any potential portal. To that point, he'll be the one who guides you. From there on, you'll guide your son. Somewhere within your memories, you'll find what you'll need to do once you're—"

Over the rainbow. Again Raoul was caught off-guard.

"—inside."

"I was going to take my family away for the weekend to catch sea bass." The rip within Bob's physical being was becoming increasingly threatening. His eyes filled with a sooty haze.

"The Sea-Brass will still be there, if you're successful."

Sue looked down at the phone in her hand, mesmerized by its very presence. There was something about the way it looked. It was a phone, right? Bloody genius! But there was *something* about it. The little holes in the ear piece appeared to be mocking her.

"I've a right to be with Bob and Josh," she said, not without some emotion. "I mightn't have shared their nightmares, but I am their wife and mother."

"That's a poor decision."

"What would you know of family matters?"

Mad dogs…

"Forgive me, Sue. You'd serve your husband and child best if you let them go by themselves."

"How so?" The phone was now firmly squeezed in her hand, her knuckles white around its body.

"Bob's going to have his hands full watching out for your son."

Sue laughed without humor. "I'm relegated to a dithering woman who'll scream at the drop of a hat and fuck the whole thing up, is that it?"

"You'd be an invaluable asset."

This derailed Sue. She stared at this stranger in her midst. The phone remained strangled in her hand. "But I equally fear you'd be used to distract Bob."

"I'm not easily manipulated."

Raoul smiled for the first time since entering their lives and destroying it. "Of that I am sure. However, Sue, you must know that whilst Patrick Nesmith may be desperate for the loop to be severed, Black Eternity *must* eat. Outside of his poisonous invitation, we do not know what other mechanisms incite its need to feed. There may well be forces that don't share Patrick Nesmith's desperation."

The house had gone deathly quiet.

Those pesky mosquitoes had returned en masse to haunt the ear canals of those within its walls.

The mix of child's play and God only knew what else was making for a weird soup. Fleetingly, Sue envied those kids for their innocence, their unworldliness. Growing up really wasn't all it was cracked up to be.

Then out of the soupy potpourri came a boy's voice. Bob and Sue were both able to make out who he was from his tone. It was their son, Joshua… Joshua in a normal world. Joshua having innocent fun, muck-assing about with his friends. Just another boy like all the rest, but unaware of the dangerous concoction being brewed for him right here, where he would come and sit and gobble down a meal, talking excitedly of the day he'd had and, perhaps, of Ethan handing the baton of his expertise in surfing the neighborhood curbs on his skateboard over to Sammy.

Their beautiful boy's birthday was approaching. Fancy that! They'd lined up the latest version of *Astra-Links*, for it was purported to be faster, with ungraded wheels and state-of-the-art design and materials. *Well, forget that crap, son. We've got an even bigger surprise in store for you!*

There was an explosion of applause and unrestrained hollering and whooping somewhere along Chasing Boulevard.

Someone swore and there was more hollering and whooping.

"I'll take my chances," Sue said, finally.

"At the peril of those you so richly love?" Raoul said without hesitation. "The lull you speak of in Joshua's nightmare is temporary. He'll be consumed by it, for I fear Patrick Nesmith will not stop until he has Joshua's undivided attention. And just before this world is lost, you will lose your son."

Sue returned the handpiece to its cradle and closed her eyes, wondering why it had been in her hand and thinking once more, *Mad dogs and Englishmen, indeed.* Bob had all but gone under the whirlpool of inner turmoil.

Raoul stood, his work done. "Time is not in your favor. The invitation incessantly urges Black Eternity to act on its instincts."

"What if we fail?" Bob looked up into the man's face, pleading. His legs wouldn't support his weight, so he didn't bother trying to remove himself from the chair.

Raoul offered an expression and Bob didn't like what he saw in it.

"Goodbye, Bob." He faced Sue and nodded.

The stranger exited their lives as mysteriously and thoroughly as he had entered it.

Bob and Sue remained motionless, silent, lost in their own thoughts.

After long minutes, Bob laughed miserably. He realized they required number seven hooks for those steroid-sized sea bass. He'd better duck down to Fernando's Fishing & Tackle just as soon as this Wednesday morning special had worn off.

In the silence, Joshua could be heard yelling from down Chasing Boulevard. It echoed like wil-o'-the-wisp through the house: "Go, Sammy! Jump the curb!"

Another chimed in, most likely Leon, but could've been either Ethan or Craig; it was hard to tell. "Yeah, jump the curb, Sammy!"

The ensemble then yelled in unison, "*Jump the curb, Sammyyyy!*"

Well after sundown, Bob had dubiously chased down the sandman. It was an effort he'd regret, because that was when the strange dreams began.

Weird developments like toffee apples and worms eating their way through the rotten cores, smothered with a syrupy red candy. Candy that had the nauseating resemblance of semi-crystallized blood.

Only there wasn't one toffee apple, there were hundreds... thousands... millions, perhaps even billions and trillions...

Each representing an Earth, and each swollen to capacity with people. With no room to move, they were like specimens in a madman's science experiment. Each hooked up to a series of pipes. And smoke twisted and curled up these pipes.

That's the essence of human beings!

And there were hundreds! Thousands! Millions! *BILLIONS! TRILLIONS!*

We need air purification, Mr. Triplow, and you're just the man for the job! Someone was yelling at the top of his lungs. Someone not connected to the torturing or the tortured; someone somewhere off in the faraway land.

Lounging above the orchids of smokestacks were massive black leeches. They puffed away, getting high on the fear and despair of their human captives.

But the real hell was that the captives knew what was happening to them. They knew and they couldn't escape… they couldn't die… they just had to endure the interminable suffering.

Now and then, someone would lose their mind and start laughing like a loon, changing form while doing so, becoming *balloon-like…* Hadn't Bob seen this before? Twelve years ago when Adelaide had been torn apart?

I forget… You knew something was wrong… the wounds never healed, **YOU WORTHLESS LITTLE SHIT!!**

Trapped for eternity—death not an option—the inconsolable faces pressed white to the inner wall of one Earth after another. Their numbers simply went on and on, making for a decoupage of horror against the syrupy membrane of blood red.

Toffee apples *should* represent fun amongst a carnival atmosphere; but here, each and every prisoner shuddered and jiggled as their essence was slowly drained.

What is a dream? Is it reality? Can your dreams come true? Got a little high back in twenty... eleven and that felt *pretty fucking real!*

Those leeches... they like what they taste... they can't get enough... more... they want more...

The late Sammy Davis Junior began dancing across the floor, jauntily delivering a macabre version of "The Candyman:"

> *...'cause they mix you with love and make you taste oh-so sweet...*
> *The toffee-apple tree, the toffee-apple tree...*

Inside one of those toffee apples, plastered against an infinitesimal patch on the other side of the syrupy red, was the terrified face of his son. Bob gasped with horror. His eyes skating here and there, not wanting to believe, but being drawn to that infinitesimal patch, the innocent face of his lovely and loving boy. Bob's feet began kicking under the comforter, just as they used to long ago when visiting The Terminus of Death.

Then, in another toffee apple, Bob saw his own face in the same white press of bottomless fear and suffering. Etched to cruel depths, and surrounding this lost world and its civilization, were fissures of excruciating hopelessness, where pure madness agitated in a writhe of glowing balloons.

> *...'cause they mix you with love and make you taste*
> *oh-so sweet...*
> *The toffee-apple tree, the toffee-apple tree...*

Though still wide awake, Sue didn't disturb him; she remained in a state of disbelief, utterly drained, if not despaired, from the day's spectacular event. Somewhere in the night, a cat cried along Chasing Boulevard. The mewling was not unlike a child who had suddenly found themselves in a terrifying ordeal.

Sue shuddered.

A high moon cast all below with their own doppelgangers. Trees clawed across sidewalks and streets, and up the sides of houses, with their sinuous shadows. Shrubs laid puffballs of darkness here and there. The streets were empty. All was still.

Bob awoke with a start and looked around, for a moment not knowing where or when he was.

"You were having a nightmare," Sue said. "Like you used to."

"Oh, shit, Sue. Can this be happening to us again?"

To that she had no answer. At least, not one that she relished to give voice to.

He eased himself from the sheets and padded into the en suite.

With the cat's eerie mewling penetrating the walls, he looked into the mirror and wondered in the same disbelief as his wife. What kind of terror was he about to lead both his son and himself into?

It was one thing to stumble into the unknown like a clueless patsy, as he did so in 2011. It was an entirely different ballgame when you knowingly walked the gauntlet. Round two would come with prior knowledge of *some* of the things that *might* lay before them. But not everything. He was, after all, going after a man in black. That was more than he'd known on his first excursion into—

Black Eternity, baby, where madness prevails!

He bent over the toilet bowl and retched.

The cat's mewling crept around him, pinching at his skin as if to test its resilience.

It was true to say that he'd tried convincing himself of Raoul's unbelievable origins, because surely he was not the genuine article? The SETI he had mentioned, the Search for Extraterrestrial Intelligence project, had been on guard for years without turning up a shred of evidence confirming alien existence, let alone visitations to Earth. It would have been easy to dismiss all Raoul had said; easy to think that such unimaginable realities existed only in the sad gray matter of a struggling man.

Perhaps Raoul had been high on something a lot more mind-bending than the suite of recreational drugs available to the addicted user.

And dreams of a man in black were the product of children's wildly fertile, attention-seeking minds.

Surely not a single word that had been uttered this morning could be the least bit taken seriously.

Baseless fabrications that would have excited the creative juices of the likes of John Carpenter or Stanley Kubrick, who'd ensure the protagonists would battle wits with creatures from exotic and far-reaching places in the universe. Playing out not just on one Earth, but an entire series.

But he couldn't do it. No matter how hard he tried, he just couldn't do it.

Because the wounds are oozing… the terror real…

Did this mean the *bitch* was still on the prowl? After all, wasn't she the one who drew him into Black Eternity?

Bob retched again.

His gooseflesh hardened, the cat's mewling pulling each nodule up ever tighter.

Sue had been little solace, her usual rock-solid rationality unable to refute Raoul's mumbo-jumbo. Not a comforting word to allay his fears had slipped from her mouth. She could've argued that Raoul was some mad bastard that just happened to choose their door and knock on it that morning. That he just stumbled up their driveway rather than that of the O'Casey's next door.

Then he could've agreed. *Yes! Yes, that's right, honey! Just some poor mad bastard stumbling about without any purpose or direction, needing to fill some other's head with the disturbances churning about his! Just like the crackpots and Roswell, you say! A weather balloon falls to ground and the world overreacts!*

What a hoot! What a riot! A bit of truth mixed with a load of malarkey! Thanks, hon, I'm sure to sleep well tonight!

What a load of shit!

I'm gonna puke!

He leaned over the toilet bowl and did just that, once more.

"How's it going in there?" came Sue's voice.

"Splendid," Bob said in a strained tone. "I've never felt so good."

Having finished his affairs with the toilet bowl, he returned to the vanity mirror. Staring into the man's eyes who stared back, he saw fear. *Real* fear. He also saw a man wracked with guilt and bitter shame. Was he prepared to lead his son to 'another dimension?'

The Twilight Zone for real?

You have no alternative. Raoul was reciting his lines once more, inside his head.

"*Boo!*" Bob tried scaring away the man in the mirror. But for all his fear, for all the crazy uncertainties, the man held his ground.

The wheels of life were turning, but sometime during the past twenty-four hours Bob had jumped off that rig. Whether simply a case of mind over matter, he couldn't shake the feeling that he'd become ten minutes out of sync with the rest of life. As if the entire world had jigged to the right and when he had tried going with it, he fumbled and staggered to the left.

The cat cried again in the small hours of darkness.

A new wave of gooseflesh tingled painfully over Bob's flesh, and a cold hand of doom caressed his vital organs.

I don't know what to expect when we go through the portal, or how to go about avoiding dangers. I don't know if I can protect my son or myself, let alone the human race.

He turned from the mirror, unable to look further upon the man staring at him, and put his hands to his face, holding back the tears throbbing in his eyes.

He believed Raoul, down to his very last word. There was no doubt. No need for confirmation. Dreams… dimensions… beings from other worlds… Crazy it might be, but where it mattered within him, instincts and intuition marked it as real as anything else in existence.

Ten minutes out of sync, with a hopeless task set before him… and his son who was yet to know.

"I'm going downstairs for a soda water," Sue said, coming into the en suite. She placed a hand gently on his shoulder. "Would you like one?"

Bob shook his head. She padded down the stairs to the kitchen and through the house, lit by the muted streetlight seeping in through the windows. She felt comfortable in this house, where she and Bob and Joshua had lived happily for all of Joshua's life.

He only knew of this house, of Corona, his friends… these had been his world. She didn't feel at all anxious in the penumbra.

His world, she thought, standing in the kitchen in some kind of swoon. Again, she pondered over the *Astra-Links* hidden away in their wardrobe; that was sure to thrill him on his special day. Almost a teenager.

She sighed heavily, went to the refrigerator and yanked open the door.

The kitchen clock ticked away in the muted light. She glanced at it and wondered why her attention kept returning to the damned thing, as well as the phone since this morning. Was there some latent suggestion interwoven amongst Raoul's revelation that had crept into her subliminal thoughts, to resurface as a point of intrigue?

She poured herself a soda water, the effervescent bubbles spitting away furiously in the ghostly light of the kitchen.

She took a sip. The bubbles tickled her nose, but she found no pleasure in either them or the cold water sizzling down her throat.

Tick-tock… tick-tock… tick-tock… The clock overhead continued its unique chatter into the night.

Again her attention went to the clock, and from there it slipped to the wall phone.

Her appetite in the soda water vanished.

Maybe it hadn't been something that Raoul had said, at all. Because… she was remembering something. Seeing something.

A hand plucked a phone from the wall in Hastings, South Australia, where she had lived with Bob and where the holocaust of 2011 had escalated frighteningly.

Why was she remembering this time, of all times?

Tick-tock... tick-tock... tick-tock...

Blow her down, if she wasn't hanging onto the phone once again at 22 Chasing Boulevard. She couldn't recall picking it up, as she really couldn't recall doing so earlier that day. One minute it was just hanging about, the next it was in her hand.

Sue looked stupidly at it, as if it'd somehow willed itself into her grasp.

And just as she'd done those many years ago in Hastings, she pressed the little green symbol, representing a receiver, and brought it to her ear.

Perhaps she was attempting to make that call again, from all those years ago... for what? A way out of the hellhole Adelaide had disintegrated into? Only this was Corona in the year 2022. Back then, she'd contacted her mother. Had she paid attention to the fact that her mother was old and shouldn't have been dragged further into the melee of 2011, there was an outside chance that she'd still be alive. That she'd have gotten to know her grandson, and Josh would've gotten to know her. As it was, he had no grandparents.

So whom did she think she was calling now? Spirits from the other side?

The soda water sitting on the island counter had lost much of its fizzle.

Listening intently to the receiver, almost believing the voice of her mother would cut through the years she'd been dead, what she heard was what she'd heard in Hastings.

The tinny voice of a man jabbering: *At the third stroke, the time will be twelve... twelve... twelve o-one A.M....*

Beep! Beep! Beep!

If penned down, depending on the time of day, and your interpretation of the stuttering, that'd read: zero-zero, zero-one. And for those with a mathematical penchant: 00:01

Sue dropped the receiver. It hit the floor with a clatter.

Her eyes snapped towards the clock ticking away like an evil son-of-a-bitch, then slowly towards the ceiling, above which her beautiful boy slept.

Whether she wanted to or not, she knew what she had to do. And hated Raoul for what he had done and herself for what she was willing to do.

∽

That afternoon... in a place where people could lose themselves

A new Ford sedan pulled into the driveway of the Comfort Inn on the outskirts of Highway 17. Though only several kilometres from the main drag in the heart of San Bernardino County, Halloran Springs might as well have been smack bang in the middle of a lifeless planet. The air rang with its own kind of empty resonance, like muffled crickets, and from where in the hell the word 'Springs' had been adopted Raoul couldn't fathom. Human beings had their quirks, and often this gave rise to names that, on face value, had little connection to that which they were, or had been, applied. *History,* he supposed; there was *history* that he didn't know about regarding the apparent misnomer.

A plume of dust had followed the car in on its wake, creeping ever higher in the still balmy air of August. For a long while, the rented ride from Avis sat below this without a single movement.

The dust hung as if in suspended animation over this flyspeck town—and it had the flies to be-speck it with. They bombarded Raoul through his open window, teasing him with their sticky feet.

From inside the car, Raoul made an immediate observation. If one wanted to get lost, this was as good a start as any. Sitting in the middle of some great plain of dust and tumbleweed, this was that typical little town made famous through schlock flicks. The type that had the knack of capturing the essence of forlorn in a single scene and carrying it on a script of less life than a plank of drowned wood.

Having recently watched a midnight rerun of *Death Wish II* (and he'd wished he hadn't) starring the nuggety Charles Bronson, Raoul's thought came in a flash: *Poor bastard had to wade through writer's block on that one.*

Any second now, he expected the bad guys—what were they called? The banditos?—each wearing a ridiculously large sombrero and a five-day growth, slung with guns the size of cannons, to materialize out of the long lonely. That was what it felt like out here: long and lonely. Perfect banditos country. Perfect to get lost in and become lost in… where nobody would ever find you, alive or otherwise.

Only in the seedy world he had become entangled with, the banditos would be dressed in dark suits and carry weapons of death that were nowhere as conspicuous as cannons. Banditos who held secret liaisons, plotting the demise of a few to ensure the obliteration of billions. Oh yes, there were things he hadn't told the Triplows.

He could have stuck around Corona, provided them round-the-clock protection, because they were under the finest spotlight ever given by the Dark Suits. But, by remaining in the area, he'd only draw further attention to them, cinch that spotlight to a pinprick, where it would bounce off the crowns of the Triplows' heads like collective lasers, signalling their prompt eradication.

What the Triplows needed more than anything else was that sliver of opportunity—to take the ultimate leap of faith. And they would. Either that or die waiting.

So this here wooden duck had bugged out of the hot-pot. With a pinch of lady luck he'd bugged out, leaving a trail of confusion for the Dark Suits to wade through before the spotlight returned to Number 22. Could he be *that* lucky? No harm trying, as they said.

He'd alluded them faultlessly thus far, of that he was certain. If he could keep this up, they'd remain distracted, because he knew he'd be their main focus, not the Triplows. Not yet, anyway.

A fly harassed his right cheek. He gave it a swat. The crumpled black-winged body fell almost comically from his sweaty skin. It hit his right thigh and bounced off, eventually tumbling to the floor, where it rocked a little and wriggled its spindly legs before going quite still.

In the time it took for the plume of dust to finally subside to ground, Raoul was satisfied that he'd not been followed, that no bad guy with or without a big hat and a five-day growth was about to materialize and say 'Hey, mister, allow me the privilege of sending you to hell'. The driver's door opened wide and Raoul stepped into the tangerine hue of late afternoon.

As if the ancient Egyptian god Ra had bobbed up at Earth's edge, the sun pendulumed in a big and bold display above the western horizon.

What could I have said more at the time? came the solemn thought. *Did I say* all *I could say? And, if I had gone on, would it only have made matters more complicated? Sue doesn't seem the type to take a back seat. How much influence would she have over Bob? I've asked her to give up everything she loves.* The answer was simple: there had been a lifetime's worth of information that could've been passed on but, even as it was, the Triplows had been utterly overwhelmed by what he'd offered. Besides, the withheld stuff… well, that too was conjecture. Most of what he'd said could neither be proven nor refuted, and Sue had teetered on the cusp of conviction as it was. Give her more of the same, she would've been apt to discard it entirely. How much influence did she have? She was pivotal in what Bob did next; *that* was how much influence she had.

In the west, the sun dipped a little more in its fiery descent.

Under the circumstances, he considered that it'd gone better than expected. It had had all the hallmarks of backfiring.

Should he have revealed that the renegades in dark suits— 'the star people' as he had called them—had an unhealthy and vested interest in their son and Bob? And if events so dictated, they'd quietly, and with the efficiency of a Sumerian sword, only with a sophistication that defied humanity, end their lives under the noses of everyone else going about their daily lives? Because the Dark Suits were masters of such deeds.

To what end would this have served, though? It was one thing to scare the living crap out of another, but to do so until they were catatonic would've been detrimental.

Raoul had also withheld mentioning the odds of success; rather he'd laid emphasis on the numbers at stake through inaction.

Regardless of Sue's impact, he'd gambled the highest of stakes on Bob's reaction, as he'd seen the other dimension, he'd *been inside* of Black Eternity. Whether he could mentally discern the what and the where—*just like Sue, but more so*—he'd been left open and raw to acceptance because of what they had endured in 2011.

Without doubt, Raoul had trodden a precarious line. Like a man on a tightrope a thousand feet above ground and without safety nets, too much one way or the other... too bad.

He took a long, shuddering breath, staring into the sun. Its sanguine body and late afternoon glare reflected in the lenses of his Ray-Bans.

Finally, the stranger from another world walked to the Comfort Inn office marked **RECEPTION** to pay the woman behind the counter for his night's stay and collect his key. The porridge-still air caught puffs of dust rising from his shoes, even after he stepped onto the thick silt that covered the cement path to **RECEPTION**.

Accommodation didn't exactly put up a struggle out here. *The perfect place to begin his own disappearing act*, Raoul told himself again.

"That'll be a double then, will it, Mister... Sampson?" the receptionist asked, laying noticeable hesitancy where she thought it counted, making a much bigger deal of the fact than was ever necessary of a single man's wish for a double room.

"Yes," he returned simply. "You don't get much action out this way, do you?"

The receptionist giggled and Raoul suddenly realized that he'd been misconstrued.

He couldn't recall precisely when life had taken its sinister turn, luring him in and trapping him in its web of deceit and malicious intent. He couldn't believe he'd willingly become part of an organization whose agenda entirely consisted of the methodical destruction of a species. Operating in a peripheral capacity, he'd never been inducted into the idealistic and clandestine core group known as the Dark Suits. For longer than he cared to remember, though, he'd been *pretending* to do their work... to see this Earth's end days through. If only he'd been able to infiltrate the core group, become a Dark Suit... But such wishes were useless.

Now he had to bug out. One way or another. And should Bob succeed in shutting down Patrick Nesmith's invitation, he might even see his days out with a loving wife and couple of kids, and actually *need* a double room.

From Corona it'd been a hundred and fifty mile dash toward the Nevada border (just where in the hell he'd imagined he was going, he'd had little idea... just an inkling to get away, leave the sleaze behind), to Halloran Springs.

"Ya have yaself a nice stay at Comfort Inn, Mister... Sampson." The receptionist broke into his thoughts. Again, she used overt hesitation between 'Mister' and 'Sampson.' "If there's anything ya need, don't be hesitating in using the phone provided in ya room—free of charge." She smiled ridiculously.

"What should I do with it?" Raoul asked drily.

The receptionist with the teased hair—*and was that a cobweb?*—stared dumbfounded. Her stupid smile evaporated into the still air.

Christ, maybe the human race should die, he thought with heavy sarcasm.

Stepping into Room 20, Raoul noted that the air's scent came compliments of San Bernardino Dust. It was *old*, the type of air that had been trapped for eons and suddenly found its escape the moment he unlocked the door. But it also formed part of an odd mixture in which the cleaner's last rites lingered. He took everything he had in with him. Since he travelled lighter than your average man on the lam, that comprised himself and the few possessions lining his pockets.

Later, lying on his bed, having beaten the sun in its race below the western horizon, his arms were crossed behind his head and the television was on. A replay of a long-ago comedy, *Seinfeld*, was playing on the 'Classics' channel.

A large smile broke over his face, although it wasn't from the show, even though Elaine had just become so excited she pushed Kramer over with a *'Get OUT of here!'* He was smiling because he suddenly had a hankering to hop aboard a skateboard and go for a ride. He wanted those little wheels to carry him far away to a mystical land of love and family… sizzling along the ground, his hair buffeted by the wind, his thoughts free to roam wherever they pleased.

He took a deep, pensive breath and made himself a promise: if it was the last thing he did, he would do that. Tomorrow, regardless of all other matters, he'd ask the teased-hair receptionist where he could purchase or borrow a skateboard, then he'd hop aboard its platform and let its little wheels roll.

And he would laugh, once again, after a long absence, and feel the spirit of the child that had been long ago repressed within.

And then he thought he might try his hand at a near impossible feat: a complete disappearing act from the Dark Suits. Not simply to elude, but to vanish.

Take a ride on a skateboard and escape the scum and sleaze. You mightn't have much time, so you'd better get cracking first thing.

Like forcing the ultimate retreat of Black Eternity, such an act had grave uncertainties of accomplishment. Neither had ever been achieved, which placed both he and Bob on their own diabolical discoveries. One honorable. The other self-serving.

True that might be, Raoul dared to contemplate there being a first.

Sure, it'd been a day of high anxiety, but the fatigue coursing through Raoul's body had rapidly overwhelmed him. First he couldn't move his arms, and when he tried getting up from the bed, he simply shuffled a little, like a vulnerable baby.

"Last hurrah!" he moaned wearily, his jaw snapping open in a huge tonsil-exhibiting yawn.

Again, he tried removing himself from the motel bed where strangers had taken their turns sleeping and having sex over the years. Again his muscles were unable to oblige. His legs were seemingly glued to the sheet, as heavy as if they had been cast in cement. His arms made him grimace and wince as he forced them down to his sides from behind his head.

Seemed he'd played his hand, and had been caught manipulating the Dark Suits' game of genocide.

He'd been *debilitated.*

But how?

His jaw cracked open for another cavernous yawn. His mind, almost amused by the deceit, jumped amongst a string of possibilities.

Then, in the struggling swill of his thoughts, came one word: *Sprite!*

Earlier that day, on his way to the Triplows, he'd pulled into a Texaco outlet to top up with the high-octane option. He hadn't known whether the need to call upon every bit of power the car could deliver would be necessary, but he hadn't wanted to risk it on a few cents extra. As he'd paid the attendant, he'd also made another purchase. Totally out of the blue and out of character, he'd felt the need for a fizzy, sugary hit. He'd reached out and grabbed the first can that found its way into his hand. Sprite. Seemed it'd been that kind of day where hankerings frequented like long-lost relatives.

That can and its contents, though having become nothing short of liquefied sugar in the heat, had been finally consumed somewhere between Corona and the Nevada border.

Raoul lived and breathed cautiousness. This he had learned the hard way. Those who became too comfortable got careless, and carelessness had been the downfall of many. Like Reynell? Maybe. But then there were others who simply fell out of favor with the core group.

For all his vigilance, though, he could not be looking everywhere at once, and had he had the slightest inkling, he might've been able to act swiftly. As it was, he was only realizing now that his drink had been spiked. His hankering his downfall.

Sneaky bastards! Have to give it to them, though, it was ingenious, since the can had remained sealed until I cracked it open.

His eyelids had become thick steel shutters, and he could repress the inevitable no longer. They closed on the vault of his anaesthetized mind.

On the tube, Jerry Seinfeld made a whimsical remark to his eccentric friend, Kramer, who'd just slid into the scene through the door of Jerry's apartment. Kramer returned with a typical oddball remark and the audience laughed. Raoul didn't hear the laughter; he was snoring loudly. Kramer left Jerry's apartment in search of a cantaloupe that tasted like the nectar of the gods… and it seemed the greengrocer down the road might just be able to offer such bounty.

In the landscape of his subconsciousness, Raoul had returned to a bright, open street. Its sign indicated that this was Chasing Boulevard. He had not done this by chance. Oh no. He was here on a mission. He had a most serious purpose to conduct.

He strolled past the address, whose residents he knew as the Triplows, to a boy further along the street.

"Hello?" he said cheerfully enough to the young boy, going on to be a teenager.

"Hello, mister," the boy returned, slightly reserved, having to veranda a hand over his eyes to shield them from the sun.

"Mind if I borrow your skateboard?"

"Well," the boy's reservation was not so well guarded now, "I don't know; it's the only one I've got, and it's *almost* as good as an *Astra-Links*."

"An *Astra-Links*?"

"Yeah—best skateboard around?"

"Fair enough, but I promise not to break it. And if by some chance I do, I'll give you the money to buy…" Raoul gave it a little consideration. "An *Astra-Links*."

"Well…" The boy scratched one leg behind the other, as if he had an itch in his left calf. "I s'pose…"

Raoul smiled and extended a hand. "My name's Raoul, and you have my word."

"Sammy," the boy said.

And so they shook.

The boy had unwittingly agreed to a very special deal indeed. Whilst not quite shaking hands with the devil—if you were inclined to believe in such things—and whilst Raoul had no intention of bringing the boy to harm, the deal had been struck. Just like that.

Too easy.

Raoul stepped aboard and took off. He threw his head back, angling his face toward the warm ball of sunlight, laughing like a loon, the wind in his hair and the spirit of child reborn within. Having been repressed to a latent seed, itching to germinate on a moment's opportunity, it sprouted like a ravenous weed. His veins and head filled with delight. He was dizzy with the essence of child.

And the skateboard's little wheels chirruped beneath him as they rolled over the tarmac of Chasing Boulevard.

"Jeez, mister, you sure can ride that thing real swell!" the boy yelled to him from behind, in a blast of enthusiasm and encouragement. His voice coming to Raoul's ears seemingly from a very long way off, as if he'd skateboarded miles from the starting point and the boy had become a mere pinprick in the background.

"I can, can't I?" he yelled over his shoulder, noting that his own voice sounded like that of a child's. The boy he'd once been: full of youthful spirit and exuberance, a sense of resounding immunity and invincibility to all things potentially hazardous. "I just want to keep going and going... I don't think I want to do anything else but skateboard, son! I reckon I'll ride into the distance and from there go a bit further!"

Sammy was bending and flexing at the knees, enjoying the man's childlike gusto as much as the man himself. He had started laughing, too. "What do you do, mister? For a living, that is? Are you a stuntman?"

"I—I don't recall!" Raoul returned hysterically. "Isn't that funny?" Tears were squirting from his eyes.

"You don't know what you do for a job?"

"I really can't remember, but I don't think I very much like it!" Raoul came zooming down Chasing Boulevard and shot past the boy, heading in the opposite direction now. "I think it makes me hurt inside! Here!" he said, tapping his sternum above his heart.

"It makes you sad?" the boy yelled, shielding his eyes from the eastern sun.

It was morning, the type that made you feel good just to be alive. On either side, Chasing Boulevard blurred past. Its neat houses of white render, orange roof tiles and green slabs of lawn, where bicycles lay like sleeping pets and cars sat in driveways, merged into a collage. Jasmine rode the air on a wistful spring breeze.

"Yeah!" Raoul returned. "*WEEEEEEEEEEEEEEEE!!!!!!!!!*" He threw his arms out to either side, as if the skateboard beneath his feet had transformed into a surfboard and he was riding the biggest tube of his life.

In Room 20, there was no one to wake him. Certain fixtures rang as he yelled in his sleep: "*WEEEEEEEEEEEEEEEE!!!!!!!!!*"

He didn't hear the *TINKLE TINKLE TINKLE* stealthily cross the room's floor amongst more laughter from the TV.

As neither did the boy sleeping soundly, revelling in a vivid dream of a man on his skateboard, in his South Lincoln Drive home in Corona. The boy giggled heartily on the sidewalk of his dream and from under his sheets. He yelled into the moonlit darkness of night, in which all had their doppelgangers to creep across the ground.

Sammy's parents didn't hear.

Earlier, Sammy had spent the day with his friends on Chasing Boulevard. And now he'd returned—or rather he'd been drawn back—to spend it with a man who could ride the board like a demon and, strangely, at the exact same time of day that he'd been here with his friends.

Just for a moment, he turned his head in the opposite direction on his pillow, a quizzical expression scrawled across his sleeping face. His ears caught the sound of tiny bells. Almost wind-chime like.

Sammy wriggled in his sleep and returned completely to the man he knew as Raoul.

He leapt off the curbing; the board launched. The ball bearings of the board's little wheels sizzled in free flight. Raoul was taking it to the max.

Any more and this baby would be lethal.

Oh yeah, those bastard Dark Suits (whoever they were, whatever he meant by that!) could go suck a rank turnip. Nobody and no one was going to touch him because he was flying… he had youthful exuberance and immunity to hold any foe at bay.

And nothing could catch the speed of this sucker.

Touchdown! The wheels sizzled as they spun madly and the speed increased. Raoul's hair was almost torpedoed back on his scalp.

"My mom says it's better to have less money and be happy in your work than to have loads and be unhappy in life!" Sammy hollered at the top of his lungs, screwing his nose up.

"Your mom sounds like a real smart lady!" Raoul turned the skateboard hard about and embarked on yet another westerly run.

"She used to work in something to do with money!" Sammy yelled after him, still giggling at the man's antics. "But now she sells coffee from a van to office workers! She reckons she loves it, but dad reckons she'll eventually return to finance 'cause she gets off on it!" The kid screwed his nose up, once more.

Raoul came speeding along Chasing Boulevard to the boy. He stopped with all the flare of a master: slamming his right foot down on the board's tail, flipping it up and catching it with a deft hand.

The boy nodded his appreciation and pursed his lips. "Nice."

There was a menacing skull and crossbones on the board's underside.

"Do you agree with him?" Raoul said, slightly breathless. "Your dad, that is."

The boy shrugged. "Can I have my skateboard back, Raoul?"

"Sure, you can, Samuel." Raoul smiled.

"Sammy," the boy returned. "Some call me Sam the Man, but never Samuel, unless I'm in *real* trouble."

Raoul smiled warmly. "I don't have a name that lends itself to that, but I know what you mean."

"Yeah—it's like, when I've done something I s'pose I shouldn't have, it's always 'Samuel! Get your ass in here right this second!'" The boy fidgeted uncomfortably. "I don't mean to get myself into trouble. Who does? It just happens now and then."

"That it does," Raoul agreed. "And, you know, *everyone* gets themselves into trouble now and then."

"But you're a grown-up! Who's about to tell you off?"

"Sammy, you don't read many newspapers, do you?"

"I s'pose I don't," the boy returned with a slightly guilty tone.

There was an odd shift to everything, as if the normal progressive lilt of time and events had stumbled a little. If you blinked at the wrong moment, it would have been easy to miss. Raoul wasn't inclined to blinking.

Nonetheless, he strolled down Chasing Boulevard and saw a kid on a skateboard. "Hello?" he said cheerfully enough to the young boy, going on to be a teenager.

"Hello, mister," the boy returned, slightly reserved, having to veranda a hand over his eyes to shield them from the sun.

"Mind if I borrow your skateboard?"

∽

Thursday, September 8, 2022
Minutes past midnight

The moon was a helium balloon floating against the night when visitors arrived at Comfort Inn's Room 20.

A beaten up rust bucket of a '58 Ford Lincoln Continental rolled up to Raoul's rental. Its engine turned off, the behemoth of yesteryear coasting to a stop. The dirt crunched under its boots and elephantine weight.

It was, as usual, a clandestine tryst of sorts where, like Marilyn Monroe, the love affair would end in certain tragedy.

Spectral figures moved amongst the flickering light just beyond the yawn of the room's door. It shut, again, in deathly silence, swallowing both the visitors and flickering light whole.

Jerry Seinfeld continued playing back-to-back in a *Seinfeld* marathon on the 'Classics' channel. This episode saw Kramer visiting the bigwigs of a company that, amongst other products, manufactured men's cologne. Kramer had the idea of manufacturing a new fragrance that carried the scent of the beach. The canned laughter was in full swing. The volume down low.

There was no need to be particularly quiet: the reception area had long closed for the night and, other than Room 20, all others were vacant. Their benighted windows were blank and disinterested in the unfolding events, like dogs at a shelter that had given up on being rescued.

Knowing Raoul would've slipped into a deep, chemically-induced sleep, the spectral figures gravitated towards his bed.

Once they'd finished tidying up 'loose ends' in what Raoul had referred to as the long lonely where banditos roamed (and right he had been! Bad banditos in these here parts, amigo! Slit ya throat, leave ya gasping ya last breath while smoking Hondurans and telling bloodthirsty stories!), there was the real business at hand in Corona.

Now that contact had been made, even the Elder would have to accede that the Triplow family had to be eliminated decisively and without hesitation.

But first things first; the little bastard brat and his procreators had to wait. Besides, breaking the bastard brat's scrawny neck would be a cinch, and disposing of his and his procreators' bodies would be a pleasure.

One of the Dark Suits in particular was relishing the opportunity to lay his hands around the boy's neck. While Jim Gillespie squeezed the kid's windpipe, so that he couldn't raise a sound, he'd watch the terrified expression in his eyes go darker and darker until finally glazing over. What a rush—what a turn-on. The more he gave the moment consideration, the more hard he became, until he was trembling slightly. He needed things here over and done with ASAP.

The end plan for Raoul was the same they had in mind for those in Corona. His rag-doll body would be slipped from the room into the trunk of the car they'd acquired. While one of them returned Raoul's Ford to Avis ('cause you didn't want any hero snooping and making waves), the other would take his body and dispose of it in America's vast network of sewers. A leg here… a torso there… let the crocs feast! This method had been used often with outstanding success. After all, once the crocs had had a munch, it was pretty difficult figuring what belonged to whom in the excrement left behind.

For now, it was time to turn up the heat in San Bernardino County.

But in the confines of Room 20, there was no body to dispose of.

The Dark Suits stood over the vacant bed.

"Bastard's duped us!" Gillespie growled, his hands tightening into white fists.

The other moved aside for no other reason than to distance himself from the man. He used his mobile phone. "We've a friendly force working for us; Raoul has been taken care of."

He listened before replying, "No, not like that. It's like what's happened before. You can see where Raoul was lying—the sheets are still warm. But he's gone. Vanished. Like before."

He listened again, while Gillespie scoffed in the background and canned laughter, yet again, drifted from the small TV speakers.

"Yes. Bed's warm and there's no possible way to exit the room but through the front door. Windows on the opposite side are locked." The Dark Suit waved a hand at Gillespie to get him to verify what he was hazarding a guess at.

The windows checked out.

Again, he listened. "Yes. The man and his child are now the priority." The Dark Suit caught a glimpse of Gillespie rubbing his genitals long and hard. He hung up and, with a look of disgust, exited the room.

On Highway 17, driving back through the long lonely, the banditos conversed.

"It's too convenient," Gillespie worried.

"What is?"

"Raoul's disappearance."

"It's perfect; whatever's snatching these people seems to be doing so in conjunction with Black Eternity. Or, maybe, it's another way Black Eternity feeds. Maybe it's got more ways of feeding than we know. There are those mad balloon things— the mad ones. But…" Gillespie's partner hesitated, "we'd have seen this happening. The sheets, I mean. They were still warm."

"I don't give a fuck. *I* wanted Raoul."

A moments' silence ensued.

Then: "Maybe the kid and his family will go the same way."

"I want to do the kid," Gillespie said, cracking an enormous, if repulsive, smile.

"You rub your balls again, and I'll—"

"Let the kid do it, just before I do him."

Raditch really would've been happy to dispose of Gillespie then and there, but he needed him. The group needed him... for now. "Why don't you shut up?"

"We *must* do the kid tonight," Gillespie demanded. "Before *he* disappears."

"Not tonight."

"You said," Gillespie whined petulantly.

"We haven't the time."

"Make the fucking time!"

"*We haven't the time!*" Raditch barked. "Tomorrow night; it'll wait until then. If the kid goes missing, our work will have been done for us. You wouldn't get your jollies, but the result would be fortuitous. And that's what counts, not your sick mind." He pressed the Lincoln's accelerator harder. It rumbled along Highway 17, leaving a fine trail of smoke twirling from the exhaust in its wake.

1958 hadn't been the best year for the Lincoln Continental— and some might have argued, "When was?"—but the uninspiring rust bucket was perfect. It was as big as they ever got, and old, a dinosaur amongst cars that nobody except enthusiasts cared for. Besides, the rightful owner was in no rush to reacquire it at present, or at any time in the future.

Nobody would expect men of such calibre to be in such a clapped-out heap. And in the Dark Suits' unique line of work, that was *the* consideration. People would remember the car because it stole the show. As for its occupants, witnesses would be at a loss to recall.

The Lincoln would serve them well until things in Corona had been taken care of, after which they'd dump the thing from whence they'd taken possession, in Mulberry Estates.

⌒

Tuesday, September 6, 2022
Two days previous

As a measure to ensure he hadn't been followed, Raoul had left it a full day before he completed his journey to Chasing Boulevard.

One could never be too careful.

Problem was he hadn't been careful enough.

This was significant, because it had lain open to the Lincoln's owner, Mister Too Much Nose, a very bad day. He hadn't realized it at the time, as none of us do just before the wheels part company from the wagon, as was so often captured in selfies seconds before disaster.

Rather than scoffing into beers and chips at a side window of his house, spying on his new neighbors, Mister Too Much Nose should've had the sense to leave well enough alone. But they had been his only neighbors for the past decade and then some in Mulberry Estates.

Besides—and more to the point—Mister Too Much Nose's intrigue had been irrevocably spiked by the two suspicious-looking characters who had moved in next door, and the other who'd taken residence directly across the road earlier. He was no dingbat, hence he'd known that nobody but *nobody* would take residence in derelict houses unless—

There were shenanigans afoot!

He knew Mulberry Estates like no other, except perhaps the town engineers who had planned this spread of failed dreams. There was a dinky road hooking round back and, if you so desired, you could sneak across your neighbor's property and come in back of your own home. Of course, this was entirely theoretical, since the houses lay hopelessly abandoned, most having never shared their walls with their intended occupants. Rodents and spiders, though, proliferated them like motels for the smaller critters in life.

The roads had long disintegrated into a crisscross of cracks from which a delicate crochet of weeds sprouted.

For reasons that confounded normal explanations, Mulberry Estates was and always had been set at a disadvantage to the main thoroughfare between Los Angeles and the procession of satellite cities and towns further south. Existing virtually alongside Riverside's main freeway, it'd been cursed with one setback after another from the very beginning. A burden, no doubt, that had escalated when its founder, known only as Moe, suddenly clutched his chest and took his last breath. His predisposition for treating people like splatter left behind after clearing one's throat, though, had spurred a string of unsavory legends. Hence, few had shed a tear on his passing. Throw a party, maybe—probably had even happened—but shed a tear, not likely.

Since then, any attempt to continue building had been met with one tragedy after another. Two entrepreneurs went in similar fashion to Moe; or, at least they were no longer surviving on God's green Earth. One had become involved in a car accident, where he lost his lunch as well as everything else upon impact. Another was shot dead in a 'gangland' style shooting (apparently drug related). And a third and last starry-eyed hopeful went financially belly-up. Mister Too Much Nose guessed he might've been shining shoes somewhere in Denver. Why not? It seemed as good as any other guess.

After that, people had kept their distance; the project was 'jinxed.' And Mulberry Estates had slowly receded into the wilderness from whence it'd been born.

That was, until now.

The fellow across the road was in casuals and he appeared watchful, whilst the occupants' actions next door were out-and-out authoritarian, dressed in their fancy dark suits without a single cease to blemish the tailored cloth that complimented their sinewy bodies. Furthering Mister Too Much Nose's self-assessment of being a creature of greater nous rather than a dingbat, he'd figured these men weren't here by accident. Only the desperate would take residence in houses with broken windows and weeds up to their assholes. This was Mister Too Much Nose's expression for 'eaves.'

When the first fellow had arrived across the way, he'd been preparing an introduction of himself, which would've been followed with something like, 'What the hell are you doing here, bud?' Being a recluse—he preferred the title 'recluse;' 'hermit' made him sound diseased in some way!—human contact didn't come easy, and so he'd been building up to the moment. Upon the arrivals next door half a day later, and with the distinct feeling that things were not right in Mulberry Estates, *again*, he'd reneged on the moment altogether.

Hurriedly—if an enormous ass that swiveled to one side, held, then swiveled to the opposite could be described as ever moving in a hurry—he cobbled together a few essentials and took possie behind a window on the side of the house.

Why, his heart was going at it like two fatigued boxers.

His breathing was hard to get, too! But after ten minutes or so of sucking air like a marooned goldfish, both his heart and breathing became accustomed to the thrill of the moment.

Espionage! And he was right in the thick of it! Right place! Right time! *Who'd have guessed in Mulberry Estates?*

Gathered around him were four cartons of Budweiser, two boxes of chips (his taste for the barbeque variety was as insatiable as that for beer), and one box of Ex-Lax. The payload often became jammed and, confronted with such intrigue, he sure as hell hadn't wanted to miss a minute stuck in the can with his head turning tomato-red. So he'd reached for the old bowel version of Drano as good insurance.

Pulling greedily from the bottle, he spilled as much of Anheuser-Busch's toast to the hops upon his mountainous stomach as what he managed to swallow. His white undershirt, stretched tight, was stained brownish-yellow from previous episodes and several weeks' worth of sweat.

Chips drizzled down this odorous landscape as he shoved them in by the handful. The teeth in his head, set crookedly like monuments in an unloved cemetery, mashed away without propriety to remaining closed.

He grunted and snorted, catching his breath as the rapid succession of beer and chips filled his mouth to capacity. A slurry of baby-pooh yellow was damn near choking him, and some of this, too, found its way to his undershirt. One day he might reconcile the situation and stop shovelling crap into his mouth. Then again, hell might one day freeze rock solid.

His newest neighbors next door had milled around back of the house. One was now perched at the house corner with a gun pointing across the road toward the newly arrived 'casual.'

Gangsters, his mind gasped excitedly.

There were several nifty ways in which to dispose of a body, and the Dark Suits knew them all. On this occasion—and the original method of choice—they'd adopted the use of a tranquilizer gun, after which they'd apply a lozenge. Guaranteed to work on sore throats… bunions… loss of hair… in fact, it'd go to work from head to toe, taking care of everything in between. It was fair to say that these exotic disposal devices were in short supply. Then again, time wasn't exactly in an overabundance for this planet, should they take care of matters efficiently.

Once the lozenge had done its job, there would be nothing left but an easy drive out of this shithole, and into anonymity once more.

Gillespie's partner had the laser pointed high on the house across the way, so as to avoid potentially alerting Raoul to their presence. His hand was on the trigger, poised.

But there were unforeseen complications.

With empty beer bottles and chip bags floating around Mister Too Much Nose like flotsam after the sinking of the Titanic, his bowels were packed to bursting, the boilers about to explode. The timing couldn't have been worse; he hadn't had this much excitement since… ever!

The sun had begun dipping over the horizon, but something ominous was rising in Mister Too Much Nose's house. He had to reluctantly leave the gangsters, but he'd be as quick as he could. Thank God for the laxatives.

First things first, though: he had to engage in the usual 'Dance of the Chair Removal.' Lifting his enormous sagging ass from the wicker base was an operation rather than an action. The fucking thing had become welded to his ass, and the chair's armrests didn't help one iota, grabbing his behemoth girth like a hysterical lover.

He had to forcefully wriggle this way, and then that, stomping about in tight circles with his stubby legs before things gave a sign that they'd part. The pressure on his system was all too much and he farted once… twice… hell, once started, he didn't really stop, like a train leaving the station with its driver yanking away on the horn as if he had a nervous twitch.

The chair creaked and groaned in protest until the separation was finalized. The webbing on its base had all but split through, and displayed a precarious crater from which his ass had decoupled.

He waddled towards the can. It was a veritable beaver dam down there. He could feel it, heavy and swollen.

It hadn't occurred to his new neighbors that someone might actually live amongst Mulberry Estates' housing. The homes were nothing but boxes of broken windows and doors, most scrawled with graffiti. But as there hadn't been a breath of wind to speak of, when a curtain shifted in a side window on the house next door, they'd discovered their error. And that was bad for Mister Too Much Nose.

The Dark Suits had bided their time overnight; acting the previous evening would've surely shown their hand, despite Gillespie's vehemence.

"It's taken weeks to track down the bastard. Now that we have, we huddle here like rats in a cage!"

"Shut your trap. Raoul's no fool; he hears the slightest utterance and we'll be made."

"So fucking what? We're not doing anything by standing here." Gillespie's thermostat had gone off the chart. There was some asshole next door who needed taking care of, and Raoul across the road who needed taking care of, and they were between the two playing tea party. "The Elder's best days are behind him. We act *now*… do the kid and his bastard parents. Matter solved."

Raditch had returned quietly and threateningly. "The Elder's worst days pale your very best into insignificance."

The stay of hand gave Raoul the opportunity to scurry from his hidey-hole early that morning.

Jim Gillespie smiled with all the threat of an insane murderer. "Run while you can… you'll get yours… 'cause some pills make you small…" He sung quietly at a front window, surreptitiously watching Raoul drive along the nameless street and out of sight.

He consulted his mobile's screen, smug in the knowledge that the GPS tracker he'd attached to his car through the night was working nicely.

And now for introductions with their busybody neighbor.

Having already dealt a winding blow to Mister Too Much Nose's cascading stomach, Gillespie was intent on unleashing his frustrations.

"We've no time for this," his partner interjected.

Gillespie took a moment's pause. "We've got enough." His smile was lurid and sickening, as typical for him. "Besides, had we taken care of business last night, we could've circumvented this."

"Bullshit. You can't help yourself."

Gillespie laughed. "Guess I'm just a hopeless romantic." He continued his assault.

And for a while his partner left him to it, having removed himself to another room. But after the house kept reverberating to one meaty blow after another, the hoots and toots of Mister Too Much Nose's sphincter releasing fart after fart, retching grunts and the odd breathless plea for mercy, he'd had enough.

"*Please!*" Mister Too Much Nose begged Raditch as he re-entered the room.

"You're a sick son of a bitch," he said to Gillespie. Even for a Dark Suit, his stomach rolled before steadying. The fellow had been worked over well.

Both eyes were swollen red gourds. The stained undershirt was splattered with blood. His nose was pushed flat against the puffed mounds of his face. There was even a lump of hair lying not too far from the mangled wreck on the floor, with a patch of flesh attached to their stand of follicles.

As for Gillespie, he wore his typical shit-eating grin from ear to ear. "Let's chop him."

Without a word, Raditch reached into his pants pocket and retrieved a vial containing what appeared to be a throat lozenge.

"They're in short supply. Let's chop the fat cunt!"

"*Please, no! God, no! I won't tell, honest I won't! I don't know who you are!*" And that much Mister Too Much Nose didn't, his words thickened by bloody mucous.

"We *really* haven't the time!" Raditch said through gritted teeth, seemingly hearing not a word from their grossly overweight and helpless victim.

"GPS tells me an entry into the sewers is less than a couple of miles off. A few hours... easy peasy, lemon squeezy." Gillespie salivated, relishing the thought of this fat geezer's dismemberment.

Raditch wasn't listening to him, either. He stooped down and applied the lozenge-shaped thing to Mister Too Much Nose's neck. He'd tried scrambling away, but like a battered whale beached high and dry, there really wasn't anywhere he could've gone.

"No! Please, I won't tell! I won't!" He slapped at the thing stuck to his neck, but it wouldn't budge. It was as if it had sent claws under his flesh and refused removal by any simple means. *"What have you done to me? WHAT HAVE YOU DONE?"*

Mercy killing, Raditch thought, looking down and backing towards the room's furthest corner.

Gillespie followed.

Just to be sure, they both stood near a broken window, through which the scraggliest of Santa Anna breezes whispered.

"How could you live in this squalor, anyhow?" Gillespie asked mockingly.

"I won't tell! I won't! It hurts! It—"

But Mulberry Estate's last resident was coming apart. Goop and fluid had begun running from his every orifice, and then some. And, somewhere amongst it, his tongue had slipped down his throat like a chunk of bologna.

"Eat that, you fat cunt!" Gillespie taunted.

His partner turned aside, appearing genuinely sickened at the thing the man had become, knowing there was every chance that he'd not have betrayed them had they left him alone. He was obviously a loner, publicity the last thing he'd have sought.

On the other hand, it was just one life; he was here to assist in the eradication of billions—a process in which he'd lose his own. He had to remember that, lest he fall into the same trap as Raoul and others alike.

Mister Too Much Nose's stained undershirt was caving in, as the physical form beneath dissolved away. Suddenly, though, it became saturated in what might've been a mixture of ketchup and mustard. A large bulge had begun pressing up beneath it. Higher the bulge went, until the undershirt rolled upwards under the strain of Mister Too Much Nose's last meal. Digested beer and barbeque chips jettisoned forth in a frizzling volcanic eruption.

Perhaps it was a build-up of gas, but this wasn't the expected developments. Usually, it went somewhat smoother.

With great amusement, Gillespie remarked, "Looks like a fucking firecracker, doesn't he?"

The man's face was sliding away to either side of his skull, and it seemed his hands were clutching at it in a desperate bid to keep it in place. But of course, that was the dying embers of his nervous system, nothing else. His eyes went Egyptian. They tear-dropped into hideous elongated slits, then finally slid to the dirty and faded carpet, oozing over the holes where his ears had been.

The stinking geyser of gastric juices and the man's staples beginning to lose steam.

His eyeballs fell back into the cavity of his head, and his ribs collapsed in like the gruesome teeth of some deranged alien thing. His lower jaw gradually opened wider and wider, until it parted company from the temporomandibular joint.

Gillespie's unbridled delight had been replaced with a sneer. He approached the destroyed thing that had moments before been a man—a lost and lonely man, but a man nonetheless. He drew his foot back and, before Raditch could stop him, rammed it squarely into the remains of the skull. Like a weird soccer ball, it went flying, exploding in a splattering crunch on the opposite wall.

"You didn't have to do that!" Raditch growled.

"There's gonna be nothing left of him in another minute. Besides, aren't we here to do just this?" Gillespie maintained his sneer and kicked again at any remaining part his foot could find.

His partner turned and walked outside.

And, just as Gillespie had mentioned, nothing remained in the minute to follow of Mister Too Much Nose. All fluids had vanished. No bones were left scattered about. Only a pile of clothes marked where the recluse had come to grief.

Nearing dawn on the eighth of September, the banditos had returned to the anonymity of Mulberry Estates. Their mission was dubiously successful; they hadn't had to deal with Raoul, as the matter had been taken out of their hands.

Gillespie continued his tirade about being blocked from 'doing the kid' earlier that night.

They hid the elephantine beast of a car in a garage, just in case, and once more took squatters' residence.

That was the way it stayed until both their mobile phones broke the silence around eleven the following night, just before they were about to take a ride into Corona. Raditch's had a ringtone of Led Zeppelin's "Black Dog" from the hard-rocking

1970s, whereas Gillespie's played Bach. He really was one messed-up son of a bitch.

∽

Thursday, September 8, 2022

Three days after Mister Too Much Nose's untimely departure, one day after Raoul's delivery to the Triplows, and less than twelve hours after his and a young boy's silent abductions ('cause sometimes you just don't have time to scream), Joshua had found himself filled with fearful suspicions that something had befallen his friend, Sammy, when he never fronted up that day.

It was out of character for him; he actually *liked* school! Which meant no one was perfect. Whenever Joshua had questioned him about this peculiarity, he'd often shrugged and had always given a similar reply, something along the lines of "I just like hanging out with my friends. It's like one big party". A reply to which Joshua invariably countered with something like, "Are you *crazy*? *Skateboarding* at the park is like one big party!".

But here it was, lunchtime, and still no Sammy. His absence had turned Joshua's legs to ice and set an ominous beat against the muscles of his heart. He was a fit boy, yet each step across Citrus Hill Elementary's recreational quadrangle threatened to catch his breath.

He'd spoken to Leon the moment Sammy never showed that morning about the nightmare they'd shared days earlier… about the old man, Satchmo, and the malevolent darkness of Sammy's house.

Leon had dismissed his fears, yet felt no less anxious. "Get a grip, Josh—he's probably not feeling well."

"Sammy? Not feeling well?" Joshua had returned, incredulous.

Lunch was the furthest thing from his mind. He *needed* to speak with Leon some more, else he might go nuts thinking his thoughts alone. And though he needed to do this before Leon got together with the gang, he had carelessly allowed them to become separated in the rush outside. Although that 'rush' was still somewhat affected by the 'thick.' Kids didn't talk about their nightmare anymore, because of past events: shrinks, doctors, medication, parents overreacting and making the situation a whole lot worse. Kids weren't allowed to watch certain things on TV, and an amount had had their computers confiscated so they couldn't hook up on Twitter and the like. Mobiles were banned. Parents would say they fed their fear, and deprived them of such things that would help stem the flow. And, if all else failed, back to the shrink, the doctor, more medications, until *it* made you sick.

So kids had developed strategies in relegating the man in black from the forefront of life with a certain degree of success. However, comparing this 'rush' to the 'rush' that had taken place same time last year, stopwatches would've testified a significant difference. Kids had slowed down.

Nonetheless, they'd still been fast enough to get in Joshua's way. He'd thought the situation could be saved until Mrs. Bruckheimer's untimely intervention stuffed it up entirely.

"Joshua, can I have a word with you, please?"

He'd pulled up sharp on his heels, and turned to look at her, exasperation contorting his face. "Have I done something wrong?"

Mrs. Bruckheimer had smiled kindly. "No, Josh, you haven't done anything wrong. You usually don't. I was just wondering..." She had hesitated before giving in to her resolve. "Whether you're sleeping alright. The nightmare you kids were having seems to have abated, but... well, I'm concerned. You don't look yourself."

Joshua had let her believe what she wanted. Perhaps then he could still get to Leon in time.

"I had an upset stomach last night," he'd said, thinking ahead.

"Has the man in black returned?"

"Uh-uh." Nonetheless, ever since Satchmo four nights ago, Joshua had been disturbed by visions of Sammy's house, and what lay around the corner in Sammy's sofa room. Visions of darkness and—

Skittery-scratch scratchy-scratch...

"Because I thought if he had, and you needed to talk with someone besides your mom and dad, that you should know you can always confide in me."

"Thanks, Mrs. Bruckheimer." Joshua had crazily sensed emotions he wasn't expecting, like he did when watching an unexpectedly sad part of a movie.

Mrs. Bruckheimer had smiled her kind smile, just sitting there observing the young boy for some time until Joshua became a little uncomfortable.

"I'd like to go outside, if that's okay."

"Of course," Mrs. Bruckheimer had conceded. "What boy wants to be stuck inside a classroom with a nosy teacher, eh?"

"Yeah." Joshua had laughed a little nervously, then, "I don't mean the part about the teacher."

"Just as long as you know I'm here if you ever feel the need to talk."

"Thanks… again." Joshua had said with palpable sincerity.

From across the recreational quadrangle, he sighed; Leon was already sitting with Ethan and Craig. On approach, he gave Leon the eye.

The other two wanted to talk about everything but Sammy's no-show, as if not talking about it made it somehow alright.

"Anybody heard from Sammy?" Joshua asked brightly, but with little hope—*because he knew.*

Ethan shook his head, digging around a tub of fruit salad. He generally didn't eat much lunch.

Craig ventriloquized "Uh-uh," stuffing his mouth with a chicken salad sandwich the size of Mount Rushmore. Unlike Ethan, Craig ate whenever food was presented, and went on the prowl whenever there was a clear absence, with one exception: breakfast. He maintained it made him feel like puking, which seemed absurdly ironic considering his current assault on the chicken salad.

Leon had seen him eat countless times, but that didn't stop him from staring in wonder, seemingly mesmerized at the demonstration, and left in little wonder as to why he had suffered a particularly nasty stomachache the Wednesday previous, his own lunch a sacrificial lamb to the flies as it sat untouched on the table.

Since Joshua had told him of his fears that morning, his own anxiety had mounted as the day wore on, and so he hadn't had much of an appetite.

Around them, kids swarmed like bees around a hive. In comparison, and despite the 'thick,' everyone seemed in a state of euphoria. Some sat, others milled, caught in their own world of jabber between interludes of food. This made Joshua feel even more alienated, as if he were some type of intruder that had stumbled across the hive. And, for a moment, he didn't know where he was or who these kids were. They were all having too much fun under the bright sun while his friend had been taken into the darkness.

If imagination was stretched that bit further, he might've been given to thoughts of the sun being a little too brassy... the type of sunlight that had fallen the day Satchmo had played his horn.

"Guys," he blurted, giving Ethan a start, making him catapult a strawberry from his spoon onto the ground. "Sorry," Joshua apologized. "I left a paper in my bag; Mrs. Bruckheimer wanted it this morning."

"What paper?" Ethan asked a little irritably. Strawberries were his favorite, and he wasn't too thrilled about feeding one to the ants.

"The essay we had to write Tuesday." Joshua's mind was going a thousand miles a minute.

"She picked them up yesterday morning; you were walking around like a crabby old man, worried it wasn't as good as you wanted it," he argued, still peeved about his strawberry.

"Yeah, but she handed it back later that day and asked me to add to it."

"She's got a thing for you, Joshy-Washy," Ethan chimed coyly, while watching the ants greedily maraud his offering.

"Don't be stupid," Joshua snapped.

"I see how she looks at you."

"I'm eleven."

"Not yet. Not that it matters; you've still got the right package."

Craig was fully absorbed in his sandwich, crumbs and salad drizzling to the table. He wasn't about to be drawn into such talk, at any rate.

"She felt the story was good, but needed completing. That's all." Again, Joshua cast an eye toward Leon, who finally got the message.

Getting up from the bench seat, he left his lunch stranded and unloved on the table. Another fly landed upon it. Glancing down at this, he thought dully, *I present to you all I have, amigo.*

Almost cross-eyed and seemingly out of the blue, Craig said around a mouthful of chicken salad, "It's waited until now, Josh. What's the rush?"

"I'm late 'cause she held me back to talk about it. And I've just remembered it's not home, it's in my bag."

"Ah-huh," Craig replied around the last of his mouthful, preparing for another assault. "And you reckon this 'cause you can see through walls like Superman, huh?"

"I really *need* to give it to her."

"Did you forget your underwear today, Joshy-Washy?"

"Shut up, Ethan!"

"Chill, Josh," Ethan said. "She'll be in the staff room, anyhow."

"Look, I won't be long," Joshua said, turning about and walking off. "I'll just pop it on her desk."

Leon gave the others a faint smile. "I'll go with him."

After he'd left, Craig uttered through a replenished mouthful, still looking bug-eyed at his partly demolished sandwich, "'Cause it takes two to pass an essay to Mrs. Bruckheimer."

"I still reckon he's got a thing for Mrs. Bruckheimer, and she has for him," Ethan said, his eyes pinched down to slits, wondering what it'd feel like to have someone else's hand up his shorts.

⌒

"I told you," Joshua berated in a whisper as he and Leon crossed the quadrangle to the main building. His voice was thready and quivering, as if he were on the run. Of course, there were no papers to hand up to Mrs. Bruckheimer.

"Josh, he'll be okay," Leon counted. His show of optimism was just that: a show.

"You don't *really* believe that!"

They hurried through one of the side entrances of the main building. Instantly, the cooler air swept around their legs. Usually this was a pleasant feeling. Today, it was just terrible, like someone had opened the lid on an ancient coffin.

"Excuse me!" came an authoritarian voice, carried on a bed of razor-sharp flower petals, from behind.

Both boys jumped and Leon screamed. Afterwards, he'd reckon his head had almost cracked the ceiling some twelve feet above.

"Are you boys meant to be in the main building?"

"I'm going to get my mobile phone," Joshua replied. "I've got to call my mom."

The school policy was that mobile phones, whilst allowed on school premises, were to be strictly used only in cases of emergency, and not *ever* carried on one's person. Any child caught talking on a mobile phone for any other reason than a genuine emergency would be summarily disciplined.

"What are your names?" the teacher asked sternly, and the boys answered. "And is this an emergency?" The teacher maintained her thin-lipped stare, arms crossed tightly over her flat chest.

Joshua felt like telling her it was none of her business, but thought that wouldn't get him any closer to his objective. "I had an upset stomach earlier, and I'm not feeling so good now," he came back quickly. "You can ask Mrs. Bruckheimer; she knows." The kid mightn't have been able to lie to save his life, but he was giving it a good crack once more.

"Come with me. We'll see." The unnamed teacher, whom he thought taught fourth grade and went by the name of Mrs. Bitch Tits, turned on her flat heels and began strutting in the direction of the staff room. "And what's your excuse?" she asked Leon.

"I want to make sure Joshua's alright."

The teacher's wickedly thin lips pinched to an even finer slit. "And why wouldn't he be?" She didn't wait for an answer.

Walking behind her in the uncomfortably cool air, they finally arrived at the faculty lounge. Warm relief, however, swept through them at the sight of Mrs. Bruckheimer, and suddenly the air didn't seem half as cold.

Without directly saying so, she seemed rather affronted by the suggestion of Jessica Something-Or-Other—not Mrs. Bitch Tits, after all—that Joshua and his friend were up to no good, skulking about the building's corridors when they should've been outside with the rest of the children.

"I held him back, Jessica. He hasn't even had time to have lunch. And, yes, he has a stomach upset," she vouched, standing in the doorway. "I'll escort the boys to Room 612."

"It's not a problem."

"Yes, it is," Mrs. Bruckheimer countered, and led the boys away without further discourse.

"I just want to call mom, Mrs. Bruckheimer," Joshua said, feeling guilty for lying to her.

Of course, Mrs. Bruckheimer was way ahead of the ten-year-old boys in her charge. Stomach upset? Maybe. Most likely not, but he was a good kid and she was willing to cut him some slack. Besides, Jessica was already a spinstery old bitch at the ripe age of thirty-something. Christ, she was old before her time.

Once at Room 612, she allowed Joshua to collect his phone from his bag. "Are you intending to go home?"

"I'll see what mom thinks," Joshua returned, feeling as if he had snookered himself into a corner.

Mrs. Bruckheimer nodded. "I'll wait outside. You probably don't want me within eavesdropping distance."

"That's okay," Joshua said.

"It's your business, Joshua. I'll leave you to it."

"Thanks, Mrs. Bruckheimer." The appreciation in his voice was no put-on.

"You're very welcome, Joshua Triplow," she said with that fond smile of hers, and walked into the corridor.

Of course, he had no intention of calling home, just as Mrs. Bruckheimer suspected.

Upon his call to the Debnars, his dread exploded catastrophically, and the nerves in his icy legs seemed to disconnect just as catastrophically. He landed in the closest chair, its legs squawking against the floor as it slid by about a foot and almost flipped over.

"*Sammy?! Oh, Sammy, is that you?*" the voice of Jenny Debnar wailed down the phone.

Joshua couldn't talk; and what was more, he couldn't think. He stared ahead, the phone slipping from his hand and clattering to the linoleum below.

Against the 'thick,' Leon snatched it up before it could skitter away in one fluid motion of such speed and grace, the incident mightn't have happened at all. He stood in front of Joshua. "What?" he asked, barely able to take a breath, overcome with dread.

Joshua shook his head. He still couldn't speak.

"What is it?" Leon demanded, his hands clenching into fists before bringing the phone to his ear. "Hello?" he said meekly.

"*Sammy?!*"

It was fortunate that Leon had foregone lunch, for his stomach heaved and he retched loudly.

Joshua took the phone. "Mrs. Debnar?" he asked. "What's happened to Sammy?"

"*Who's this? Is that you, Joshua?*" Jenny Debnar was insanely distraught.

"Yes," Joshua whispered.

"*Where's Sammy, Joshua? Where is he? Is he with you?*"

"No," Joshua could barely speak. "I… I don't know where he is." But that was an out-and-out lie. Now it was Joshua who felt like losing his stomach.

Sammy's mother screamed a scream that turned Joshua's blood to ice, and then the phone went dead.

Leon swallowed hard, a click rising up his throat and out his mouth. He looked like a bird in desperate need of a drink.

With damp eyes, Joshua looked up, and the fear on his face was something Leon had only ever seen once before. He'd been flicking through a publication from a thousand years ago and locked between its pages were scratchy black-and-white pictures. In those pictures had been the harrowing faces of hopelessness and destitution, but beyond all else, anguish and fear. They were the victims of the cruellest expulsion of people in recent history. It'd been World War Two and they'd been the victims of Germany's concentration camps. Now, looking down at Joshua, he was reminded of the many people in those pictures... being lead, humiliated and naked, to bathrooms of sorts. Their appearance as innocuous as any regular shower facility, with one major difference. Since the Nazis weren't particularly interested in personal hygiene, water had been substituted for something called Zkylon B gas. Piles of what Leon had desperately wanted to believe were mannequins had been crammed into crematoriums and incinerated by the *thousands!* But they weren't mannequins—they were *people*. People who had once walked the streets... who had gone shopping... who had raised families and loved...

Leon's stomach was churning, his head swimming.

"She was crying, Leon... asking if I knew where Sammy was. I told her I didn't." Joshua looked desperately at his best friend. His eyes harrowed like those that had stepped into a shower for the last time. "But we do. We know exactly where Sammy is."

"Josh, you don't know that." Leon said, stumbling backwards and knocking into the desk behind.

"You keep saying that, Leon, but you know it's not true."

Though he'd warned Sammy, this did nothing in mitigating the grief, guilt and feeling of all things lost. One of his friends had been taken, and God only knew what was being done to him, as he sat in this classroom while its kids played beyond its walls and ate peanut butter and jelly sandwiches.

Skittery-scratch scratchy-scratch...

Later that night, after Joshua had gone to bed, Bob found himself staring into the en suite's mirror. Again. There was an inquisitive knock on the bathroom door and Bob jumped with a start. Often he would leave the door ajar, but felt it necessary that evening, as he had the evening before, to shut it completely. The leading portion of a yelp escaped his lips before he could rein it in.

"Bob?" came Sue's inquisitive voice.

The bathroom door whispered back on its hinges.

"Couldn't sleep?" Bob asked lamely.

"I should be asking the same of you," Sue returned. "Coming back to bed?"

Both lay full-length atop the sheets, propped up on their pillows. Looking to Sue's bedside cabinet, Bob noticed a novel perched upon it. A paperback by someone who went by the name of David A. Neuman. *KALEIDOSCOPIC SHADES –* WHERE ETERNITY BEGINS.

If only, he thought with miserable envy. The privilege of placing 'The End' at a point both publisher and writer felt comfortable with was a luxury he did not have.

Sue was staring at the ceiling.

"What are you thinking?" Bob asked.

"That you and Josh have an ordeal before you." They hadn't discussed the events of the previous morning until now, each avoiding the subject as if by magic it'd disappear, taking care of the matter.

Unfortunately, life didn't work to such conveniences.

Her reply was confusing, as it wasn't what Bob had expected. "I..." He hesitated. "I didn't think you'd be so willing..." He looked at her with close scrutiny.

No answer.

"Sue?" he prodded.

Quietness continued to hold sway in the Triplow bedroom.

The night was soundless, and it seemed those fey mosquitoes and their fey buzzing from the previous morning had returned. The air rung with quietness.

"Raoul didn't say *anything* that couldn't be researched from old gazettes. 2011 made the history books. With a bit of license, *anyone* could've made up such wild stories." Bob laughed. "Star people."

Only Sue didn't join in his flimsy humor.

He drew a deep breath; it ran down his throat like the cold hand of death. "If we're to return to Adelaide, we *all* go. *Together.* As a family. Hell, Sue, we've been there before. We came through it—"

"Mum didn't," Sue said bluntly, continuing to stare at the ceiling. Then, slowly, she turned her attention to him. "I believe Raoul."

"What?" Bob felt himself beginning to slip into an emotional ooze, not dissimilar to the morning before. "Are you serious?"

But she was. He could see that.

"We *all* go," he repeated.

"No, Bob. I can't."

"Why not?"

"It's how Raoul put it: I'd be a distraction."

"Honey, Joshua needs you, his mum, to be there with him as well."

"*You* went through this before. Not me. Faded pictures are all I have, but what I *can* remember is that I *was* a distraction." Sue paused. She felt like bursting into tears, but that wouldn't do at all. "The last thing I want is for our son to be thrown to the wolves, and that's what this feels like. But to ignore those things that *will* unravel and seal his fate, is unconscionable."

Bob was shaking his head. "If it weren't for you, Sue, I'd never have made it so far."

"Raoul *is* right. Wouldn't it be terrific to think he was just some loony off the street? But he isn't, and the story he imparted scares the shit out of me. But I believe him down to his very last word."

Bob was still shaking his head. "What the hell has happened?"

Sue glanced at the mobile phone on the bedside cabinet. Bob couldn't but two and two together because, yesterday morning, when she seemed to have some sort of affinity with the phone in the kitchen, he was too busy managing his own inner turmoil. A little like he was currently doing. Of course, she hadn't realized the 'why' herself until her one-way chat the night before with a man:

At the third stroke, the time will be twelve... twelve... twelve o-one A.M....

"Sue?" Again Bob prodded, not really wanting an answer. This was good, because none came.

Minutes dragged on.

The silence dragged on.

Bob shivered, though the night air was tepid.

Then, out of the ringing quietness: "I need to stay. You and Josh need to go."

Maybe Sue had been abducted and the woman lying in their bed was an imposter. A star-woman. Their limited discussion set to just one resolve, whilst, unknowingly, the man who had opened Pandora's box, Raoul Zimizen, was trapped inside an infinite bubble, furiously scribbling away as did Joshua's man in black, aka Patrick Nesmith, surrounded by the lost souls of umpteen Earths.

Bob quietly laid against his pillow with a head full of thoughts that blew in fitful starts and stops. What a week this had turned out to be. Beginning with the excitement of Lake Welland and the attention to the boat and fishing tackle with Josh, it had since degenerated into a surrealism rivalled only by that of 2011.

As he slipped into a disturbed sleep, he began dreaming an old, familiar nightmare. Tormenting him through his years until the early months of 2011, it was identical, all but for one exception. The young boy chased through the sad walls of the orphanage was a collage. He was Joshua. And Joshua was him.

A superimposition. Two boys in the one.

And he—*they*—ran.

Their legs pumping hard. Their lungs burning, on fire. Terror distending their eyes into wild orbs.

The *bitch* was in hot pursuit. The *bitch* who ruled this place for lost children, gaining pleasure from the terror and misery she wickedly imposed, the children always on guard to steer clear. But sometimes, that was not enough. Sometimes, it didn't matter how hard you ran or where you tried to hide, she would hunt you down, enveloped in an aura of outrage and spleenful vengeance.

But she had her favorites.

Never a moment's rest. There was no assuage to be found in the place for lost children.

So the boys ran for their lives. He ran for one… He ran for two…

The chase, futile.

The *bitch* hot on their heels.

COME OUT, MASTER BOBBBBYYYY! IT'S HIGH TIME FOR YOUR PUNISHMENT! YOU-WORTHLESS-LITTLE-SHIT!

The sound of her evil feet against the stone floor—

CLACK! CLACK! CLACK!

—like some insectile beast.

Bob's eyes flew open, and there he lay in a paralyzed state until the nightmare ebbed from his soul, leaving him wrung out and slightly feverish.

He slipped from under the sheets and into the en suite to find himself staring into the vanity mirror, yet again.

This was becoming a habit that he'd rather leave alone.

Could Joshua's man in black and the *bitch* be one in the same?

He didn't think so. And how would that even be possible?

He placed his face in his hands and wept silently.

Sue opened her eyes. She remained silent. She did not move.

Raoul had opened wounds that, whilst they should've remained undisturbed, were bound to eventually catch up to them.

And perhaps it was better that it had happened sooner rather than leaving it till later. A privilege that might well be beyond everyone's reach.

At the third stroke, the time will be twelve... twelve... twelve o-one A.M....

❧

The Dark Suits' mobile phones rang simultaneously, Led Zeppelin duking it out with Bach amid a lost part of the world in Mulberry Estates.

Both answered, but it was Gillespie that spoke.

The Elder was telling Gillespie things he didn't want to hear.

"*Why?*" he shouted down the phone.

"Raoul's disappearance is a sign, Jimmy My-Boy. Lose the attitude."

"That doesn't explain the kid!" Gillespie wasn't listening. Enraged.

"If the storm is this close, it'll do our business..."

"*But we knew that before!*" Gillespie continued shouting. He glared at his partner.

"*Do not act.* Got it, Jimmy My-Boy?" There was something in the Elder's voice that was meant to be unmistakably offensive, as if Jimmy My-Boy might have played his final card.

Festering silence.

"If the kid remains untouched, *unclaimed,* after three days, you may have him, but not before. If we don't have to get involved, we won't, which means you *will not* make a move until Monday morning."

"I'll see to it," Raditch interceded.

"Well done." The Elder paused, before adding, "Time is near done, that I can sense."

Gillespie's seething continued, but what came next was like merrily pouring gas onto a flame while scratching one's ass. "You'd do well to listen to your partner, Jimmy My-Boy. There's a fellow with sense."

Then the conversation was apparently finished. There was a click and then nothing, as if the Elder had been swallowed into an abyss.

Raditch hung up.

Gillespie himself was hanging on, as if waiting for better news to come. Eventually, he pressed the button stamped with the little red phone. There was a strange moment where everything seemed held in suspended animation, or perhaps a vacuum, and then Gillespie's face reddened, his eyes bulged and he went on a ranting tirade. "*You phoned the old cunt! You shouldn't have phoned him! Why the fuck did you phone him?*"

Raditch put distance between them, thinking, *Mad son of a bitch should be put down!*

Things were being destroyed throughout what remained of their squatters' residence. Shrapnel was flying, and so was Gillespie, his rampage a typhoon. He couldn't have the kid. *Hands off, Gillespie!*

By the time Gillespie had spent his energy, the house's interior was in complete ruins, having gone so far as to demolish several pre-fab dividing walls. Almost all the others sported enormous holes which had been punched into them. Plasterboard and studs hung like the broken bones and flesh of a mangled creature. Insulation poked through in wild tufts.

Slumped in exhaustion, from which an acrid odor rose in an invisible bloom, as if the man had been on the turps, Gillespie's moderation was merely taking a breather.

In the illumination from his partner's LED torch, dark and tortured geometric shadows clawed about the tattered rooms.

And even before the thunderous commotion abated, Raditch had considered simply taking a side-step and leaving the madman to himself. But of course he couldn't, because he had become his responsibility, whether he liked it or not.

A MISSING TOWNSHIP

~~~

Thursday 8, September

The day of Sammy's disappearance, a watershed story of another kind was in progress at El Mejor Café in Brazil. The news clipping that shouldn't have been:

THOUSANDS DISAPPEAR UNDER CLOAK OF MYSTERIOUS CIRCUMSTANCES
By Emilio Rodriquez, as told by Pinon Rebisso

In a small township secluded at the mouth of the Amazon in Brazil, the people of Bonatares were never far from mystery. Being of rural persuasion, surrounded by dense jungle, these people thrived on folklore and legend. They also had their share of the paranormal. In 1977 strange lights blitzed the skies over Bonatares, just as they did in the same year over Colares, a small village in the same region. Many people were affected, some even died. The Brazilian military dispatched an infantry to both the township and the village following months of terror. Strangely, and in keeping with the mysterious events, the military went in armed not with the latest weaponry, but with cameras. Sanctioned by the government, they were on a filming safari to capture the strange lights that buzzed and sometimes killed. The project was known as Operacao Prato (Operation Saucer).

Now, almost fifty years on, it would seem that strange events have claimed the township of Bonatares.

On the night of August 4, 2022, it seems that abductions took place on an unprecedented scale and Bonatares ceased to exist...

Daniel Mayson's intrigue had been catapulted into hyperdrive. He had to know more. His efforts had been mainly fruitless, but they did lead him to Brazil.

He entered El Mejor Café, scanned the pools of tables, and approached the one where just a single man sat. "Emilio?" he asked. "Emilio Rodriquez?"

"Yes."

"I'm Dan," he said, holding out a hand.

"Pleased to meet you, Dan," Rodriquez said as the men shook.

"As I've explained previously, I'm a ufologist, keen to further investigate the missing township. Although," he said, taking a seat, "I'm puzzled that I had to stumble across this news in a small article that was almost a last-minute thought in a gazette. With my interest piqued, I've researched this incident further."

A waitress came to their table. "Would you like to order?"

"I'll have a cappuccino," Dan said immediately.

Rodriquez felt he might need something with a little more kick than caffeine. "Dos de tequila. Por favor, no sales el vaso."

The waitress smiled and receded into the bowels of the cafe.

"Early in the day for eighty proof."

"I don't normally indulge at this time, but this is a special occasion," Rodriquez returned. "What did you find?"

"Sorry?"

"In your research?"

"Oh… nothing. Not a goddamned thing."

Rodriquez lacked surprise. "The story was hushed up."

"How many people *actually* went missing?"

"'Bout five thousand," Rodriquez said in a monotone.

"*Five thousand?*"

Rodriquez merely stared at his new friend.

"How can five thousand missing be hushed up?"

"When I attempted to run my story, I was intercepted. These people refrained from small talk. Who they were, where they were from, they were not about to say. And I was not about to ask; their very presence left no doubt as to their capabilities. They confiscated all of my work, destroyed my computer and flash drives, even those of my family… going from room to room systematically destroying or claiming thousands of dollars of personal belongings." At this point, Rodriquez laughed. "They even destroyed my mobile phone." He leaned forward. "Why the fuck would you destroy a mobile phone?"

"The gallery… could've taken pictures."

The waitress returned. "Your cappuccino and tequila," she said pleasantly and handed them the bill. "If there's anything else, just raise a hand and you'll be attended to."

"Muchas gracias," Dan said, smiling, and took the bill. He didn't bother with glancing over it, but would later think that fifteen smackaroos for a double shot of tequila was an out-and-out ripoff. The bills, however, mounted over the course of their conversation.

"You didn't pursue the matter further?" Dan asked after taking a sip of the coffee.

"No." Rodriquez downed the double shot in one gulp.

"But you have your knowledge. I dare say they didn't take your memory?"

"Dan, have you ever been threatened in the severest of ways? Have you ever *known* in here—" Rodriquez tapped his chest. "That you had better do as you're told?"

"Can't say I have."

"I adore my family. And I don't mind admitting that, at this stage in life, I'm rather partial to breathing." Rodriquez rolled his eyes skyward before bringing them upon the man with a steely gaze. "I've agreed to meet you strictly on those terms I set out in our last conversation."

"You have my word."

"I need more than that. I'll tell you what I know, but you'll neither write nor record what I'm about to reveal."

Dan thought on this for a while. He was a man of his word. In his game, if you weren't, you basically had no future. It was poor form to go mouthing off about sensitive information. Such behavior would rapidly alienate you, and any credible source would just as rapidly dry up like a riverbed in an African savannah. So of course he wouldn't betray the man. But what to do with the information imparted? He supposed he could act on any thread he saw as a potential lead, and if ever cornered play the hapless guy with a nose for a good story. And so he agreed. "You may have been silenced, but what of Bonatares' family members, relatives, and disgruntled exes? Somewhere out there must be others who didn't live in the township, wondering what happened to their loved ones. People simply don't vanish from existence."

"Dan, I once learned of a cousin of mine who went missing years ago, never to be seen again. *He* vanished from existence. There was no outcry. There was no investigation. He simply walked out of life, never to be seen again. Go to any law enforcement bureau and they'll tell you of the staggering amount of People who vanish without a trace. No clothing. No bones. No witnesses. As if they simply strode down the road and were swallowed whole. It wasn't until years afterwards that I even learned of my cousin. When I did, there seemed no point in pursuing the matter. Where to begin? Even for an investigative journalist."

"Rodriquez, you're talking about one solitary person. An individual. There are five thousand missing, erasing the population of an entire township. Plus, it's hardly ancient history." Dan drank more coffee. "It was last month, for Pete's sake."

Rodriquez nodded. The tequila had hardly hit the spot. He raised his hand. But he understood that whilst it was okay to indulge, it was equally prudent to keep watch over what was said. Remaining prudent was top priority, even though he had agreed to meet Dan... a man he knew nothing of, except that he had an interest in the paranormal, the unexplained. "The township is remote. There is every chance that most living relatives of those missing outside the township may not know, even today. And they may not for years to come. You read a tiny piece in some newspaper because, and only because, of your interest in UFOs. After all, had you not been looking—and even if you had—you'd most likely have wrapped your vegetable peelings in it and tossed it in the garbage without noticing it."

Dan conceded. "I s'pose I could've at that."

The waitress returned.

"Iqual ques antes," Rodriquez said.

The waitress turned to Dan.

"Oh, gracias, estay benie," he replied. "Estay... I'm still finishing my coffee." His Spanish wasn't all that it could have been and he was left a little red-faced.

The waitress smiled benevolently, "Don't worry; I'm not that good at it myself." She turned, and disappeared into the cafe. Dan watched her sink into its murky depths, where he could barely make her out before rounding some corner. Disappeared, but not gone.

"People in remote Brazil are a superstitious lot, and whatever can't be explained is left to the imagination. *They* know it's true because *they* have seen it." Rodriquez said, tapping the side of his head. "Just as people are convinced of the existence of the Moth Man or Chupacabra. Just like people are convinced of UFOs."

"You don't believe?"

"There are many who'd claim you to be a foolish man, running about looking for creatures , including in green skin."

"And you?"

Rodriquez laughed softly. "Dan, I believe. But then, I believe in the Moth Man and Chupacabra. Regardless of my beliefs, any others who may know of the missing may well fantasize of exactly how that came to be. No one outside of that belief is going to take such wild explanations seriously. They'd be scoffed at, and people told that they were given to hysterics. And so, some may well have spoken, only to be ridiculed and discredited—or threatened—into silence."

"You've spoken to such people, besides Rebisso?"

"Yes," Rodriquez said simply.

Dan's intrigue was, once more, jacked so high that the waitress's return went completely unnoticed. He didn't recognize that she'd delivered the double shot of tequila, nor the bill on the table. Staring at Rodriquez, he waited with barely refrained patience.

Rodriquez once more tipped the alcohol down his throat in an instant. "I drew from what others said and discarded much of it. They were not witnesses, Dan, you must remember that. So, what is needed are corroborating stories, or at least parts of stories that corroborate each other from sources unknown to each other, and that have not been compromised or tarnished through indirect associations." He leaned forward, his eyes turned down to slits. When he spoke this time, he did so in hushed tones. "There was the one man of whom you spoke."

"On which the news article was based?"

"Pinon Rebisso," Rodriquez confirmed. "He wasn't someone who was merely given to superstitions. He was a resident of Bonatares."

"He survived?"

"He had a very sick family member in Colares, which you'd have also glimpsed in the news article. Dan, out of five thousand, how is it that just one man would seem to have been out of town when the final assault occurred?"

Daniel Mayson wasn't quite sure how to answer, so he didn't.

Rodriquez laughed mirthlessly. "I mean, it's one thing to *live* in another township and not know. It's something else when you *lived* in the township to find upon your return that *everyone* had vanished."

"There may be others who'll eventually come forward."

"Maybe." Rodriquez looked at him closely, delivering little hope in his voice. "Just another mystery, right?" he said sadly. "Rebisso said that the incidents started slowly when he looked back on it. Temperatures began rising unexpectedly and time started going haywire."

"What did he mean by that?"

"He said that watches and clocks started acting strange, and that it was increasingly difficult to accurately tell the time. But such events were blamed on the month of August. *El mes de la tristeza y el dolor*—the month of sorrow and grief."

"But as you say, these are all part of superstition."

"Have you taken notice of your watch of late?"

Dan glanced at the Omega happily strapped around his left wrist through a stainless steel band that damn near reached his elbow. He went to say that he hadn't noticed anything amiss when he was cut off.

"People had begun donning white to ward off such evil, Rebisso included, as white is reputed to have such powers. But, as we know, their efforts were futile, and they might as well have continued wearing whatever they had been before."

"Rebisso survived."

"Only because he wasn't home when the spirits came knocking. And, who knows, Daniel Mayson? They may have well been creatures in green skin."

"Did he see anything?"

"Besides a noticeable increase in the temperature, and the fact that time seemed to go off-kilter, he didn't see the abduction of the township's people, but he *did* see things." Rodriquez was feeling a little ill; retelling the tale was a test of his own fortitude. "He said he saw balloons."

"Balloons?"

"He said that many others had seen the same thing, and so everyone started talking about them and wondered who was releasing balloons into the skies, and what they were releasing them for. But as they glowed white, they were seen as another way to ward off the evil spirits that seemed to have chosen the township to molest."

"And were they?"

"The more this was witnessed, the more people started hearing a strange kind of laughter. No one knew for sure where this was coming from, but the laughter wasn't the kind that came from humor. Rebisso said it was the type to snatch your soul and give it to the Devil."

"Could it have been someone messing with them?"

"It was witnessed over a large area."

"A cult of sorts in Bonatares, celebrating the month of sorrow, perhaps?" Dan really was clutching at straws, but it was reasonable to speculate. He'd seen such things. And knew of such things, as most did, like those fallacious teenagers that satanically murdered the Lillelid family in April 1997. Husband, wife and two small children were ritualistically sacrificed in the belief of attaining a closer bond with the Devil. Three family members had died immediately. Their young son survived, only to be both disabled and without a mom, dad and sister.

"Rebisso firmly believed that these balloons were associated with the disappearances, all five thousand of them. In that way, it was a celebration of sorrow, but I doubt if it originated on Earth."

"Could they have been UFOs?"

"Unidentified flying objects? That is certainly what they were. But I feel what you and I are referring to are vastly different. If you mean 'spaceships' piloted by creatures in green skin, I think not."

Dan shook his head. *If this is UFO related, as it appears to be, it's the first encounter ever that indicates deadly consequences.*

Strangely enough, Emilio Rodriquez felt no side-effects from the four shots of tequila he'd poured down his throat. So damn if he wasn't raising his hand yet again. At this rate, he might as well order an entire bottle. Get it over and done with, sans the foreplay.

"Where did Rebisso think the balloons took the people?" Dan asked. His intrigue was sprinkled with pangs of anxiety.

"He was convinced that these balloons came from the sky and left the same way."

Dan stared at the man, dumbfounded. "UFOs," he uttered louder than he'd intended.

Rodriquez found this amusing. "You should live in Brazil. You've got the mind for it."

The waitress arrived at their table. Emilio Rodriquez ordered. Dan did not. She went away.

"Think about it, Dan. Five thousand is an extraordinary amount of missing people. Where did they go? You can't hide this amount in the back of semi-trailers. Five thousand people must have gone somewhere."

Silence ensued before he added, "And there was more thing." For some reason, *Oliver Twist* popped up in Dan's mind.

'Please, sir, I want some more.'

'You can't have any more!'

"These balloons seemed to have had company," Rodriquez continued. "Rebisso said he hadn't heard the bells himself, not at first, but knew of many who had."

"Bells?"

"Fairy goblins, Daniel Mayson. And, no, it was no festival. Not for the town's folk, at any rate. Rebisso said these were only ever heard upon waking from sleep. Like how you remember fragments of your dreams immediately upon opening your eyes, the sound of bells seemed to dissipate into the walls. There and then gone. But enough heard these bells to make it a phenomenon which accompanied the balloons, the destabilizing of time, and the rising temperatures. It was around this time that people started going missing. Just the odd one here and there."

"Did Rebisso know of any?"

"No," Rodriquez said with an air of finality. "You must remember, none of this was a drawn-out process. Less than a week, from beginning to end, had transpired. The abductions clean and ruthlessly efficient in a surgical manner, leaving people little time to react beforehand."

The waitress returned and handed Emilio Rodriquez his glass. He held up a hand. The waitress waited. He downed his drink and handed the glass back. She said, "Should I delay giving you the bill until you're ready to go?"

Rodriquez looked at her in a very honest yet quizzical manner. "I was ready to go before I sat down. And once I did, I immediately wished I'd taken heed of my senses."

She smiled, not sure what else to do.

"Leave it," he said, noticing her confusion. "I'm about done here, at any rate."

"Okay, just remember—"

"If I drink any more, I'll be under the table." He smiled, and the waitress smiled back and left.

It was Dan's turn to lean forward and ask in hushed tones, "Is there any chance that I could met this Rebisso fellow? Perhaps you know of his whereabouts, and I could inquire to see if he's willing to talk to me?"

Rodriquez nodded with that same honest yet quizzical countenance. "I am sure Rebisso would be most willing to speak with you."

"Good."

"If he could be found."

"He disappeared too?"

"I remained in contact with him for days after our first meeting. He knew of me and sought me out. Apparently I'm known for my honest appraisal and handling of situations that are delicate in nature. And as this was a most delicate situation, he decided that I was the one to turn to and reveal what he knew."

"As you meet on several occasions, was he able to tell you more?"

"He began having his own dreams, Daniel Mayson. He began to hear his own bells. That was when I lost contact with him."

"You mean he cut ties with you?"

"I visited his home and, when there was no answer, I was forced to get outside help. The police finally came after some persistent persuasion. A few days of rudimentary investigations transpired. They discovered nothing and chalked it up to just another disappearance in Brazil. No big deal. Before filing their reports, putting the matter to rest, they thanked me for wasting their time. But Rebisso's bed, there was something about it. Even the police acknowledge as much."

"What?"

"It looked as if Rebisso was still in it. There seemed to be a perfect impression outlining his body. But there was no body. The bed was cold. He'd been gone for some time."

"What do *you* imagine these balloons and bells were, besides green-skinned aliens?"

"As I was not in Bonatares, that is difficult to say. But what happened was real. These people deserve to have this explained properly and not simply filed and stamped as cases of 'missing people'. They are more than missing. But the explanation is convenient. Law enforcement has *real* matters to deal with, things that they can actually get their heads around, like murders and rapes and domestic violence. But disappearances? Too time-consuming for little if any results. *Ever!*" Again, Rodriquez leaned forward, keeping his voice low. "What I do know is that five thousand people are in desperate trouble. Where? How? Why? These are all unknowns and it gives me the creeps. I don't believe they are dead, but I can't tell you why I think so. I just do. But I'm not about to act on these thoughts. As I've told you, while my family remains unaware, believing their computers were vandalized by an intruder—which is true... in part—their lives have been, as has mine, threatened by people I don't know. People I do not *want* to know. People who came out of the darkness and went back into the darkness."

Dan sat in the aging hours of the day, somewhat dazed. How time flies when you were having fun! And he knew exactly what his next move was going to be. He had to visit Bonatares himself. He had to see the aftermath of five thousand abductions. Not in a macabre way. He just had to see for himself.

As if reading his mind, Rodriquez said, "Daniel Mayson, it's a bad idea."

"Don't you worry, Rodriquez, I'm not about to take residence, and I'll be acutely circumspect to balloons and bells."

"You can't run from what you don't understand, nor can you deprive yourself of sleep if you start hearing bells. Either way, you may take the Bonatares disappearance tally to that of five thousand and one."

And while Dan gazed into the sky, maybe to catch a glimpse of a balloon, Rodriquez said something that made him almost cry out in terror. "Bonatares isn't the last and it wasn't the first. The balloons, they'll return. A precedence was set in 2011, in Australia. This is the same phenomena, of that I'm certain."

∽

Friday, September 9, 2022
Early morning

Today's sunrise was fierce. Very fierce. Shepherds take warning. Kids were packed into cars and trundled off to school. Adults packed themselves into cars and trundled off to all kinds of workplaces. Lawnmowers enthusiastically burred across expanses of lawn, here and there, spitting out the scent of freshly-cut lawn, some of which speckled the deflated souls doing the pushing. Arturo was deeply regretting not putting hold to those bookings for the day as he had slogged his way through the last customers and out to the caged flatbed of his pick-up, which read: *Arturo's Complete Gardening Specialist. Free Quotes. First Service Free.* Others were proving how fit they were and powering through an early morning jog. Their favorite tunes coming through their earbuds apparently frying everything between each ear as their faces glowed a glistening cherry-red. Just the usual rhythm of the mundane, albeit weary, under the every increasing blaze. But for those at 22 Chasing Boulevard, it was the mundane they would've loved to have been truly a part of.

The daylight hours had brought a veil of hazy torpidity with them and a warring of emotions that went way beyond the responsibility of the heat. Each member of the Triplow family moved about in what Joshua had come to think of as the 'thick.' It had returned with a vengeance. He fancied that he recognized this in his mom and dad as well, and then discarded it as the hypothesis of a rather distraught mind.

He got ready for school in the usual way, except everything seemed a plod, as if he was walking through some auntie's worst rendition of porridge—the type which could break spoons and keep you chewing for hours.

Once ordinary affairs, such as glancing at a clock, or mobile phone, even the little readout in the bottom right-hand corner of the computer screen, had become one born more of unsettling fascination.

The doorbell sounded, but Joshua's attention remained transfixed on the kitchen clock.

8:35 A.M.... 9:20... 6:10... 5:33... 2:19... Seemed whatever was influencing time was becoming more powerful. More influential.

"Hi, Mrs. Triplow," Joshua heard Leon say from the other room, forced brightness in his voice.

"Hi there, Leon," she returned, not pretending to be anything but on the ball, albeit in the same weary fashion as the rest of humanity. "Josh, your soulmate's arrived!" Her voice dully rung through the house and up the stairwell close by. "Before you go, just as a reminder, I'm going to pick you and Josh up from school, so please don't forget or I'll be left stranded and looking rather foolish."

"We won't," the boys said in unison, Joshua coming up behind.

"Are you sure you boys wouldn't mind a lift to school?" Sue asked, gazing out to the road with an expression of trepidation.

Joshua shook his head. "Thanks, Mom." He needed space to share his grief, and since his folks had yet to learn of Sammy, he had to do so in relative privacy. So why not the sidewalks full of bleached bones? At least, that's what the sparse number of joggers would be if they kept it up under the heat. As much as saving his legs the trudge to school was irresistibly appealing, the reward just wasn't worth it.

"Okay, then. Off you go and take care," Sue said, because it seemed necessary. "And, remember, drink plenty of water!" No sooner had she voiced her admonishment than she was remembering *The Curse* with Joshua Triplow standing in for Wil Wheaton. She watched her son and his soulmate saunter into the southern end of Chasing Boulevard, wondering what kind of mother she was.

Drink the water, Josh. Go to Australia with your father, my handsome young man. Drink the water and shake hands with the man in black before your blue eyes close, never to open again!

"We will," the boys had said, once more, in unison, and Sue had raised a half-wave, truly terrified for her son, just a boy. An innocent boy whose greatest wrong in life had only ever been to inadvertently run over an ant or two while on his *Astra-Links*.

They were heading off to join up with what remained of the team at Citrus Hills Elementary. Sammy, of course, who'd confessed frequently to liking school, wouldn't be there unless by some miracle. *Or in spirit*, Joshua cursed himself for harboring such a thought. Unintentional or not. It must have been lurking somewhere in his mind else it wouldn't have made an appearance, at all.

Both Joshua's and Leon's hearts were pumping pure lead through the passageways of their veins. Sweat coursed down their bodies as if the heavens had opened up, rather than the sun beating down.

"I like the heat, but this is a bit much," Leon confessed.

Head down, Joshua remained silent, his hair a bedraggled screen hanging in his face. It was damp, and he could taste salt in his mouth where sweat trickled into it. He rubbed his nose as it dribbled from the tip and made it tickle.

They both walked as if through that auntie's torrid porridge, in a fashion that suggested they were participating in Sammy's wake. But Joshua wouldn't have it. None of it. He was still, deep down inside, determined to rescue—*somehow*—his friend from the man in black.

"Did…" Leon began hesitantly. "Did you have another dream last night?"

No, but I masturbated then I cried, Joshua thought cheerlessly, distantly, his soul drifting a billion miles from home-base. He was the ball that'd been hit clear into orbit, never to be seen again. "No. I tried. I really did. I couldn't dream, even though I told myself that I should, because I wanted to—" He broke off. "Funny, huh? I actually wanted to dream."

"I did," Leon offered. "I dreamt I went to Sammy's."

Joshua stopped immediately and grabbed his friend by the arm. "Did you go inside? Did you see him? What about the man in black?"

"I didn't see Sammy. I didn't see the man in black. I didn't hear that man with the trumpet, Satchel—"

"Satchmo."

"Yeah, right," Leon said, as if his mind too was drifting. "Honestly, I don't know what I was doing there. It made me feel weak, as if all my energy was being drained away by an unseen force." Leon whispered in fear of them being overheard, though not another soul braved the sidewalks, not since the joggers seemed to have rediscovered their senses and sought refuge from the sun. Either that or had simply died mid-stride. The boys supposed all the other kids had hitched a ride to school due to the heat.

"So what did you do?" Joshua flicked his hair, darkened and ropey with sweat, from his face.

"Nothing. I just stood there, like a dope, at his front door. It was as if I was hypnotized by it." Leon frowned. "When we went there before in our dream, what was on the doorbell?" His heart hammered in his throat, making his voice warble.

They'd began their trudge towards school once more.

"What d'ya mean?"

"Whose name was written in the doorbell to alert others of whose house they'd arrived at?"

"Debnar."

"Yeah."

"Why?"

"Well… it *was* a dream. Right? So I guess the word 'DREAM' shouldn't be unexpected. Right?"

"I don't know," Joshua said. This did little to allay his friend's fears. "It's *Peter Pan* meets *The Twilight Zone*," he added, having given it some extra thought.

The show he'd so delighted in watching with his dad floated in his head, just as the door floated in the screen upon the show's introduction.

You're moving into a land of both shadow and substance... where men write and steal your dreams and your best friends... where ghouls stalk the dark passages and boys are held captive never to grow old... holidays become nightmares and the cycle goes on... you just crossed over into the Twilight Zone...

"*Peter Pan? The Twilight Zone?*" Leon asked, breaking into a shivery sweat. "You mean like on TV?"

"No, Leon, *nothing* like TV."

⤴

8:45... 5:19... 7:21... 12:10... 9:34... 8:46 A.M....

They should've reached Citrus Hills Elementary by now, but the walk had taken much longer than usual. Joshua was in an ambivalent state of mind. He'd needed, desperately, to talk and be with Leon, best friend and soundboard, but a lift to school would've saved his tired legs, made no better as the heat sucked what little was on offer from them.

They were two streets from Citrus Hills Elementary when—

"What's going on here?" Joshua asked, and suddenly the porridge had turned to cement, his legs incapable of pushing through one more step.

The street was choked with unmarked police cars and ambulances. Though the sun was stringently bright, the pulsating flashes were demanding. As a collective, they were also strangely claustrophobic in the morning's breathtaking fumes.

Snowbird Lane had been barricaded. Traffic was strictly barred from coming in or going out. Both plainclothes officers and patrol police milled around the perimeter of one particular house, forming a scrum at the centre of which a team of paramedics seemingly ambled about.

Police and those in suits and ties—ridiculous attire under the conditions—combed either side of the street, peering here and there, looking into this and that, searching for something. Clues, the boys guessed without a second thought. As to what, though?

"That's old Mister Grouch's house," Leon whispered to Joshua, hitching his school bag onto his shoulder.

"How old was he?" Joshua's sickeningly uneasy feeling, churning in the pit of his stomach, intensified tenfold.

"I'm not sure, but he was *really* wrinkly."

"That old, huh?"

"Yeah," Leon half-laughed. There was no humor in it. "I heard he once chased after a kid because he stepped onto his lawn. I heard he was really pissed and threatened to break the kid's legs. He chased after him and scared him so much, he never walked this street again."

"I heard the same, but didn't the old man catch the kid and break his legs?" Joshua asked.

Leon was nodding. "It wouldn't surprise me." Words of a wise boy.

They stood to one side of Grouch's verge, in the belief that all stories from other kids were irrefutable facts… facts that gain their own life and become bigger than the incident that originally spurred them.

In truth, Old Mister Grouch, whose true name was Alexander Reilly, might've done nothing more menacing than make a friendly gesture to the 'kid' that he'd just laid new seed, and would appreciate it if he kept off the grass.

However, amongst the kids in the neighborhood, as with Lucille Goldman, the rumor had been long-established. And, whilst Goldman's reputation was deserved, baseless talk from the mouth of one boy had become hardened fact, condemning Alexander Reilly to Old Mister Grouch with an iniquitous penchant for causing harm to innocent children.

The coordinated search through the front yards on either side of Snowbird Lane ensured that every square inch was thoroughly covered, leaving no patch overlooked.

One officer started waving frantically. Others rushed to where she was.

"What do you make of this?" The policewoman was pointing to the ground.

Neither Joshua nor Leon could see what she was pointing at, which was rather annoying. Their 'thick' was currently washed aside by disquieting intrigue.

Another officer said, "It looks like a balloon."

"So we can assume, at this stage, this was a party that got *way* out of hand?" another was asking, as he too was pointing to something on the ground.

The police went over to him.

Before long, they all began to discover the same thing.

Balloons.

Not your regular variety of balloons, either.

"Can you see what's happening to it?" another was saying in stark wonderment, having pulled away a branch of a shrub which the balloon had fetched up on. "It's disintegrating."

"You just exposed it to direct light," one of his team said, harboring a theory.

"Yeah."

"That might explain why we're only seeing these balloons in the shadows. Look around; there are none in direct sunlight. The only ones we're seeing are under shade."

"Maybe they're made of a different type of plastic that breaks down under ultraviolet light?" another speculated.

"Balloons that can't tolerate the sun... nope, that makes no sense. Imagine daylight parties without balloons. Besides, there's something rather odd about them, wouldn't you say? It's as if they're somehow alive."

This drew an amount of sniggering despite the situation.

"No, listen! *Please—be quiet!*"

As if in telepathic collusion, each one held the same peculiar countenance. It was a mix of confusion and intense anxiety and this, beyond all else, reinforced the cement that had encased Joshua's legs. If the entire police force couldn't figure out what was happening, they were all in trouble.

After a moment, someone said, "What's that noise?"

"I have no idea. But if forced to put this in a report, I'd say it was some kind of talking."

Another was shaking her head. "No—listen closely. That's not talk. It sounds like... giggling."

They listened a bit more.

"How the *fuck* can something like *this* be making a sound like *that*?"

"They make birthday and Christmas cards sing and talk, don't they?"

"This is no goddamned Christmas card, Barry." The nervousness in the policeman's voice was palpable.

Old Mister Grouch's lawn now swarmed with plainclothes officers who had joined the paramedics at the centre of the scrum, relegating the police to the outer perimeter.

One officer was shaking his head. "How's this even possible?" he said, looking up to the sky. "I mean, there's nothing—not a thing—he could've fallen from."

"It's got me," one of his colleagues agreed. "Even if there was a tree, this would still be impossible, unless it was a pretty fucking tall tree."

The boys could hear that the man was unsettled even from where they stood. Again, the disquiet in them amplified.

The first plainclothes officer was still looking skyward. "He had to drop from a helluva distance. The human body doesn't simply pancake like this by taking a header from a few feet up." He swallowed hard without looking down. "What do you reckon the distance would've been to cause this much devastation?"

His colleague was shaking his head. "Ten, fifteen stories. At least."

"Christ, he's even left an indentation in his lawn," the first was saying, now stomping one foot against the ground, bringing up small puffs of dirt and grass. "It's pretty hard to leave a dent this deep!"

"Could he have fallen out of an aircraft? Could we be looking at murder?"

"Er..." the plainclothes officer stammered. "It's murder, but I'm not convinced it's the common sort we're used to dealing with." He paused, then said, "And to land in his own front yard?" He turned to another. "This is the poor bastard's residence, right? Or was?"

"His neighbor said he'd lived here since her family had moved in, some eight years ago. And from what she knew, he'd lived here much longer than that. His name was Alexander Reilly and he'd been retired for as long as she'd known him. She was pretty shaken up."

"*I'm* pretty shaken up! Don't worry about the neighbors. This doesn't make sense. None at all!" He gathered himself. "This is going to be difficult for her, without doubt, but I'm going to have to speak with her myself. I need to hear what she has to say. Start another round of door knocking, and keep asking questions until it jogs someone's memory, even though they'll complain about having been asked a hundred times over. I don't care; we need answers. Someone must've heard or seen *something*. People just don't land in their front yards looking like the Hunchback of Notre Dame, no matter how crazy the party the night before was. I'm baffled, and I don't like being baffled. I can't even start to think of where to begin, except looking up to the... sky. And that's about as useful as doing nothing at all."

"If the other neighbors are anything like those next door, they'll be as helpful as you looking into the sky."

"*Just do it!*" the plainclothes officer barked.

Off to the side there was a horde of news crews, getting their grisly scoop for the day. Cameras were rolling and journalists were talking excitedly. Only problem was, no one knew what they were talking about. Everyone from the paramedics to the news crews were desperate to make sense of things that scrambled the senses. What to think, say or do was all a matter of clutching at straws.

Leon and Joshua craned their necks to catch a glimpse of what lay at the centre of the scrum, not exactly knowing what they'd see, nor prepared for what they did see. Of course, neither had wanted to see, but they couldn't help themselves.

Through a gap in the officers standing around in their suits and ties was something flat on the ground. It wasn't the body that assaulted Joshua's mental processes, but the head. The face. It was flat. Literally. There were no contours to it. There was no nose or bridge of the forehead. There were no lips or cheeks. No ears or earlobes. It was as if someone with a herculean steamroller had decided to squash Old Mister Grouch's head into a patty the size of a dinner plate.

Joshua felt his stomach roll.

Leon went one step further by retching.

This gained them unwanted attention.

"How the hell did those boys get in here?" the plainclothes officer who seemed to be in command (of what was another matter altogether) was shouting. "Get them outta here. This is no place for kids… shit, it's no place for adults. *Get them out of here!*"

A policeman came rushing up to them. "Move along, boys. Now!"

The boys struggled to break free of the stranglehold on their legs. They'd seen more than they had wanted, at any rate. Old Mister Grouch might've been a tyrant, but no one deserved to end the way he did.

Once away from the authoritarian attention of what seemed like the entire police force of Riverside County, Joshua turned to his friend. "Did you see his face?"

Leon nodded, groaning, "I don't think I'll eat another hamburger for as long as I live!" He then spun on his heels and threw his breakfast up in someone's beautifully manicured shrubbery. "What happened to him, Josh?" he whined, wiping moisture from his lips.

"Leon," Joshua started gravely.

"Josh, if you say we're in another nightmare, I'm gonna scream my head off."

"No," Joshua murmured, much to Leon's relief. "There's none the weird kind of stuff that's associated with nightmares."

"What?" Leon barked. "Old Grouch is pretty fucking weird. I'd say what happened to Old Grouch is totally deranged!"

"But not dream kind of weird." Despite all that was happening, Joshua Triplow was holding his mettle. "The sun's not like thickened orange juice. The streets are pretty quiet but we can still hear all kinds of normal things, can't we? In nightmares you can't. It's like tunnel vision of the mind. Nothing exists around you except what you're focused on."

"I s'pose." Leon's tone lacked conviction, and his mouth tasted sour. Perhaps he should follow Joshua's lead and forego milk on his breakfast cereal for orange juice. Then again, that too would taste pretty sour after a little massaging of the stomach before expulsion. *No more Joe-Joe's hamburgers,* he thought again.

Joshua stared at him and Leon's face took on a deep patina of horror. He didn't like what he saw in his friend. Other than running from him, he knew he was about to get it with both barrels blazing. "Can you remember what Old Grouch looked like?"

"Why?"

"*Can you?*"

Leon hesitated before finally saying, "I think so. He wasn't the kind of man you wanted to see, so I hardly ever saw him." He paused. "Why did we take that street? We hardly ever take Snowbird Lane. Why did we take that street today of all days? We know what Old Grouch is like. We *never* take that street."

"Leon," Joshua said sternly, "calm down. It's not helping."

"But *why*, Josh?"

"I don't know. But you can remember what Old Grouch looked like?"

Leon was nodding. His head felt fat and likely to fall from his shoulders. At least, then, he wouldn't have to be bothered with what he poured over his cereal.

"I guess I can, too," Joshua said. "His house… that was kinda like the one in our nightmare of Satchmo."

"So this *is* another nightmare," Leon could hardly prize the words from his mouth.

Joshua was shaking his head. "No, forget the nightmare, Leon. The house was similar. Remember we said that we'd never seen it before; but I think it was just like the sun that looked like thickened orange juice and the lack of all sounds. I think what we saw was his house but it just *looked* different. I think the old man was Old Grouch."

"What are you getting at, Josh?"

"I really don't know, just that we probably dreamt of him in our nightmare because of the messed-up state of affairs all around us. Old Grouch we placed into it because of what we thought of him. He was a scary man. The environment was weird and scary. I reckon if we went through his house, we'd find that he played Satchmo."

"We're not going through his fucking *house*, Joshua! Not on your life!"

"I'm not saying that's what we'll do, just that at some point in time, we might've heard Satchmo coming from his house and just placed it into our nightmare."

"So where does that leave Sammy?"

Joshua sighed with a heavy heart. "Sammy," he repeated, and suddenly all the steam was lost in his voice.

"Do you think he's like... Old Grouch?"

"No, I don't."

"Why?"

"Because it doesn't feel right. Sammy's not dead, just gone."

"Come on, Josh, after what we've just seen, what *does* feel right?" Leon reasoned. "I feel like going home. I don't feel like going to school. I don't reckon I'll be able to concentrate, not after that. All I'll keep on seeing is what was left of Old Grouch. All I'll keep thinking of is Sammy."

They walked on further, running hopelessly late for the start of school, neither caring much. They had, after all, a pretty good excuse for their tardiness should Mrs. Bruckheimer put the hard word on them, which she probably wouldn't.

Joshua stuck out a hand to stop his friend in his tracks. "Look," he gasped.

They both stared at the side of a house. The sun was in a position where it couldn't reach this area. The shade was complete, whilst all around it, the sun bit into everything with vicious teeth of some forty-plus Celsius (roughly 108° F).

There was a mound of plastic; or to be more precise, there were more of what the police had described as balloons. They hadn't actually seen what the police were referring to, but this was the only conclusion they could make.

The mound was writhing pathetically, as if being blown by a fitful breeze. But there was none to speak of. The air hung like a winter's blanket in the morning's furnace.

The boys stared in wonder, each inferring the one thing none of the officers on Snowbird Lane had seemed to; by their very appearance, these 'balloons' displayed a warning, like any deadly creature of nature, to keep your distance or dare take a chance with your life.

"What are they?"

"Leon, if I knew that, I'd be a plainclothes detective… only better, 'cause even they couldn't figure it out."

Once their adrenaline had worn off, the rest of the day was marked with fluctuating anxiety. Like the LED frequency bar of an equalizer, the sensation continued surging and dropping, one frequency rising, the other falling. It pushed aside any attempt of subjugation, and was by no small means helped by the 'thick' which had, once again, escalated. They were back in auntie's porridge. She had watered it down somewhat and, though no longer the consistency of cement, its counter-force to whatever they tried to do was unrelenting.

Leon had gotten it right when he'd said he'd not be able to concentrate.

Neither boy discussed the weekend affairs, each assuming what the other was doing: a wedding, a fishing trip. Such distractions were insignificant, unlike a week earlier when fishing was all Joshua had been talking about, and Leon bemoaning the fact that he had to get dressed up in a daft suit and tie to attend someone's wedding, hoping the food would at least be good. Still, fishing sounded a whole lot better. At one point, he'd said ruefully, "They really should've more consideration. After a hard week at school, what kid wants to attend a wedding dressed up like a demented flamingo?"

Then Sammy disappeared and the world had disintegrated.

Leon and Joshua decided not to tell Craig or Ethan of that morning's events, on the grounds that Craig would completely freak out and Ethan might or might not make a joke of the whole sordid affair. *Was that* just *power of suggestion, Ethan? Would your folks convince you that Old Mister Grouch was* all *inside your head since he didn't have one to think with himself?* And the boys could do without that.

Joshua's mom picked them up as promised, including Ethan and Craig, and drove them home without much chatter between them.

Craig couldn't stand the heat, and he was beyond 'thick,' at almost 'out of it' by late afternoon.

Ethan started jabbering some crap, and Joshua had begun sweating greater quantities than even the wretched heat could account for, in fear of him spilling what each of them carried, like the remains from an exhumed loved one. Relief swept through him when Ethan finally shut up.

For all his bravado, it was merely a front. Ethan was tormented by the dark hands of sorrow, despite his projected optimism. Sam the Man was off somewhere goofing around. Right? Sam the Man would appear out of the blue soon, and his friends would look downright silly. Right?

There was something, else, though. Something he couldn't quite put his finger on. He wasn't diseased with an unhealthy liking for school, like Sam the Man, but it seemed as if he was being driven away from a place he'd never return to or see again.

Funny, isn't it? How the mind plays tricks?

The heat. It had to be the heat.

⌇

Saturday, September 10, 2022
Early morning

The occasions that Joshua wasn't the first to the breakfast table were a rare occurrence.

This morning was one of them.

By the time Sue padded down the stairs and into the dining room, Bob was already on the phone to Malcolm Edwards, talking business. He saw what was in her hand and rolled his eyes. "What a dickhead," he muttered.

"Sorry, Bob?"

"Oh, Malcolm, sorry, I was miles away."

She carried *The Sentinel Weekly News* upon whose front page smiled the face of a young boy. A boy they both knew well.

He'd left the paper on the bedside table with every intention of secreting it away before she could see. He was going to gently confront his son, but before he could do so the phones had started ringing. He had successfully ignored this, but when his mobile joined where the phones had left off, Bob felt compelled to answer. Before he raised it to his ear, he could see it was Malcolm and knew he would want to talk business, when all Bob wanted to do was hold his son in his arms and hug him for dear life.

"Tenders have been closed on the purifiers for months. Your design won, Bob. I don't mind reminding you that this is a very big deal for us all, which surprises me that you've been so quiet. It's not usual that I've to chase people when the situation is so lucrative to them."

"I'm sorry, Malcolm, it's been… a bizarre few days."

Sue approached Joshua, who sat at the breakfast table. "Honey, did you know about…" She hesitated. "Sammy?" She chose not to show him what she held.

Joshua opened his mouth as if to say something, then closed it, tears silently trickling down his face.

Bob didn't see this, and that was just as well for Malcolm Edwards, who might have been rudely dispensed with.

"Well, all isn't lost. But there's the proverbial outstanding billion and one trivial details needing to be trimmed, binned or tidied up. I don't know where to start without you. I may be the CEO of this corporation, but I'm hardly the brains behind these state-of-the-art purifiers. I must say, in a world which is going more and more green, this is an outstanding achievement on your behalf, and one which Crystal Bell eagerly awaits. These should place us well and truly in front of carbon emission reduction. What are the figures, Bob?"

"Um, carbon emissions are reduced by approximately twenty to twenty-five percent."

"Cracking good stuff, I must say. Impressive, particularly as the design has been independently assessed and the claims you make verified as conservative. The estimates I've in front of me suggest reductions are more in the vicinity of thirty to thirty-five percent. You're a bloody genius." Malcolm's British heritage was never far below the surface. Though his accent was a pretty good American rendition, it was in the subtleties that his true origins could be discerned.

"Thanks, Malcolm." Bob was intently watching the interaction between his wife and son, his words dribbling off his lips.

"You don't sound too excited. I like that. People who get too excited tend to be less than grounded. Remaining grounded is a mighty good attribute. But I must say, there are those here getting somewhat nervous with regards to your absence."

You might change your tune if you knew the world's future was in the balance. You might think that a reduction in carbon emissions was quite trivial.

"I can't say I'm getting my backside kicked, but it's not far off."

Bob placed his fingers under his glasses and rubbed his eyes. They felt tired, though it had yet to go 7:00 a.m.

"Therefore, I'd like you to grace us with your good presence *today*. It's only a forty... forty-five-minute flight. And at this time of the year, flights are readily available."

It'd have been simpler to have told Malcolm to shove it. It'd have been ethically balanced with his main concern leaning heavily to the welfare of his family, if not the entire human race. But in the same breath, he realized such an act would put a severe dent in his reputation, and inventions that brought in the big bucks didn't come thick and fast. Frankly, he had two claims to fame: the Hydraulically Collapsible Parking Lot and, now, the smokestack purifiers that could be converted to purifiers for any air pollutants from industrial businesses. The latter was a game changer. It'd provide for his family indefinitely.

If there is a future...

Joshua's head was buried in Sue's stomach. The sight broke Bob's heart, and he really was a conflicted man. If Raoul and all he said proved nothing but empty bullshit... and he told Malcolm Edwards to go find himself a pole and use it, there'd be *no* future, that much *was* certain. Reduced to once more penny-pinching just to survive from week to week lacked the appeal of being a man who stood his ground on ethics. He was damned if he'd force such a lifestyle onto Sue again, and onto Joshua.

"Okay," Bob found himself saying against his will.

"Good on you, Bob. I'll be expecting you around... What's the time now? About five past seven. If you get cracking, you should be here by ten tops."

"I won't be staying, though. I do need to come home to attend to family matters," Bob said, his eyes never leaving his wife and son.

Sue stared at him, her eyes blazing with reproach.

"Not a problem, Bob. Promise you won't be detained any longer than necessary. The usual pesky issues that, I dare say, will crop up during the day can be either prioritized or allocated to future handling over the phone. Now, that doesn't seem so arduous, does it?"

Bob hung up. If only the silly bastard knew. But, of course, if he got an insight into what was scattered throughout Bob's head, he'd be written off as a severe liability to the corporation, and not at all grounded as Malcolm was so enamored with. Quite the contrary; he'd descend from this lofty status to someone with a little too much junk in the attic, like toys in a kid's playroom, any one of them a potential hazard to the conscious well-being of a CEO.

He walked over to his wife and son, shaking his head remorsefully. "I am so sorry, but I have no choice."

Sue's eyes coruscating blue razors.

He knelt beside his boy who was still crying silent tears and ran a hand through his hair. "How long have you known?"

Joshua sniffed several times. "Since Thursday." His words were muffled in Sue's T-shirt that, ironically, displayed the phrase *Make Way For A Happy Day*.

"Why didn't you say something?"

Joshua wasn't about to tell his parents that he was guilty. That he had known from the outset, since before dreaming of entering Sammy's house where the man in black sat scribbling away like a crazed man. He had known then, he had known since, and it'd been confirmed with Jenny Debnar pleading with him if he knew of Sammy's whereabouts.

That he did. Sammy was now with the man in black.

He was now in his house, not around the corner at 17 South Lincoln Drive, but somewhere that was haunted by the man in black and, perhaps, a man who played the trumpet.

But if quizzed on the dream he'd had of Satchmo, Joshua would've given an honest evaluation and stated confidently that Satchmo was merely a by-product of his nightmare of the man in black. He was like an alleyway that went off in some other direction. A diversion to serve no other purpose but to ensure confusion reigned.

Joshua's reluctance to answer said it all. At least, so his parents thought.

"Mate," Bob said quietly. "Mate, I've got some affairs to take care of today, but I'll be home by late afternoon, early evening at the latest."

Joshua nodded, his head remaining buried in Sue's stomach.

As much as Sue didn't want to, she drew Joshua away from her, looked him in his watery eyes, and said, "Baby, I've got to have a chat with your dad. Just for a moment. You'll be alright for a few minutes?"

Joshua nodded.

None of them heard the kitchen clock's rhetoric:

Tick... Tick... Tock... Tick... Tock... Tock... Tick...

In their upstairs bedroom, Sue was seething. "How *could* you? Your son needs you more than ever, a lot more than Malcolm bloody Edwards!"

"Hon, it's only for the afternoon. You stay put, I'll catch a taxi—"

"Don't 'Hon' me. I'm not in the mood. He could wait!"

"He has a point, Sue. This deal is worth close to two billion over the course of time to them, and countless millions to us."

"Sometimes, Bob, there are things that no amount of money can buy. Do you understand that? Do you get that? You're abandoning your son when things couldn't get much worse, and you're catching a flight—not to Adelaide, but into the arms of Malcolm *bloody* Edwards!" Sue paced the room.

Bob understood her anger, but he'd never seen her this enraged.

"You catch your flight. But you'd better be home before sunset, mister. You'd better remain true to your word that you gave your grief-stricken son moments ago."

"I promise."

"Do you? Do you *really*? Guess Betty Mae might've had a point after all... adults, *parents*, break promises all the time to their kids, leaving them stranded and helpless."

Bob could've argued this point, but for as much as he was determined to make good on his promise to Malcolm Edwards, he was equally sure he was doing so in the guise of reprehensible double standards. One that Malcolm would be blind to see.

∽

The afternoon of September 10th slowly dissolved into evening. Still no Bob.

A situation that did not improve Sue's demeanor. She sat on the sofa with her son, not having let him out of her sight all day. Joshua had hardly protested.

Since the front page of the newspaper made Sammy's disappearance official, as if before there might've been the tiniest of chances that he had been wrong, he didn't have any desire to go anywhere or do anything. Besides, his best friend was out playing dress-up for some distant relative's wedding, leaving him alone and with no one to confide in.

Deep in his mind, a dark well-spring bubbled, and from its depths rose an absolute intention to make good on his disastrous inaction. He had a most definite destination in mind. A horrible destination, one that was not what nightmares were made of. This went one step further. It was an intentional intrusion into a place that should never be contemplated.

The nightmare.

His mom had inadvertently left *The Sentinel Weekly News* on the kitchen table, as she'd escorted her husband upstairs earlier that day to tell him a few home truths about himself.

Joshua had wiped the tears from his eyes and snot from his nose. He'd thought whimsically that he must've appeared a derelict child sitting abandoned and destitute at the kitchen table. Unloved as there was no one there to love him.

He'd picked up the paper and read the article on one of his closest friends. The kid he'd often skateboarded with and was, arguably, rivalling Ethan as the best of the group on the board. He'd even nailed the *Cha Cha*, whilst the others were left struggling, yet enthralled that someone had the talent to master such a series of moves. He must be an up-and-coming skateboarding god.

Sammy's front-page headlines beamed with no intention towards subtleties. Here was an eleven-year-old boy who'd been abducted from his bedroom, upstairs, in his own house. How could that be? How had his parents failed to hear that an intruder was in the house? How was it that there were no witnesses? There were *always* witnesses. It didn't matter the time of day or night, there was always at least *one* witness. These were nasty implications, no doubt, of which the article was unapologetic.

Now, as darkness descended outside, both he and Sue sat before the flatscreen. It was tuned to Nickelodeon. They weren't watching cable, as they weren't watching the screen, so there seemed little point that SpongeBob SquarePants was goofing around with his friend, Patrick, across the sands of Bikini Bottom, his popcorn laughter jumping throughout the sofa room.

Time rolled on. It had started getting late.

"Honey?" Sue said to Joshua.

"Yes, Mom?"

"I'd like you to sleep with me tonight."

"That's okay, Mom. I'll be fine."

Sue stared at her boy for a long while as SpongeBob managed, yet again, to piss off his boss, Mr. Krabb. "I want you to leave your door open, then. And I'll leave mine open."

"Okay, Mom."

"You feel tired?"

"No," Joshua said flatly. "But I s'pose I should go to bed." Yes, indeed, because he had unfinished business with the man in black.

Sue reluctantly agreed. "I'll be upstairs soon."

"Okay, Mom."

"But, hon?"

"Yes, Mom."

"Holler if anything doesn't seem right."

"I will, Mom."

"Would you like me to leave the cooler on? 'Cause it feels rather warm, don't you think?"

"I don't know, Mom."

"Okay. Off to bed, then. Remember, leave your bedroom door open." With that, Joshua left, although he was certain that it'd not be a pleasant night's sleep.

She speed-dialled Bob and, once again, didn't hear the commotion from the clock above the refrigerator in the kitchen.

Tick... Tick... Tick... Tock... Tick-Tick-Tick... Tock-Tock-Tick...

Hi there, you've successfully reached Bob Triplow. I'm all ears and keen to hear what you've got to say, so don't be bashful and leave a message.

BEEP!

"Bob Triplow, you're breaking your promise. You might be all ears, but you need to look into your heart." Sue's message lacked all pretence of 'Honey, hope all's going swell and you'll be home real soon.'

～

Saturday, September 10, 2022
The dark hours of night

Sometime in the early hours of morning, the thready fragment of Gillespie's patience, perhaps his sanity as well, and the irrepressible urge to deal with the boy, became all-consuming.

He sent a tranquilizer dart into his partner whilst he slept, thinking, *Raoul's fortune becomes your honor...*

"What the...?" Raditch awoke with a start, and saw Gillespie standing at the foot of his bed, holding the tranquilizer gun. "You've taken leave of your..." His partner's voice trailed off, the potion sent into him going to work fast.

He wriggled his right fingers over his mobile that'd fallen from his pants pocket. It lay hidden, as it was tucked under his right hip. He had enough dexterity in those fingers to open the phone. The last call was to the Elder. He pressed the bottom left corner to engage PHONE. Pressed the top of the screen to engage LAST CALLER. Slipped a finger to the bottom of the phone's screen and made the call.

Gillespie wasn't taking notice of what his right fingers were doing under his hip as he was a little too preoccupied with leaning over him while prizing a vial from his shirt pocket. "What have we here?" he said, feigning eager surprise. "Why, it's three lozenges. One for the kid's daddy. One for the kid's mommy... the kid I'll deal with myself," he said with sinister implication and a downright dirty wink. "And, looky here, there's one left for the little pig that lives down the lane. So come here piggy."

Tranquilizer or not, his partner's eyes swelled, the pupils rapidly dilating.

Gillespie pressed one of the lozenges firmly into the left side of his partner's neck. "Pity you're so drugged. You could've tried swiping it off. Then again, you of all people know the futility of such actions. You'd merely look like a wild pig with its head cut off. Then again, you *do* look like a wild pig with its head cut off!" he cackled.

Raditch tried to say 'no' but all that came forth was a gurgly groan.

The lozenge's payload spread into his veins, where it was immediately swept throughout his cardiovascular system. He could *feel* it. And it felt *good*. It felt *grand*. The sensation kind of tingly, his head spinning. Though it could've been a mixture of both the lozenge and tranquilizer.

As his thought cascaded into a well that had opened inside his head, Gillespie started…

Dancing…

He was also singing.

Whilst Bach was his go-to mobile ringtone, he had a partial liking to late 1960s Jefferson Airplane, and in particular to 'White Rabbit.'

He was singing about pills and about a ten-foot-tall Alice, his arms outstretched, his long legs spidering this way and that in an obscene parody of Olive Oyl from Popeye.

In the last vestiges of Raditch's mind, he thought, not for the first time, but most definitely for the final time, *You really are one fucking weird, messed-up son-of-a-bitch.*

And with that, his eyes fell into his head. His face slipped off his skull like runny toffee. His skull collapsed, followed by the remainder of his skeletal system.

Still Gillepsie sung at the top of his voice. After all, the only resident of Mulberry Estates had gone up like Mount Vesuvius several days before, and Gillepsie had to let off some steam after being trapped in this shithole like a cornered rat. Unlike the lozenge, the pills that mother dished out, according to Grace Slick, didn't do a fucking thing. So go chase a white rabbit before you take a fall...

The Elder, as was his custom, had answered without speaking, because a wise man listened before committing himself.

And listen he did, with unwavering intent. And what he heard was Gillespie coming undone.

In the bowels of the Earth, he decided that Gillespie needed to be dealt with. Should've done it earlier.

Despite the storm's intensity rapidly increasing, putting the matter to bed would be quite satisfying.

And... necessary.

∽

In Mulberry Estates, a 1958 Lincoln Continental was pulling out of the driveway of some forgotten house, leaving a trail of smoke behind it. Curling up in the hot night air, it passed the shattered windows, the peeling gutters and eaves, and disappeared over the roofline, marked with darker squares where tiles had long gone missing.

Mulberry Estates regressed into a state that had long challenged it and, in an instant, became a ghost-suburb, where no human life existed.

❧

Having laid awake for some hours, wracked with guilt and tortured by feelings of failure, Joshua had found sleep impossible to catch. Eventually, though...

In a place far over the rainbow...
10:49... 3:14... 2:11... 4:51... 3:28... 8:09... 1:15 A.M...

The phone rang. Its burst of enthusiasm rudely rattled through the morbid quietness.

Doped on a lack of sleep and highwire tension, Joshua's mom picked up from the kitchen. "Hello?" she whispered, her voice as hollow as a rotten tree trunk.

It was Leon. He needed to speak with his best friend.

"I don't know where he is," she said. But that was an out-and-out lie, because he was standing right next to her, as he'd been about to grab the phone before she pushed him aside. And she did this wearing bells. She must've been wearing bells, because he could hear them:

Tinkle... tinkle... tinkle... tinkle... tinkle...

The sound of bells filling the kitchen space and beyond.

Joshua looked through the windows. "Mom, those bells are outside, too," he said, very afraid.

An earthquake you could deal with, because it was earthly and tangible, albeit often deadly. But this, this was everywhere and nowhere. Like something you could almost reach out and grab, except that it kept shifting away from your hand.

Joshua's mom didn't answer him. She continued to chat with Leon in that hollow voice of hers. "Oh... Goofy Foot and

Ollie… I didn't know they were skateboarding moves… my, you must tell me more."

"Mom." Joshua's nerves fetched up as if on thin spikes of ice. "Has Leon returned from the wedding?"

"Oh, you want to meet Joshua at Sammy's house?"

At Sammy's house...

"Oh, you want to catch up with Sam the Man and do the *Cha Cha* to plan." Sue's voice became more lost to those hollow tones. "That's a funny name." She laughed as if reading it from a script and lacking the finesse to act, so it stammered forth as *Ha—Ha—Ha.*

"Sam the Man," she was now saying very slowly, very deeply. "What a plan."

"Mom, what's wrong with you?" For that matter, why was Leon bothering with a landline, when he could have simply called him direct on the mobile? Or how about walking down the road. Worked every other day of the week.

Joshua's mom continued ignoring him.

He left the kitchen through its door. The ringing commotion beyond the house… stopped. Just like that.

And there was nothing. No noise.

For a while, that was how it'd be, and Joshua would wish it had remained that way.

The door closed behind him and there was a single ringing, as if the door was fitted with a bell, the kind that alerts others to someone's presence.

The lack of noise folded back on itself.

Joshua looked down. He was holding his *Astra-Links*. This was handy: saved him racing inside and upstairs to fetch it from his room.

He shook his head, in the biggest grip of the 'thick' he'd ever experienced. If he didn't know better, he might've said that the 'thick' was beginning to consume him.

And he didn't know better. That much he knew.

The board had found its way under his feet, and he was gliding along Chasing Boulevard.

Across the way, his nosy neighbor was in a flap behind her upstairs window. Had he noticed this, he'd have thought Lucille Goldman—whom his folks called Dorothy Evans, which he'd guessed meant 'nosy parker'—was throwing a party. Doing some kind of crazy dance and hanging about with a whole bunch of balloons.

The *Astra-Links* wheels chirruped over the cement and strummed over the expansion grooves, each particle of grit under their weight exploding and reaching Joshua's ears, as if several children were mashing away at their breakfast cereal on either side of him.

Now there were other sounds. They came to him like a distant image, rushing headlong toward you in a flash. Not there. Then there.

He was being chased by bells.

And the further he cruised along Chasing Boulevard, the grander the sound became, until it became a soft yet impenetrably pliable cacophony. As if this too was affected by the 'thick.'

Just as it had happened with the bells, there was a sudden rush of people. They swarmed their front yards, parks and sidewalks, except for where Joshua's board wanted to go. That pathway was left clear.

'Cause he had to get to Sammy's…

The swarms were having a rip-roaring festival. Everyone was rejoicing with bunches of balloons. And they raged with laughter.

Who's laughing, Josh?

The kids? The adults?

Joshua's mouth was agape. It was at this point he might well have screamed, but couldn't. Whether a symptom of the 'thick' or his innermost nerves having become entwined in a great big bundle, like fishing line that had fallen off the reel to become an instant contender for the Rubik's Cube, anything he might otherwise do or say had become ensnared.

Regardless, his *Astra-Links* kept right on rolling.

The bells are ringing and the balloons are laughing!

They are doing all *the laughing!*

Each one had a stick-figure face that was highlighted by their inner glow. A soft white garishly emphasized the way those stick-figure faces moved, twitching and popping like hot fat on water. Their little round eyes jumping up and down. Their little slit noses jagging one side then the other. Their little slit mouths working, changing shape, in near imperceptible succession. Together it made for a complete confusion of movements.

And their laughter...

That's no laughter, Joshua. That's not the sound of fun...

It was like no sound he'd ever heard.

If asked to define it later on, he might say that it was a festival for everything mad. The laughter... the bells... the frenetic running and mortified screaming. Kids, adults, grandparents, all running amok. They ran to the left. They ran to the right. They ran forwards and backwards.

And a lot were running *upwards*. As if on invisible staircases.

They flapped about as if having given into mass spontaneity of the Chicken Dance, the tune Joshua had never been able to stomach. Bearing witness to this was enough to make him sick to his core.

There was a mother rushing along the street, pram out in front. She was trying to shoo the balloons from her precious cargo. One balloon after another was knocked aside.

But they kept on coming in the rip-roaring festival.

Her baby was screaming. She was screaming.

The balloons… they kept right on laughing…'cause the fun kept right on coming...

In a suffocating assault, she and her baby were smothered.

The screaming intensified, the pram's wheels almost smoking, they were spinning so fast, until they left the ground. The mother thrashed wildly amidst the writhing attackers.

Her baby's blood-curdling mewling pushed through this obscenity and split the syrupy sunlight, its brassy hue pulsating in response.

A shoe flipped from the mother's thrashing feet, like a morsel spat from a bait-ball in the bombardment and after a morning of changing diapers, having breakfast, putting on the washing and talking sweetly to her infant child. Who'd ever have known that by simply leaving the house that morning, they'd end up on the breakfast menu?

The shoe flipped end over end and clattered to ground.

Their screams, whilst powerful, were infinitesimal in the symphony from Corona's former residents that shattered the atmosphere, shattered this once 'best place to live.'

The bait-ball of baby and mother rose ever higher.

Another shoe was rejected from the pack, upon which mother and baby abruptly ceased screaming. Since they couldn't beat their assailants, they joined them with their own brand of mad laughter.

The shoe clattered just before Joshua's path and skittered off to someone's patch of lawn, where it lay like a rejected scrape of someone's meal on a plate, ready to be brought to the attention of the chef for being somewhat overdone.

The *Astra-Links* passed by, not to be deterred in delivering Joshua where he was meant to be.

He craned his neck, bending his head back so far that the vulnerable underside of his throat was exposed to the syrupy sun. Under the circumstances, a rather stupid thing to do. After all, he was no less vulnerable, yet somehow managed to avoid the mayhem and carnage.

He hadn't wanted to see, but he *had* to see.

And what he saw made his tears flow. Beginning as disjointed dribbles, they soon transformed into rivulets. His chest hitched with terror and profound sorrow atop the board that merrily tootled headlong to Sammy Debnar's, house of the skittery-scratch and long-black hallway.

Mother and baby no longer existed.

The woman's appendages had dissolved. Her body had become swollen and spherical before collapsing in on itself. She was left not a woman, but a balloon.

Deranged laughter contorted her stick-face; she was beside herself with madness. No more diaper-changing days for this lady.

Which was just as well, as the remnants of the baby floated from the pram. It shilly-shallied, like an alien spacecraft unsure whether to take to the cosmos or land, before plummeting to the ground, exploding into smithereens upon impact. One of its wheels sizzled overhead and could've ripped Joshua's head clean from his shoulders, but didn't. Managing to miss him by mere fractions, it sliced through a thicket of shrubs, hit a wall behind, and ricocheted into the middle of the road. Here it slowly lost inertia.

Buckled and bent, it lay amongst the screaming, the laughter, the ringing, the thrashing and hollering. It lay there whilst Corona came apart.

The *Astra-Links* nonchalantly negotiated a corner into South Lincoln Drive, heading directly, as it had from the start, to number 17.

Leon was standing at the front door, dressed in a tuxedo and appearing as if he'd just bugged out of the wedding to leave the formalities to proceed without him. His posture was rather odd; but then, what wasn't?

People were either flying about, as if on an entanglement of trapeze wires, or stampeding hither and thither, flapping about as if alight with methanol. So Leon standing at Sammy's front door looking somewhat peculiar was hardly out of order.

He looked as though he was peering into the cavity of the house. But the door was closed.

Joshua dismounted his board rather clumsily. He wasn't in the mood for fancy moves. The *Astra-Links* tootled away, to come to rest amongst some bushes off to the side.

"Leon?" he gasped breathlessly, the last washes of his tears subsiding.

No answer. Leon remained staring at the door in that odd fashion. A finger was poised at his lips as if he were attempting to figure out how best to press the button on the doorbell.

"Leon?" Joshua asked again, coming up to his side. "You rang mom and asked me to meet you here?"

Leon never turned from the door. "No," he said, his voice that same hollow tone as his mom's.

Joshua gazed at the doorbell with the name tag inside it. His tears beginning to dry on his face. The name had been changed from DEBNAR to DREAM SORCERER.

He pushed against the door. It opened in a whisper, as he'd known it would.

Skittery-scratch scratchy-scratch…

The sound immediately drifted out from the interior. He'd known that this would be the case as well.

Moving into the pitch darkness of the hallway, he left the cacophony of madness and his friend, who continued peering into the house, wearing his tuxedo, finger at his lips in a 'golly-gosh' manner.

Skittery-scratch scratchy-scratch…

Assaulting his ears. Passively demanding. Needing his attention.

But Joshua wasn't here to pay the man in black a visit. Not yet, anyway. His friend's safety and whereabouts were the prime objective, and he suspected he knew where he could be found.

He walked further along the hallway's near-impenetrable darkness. The brassy sunlight once more struggled to establish its presence before being entirely consumed.

Joshua knew Sammy's house well, so even though he couldn't see, he knew the alternative route to the stairwell was coming up. Taking the other route through the sofa room, where the man sat, was not the plan unless his friend could not be found. His heart rammed against the inside of his skull. Any second now, his chest would explode as it slammed into his ribcage. Every vein in his body pulsated with painful intensity, his breathing coming in hot geysers.

He slowly made his way through the darkness. God, if he fell and hurt himself

Skittery-scratch scratchy-scratch…

the man in black would surely set upon him with those bottomless eyes wherever he came to grief.

Feeling his way up the staircase with one hand on the handrail, the other groping blindly in the darkness, and his feet testing each tread, one emitted a loud *creak*. He stopped cold and proceeded on only when sure nothing had joined him for closer inspection. It was said that when rock-climbing freehand, you should always have three points attached to ground. He maintained such a grip, lest he fall and become a bait-ball of a different sort.

He reached the top of the stairwell by the way the tread flattened into a wide expanse.

Again, that feeling of vulnerability. Always in t-shirt and shorts. He really should start taking to wearing jeans and long-sleeved shirts. Maybe a suit of armor and nuclear weapons would be of some use amongst the fray that was as dark as it was silent.

Nothing seemed to exist here except for that

Skittery-scratch scratchy-scratch…

And even that was fading, getting smaller, as if the man in black was rapidly moving away from him.

Well, at least there was something positive coming out of this.

Through this silence came a *squeak*.

Joshua's bladder let go.

A patch of muted light, tinged a shade of green, fell into the upstairs hallway at the far end. It was oblong in shape, the outline of an opened door. But what kind of light was burning behind it? Perhaps a green shade had been hung around the globe to make it look that way.

And what way was that?

Sickly, like bile.

Joshua didn't dare breathe. So he stood there in his wet shorts, urine freezing against his legs and in his shoes and socks.

Something was moving along the hallway, toward that oblong patch. He could make out no more than an apparition that slowly swayed from side to side, as if a large wind-up toy was swaying from one robotic leg to the other and way from him.

Had Leon somehow snuck around him? He was certain that he hadn't. Then again, his mind was chugging along like a wrecked train, all its passengers bloodied and dead, the apparition's definition becoming increasingly clear as it moved closer to the light, to hold up directly before it.

It was his friend, Sammy, and he maintained that shifting from one foot to the other as if enchanted by what he saw beyond. His hair was a little dishevelled, his clothes as untidy as usual, his face a petrified mask and highlighted in bile-green.

And, for a very brief transition in time, Joshua thought he could hear the sound of clocks.

He sharpened his senses so his ears hurt with strain, and all he got was the typical ringing that accompanied utter quietness, besides the gushing blood through his veins.

Maybe it was nothing. Besides, it wasn't important, was it?

"Sammy?" The word was a rising gourd, squeezing between the soft tissues of his throat.

"*Yes,*" came a crooning voice, not from the boy but from off to Joshua's right.

He yelped and stumbled, managing to catch himself before his feet found the very top of the stairwell. His heart thwacked even harder in his veins, chest and skull.

Here lies Joshua Triplow, aged not quite eleven and taken too early by a shattered heart. Let's bow our heads and pray...

The sound of bells began like baby rattles that tinkled in a shroud of invisibility, going off here and there and somewhere else.

A face of hideous proportions peered from the darkness to his right.

Joshua felt himself sinking into a swoon and fought hard against it.

"*Your friend needs your help, so why aren't you helping him?*" This man-thing had enormous eyes, a huge mouth with gleaming teeth, and a long protruding chin. He looked like a fucked-up man in the moon. When he came a little closer, those bells tinkled darkly once more throughout the hallway. Maybe the house. Joshua was in no mind to care.

"*Why aren't you helping, Joshy-Washy?*" the man-thing crooned. "*There's nothing to be afraid of. Just as there was nothing to be afraid of when you met Satchmo.*"

Joshua's eyes swallowed his face, his tears having dried to crusty riverbeds on his cheeks. "Satchmo?" Strained.

The man-thing tutted. "*He was a bit of fun, wasn't he? Just like old Mister Grouch. So sad what happened to him... if only he'd listened and taken my advice. Instead, he allowed those mad ones to have their way. Oh well, such is life. Now, I feel I must confide in you, Joshy-Washy, because I'd hate to see the same happen to you. Besides, you do like having fun, don't you, Joshy-Washy? You like having fun because you're a boy of ten. Oh—*" A spidery hand came up to the man-thing's mouth. "*I do beg your pardon. You're a boy of near eleven. Isn't that right, Joshy-Washy?*"

Joshua remained silent. He couldn't speak even if he'd wanted to.

"*I can make you have fun.*"

"Like Sammy?"

"*Sammy needs help.*" The man-thing nodded as if Joshua should heed his words and do the honorable thing. "*I can make your dreams come true, just as I can your friend's.*"

"This is," Joshua croaked, "a… a nightmare."

"*Mm, I see your point and I understand how all this must appear. But,*" the man-thing said brightly, "*appearances are but skin deep. Once you get past this dark patina, you'll see how bright and vibrant your dreams can be.*"

The man-thing receded into the darkness, and an implosion of bells seem to follow in his wake, as if tumbling into some vortex. There was a scratching sound, not that of the man in black. This was something more earth-like. Joshua had heard it before; the sound of a needle hitting the vinyl of a record, which used to be all the rage before MP3s and USBs.

Suddenly the hallway was filled with soft tunes of yesteryear. Joshua thought he recognized it as the type old people played when sitting in a sofa room, bored out of their heads and with nothing better to do but stare at the walls or read the paper while their wife knitted a pair of socks.

The man-thing's face reappeared in darkness and It was humming along with the song, softly swaying from side to side, as Sammy continued to do at the far end of the hallway. Then It broke into the chorus: "*Dream a Little Dream of Me.*"

The music and lyrics continued to drift through what had become of the Debnar's house.

"*Now, that doesn't sound too scary, does it?*"

To hell it didn't! Had Joshua more to give, he'd have given his shorts a second round of urine.

"*The sweet sounds of... Who was that lady?*" A spidery finger came up to the hideous face. "*Oh yes, Doris Day. Do you remember Doris Day?*"

No answer.

"*Probably before your time.*" At this point, the man-thing laughed and it sounded downright nasty. "*How can that be scary to a boy almost eleven?*" The man-thing pushed Its face further through the darkness, and Joshua could see that It wore a hat which ended in three points, each terminated with a bell.

"You've been stalking me?" he said with such thready utterance that it came as some surprise this creature was able to decipher it.

"*The mad ones you witnessed before getting here, they'll stalk you, and they don't offer little boys pleasant dreams. They only offer nightmares of madness... eternal madness.*"

"What do you want with me?" came Joshua's thready voice once more.

Sammy had started moving toward the oblong patch of bile-green. Joshua caught a glimpse of this out the corner of his eye.

"*WAIT!*" His scream crashed through his mind-numbing terror. But Sammy wasn't listening. Either that or he couldn't hear him.

TINKLE-TINKLE-TINKLE...

"*GET AWAY!*" Joshua stumbled again. One foot slipped over the edge and onto the top tread. He almost went careering down the stairs.

"*Oh, do be careful,*" the man-thing crooned. "*Don't want to go hurting yourself. That wouldn't do at all. Now, be quick and run to your friend before it's too late.*"

"What's behind the door?" Joshua asked. He was gripping the top balustrade so tightly, his fingers had locked into a white-knuckled clamp.

The darkness surrounding him was absolute. It'd swallowed everything except for the light into which Sammy was heading and the man-thing's face which seemed to float against it.

"*All the wonders of the rainbow.*"

"That's why it's green," Joshua uttered under his breath.

The man-thing heard him nonetheless. "*Yes, that's right, Joshy-Washy. A most beautiful rainbow where your dreams come true.*"

"Then why does he need saving?"

"*Because he needs a friend, and I am the Dream Sorcerer, where wishes come true,*" the man-thing said. "*And you, Joshua Triplow, you are his friend, aren't you?*"

Joshua was here to rescue Sammy, regardless of what this creature was asking him to do. Without leaving his eyes from the enormous orbs of those belonging to the Dream Sorcerer, he sidled along the hallway. "Sammy?" he tried calling out, but it had no quality.

Sammy was almost through the doorway. His face... what had happened to him? He didn't know what he was doing... he was in a trance... something had worked him over so well, his mind had snapped...

Joshua lunged forward and grabbed his friend's arm before he slipped the entire way through, chancing a look into the bile green.

The room was filled with people sitting at desks, for which there was one to each of them. In the style of the man in black, they were all frantically writing

Skittery-scratch scratchy-scratch...

The sound was both soft and enormous, like a massive conference room choked with delegates, each one whispering their opinions. One on its own. Nothing. So many; countless many. Enormous.

This room seemingly had no end. Continuing out of sight and

Over the rainbow... lost in a lullaby...

There was no fun to be had here. They were *trapped*, their hands furiously at work...

Skittery-scratch scratchy-scratch... Skittery-scratch scratchy-scratch... Skittery-scratch scratchy-scratch...
Skittery-scratch scratchy-scratch... Skittery-scratch scratchy-scratch... Skittery-scratch scratchy-scratch...
Skittery-scratch scratchy-scratch... Skittery-scratch scratchy-scratch... Skittery-scratch scratchy-scratch...
Skittery-scratch scratchy-scratch... Skittery-scratch scratchy-scratch... Skittery-scratch scratchy-scratch...
Skittery-scratch scratchy-scratch... Skittery-scratch scratchy-scratch... Skittery-scratch scratchy-scratch...
Skittery-scratch scratchy-scratch... Skittery-scratch scratchy-scratch... Skittery-scratch scratchy-scratch...
Skittery-scratch scratchy-scratch... Skittery-scratch scratchy-scratch...

The dainty tinkling of bells begun rushing at Joshua from behind.

Skittery-scratch scratchy-scratch... Skittery-scratch scratchy-scratch... Skittery-scratch scratchy-scratch...

Skittery-scratch scratchy-scratch... Skittery-scratch scratchy-scratch... Skittery-scratch scratchy-scratch...

Skittery-scratch scratchy-scratch... Skittery-scratch scratchy-scratch...

He pinwheeled from the door, his grip slipping from his friend's arm. *"SAMMMMYYYY!"*

The Dream Sorcerer went flying as Joshua's arm flung into Its malicious face.

*"**WORTHLESS LITTLE SHIT!**"* It yelled, Its voice on fire.

Joshua stumbled down the hallway, while Sammy slipped into

Somewhere far over the rainbow
The Boogaloo is out of sight
In a place far over the rainbow
Everyone's lost in a lullaby...

Bells immediately gave chase, pursuing him to and down the stairs into the lower hallway.

Joshua ran for his life. Blinded by fear, his legs pumped hard toward the front door, at which a boy in a tuxedo stood, looking for all intents and purposes as if he were watching a magnificent development of nature. But he was losing the chase to the malevolent *intent* rapidly coming up from behind.

The Dream Sorcerers, masters of opportunity, were keen to secure this one. Spidery fingers of a multitude worked the air, as if in preparedness of cocooning Their victim. They verged on clasping the boy by the back of the skull and dragging him into the Boogaloo, when he exploded from the darkness and into the brassy light of day.

Corona's residents continued flying about on their trapeze, below which Joshua continued to run blind along a sidewalk he would no longer have recognized. Wrung through with the terror, he belted from South Lincoln Drive and...

Into his mother's arms.

"*Joshua!*" she was shouting, scared out of her wits. "*Joshua!* Jesus, wake up!"

But he wouldn't. He kept thrashing and screaming.

Sue shook him hard, tears in her eyes, frantic blooms of outrageous panic in her head.

"***JOSHUA!!***"

Despite this, he remained in the grip of his nightmare.

"***JOSHUA!!***"

With that, his eyes finally snapped open, his thrashing beginning to settle. His heart was pounding so hard, Sue could feel it sending seismic waves through her body and into the bed, resonating in the springs below. He was saturated with sweat, and he'd also wet himself. "Oh, baby," she said, and hugged him with the strength of a distraught and extremely frightened mother.

She couldn't shake the feeling that this nightmare had been close. Exactly what did she mean by this?

Her thoughts went out to the Debnar's, to Sammy who remained missing.

She couldn't dismiss a connection between such disappearances and nightmares.

Raoul had said that Joshua was important to Patrick Nesmith... maybe he'd used his friend to get to him...

Maybe this whole fucking mess had been delayed way too long.

$$\backsim$$

Sunday, September 11, 2022
Just before 2:00 a.m.

Bob's mobile was ringing.

He answered groggily, "Hello?"

"If you have to crawl on your hands and knees, you'll get your ass back to Corona by early morning."

"Jesus, Sue, what?"

"Your son has just had the worst nightmare I've seen. I didn't think I was gonna be able to wake him. *That's* what."

Bob breathed heavily. "I'll see what I can do."

"Not good enough. You *will* be here by early morning, or I'll take Joshua to Adelaide myself, and screw what Raoul or anybody else might think, say, have said, will do or have done. Get it?" Sue hung up abruptly, leaving Bob in a swill of vaporizing sleep.

He was on the phone immediately to Malcolm Edwards. "I'm sorry, Malcolm, but my wife has just told me that Joshua had a… a grand mal seizure. I've got to return to Corona. I don't know how, but I must."

"Now, hold your horses, there, Bob. Getting back to Corona at this time of the morning isn't going to be easy. Flights aren't operational—"

"I'll see if I can hook up a charter flight." Bob's mind was firmly on his son and not much else. He wasn't making a lot of sense.

"Fortunately, I happen to know someone who has a charter plane, and that traffic controllers will, if the circumstances are explained appropriately, allow such mercy flights to run."

"Who do I contact?"

"It so happens that you don't need to bother yourself with that, as I happen to be the pilot and owner."

"Thanks, Malcolm." The relief in Bob's voice was unmistakable.

"And who said that CEOs were complete assholes?"

"I… never," Bob stammered.

"Doesn't matter. We need to get you to Corona. Now, you live on..."

"Chasing Boulevard."

"Righty-oh. Closest airport is Corona Municipal Airport. Not a problem for light aircraft. I'll arrange affairs. You come here. Leave your rental; I'll fix that up. I'll also ensure there's a ride for you from the airport to your house." Malcolm Edwards' CEO instincts were flying high. "It's a short distance to your address; so all up, if we're ASAP, you'll be well and truly on home turf by 4:30 a.m. tops."

"Thanks so much… for everything." Then, "Forgive me, Malcolm, but have you gone home yet? Sounds like you're still in your office."

Malcolm chose to avoid answering. Instead he replied, "How is your son, anyway?"

"He's in trouble, Malcolm. Desperate trouble."

The Lincoln Continental growled along Highway 17, heading towards Corona.

Gillespie's hormones were fat, his pants full. Sick sweat stood out on his pores, glistening in the passing streetlights. He didn't give a shit about the order; he cared only for one thing: to get his hands on the boy... the sweet, tender young man.

∽

Sunday, September 11, 2022
Early morning

Just ten days before Joshua Triplow's eleventh birthday, his family found themselves sitting around the dining table. They were about to engage in a most interesting conversation, not one that your average family would generally have.

But then, according to Raoul, man from the stars, they weren't your average family.

"Mate, your mother says that your nightmare last night was the worst she'd seen you react to."

Joshua stared at his dad.

"Is that correct?"

Joshua shifted uncomfortably in his seat.

"Mate, are your nightmares getting worse?"

Joshua looked at his mom sitting right beside him. This was the point at which she'd usually interject with words of compassion: *Bob, leave the subject alone.*

But she didn't this time. She sat there looking compassionate, but didn't open her mouth.

Joshua waited until it was obvious that she wasn't going to, then turned to his dad once more. "Maybe," he said, and huffed sadly. "Last night was pretty intense."

Bob leaned into his seat and drew in a deep breath. He went to fiddle with his glasses and thought better of it. "Has the man in black ever said anything?"

Joshua shook his head, his fingers in a mash atop the table and fiddling amongst themselves.

"Has he ever told you who he is and what he wants from you?"

A cold hand of dread punched up through Joshua's stomach and placed its spindly, frozen fingers around his throat like a garrotte. His dad was talking about the man in black as if he was real, as if he knew more than what he was saying.

Bob waited patiently.

Tick-Tick-Tick… tock-tock-tick… tock-tick-tick…

The Triplows gazed up at the kitchen clock.

Sue thought with utter dread and despair, *Christ, it really is happening again.* But then, she already knew this.

Bob returned his attention to his son, who seemed enchanted by the clock's antics. "Do you know why he's so interested in you?"

If Joshua said what was on his mind—that Sammy was with the man in black—they might send for the paramedics, who'd cart him off because he was a sick boy in desperate need of medical intervention.

Bob took in another deep breath. "I… I used to have a recurring nightmare myself. A dreadful nightmare that chased me through my teenage years and into adulthood. It was relentless, Josh. And damaging. I wasn't able to live, not properly, until I managed to rid myself of it. The only memories I have of being a boy of your age is one of misery and terror. My nightmare was not of a man in black; but…" He hesitated, gathering himself. "I believe they would have sent me mad. And to this day, believe that they *were* sending me mad."

Like an oil-patch of recognition, Joshua's eyes expanded over his face. He wasn't sure how much longer he could prevail over the man in black, to deal with his onslaught. Until his dad had said what he said, he hadn't considered the man in black could send him mad. Until this point, he'd made off-handed reference to it, never believing it. Not for one second.

But he could, couldn't he? Wasn't that what last night's nightmare had been about?

"Until last Wednesday, when you had your student free day, I considered it a thing of the past. That I had succeeded after years..."

Joshua's concentration was almost mind-bending. He knew his dad was leading up to all things unsavory, but it was imperative that he took it all in.

Bob fiddled with his glasses and rubbed an eye, despite his previous misgivings. He hadn't wanted to but he did. Just as he had never wanted to dream of the *bitch*. Some things in life were inevitable. Some things you could manage. Others managed you. "Seems I was merely fooling myself. A stranger called that Wednesday morning and spoke of things that, had it not been for your nightmare and mine, and... past experiences, would've reduced him to some delusional vagrant. However, it appears my nightmare may not have been so well conquered, as yours continues to ravage your life."

The day was unusually warm; uncomfortably warm. The news man on the radio that morning had said the temperature would reach some 60 degrees higher than average, tipping the mercury at an oven-baking 130 degrees Fahrenheit. Which was kind of funny, because Joshua couldn't stop shivering.

Sue moved closer to her son and wrapped her arms around him. She kissed him on the head, and breathed deeply the beautiful clean boyish scent of his hair. *Christ, she wished there was another way.*

"Joshua, mate, do you know where the man in black comes from?" Bob asked, allowing time for the interaction of mother and son to take its course.

"Comes from?" Joshua frowned.

"Yes," Bob said. "Do you know what draws the man in black to you?"

"Dad, you talk like the man in black is real." Joshua's voice trembled. Maybe… just by a slender chance, the paramedics weren't required. But maybe… just maybe, they were *all* in need of some serious medical intervention. In that case, who was gonna make the call?

"I think that at some point in time, perhaps a very long time ago, the man in black *was* real."

"*What?*" Joshua asked hoarsely.

"I think he wants something from you."

"*What does he want?*" Of course, Joshua knew; so, what did his dad know?

"I wish I knew, son. I really do. But I don't," Bob said sadly. "Do you?"

"No." Joshua felt himself beginning to panic, and sat down hard on this unwanted emotion.

His mom hugged him harder. She felt so utterly helpless.

"You certain of that?"

"Yes, Dad." But he wasn't and it showed.

In the lull of this terrifically enthralling tale, they looked at the kitchen clock simultaneously once more. The clock seemed to want to make its presence felt, as if it was dipping out on the fun. Since it hadn't been given the notice it demanded on the initial occasion that morning, it became more insistent.

Tick... tick... tick-tock-tock... tick-tock-tock-tock... tick...

"What is the matter with time?" Joshua asked, frowning. Just another nifty element to this most fascinating of mornings. Nonetheless, swimming close to the surface of all his frazzled emotions was his friend who had joined the man in black. *What does he want? Me. Just as he wanted Sammy.*

Neither his mom nor dad answered.

The clock resumed its usual lilt. Merrily ticking away, as if nothing was amiss; just a little mechanical tickle in the throat along its ceaseless journey.

"Mate." Bob started the part of this conversation he didn't want to have. "You and I, we need to take a trip to your mum's and my birthplace."

"Adelaide?"

"Yeah—Adelaide, South Australia."

Whew. For one moment, Joshua had honestly believed his dad was going to lay something heavy on him. A trip... that didn't sound so bad.

"We've got to go because, maybe, the man in black can be put to rest there."

"So he *is* alive?" Joshua asked, again his voice trembling badly.

Bob nodded. "Kind of. I don't know how else to explain it. I don't know exactly what we'll do when we get to Adelaide. I guess, when we do, we'll find out. But it may be a means to an end of the man in black nightmares." Bob hesitated. "And mine."

Joshua couldn't remember his dad *ever* having a nightmare; but then, maybe he did and wasn't such a wuss.

Besides, if going to Adelaide got him closer to the man in black, he had a second chance to put wrongs to right. He had a second chance to find his friend and lead him back to his skateboard in Corona.

Bob had hit the internet that morning at approximately 9:00 a.m. He might as well have hit the proverbial brick wall with a sledgehammer. The service provider seemed to be having *issues*. This really pissed him off. Typical! The internet's reliability always had *issues*, especially when needed the most. However, that wasn't the worst of it. Because, though it ran, if like a bucket of bolts, it did manage to finally hook up with his objective. Jerking and jagging its way to the airline site, there was an outstanding message that greeted him:

This service is temporarily unavailable.
Please try again later.

He swore, which was unhelpful, yet seemed to improve his mental status. However, after hopscotching from one airline site to another, the result was no less frustrating. The swearing lost its effectiveness.

He resorted to the only thing left at his disposal: he picked up the phone.

"I'm sorry, sir. You may wish to try another airline, but I doubt if you'll have any better luck," the Air Canada operator was saying.

"I *need* to book two flights to Adelaide, South Australia," he said, having to withhold telling this woman, who could hardly be blamed for the situation, to go take a fucking flight of her own. Bob was feeling a tad frazzled, and saying such things would've been wildly out of character and hardly progressive.

"I'm sorry, sir. I understand how frustrating this is, and the inconvenience it's causing. Rest assured the matter should be resolved soon."

"How soon?"

"I'm sorry, sir, I can't say for sure."

If she says 'I'm sorry, sir' one more time, I will let lose with some advise on the type of flight she should take, he thought, fiddling with his glasses and rubbing his right eye hard enough, he might just punch it through the back of his skull.

"What's the problem?" he asked after gritting his teeth and casting the stars in his right eye away.

"I believe all airlines are grounded due to a technical glitch in the flight towers."

"A technical glitch?"

"Yes, sir. The power grid is fluctuating, therefore flights can't be managed safely. And without the towers fully operational, it's simply too dangerous to the public."

"Thanks very much," Bob said, probably more ungratefully than the woman deserved. But his mood was somewhat on the shabby side, so he considered his temperance a good effort. He hung up.

No one in the household noticed. No one could care less what was going on outside.

Parked parallel to the verge of 22 Chasing Boulevard was a beaten-up 1958 Lincoln Continental.

Mrs. Goldman, across the way, wasn't so preoccupied with her internal thoughts of saving the world and the potential loss of loved ones. In fact, Lucille Goldman—aka Mrs. Dorothy Evans—had a rather impolite habit of invading the privacy of her fellow neighbors. Never by face-to-face interruptions, but rather from behind the panes of glass adorning the front of her house.

She was well known for her proclivity. The kids used to make fun of her. The adults used to curse her. Some would wave and smile whilst calling her 'a nosy bitch' as they strode past.

Her giveaway: the curtains. Whilst they were drawn back with sly intention, Mrs. Goldman lacked the cunning shrewdness of doing so in such a fashion as to conceal her movements. As good as she was with keeping tabs on the neighborhood, she was extremely poor in her execution. At age 77, her habits weren't about to change.

And so on the Sabbath of September the 11th, she was most curious about the titanic rust bucket parked out front of the Triplows. She couldn't see exactly who or how many were in the car—frankly, it was big enough to fit an entire football team!— but she found it rather odd that it'd pulled up and remained on the spot under the bay laurel since early that morning.

From an upstairs window, she could see movement in the car. So that meant someone was inside it, if not the entire LA Rams. Like Mister Too Much Nose, she kept a close eye on affairs. However, unlike the late Mister Too Much Nose, she wasn't apt to blinking at the wrong moment. She was positive no one had gotten out of that piece of crap on four wheels since pulling up.

Should she call the cops?

Yes, she thought she should. After all, it was her civil duty. And so she did.

Only, when she picked up the phone, it seemed there was a little man sitting inside it, jabbering his stupid head off.

At the third stroke, the time will be twelve... twelve... twelve o-one A.M....

The stupid prick kept yapping this over and over. So she hung up and tried her mobile.

Nothing.

The service was down. And, like Bob Triplow had earlier that day, she cursed the fragility of technology.

By half past three, Lucille Goldman's stave of the hand could no longer be restrained. She had that civil duty to uphold. Her pangs of compulsion both uncontrollable and unstoppable, as were those of the occupant in the rust bucket below.

She picked up the phone. Dialled. Listened.

The little prick had gone.

The phone was ringing. *Thank God for small mercies.*

"Corona Police Department, how may I assist you?"

"I'd like to report a suspicious looking car," Lucille said, peering out onto Chasing Boulevard from the upstairs window, as if at any second, the LA Rams were going to flex their muscle and take over the street.

There was a pregnant pause before the operator drily responded, "Lucille Goldman?"

"Yes," Mrs. Goldman replied, instant annoyance of her name in the operator's voice sliding by without recognition. Her eyes turned down to slits, yet full of excitement. There were serious matters that required urgent attention. If not for the likes of her, who else would keep the world safe?

"What can I do for you *this* time?" The weariness in the operator's tone was palpable.

"A car's been parked on Chasing Boulevard that I've never seen before. And it's been parked on the spot since morning, not having moved. Not *once*."

God, give her strength! the operator thought. *Does the old cow never sleep, take a dump or eat? Is she* always *plastered to her windows?*

"And what would you like the police department to do about that?"

"They need to take charge. The occupants of that vehicle need to be moved on, as they are loitering and becoming a public nuisance."

"Lucille, *they* are *not* the public nuisance."

"You wouldn't know. I'm the one who keeps watch over Chasing Boulevard."

"That you do." *Wish* you'd *move on,* the operator thought, not without malice.

"Well?" Mrs. Goldman asked, irritated, her eyes glued to the behemoth below.

"There are serious and important matters that require urgent attention by our dedicated force. A car parked on the side of the road for less than a day hardly qualifies. Is it parked illegally? Is it blocking someone's driveway or awkwardly positioned on the road?" *Do I give a shit?*

"I've seen this rust bucket before," Lucille said, implicating dire straits. "It's an old Thunderbird or something like that. Reckon it's from the 1950s. It's so big it *almost* blocks the street."

"Is it actu—?"

"*Almost.*"

"There is no crime in driving such a car. Some may even cherish and highly value such as a work of art."

"What if I told you the occupants were toting guns?"

"Are they?"

"No."

"It *is* an crime to lie to the police, Lucille Goldman, with serious ramifications. Are you aware of that?"

"If one of my neighbors dies, *you'll* be responsible." Lucille jerked to one side. Were the LA Rams of said rust bucket disembarking, carrying weapons?

No. False alarm. This time.

"It's feasibly impossible to dispatch a unit in response to a car parked on the side of a road. Now, I'm afraid this conversation needs to end. I've got serious calls to attend."

With that, the operator hung up on Lucille Goldman, who was left gobsmacked.

"*Bitch!*" she spat, slamming down the phone.

Roughly five minutes later, at 3:35 P.M., Bob Triplow finally hit pay dirt as well. The internet, bless its generosity, had reconsidered the disruption to all of mankind, to which each and every one should be devoutly thankful. He searched for the earliest flights possible. It seemed Air Canada came up trumps. However, none were available until 9:15 a.m. the following morning.

He would have to compare several timepieces, as all were running amok, as they had done in Adelaide in 2011. He went about setting his mobile next to the bedside clock. Got a travel clock and placed this with them, as well as Sue's mobile; it was doubly good, as she was with a different carrier, so if one was 'having issues' the other might not be.

Catching the 9:15 Air Canada flight to Sydney and connecting flight to Adelaide was crucial. Whether it was to hell or not, they had to make it.

∽

Monday, September 12, 2022
The early morning hours

If there was ever a phone call that had the power to change the course of history, such a call was made that night around 12:40 a.m., to a man who'd no suspicions of the audacity and implications of his actions until it was too late.

Lucille Goldman wasn't the only one who'd been keeping tabs on the '58 Lincoln Continental the day before.

As with any organization, regardless of size, there'll be faction groups that don't entirely see eye-to-eye with the policies and politics under which they operate. Therefore, organizations often inspire sub-organizations within that evolve in silence, like eddies swirling through the great blue depths of oceans. Further still, some members become involved in an organization because of their vehement opposition to its mission. Positioning themselves with strategic observance, they are set to thwart sorties and passadoes as they promulgate. In other words, to stop the shit from hitting the fan… or at least cast some sort of net between said shit and fan.

In this case, the sub-organization started at the very top, because Earth wasn't such a bad place to live. And Black Eternity, as much as it could be known, was madness in the most literal of senses. The decision to turn had been made many years before.

At 35 Chasing Boulevard, Zachary Mendoza's mobile phone began ringing in the dead hours of night.

Marlene flopped over in bed and said in the swoon of sleep, "Tell Diego Gas… to shove it."

Zachary stuck out one arm and blindly fumbled for the phone, clumsily taking hold of it. It rattled across the bedside cabinet before he managed to grip its plastic girth. In a rather irritated manner, he jerked it to his ear. He'd been miles away in that rare species of comfortable sleep, the type in which all the planets had aligned in perfect harmony: the sheets caressing his body and the mattress a soft cloud beneath, while the pillow hugged his head in a perfect cradle. No need for tossing and turning, or those annoying micro-adjustments that seem endemic in seeking the perfect sleep. However, when he heard the voice on the other end, he snapped to full alertness. If ever asked later, he'd have said something along the lines of that it was the voice of authority. A voice not to be trifled with.

"Zachary Mendoza, your services are required."

"Do I know you?" But Zachary thought he did. The voice; he'd heard it before, hadn't he? Somewhere. Some time ago. Its timbre sent waves of disquiet through him.

He eased himself from the bed.

"You know me from a conversation we had some years ago. Under ideal circumstances, I'd have foregone bothering you."

Zachary's eyes sparkled while his caller talked. With a glance over his shoulder, he was relieved to see that Marlene had not woken. Thanks to the climate control, the house's cool interior had allowed her to descend into deep sleep without further arousal.

He slipped like liquid grease from the room into the upstairs hallway, the door whispering on its hinges.

"There's a problem which you're well-positioned to take care of," the voice said, and there was no room for humanities in that tone. This was serious business. In fact, it didn't get any more serious. The voice made no doubt of the fact.

"Take care of what?" Zachary asked in a nearly inaudible tone.

"You made a promise all those years ago. A promise you now must keep."

Zachary shut his eyes. He could barely remember making a promise, but he could remember something. "I can't—"

He got cut off by the voice. "It matters not."

Suddenly, he was wishing all this away. It was as if he'd walked along a beach, found a beautiful blue bottle, and picked it up to discover it wasn't beautiful at all, its tentacles sending poisonous barbs deep into his flesh.

"You've no choice but to embark on a short errand."

Zach shook his head and leaned against a wall. Nearby was his son's bedroom door. It was closed. He was grateful.

"You recall being told that Bob Triplow and his son were 'special' people?"

"Vaguely," Zachary said, while his family slept soundly.

"Their specialty has attracted the wrong sort of attention, and so you must make good on your agreement."

Zachary Mendoza felt as if he was about to go into a battle he was neither prepared for nor understood, like wielding a papier-mâché sword to thwart the beast. Whatever in the hell he meant by that. Regardless, it seemed the day had come to make good on a promise he couldn't quite remember.

"You recall receiving a package some years ago?" the voice on the opposite end of the line was asking without emotion. Just mouthing words. The man delivering these words, however, was full of rage and purpose.

"Um…" His head was spinning. Just moments earlier he'd been enjoying a rare species of sleep, and now this. "I guess."

"You must be more specific. I trust you've secreted it well and are able to readily access it."

Zachary screwed his face in tightly. Recollection was hard to come by. But then, "Yes. It's in the safe." He left out the crucial words: *I think* it's in the safe.

The safe he and Marls had purchased to keep their valuables secure; only, immediately after purchase, they'd decided they really didn't have much in the way of valuables. Except their son... and that'd have been just downright cruel. So the safe had been relegated to the back of their walk-in wardrobe.

"Good," the voice said. "I want you to be very careful with what you find inside it. Handle it with extreme caution and gift it to someone. But it's highly important you do so without their knowledge."

"Someone?" Zachary ran a hand across his forehead. Despite the climate-controlled air, sweat stood out on him in large globules.

"It's not important who the recipient is, just that it's carried out." There was a momentary pause. "Bob Triplow and his son are in grave danger from this individual who's positioned himself outside their house. He must be neutralized, immediately."

"What do you mean by 'neutralized?'" This call was something he wished he could hang up on. But he couldn't; he'd made a promise. And Zachary Mendoza was a man of his word, even if he couldn't remember what that word was.

"This individual intends to murder Bob Triplow and his son. He intends to do so tonight. There is no time for delays. Once the artefact is applied to this individual, he'll drift off to sleep and you'll need not concern yourself in the matter further."

"What are you asking me to do?" Zachary's nerves danced across his vocal cords, which was an odd sensation to him, as he was usually the last man in the room to ever become nervous.

"I am asking you to save the lives of Bob Triplow and his son."

"And what of this individual?"

"He's a wayward agent of the government, and forces within the government will ensure he's dealt with fairly and appropriately."

"Then why doesn't the agency whom he works for take care of this business?"

"There's not the time. Even as you stand debating facts with me, the situation grows increasingly grave. It has only just come to our attention through an informant who wishes to remain anonymous, and whose involvement goes no further. All will be lost if this agent finds his way into the Triplow household. I'm hoping that hasn't happened, and that this agent remains in his car outside 22 Chasing Boulevard. It's an old Lincoln; you can't miss it."

"What do I do with this 'artefact?'"

"It'll act as a tranquilizer. It must be attached firmly to his skin, *only* his skin, and without inadvertently attaching it to yourself."

"I've got to get that close?"

"Given the chance, he'll get much closer to Bob and his son. The result: a lot of blood spilt. Lives taken."

With that, there was a polite *click*, leaving Zachary Mendoza momentarily lost in the communication abyss, wondering what in the hell he was about to commit.

Whatever in the world had compelled him to make such a promise? Obligation? He supposed that must've been what had forced his hand. But then, he'd hardly known Bob ten years ago, and there was no reason to think that their sons would become joined at the hip. So why the obligation? It might have come down to that genre of conversation you started having with another and, before you knew it, you were agreeing to things that wouldn't have been normally on the radar. Things that you immediately regretted once the conversation ran its course.

Furthermore, promise or not, what would've stopped the Triplows from picking up stakes to head anywhere in the world? What would've that meant? Would've he been obligated to chase around the world to pin a fancy medallion on a complete stranger whilst whispering sweet lullabies? That seemed illogical, if not utterly ludicrous.

After a decade, he still had this artefact. That, too, was illogical, in every sense of the word. Who'd be expected to hang onto something that was ostensibly useless for a year, let alone ten? He didn't recall ever being asked to safeguard it. He couldn't actually remember anything that specific about its arrival. He'd made a promise, obviously, and had been delivered a package. Which he'd kept! Illogical.

If he'd ditched it, what would've he been expected to do now? How would he have been expected to handle this situation? With a rubber mallet? *Here, sir, please hold still whilst I belt you one.*

And just what made Bob and Joshua so special that such actions were required? Out of all the people in the world, some six billion, why Bob and Josh?

He could wrangle the tos and fros all he wanted. Fact was, their lives were apparently in immediate danger.

Jesus, how in the hell did I get into this?

Obligation...

For some inexplicable reason, he had wandered down into his garage whilst deep in thought. Except for his underwear, whose fly was undone and—*why, would you looky there! How ever did you manage to spill an entire pickle down your front!*—he was naked and not appropriately dressed for sojourns under the midnight moon. Just as well that he had to duck upstairs to grab a little 'artefact' from the safe.

Before he slipped past his son's bedroom, he hesitated momentarily. *Bob's son is a good kid. A great kid! I don't know what I'm about to do, but I'd never live with myself if, as the man on the phone stated, this bastard's about to murder Josh. I'd have to live with that for the rest of my life. I'd have to live with that knowledge. I couldn't do it. It'd eat me up and I'd go mad with remorse. Utterly mad.*

He got dressed and retrieved the package from the safe. Only when he'd made it downstairs into the garage once more did he open it.

A strew of bits and pieces laid about his feet in his latest grand scheme, the upstairs' bathroom renovation. There were varying lengths of wood, sawdust, a table saw, hand saw and circular saw, plus a variety of chisels and a coping saw. His Triton workbench looked somewhat like a prehistoric sea urchin, with wood chips and curls decorating it.

You can't hide from me that easily, he thought. Perhaps he could forget going out tonight and get lost in his project. He sighed ruefully.

Who the fuck was he kidding?

He reached inside the mundane cardboard box to find a glass vial. In the vial was... something. He didn't know what. He shook the vial, because apparently when you didn't know what you were handling, such an act was guaranteed to get results.

The 'artefact' rattled innocuously, but did nothing spectacular, like manifest into a mythical beast or light up the room in a ghostly incandescence because it'd been rudely awakened from its ten-year slumber.

It just laid in the glass vial, looking rather pathetic, really.

I've got to stick this thing onto someone? He thought a little hysterically. *This should be fun.*

Zachary Mendoza, besides not being given to nerves, was an equally bright fellow. If this artefact caused the recipient to fall asleep, it'd be best handled with the utmost care, as he'd been instructed. But it looked like a tricky exercise in itself. The thing was like a lozenge: round, not all that thick. How did you handle something like this, which required pressure in application, and not risk yourself in the process?

It'd remain in the vial until he needed to apply it to its host. Carrying this little fucker any other way might just put him to sleep, from which the world would be a different place. A little emptier. He'd have lost a good friend and Leon his Siamese twin.

I could never live with that. I couldn't lie to Leon over and over. I couldn't look into his eyes and do it. I'd lose my mind. He considered such implications once more.

Zachary swallowed hard, sized up the garage's side door, and headed towards it on a journey. One that whilst short in distance was nonetheless potholed with trepidation.

Stepping into the moonlight and the unimaginable heat, he had to slap a hand over his mouth to shut himself up. Laughter and tears had boiled to the surface, fiercely wanting to wash away the dread within, on the image of skulking about in his scant underwear whilst playing Inspector Gadget.

And what would you be doing, Inspector?

Oh, just taking a typical moonlit stroll in the nude. I like the way the light reflects off that wayward pickle, don't you? Makes me look rather like a Lebanese cucumber! Go, go, Gadget!

It was all down to nerves, didn't you know?

Slipping from one neatly manicured frontage to another, Zachary was one with the shadows. Even for those whose sole duty on earth was to resolutely maintain ardent neighborhood watch on Chasing Boulevard (aka Mrs. Goldman at her windows, across the way from the Triplows) would've been fooled. At worst his vulnerability might've lain in being caught as a flicker in the corner of one's eye. There and then gone… will-o'-the-wisp stuff… a dust particle floating in one's peripheral vision for a momentary second.

Around him shadows stirred on a hot Santa Ana breeze.

He passed Number 24 before doubling back. His heart had risen, full and bloated, into his throat. The breath at the back of it tasted slightly rancid with anxiety. High anxiety. This wasn't fear, because Zachary Mendoza—who'd come to the conclusion that yours truly was in way over his head—couldn't allow such emotions to take residence within.

He nestled into the O'Caseys' golden diosmas. There were four in all, bunched together but far enough apart so that they each had their own space. Having been meticulously clipped into smooth topiaries that weren't quiet oblong and weren't quite round, they provided the perfect camouflage.

Zachary breathed deeply, savoring their spicy scent.

Only hours ago I pulled into the driveway after a long haul and listening to 'Here comes the Bride.' Whose grand idea was this? He asked himself a most fateful question. When at the battlefront of such high-stakes business, the airing of one's laundry often came with a tag, the kind loved ones found carefully hung over your big toe with your name scrawled across it. If this Lincoln-driving murderer was happy to kill a father and his child, he was no less immune.

The moon was high, and before a friendly cloud happened by its path at a fortuitous moment, the beads of sweat adorning Zachary Mendoza's forehead shimmered like the sequins on a bridal gown. His every sense hummed, as if hooked to a generator capable of delivering a lethal dose.

The O'Caseys' diosmas sat near the boundary of the Triplows' and, now with the moon cloaked, he sidled through other plants, at a total loss as to their botanical names but acutely mindful of the limited cloud cover.

He then slinked across the upper end of the Triplows' driveway before sliding on his belly over the grass.

Look at me, Ma, I'm Inspector Gadget!

A curved garden of plants, on the opposite side of the frontage, provided the next camouflage. Once there, he turned on his belly towards the sidewalk and was about to crawl on all fours to the curb, when the moon recommenced wrapping the neighborhood in a sheet of thin aluminium.

Careful, old son, on who your allies are!

He'd have to wait up.

Casting his eyes skyward, relief swept through him on seeing another fat cloud cruising towards the moon's pregnant exposure.

Under the relative safety of darkness, he made his way to the curb once more.

Here was the car, a late 1950s Lincoln Continental. If he wasn't mistaken, this particular beast had incurred a nickname: the massive, slab-sided Lincoln. For good reason. Never a graceful-looking stretch of sheet metal, this thing had seen better days. Hardly the rare species sometimes rescued from the pack and restored through shows on cable like *Hot Rod* or *Classic Street Cars*. Oh no, this was your common rubbish-dump variety. Nothing to look at. Nothing to show for itself. Just loads of faded metal fashioned by overly zealous men wearing hugely bright cravats against a forest of chest hair.

In the heat of the infant morning, odors were amplified, as with the O'Caseys' diosmas. Here, he could smell the rancidity of ancient oil rupturing from this hulk, the smell of dead machines and history that the rest of the world had left buried and forgotten in the past. This *thing*, once the pride and joy of its very first owner, now sat like a diseased citadel.

Music drifted from its interior.

Zachary listened despite himself. Gooseflesh rippled through his body, together with the hum from that generator. The music seemed grossly out of place, yet perfectly suited at the same time.

Zachary was forty-two, and so hadn't enjoyed the pleasures of the psychedelic era that marked the late 1960s; and even if he had, he probably wouldn't have remembered them, anyhow, due to cocktails of experimental hallucinogens. But he knew the song. He couldn't quite remember who sung it, and would only later recall that it was Grace Slick from Jefferson Airplane. But there was no mistaking or forgetting the song itself: 'White Rabbit.'

The song was at the point where someone was chasing a white rabbit just before their fall.

Zachary fought hard to shrug the song off and desperately hoped it wasn't a reflection of things to come. Though he couldn't see the car's interior, he was hoping he hadn't arrived too late.

Now, according to Jefferson Airplane, there were caterpillars getting stoned out of their minds in the Lincoln...

Fresh beads of sweat shimmered on his forehead and dribbled down his face, threatening to get in his eyes and momentarily blind him. The front of his shirt was damp with his own fluid. Like black oil, he slid past the rear quarter panel to hold up at the rear passenger door, where he deftly withdrew the vial from his shirt pocket. He uncapped it and rolled the small object into his palm. Exerting great care, he picked it up with the tips of his fingers, careful to maintain a gentle yet firm hold.

Again, he marvelled on its resemblance to a throat lozenge. Maybe the occupant of the massive, slab-sided sheet metal was coming down with a cold. Zachary sure felt as if he were. His heart, rising higher in his throat, was near suffocating.

He caught a break. Because he was one of the good guys. And good guys always caught a break. The driver's window was fully open. The driver's seat was occupied.

Jim Gillespie had taken his eye off the ball. At least, the one that surrounded him, his attention completely on what he was about to do. He'd revel in the sound of their necks being broken, like a meaty stick. It'd be most satisfying. Of course, this would only happen to the boy after his time with him. His grin widened, while he pleasured himself as he had done since nightfall. His appendage had been rubbed to a state of numbness which would make his time in the upstairs bedroom all the sweeter as it plunged in and out... in and out.

Gillespie reached for the door handle as Zachary reached a hand up as high as he could, with the artefact between his fingertips, his arm like a periscope from the depths of the verge. At this moment, a frantic thought ripped through his head like a lightning bolt: *What if this needs to be applied a specific way? What if I get it wrong?*

Too late!

He pressed the artefact into the stranger's upper left arm, just below the hem of his short-sleeved shirt, at the moment Gillespie was about to open his door to satisfy his outrageous urge.

Grace Slick was telling both men about players on a chessboard, and how they were about to tell them where to go.

Zachary Mendoza drove the artefact home harder than necessary, just in case.

"*FUCK!*" Gillespie yelped. The sound carried off on the soft Santa Ana breeze, rippling along Chasing Boulevard before fading fast.

The driver's door slammed into Zachary, who went sprawling onto his back. The streetlights on either side of the road wigged in and out, their craning bodies and illumination doing the hula before steadying. The wind had been knocked from him and, for a moment, there seemed more stars in his eyes than the night could account for.

Gillespie turned on him like a rabid dog. "*What have you done, you fucking cunt?*" He went to lunge at Zachary, to throttle him, break his neck like a meaty-stick. But he knew he had to rid himself of the lozenge.

He gripped it and began yanking at it frantically. Turning on his heels like a cat chasing its tail, saliva thickly rained from his mouth. Outrage mixed with terror filled his head; he'd become a victim to this asshole sprawled on the road.

The lozenge had stuck hard and he sensed it burying itself further into his flesh.

"*NO!*" he screamed. "*NO! NO! NO! NO! NO!*"

Spinning around and around, his arms were in a diabolical self-embrace, as if he were attempting to give himself a hug by a thousand lashes, just as Grace Slick in the Lincoln Continental was experiencing the heady delights of eating a certain kind of mushroom.

Her voice was a psychedelic chant, the music churning the air, while Gillespie kept screaming *NO!* and pirouetting along Chasing Boulevard.

Lucille Goldman had been in the uncustomary act of catching some shut-eye. Upon hearing the commotion outside, she was all over her upstairs window.

The little upstart is gonna have to send a patrol unit now, she thought with an arrogant grin and unbridled excitement and justification.

But when she picked up the phone, all she got was: *At the third stroke—*

She hung up.

Redialled—*the time will be—*

"Shut up, you little prick!"

She tossed the landline across the room and opted for her Nokia. That'd do the trick.

Dialed.

Silence. She resumed her arrogant grin, before:

At the third stroke the time will be twelve… twelve… twelve o-one A.M.

Lucille Goldman was having no joy. None at all.

Neither was Jim Gillespie, who'd begun to experience the heady delights of self-destruction from a lozenge. No need for a mushroom, regardless of its intoxicating effects.

Zachary kicked in a manic style of a frog-paddle. His butt scooted over the grassy verge, the cement sidewalk and the Triplows' driveway, while transfixed to the man who seemed to be melting into the tarmac.

Gillespie's feet had dissolved, and the thing he'd become fell to the ground like a lumberjack's tree. He kicked and thrashed on the road, slapping at the lozenge that had eroded away his flesh while sinking into his humerus. There was nothing humorous about this, though. And there was no point in Gillespie attempting to rid himself of it. The task—impossible. The game—over.

He shouldn't have taken his eye of the ball. But he had; and now, all he saw was a blur of light down two long tunnels into which his eyes had sunk.

Zachary had managed to get onto to all fours, horrified by the sight and what he had done.

And for naughty boys, your teacher will present you with a very special treat.

Beads of sweat continued rolling down his face. Part of him was urging his legs to pole-vault him from the ground like a full-sized, living and breathing jack-in-the-box.

But of course, he wasn't about to do that, was he? Because the boy, having been offered a very special treat indeed, was flattening against the ground.

Sinking into it? Zachary thought wildly. *Some tranquilizer!*

The man's denuded skull formed a death mask atop the serrated pole of his cervical spine. His sunken eyes wobbled. Held. Wobbled again, and then rolled into the cavity of his skull. Dark sockets stared blindly ahead, while exposed teeth bore a Davy Jones' locker grin.

Whatever remained of Jim Gillespie somehow moaned through pipework that no longer existed. His skull turned in Zachary's direction, bearing those eyeless sockets on him. Through the dark hole where his nose had been, the last of his brains leaked like chunky snot. His toothy grin snapped open further, and his lower jaw promptly fell onto the road.

The vestiges of the man's central nervous system cast remnants of electrical signals through the ravages, ensuring he thrashed until his arms were no longer, whilst his body writhed before that too dissolved completely away.

Grace Slick was chanting from the Lincoln's vast interior that one should never forget what the dormouse said… something about feeding your head.

Did that. Didn't do much good, so tried for an all-over body exfoliant.

Zachary was feeding his head, alright, like never before. Man, he was tripping. *Kids today are such an unruly lot.* He resorted to wit. Either that or return to his wife and son a man who'd seen and done things that had disconnected his sanity.

Like the caterpillars… he was *off* his head…

Within less than a minute, the man Gillespie had been was no more. For Zachary Mendoza, he'd have testified that the duration was far greater than that, perhaps hours.

Jefferson Airplane had finished their opus to all things psychedelic. In the lull, Zachary Mendoza found a strength within that seemed to have left him, and rose to his feet. The weight of ponderous moments passed before he could find his mind.

Go ask Alice, the thought bubbled up in the mire of other nonsense. *I must remember to congratulate the new bride and groom on a splendid occasion. Who were they again? Relatives? Distant or close? On whose side?*

He shambled his way over to where the body had liquefied. Nothing was left but clothes. There they were, still in the same place, as if adorning a body. Short-sleeved shirt almost too neatly atop a pair of black pants. A watch lay off to the left, its tiny hands jerking across its face. The shoes and socks were a little further behind.

Because his feet had departed his legs and he fell away from where he was standing, Zachary thought, and with that, threw up.

No more mushrooms, came yet another nonsensical thought in the swill of weddings and dismembered body parts.

Lucille Goldman was determined to raise the Corona Police Department. Dialling in a frenetic, obsessive fashion, she *had* to make the call. She *had* to tell the little *upstart* how *wrong* she'd been... should've sent a patrol around when she'd contacted them the day before... now, see what you've allowed to escalate! I was *right*. You were *wrong!* When I call next, you'll take *notice!*

But upon every successful dial, the little prick was there to stymie her efforts:

At the third stroke the time will be twelve... twelve... twelve o-one A.M.

Zachary knew nothing of this, of course. Wracked with high-voltage horror, and the fact that he was now an accomplice to murder—the very thing he was meant to stop by passive means—he thought miserably, *Christ, what have I done?* Again he retched. Nothing came of it but strands of gastric fluid.

He realized that he'd been duped.

Gathering himself, whether necessary or not he used the shadows, as he had before, to retrace his steps home, where his wife and son peacefully slept. Unknowing. Never to know. This was his secret that he'd die with. This was his burden, regardless of whether the man was there to murder or not. This was his to keep and keep alone. Of that he was certain.

Nasty business had been done. And the world still turned on its axis.

He whispered through the house, barely disturbing the air as he went, and slipped beneath the bedclothes after rinsing his mouth.

The bedroom clock indicated it was a little past 1:10 a.m. in short, strobing bursts. He frowned. *Why?* he thought miserably, implying much more than the antics before him.

He would never truly get to sleep that night. At one point, when success was within his grasp, he'd dream in his half-swoon of schoolboys dying at their desks, pens and paper spread before them, their despotic teacher claiming, *Never let it be said that this teacher is an easy pushover...*

If only Zachary Mendoza knew the terrifying tragedy ironically woven through his mental caricature, he might've well had a rethink.

As it was, with his head nestled firmly in the pillow, his eyes began fluttering shut when

Tick-tocktocktocktock... ticktick-tock-ticktocktock... ticktick...
They snapped open and turned to the clock. He swore under his breath.

Yesterday I was eating lobster and shaking hands with people of the family I barely knew. Christ, what have I done?

MITCHAM'S PORTAL

~

Monday, September 12, 2022
6:00 A.M.

Bob pressed the standby button on the remote, and the hi-fi awakened from its slumber. He was keen to hear what the newsman had to say.

WELCOME

popped up in the unit's display.
That was the last of the good news.

"Good morning, folks of Riverside County. You're listening to Real 93.3, home of the Hip Hop with Dylan Carruthers…"

"And Ashly Cummins."

"Top of the news, weather, and more weather," Dylan said, way too enthusiastically. "It's predicted to tip the mercury at staggering one hundred and thirty-five today, and that respite we've been all enjoying at night is about to *vamoose*. At least for the next week."

"Yes," Ashly chimed in, also sounding chirpier than he had any right to be. "The seven-day forecast is extreme, folks. Temperatures both by day and night are not expected to dip below the mid-nineties, and reach as high as a body-melting one hundred and forty!" He made an exaggerated *whew*, before, "That's right folks... one... forty."

"Wow, that *is* extreme," Dylan said, finally indicating some trepidation. "This calls for us all to be extra vigilant of others and take necessary precautions for ourselves. Under these conditions, we're advised to drink at least six pints of water daily and stay out of the sun."

"That's right," Ashly agreed. "If you've older folks in the family or you know older folks, it's imperative that they're made aware of these precautions. And if, like me, they don't like drinking water, find strategies that'll ensure they're taking in the required amount of daily fluid."

"Preferably not alcohol," Dylan said brightly, retaining a degree of gravity. "Dehydration and heat stroke are killers. So stay alert. Make good use of air conditioners and fans. If you own a pool, use it."

"Like yourself?"

"That's right, Ashly. Had it installed several years ago and, until now, had some regrets on whether it was worth it."

"Dare say a pool is gonna help a lot of families endure this heatwave. But, please, remember, avoid being out in the sun—even in a pool. The UV predictions are just as extreme."

"To other news," Dylan pushed forward. "A most baffling case has emerged across wide parts of America concerning the instability of timepieces."

"It seems as if it doesn't matter if it's a mobile phone, a watch, or the clock in your car, they'd all seem to be under some extraneous influence."

"Reports are coming in from across the world of the same strange phenomenon. There's talk already as to what the cause could be, and some are speculating that a spike in solar flares might be to blame."

"All's not lost, however," Ashly said, as if he knew his subject matter intimately. "Timepieces seem to be righting themselves. However, do expect delays across many sectors as businesses and services are coming to grips with all amount of disruptions."

"A sundial might be your most likely go-to option," Dylan was saying, and Bob imagined him shaking his head. "Regardless, we need to show respect and civility as reports come in of a spike in violence due to frayed tempers. This is hardly anyone's fault, so please, remember that we're all managing this together. Everyone's doing the best they can. We'll all get through this; we just need to stay calm and respectful of each other."

"At this stage, we're told there is no reason to believe this will last as the cause is further investigated."

"Sounds authentic," Bob muttered. "Pity it's a load of bullshit," he continued on, as if Dylan and Ashly could hear him.

"Closer to home, a woman has been charged with three counts of murder after going on a deadly rampage overnight through Jurupa Valley. One of her victims was a child of just thirteen. She'll be remanded in custody until an expedited hearing in just three days. When questioned as to why she did it, she blamed her mental state on the heat."

Bob pressed the standby button and the hi-fi shut up. So much for the news and so much for hip hop.

In hindsight, he should've left the news well alone. Listening to such depressing and evocative tales was a bad idea, prior to catching an Air Canada flight to Sydney, Australia. In his defense, he'd no idea the news would be quite as bleak.

Then again, was there ever any good news on the news?

Wednesday September 14, 2022
10:50 A.M.

Outside Adelaide International Airport, as the Triplows were boarding their flight in Sydney, the time had steadied and planes had returned to the air. Many carriers were feeling pressured by their customers to do so, because the responsibility for their safety lay squarely with their airline of choice, and that included getting them to their destination in a relative timely manner. If the plane went down, however, there'd be hell to pay.

"Come on, fella, move ya ass!" The taxi driver was coming up behind the first in the rank, which had just waved off a customer. "If I didn't know any better, I'd say you were an Uber driver."

A tall, dark, slender man gracefully slipped out from behind the steering wheel. "And what is wrong with being an Uber driver?" he said.

"I don't like 'em."

"Oh, have they done something to offend you?"

"Do you mind moving ya ass… Malinda?" the taxi driver said while glancing at the man's ID in the windshield. He was in no mood for chitchat.

"I am sorry, but I am waiting for someone."

"Yeah, aren't we all? Now get a move on."

"It is very important that I wait."

"You're blocking the lane," his unfriendly counterpart retorted.

"Well, dear sir, if you had not parked so close, you could have moved around me." The man spoke with a distinct African accent, which imparted a disarming calmness. "Tell you what I will do, so you can help someone out by giving them a ride. I will move up a little. That way you can get around."

"Thanks," the taxi driver said, somewhat flummoxed. He really wanted to knock the guy's block off, but the dark-skinned man had somehow dampened his fuse.

That should've been the end of that, or so the African-speaking taxi driver thought, but the following taxi drove directly up to the rear bumper of his. Once more, he exited his taxi with an air of unshakable decorum and walked up to the driver's window. "Excuse me, sir, I am waiting for someone and need to remain here. I have already pulled up a little, and I can do so again, but if I keep going I will finish outside the terminal."

"You should've thought about that before, you fucking asshole. I'm sweating my ass off here and you're playing tiddlywinks."

"Tiddlywinks?"

"Yeah. You're being a fuckwit, in other words."

"Oh, I am so sorry. I was not meaning to be a fuck quit. I will move once more."

"Why the fuck don't you just get your ass out of the fucking way and let us make some money, for Christ's fucking sake?" The driver was about as surly as you could get.

It seemed the word 'fuck' resonated well with this fellow, so Malinda returned, "Do not worry, sir. I will move my fucking taxi so that you can get on your fucking way."

Once more, he creeped his taxi forward.

The surly driver took a ride and drove off with his finger in salute. Malinda smiled his brilliant white smile and called out in his disarming tones, while waving back: "May you fuck all day!"

After a similar scenario happened yet again, sans the 'fuck'— because no one seemed to be taking any notice of proceeding matters and, poignantly, people seemed somewhat stupid— Malinda scrummaged around for paper and pen.

He had papers on the floor of the taxi to keep it nice and clean. These he used and, by the grace of the universe, found a wide-tipped felt pen in the glove compartment.

Perhaps others had had to deal with similar circumstances in the past, Malinda thought. *Happy fucking days.*

On the paper he wrote:

HIRED

He stuck one on the rear window, the other on a window facing the terminal.

That seemed to do the trick.

And so he waited while the mercury kept rising and the morning wore on.

At exactly 9:15 a.m. on home soil, Bob and Joshua Triplow boarded the Air Canada flight to Sydney, Australia. Their expected arrival into Sydney Airport was approximately 9:15 P.M. Eastern Daylight Saving Time, Tuesday the 13th of September.

They would hole up in Rydges Sydney Airport hotel, directly opposite the international terminal, until their Virgin Australia connecting flight the next day at 7:30 A.M. At least, that was what the itinerary said.

It was a rather uneventful flight over the Pacific Ocean, except for a man claiming he was Jesus and wanting to open the middle emergency door to prove to everyone how he could fly. Obviously not a religious man, and neither was Bob. However, even he knew that while Jesus might've walked on water, as much as he could recollect He wasn't reputed for His feats of daredevil skills from jets at thirty-nine thousand feet.

Neither Bob nor Josh had slept well, so when Bob woke at around six the next morning, he didn't so much get out of bed as rolled out it.

He woke his son and told him that they had to get a move on, as there was an hour and a half before they boarded the Virgin flight to Adelaide.

Bob had once experienced the joys of too many drinks the night before. This reminded him of that hangover. He felt like crap. His mouth felt like crap. So, rather than trundle over to the domestic terminal and wait for their connecting flight, feeling like crap, he took a refreshing shower. He even brushed his teeth. As he got dressed, he reflected on the fact that he still felt like crap. He reckoned it had as much to do with jetlag as with the fact that he was actually in Sydney, en route to Adelaide; it was pointless delaying the inevitable. He could squeeze in another shower, but what for? He could miss their flight altogether, but what would that achieve?

Joshua had taken a shower first, and was waiting for his dad when he exited the bathroom.

"How are you feeling, mate?" Bob asked him.

"Jeez, Dad."

"Mm," was all Bob offered. Didn't he know it? "Come on, we best get going. I tried giving your mum a call to let her know we're still in the land of the living, but couldn't get through. I'll try on the way over." Meaning over to the domestic terminal.

The digital display in his phone was impossible to read until it finally settled. It was about 6:45 A.M, making it about mid-afternoon Corona time.

After 5 minutes of

At the third stroke the time will be twelve… twelve… twelve o-one A.M.

frustration and wading through the residual heat rising from the tarmac between Rydges and the airport, Bob gave up, resorting to the idea of calling Sue when and if he had the chance later on.

They presented themselves to bookings. The fellow behind the counter took their tickets and asked if they had any luggage, to which they replied in the negative.

"Travelling light, huh?"

"Yeah, less hassle."

They'd managed to get through this process and make their way to the waiting area for the call to 'All passengers flying Virgin Australia to Adelaide'.

Joshua was almost spellbound by what he saw, and Bob followed his gaze. Although, take your pick in what direction.

An electrical gremlin was playing havoc yet again, with every conceivable service that relied on the power grid.

Flights were immediately grounded.

The public announcement—courtesy of an inadequate microgrid: similar to a home solar backup battery lacking in the grunt department—which echoed throughout the complex was hardly required. With every overhead light, restaurant and store as well as every flight schedule display convulsing in rapid succession, a rainbow of color spewed through the terminal in psychedelic patterns, to which some had violent reactions.

One woman suddenly collapsed to the floor and started thrashing and choking on her own spit.

Security and medical personnel rushed to her aid, telling Bob to stand clear when he asked if he could lend assistance.

Her susceptibility to epileptic fits had been incited by the extraordinary demonstration of near mind-bending color arrangements.

Another who'd been diagnosed several months earlier with early-onset dementia completely lost the plot. They later apologized and said, "The lights… they took total control of me."

Further unnecessary announcements blared the obvious, and it seemed to Bob they were missing their desired objective. The agitation meter seemed to keep rising on each subsequent announcement. He wondered if anyone had had the bright idea to say it a few times before giving it a rest, rather than stirring their valued patrons into a pack of vigilantes. "We apologize to all who are awaiting to board flights. However, due to circumstances beyond our control, flights will be affected until further notice and reinstated as soon as it is safe to do so. Until then we thank you for your continued patience."

Five minutes later: "We apologize to all who are awaiting to board flights. However due to circumstances beyond our control…"

One couple passed by, venting their spleen in such quantities that Bob fancied he could see steam belching from their ears. Needless to say, they probably wouldn't be flying their chosen carrier again, even if offered free flights to Mars by Robert Bigelow himself.

For the next three hours, until the glitch ran its course, and with the microgrid having stabilized the light show, Bob and Josh sat in the domestic terminal lounge, listening to the hum of agitation and the silly woman on repeat. They were finally able to board their Virgin flight at approximately 10:35 A.M. Sydney time. During the wait, they'd taken the opportunity to have breakfast and drink a coffee or two, as well as a Red Bull.

"Don't worry, Dad. I've had a can of Monster now and then," Joshua had said as if to persuade his father into making the correct decision.

"Monster?"

"Yeah—you know, the stuff that allows you to walk through brick walls."

"Thought it gave you wings."

Joshua had rolled his eyes, saying, "Dad, that's Red Bull," whilst holding up the can.

"Well, strike me down and call me shorty for mixing up my energy drinks," Bob quipped. "Besides, when did you feel the need for an extra kick?"

"It helped me get through some days at school."

"Oh, that bad, huh?"

Bob had allowed him this; after all, he was about to lead him into his nightmare, so what was one can of Red Bull going to do? If the advertising machine had it right, wings might be a distinct advantage.

"Dad?"

"Yes, mate?" Bob had answered, staring at the stupid antics in the arrival/departure boards just beyond the cafeteria, puzzled by the fact that even the cafe's lights operated, as well as their coffee machines, cooking appliances and refrigerators, but not what he'd have considered the most important feature of an airport. Engineers, he supposed, were likely to be an eccentric bunch who got their kicks through the niggling things they purposed-built into their work and, in this case, you could all the cafe lattes you desired, just so long as you weren't in a hurry to board a flight.

"Why are they doing that? It's like it was with the clocks back home," Joshua had continued, wanting his dad to say something.

"Time's being affected, Josh."

That wasn't quite what Josh had in mind. It made not a dent in his anxiety, and it could really use some denting about now. "By what?" he had asked and wished he could keep his trap shut. As much as he was a curious boy, he was smart enough to know when he didn't want to know.

His dad had drawn in a deep breath. *He's seeking atonement… he's seeking this through you, son… he's seeking this for the dreadful thing he perpetuates.* Bob was thinking of Raoul's sermon. Jesus didn't fly at thirty-nine thousand feet, nor did He intervene in the personal affairs of a man of theology. Jesus must've been a busy man nonetheless. Bob had laughed, despite himself and the dire circumstances.

"What's funny, Dad?"

"The man in black."

Joshua had shaken his head. "No, Dad, he's not," he said gravely.

"He's the one affecting time." Bob had refrained from using his name, Patrick Nesmith, for that'd make him seem more human than he had any right to.

A fellow traveller sitting close by silently removed themselves from their seat to reside several tables away to continue their cafe latte in substitution for a seat aboard a flight.

"The man in black's doing this?"

Bob had looked at his son, wearing an amalgamation of guilt, helplessness and a rare species of anxiety, the type that physically changed one's appearance. "I believe so."

"So is he alive or is he a ghost?" Joshua had pressed once more, picking up on the conversation they had had around the dining table two days ago.

"Neither."

"So he's haunting some place in Adelaide, and that's where we're going?"

"Something like that, mate." *Frankly, son, I haven't the faintest idea. Apparently it's linked to another dimension.*

"Dad?"

"Yes, mate."

"He took Sammy, Dad." Finally, the admission Joshua had been painfully debating on how to broach. "And it was my fault."

The revelation had come as no surprise. Bob had drawn him close, wrapping an arm around him. "Josh, let's just get through one thing at a time and see what happens in the end," he said with an aching heart.

If a single phone call had the potential to change world history, then a single moment in time can mark that change. As it is with all incidences that become a series of major, perhaps even catastrophic events, there is that one fleeting moment that defines what is about to unfold. Hitler made leader. Genghis Khan pissed off by the Christians. The Gaza Strip acquired by the Israelis during the so-called Six Day War. And so on. All are markers, if you like, each a fork in the road of time, where the pendulum swings between what was and what would be.

Despite so many losing their lives in Bonatares, Brazil, that moment did not rightfully belong to them, but to a few: a girl, a boy and his faithfully restored 1972 GTO.

∽

Monday, September 12, 2022
Approximately 4:45 A.M.

Some four hours off Bob and Joshua catching a flight into the most exotic of lands, sound waves of terror hit the ionosphere and lit up radios throughout South America. From cost-effective RadioShack systems to outrageously expensive Bang & Olufsens came a rude yet brief interruption to the morning's broadcasts. Although listeners were sparse at this early hour, and the incident's duration less than sixty seconds, it was picked up clearest in a Peruvian village on the fringes of Cusco.

One fellow who suffered chronic insomnia, of which only the high-octane juices of the agave could combat, tumbled from his bed. Its wooden slats creaked dangerously beneath his mammoth weight. There was even one loud *crack,* which kind of matched the one exposed from his striped underwear. He took no notice of either; personal presentation didn't rank terribly high on this fellow's list of priorities. You either took him as he was or could you get stuffed. Between his pie-plate hands, he almost shook his RadioShack into oblivion, ranting in tones given by a little too much imbibing.

A tequila bottle, whose contents surely came from the gods and not a cactus, lay empty by the side of his bed. In his delirium and anger he staggered about, kicking it so that it went skittering across the dirty floor, his legs barely holding the veranda of fat above them.

"Piece... piece... shit... yar a... shitty... piece!" He ranted slurred damnation in the face of his RadioShack. It just sat there mocking him whilst having a meltdown. Nothing else could account for the blast from its three-inch speaker. If he hadn't known better, he could've sworn this shitty piece of shit was screaming in mortified pain.

Through the dead quietness of Peruvian darkness, the noise shattered across the plains. It blared from the small square windows in his mud-walled adobe, together with his ranting. The accompanying yellow light of a kerosene lantern flickered through them.

After the umpteenth shake, his RadioShack returned to the usual program for this time of the morning: '*Who Cares for the Charango?*' It was the kind of show where political debating thrived with earnest spiel; once there was even a dust-up.

Following a protracted belch, in which enough volatile gas was expelled to have refloated several Hindenburgs, this fellow drifted back towards his alcohol-induced stupor, oblivious to another hard day's work which lay before him and that time was getting on. Not quite late enough to be getting up; not quite early enough to drift into a deep stupor.

On the other side of the small village, Rosa Marquez had promptly fallen to her knees and prayed El Chupacabra would not take an interest in the village's livestock. The alpacas had born few foals this year, and meat was in short supply. Besides, should El Chupacabra find the flesh of the animals in short supply, what would stop it from turning its attention to her people? There had been talk that this had happened in the past, that El Chupacabra was not always merely content with gorging on the odd alpaca. Please, not today. Please, not tomorrow. Please, not ever.

Rosa was an early riser and had been preparing her wares for the local bazaar, where tourists would sample her cuisine.

Having experienced El Chupacabra's explosion of anger from her radio, though, she'd have to force herself to complement each scoop of live bugs into the cups of tourists with a broad smile.

Juiced up on excitement, the tourists wouldn't care. They wouldn't know. Jabbering on what they'd seen from their flights over the Nazca Drawings, they'd be looking for something a little on the exotic side to quell the lunchtime munchies. Her most popular line: the peppermint bug. Just the thing for those looking for an after-dinner mint that wouldn't sit still in the mouth.

But, maybe, they'd be the lunch!

Though she continued her preparations, her trembling hands wouldn't be still. They shook so badly that she dropped almost every second item she grabbed, including a jar of peppermint bugs. They immediately scampered away. "Oh, you silly woman," she berated herself while fussing about the floor, meticulously scooping up the would-be escapees.

Rosa had talked herself into believing El Chupacabra had returned, bloodthirsty, long-fanged and red-eyed. That somewhere, this monster lurked amongst the plains… and it was only a matter of time before lives were lost. Animal or human? *Or both?*

The hands of time were rapidly deteriorating, trip-trapping around the face of analogue and digital pieces on a global scale. Unlike the goats of the Three Billy Goats Gruff, who trip-trapped across the troll's bridge, their story had been long in the making.

It was approaching 4:45 A.M. across the Peruvian Desert, and events were careening toward that fork in the road, the pendulum swinging against the survival of this Earth and mankind.

Events both known and unknown were spiralling irreversibly out of control.

"*Faster! Go faster!*"

"*I'm doing one twenty now!*" Paul screamed back. His Judge howled through the desert night, streaking northward along the Pan-American Highway.

"*SHIT!*" he yelped, snapping the wheel one way and then overcorrecting with as much force. His panic-stricken mind was unable to cope with the usual task of making his hands steer a true and safe course. The 1972 GTO, surely a showroom pony of yesteryear's American muscle pride, unlike the late Gillespie's *acquired* Lincoln Continental, twitched dangerously. A straight stretch of highway laid before it, which was fortunate. For now.

"*You get us away from those… those things, Paulie!*" Annie was entirely beside herself. "*You get us away from 'em!*" Each hand was a white-knuckle clump buried in the top of the back seat. Like bookends to a collection of horrific stories, they pinned her face, an alabaster orb of terror. Staring through the GTO's rear window, her head wobbled at the slightest bump in the road, like a life-sized caricature of a rear parcel-shelf dog.

Annie was smelling a little rich, too, running on her own brand of high octane.

And for all his panic, Paul still had that special place in his heart and mind which rued the state of his beloved machine.

You see, Annie had had an orgasm of a spectacularly different kind. Whether it was the hamburger having sent forth disagreeable quantities of saturated fat amongst her gastric juices, or the *thing* that had slipped through the car's metal roof and into its interior, didn't really matter. Annie had thrown up and, by pure luck alone, Paul had ducked in perfect synchronization with the projectile, each passing the other like well-choreographed ballerinas.

One moment she'd been in ecstasy, nearing the usual variety of orgasm. The next, she'd looked up, not into the deep brown eyes of the boy who currently had his rather large appendage shoved inside her, but into the face of some *thing*. That was the only way her baffled mind could describe it: some *thing*.

As for Paul, he couldn't recall just what had happened… and never would.

From that point on, the wee hours of September 12th escalated into speed that defied reason.

Some *thing* had begun *laughing* in Annie's face, its own mean little face almost plastered over hers. It was the kind often drawn on stick-figure men, only this one had been on the fucked-up side, obviously the result of a wannabe artist with a penchant for the nasty.

The night had started out with a bite at some greasy hamburger joint, followed by a drive into the desert. The idea had been good. More than that: it had been fuelled on the raw power of hormones. The only power now, however, came from 455 cubic inches, compliments of General Motors.

Paul had his foot jammed on the accelerator; whatever was chasing them easily maintained the Judge's speed. He was soaked through in sweat, and had to blink and rub his eyes like a kid with a nervous twitch. It did no good: the salty droplets kept right on coming, aggravating the bejesus out of his sight. There was two… three… four of everything.

Though set in a hard mold of desperate determination, his driving style had gone to pot. Both young and full of confidence, Paul was nonetheless sure he could outrun the balls of light. After all, this *was* his Judge… and nothing on this earth could beat it.

Maybe if his mind hadn't been traffic-jammed with panic, and maybe if he'd listened to his friends' doubts of his behind-the-wheel panache, he might've wisely reduced his speed. But at 19, his skewed sense of confidence, poor visibility and lack of mental acuity was a volatile concoction, rendering the Judge a skittish beast, its needle hovering over 125 MPH.

"*I can still see 'em!*" Annie was screaming. "*I can still hear 'em laughing!*" This was, of course, mindless bullshit: the only thing Annie could hear was the howl of 455 cubic inches at high tilt.

But she *imagined* she could hear them, and that was all Annie needed.

The Judge twitched violently again.

Her alabaster face, surrounded by a wild entanglement of hair, wobbled. This time the vomit didn't simply come in a steady stream, it came in a wall of mind-altering colors, hitting the rear window in one massive splash. From there, like a spider's spreading web, it grew. Chunks of hamburger fanned along the glass like satellites, before dropping to the parcel shelf.

"*Jesus!*" Paul retched against the stench and damn near lost it himself, his eyes watering up worse than ever.

The next bend in the highway was fast approaching.

The needle in the speedometer continued its hover in the stratosphere.

When Paul cleared his eyes to the extent that, at the very least, blurred images could be seen, he noted his Judge was somewhat off-centre. The white lines in the middle of the road were travelling diagonally beneath the car rather than alongside it. At this angle he was heading for an off-road excursion. That would be bad. In fact, that would be *very* bad: it had been a few short months since he'd forked out thousands to have the paint restored to its original Orbit-Orange. Heading off-road would undo his favorite girl's looks, giving her a 'dent-and-scratch sale' appearance.

He snapped at the wheel again. His friends could've told him that this, too, was very bad. That, perhaps, he was no boy racer, despite his assertions to the contrary. The tires caterwauled across the tarmac, and the Judge slewed dangerously and violently.

It was an instance where seatbelts were a must. And though Paul had, in his delirium, strapped himself in, Annie hadn't. Obviously, she'd been, and still was, that bit too delirious.

She screamed nonetheless, as if assisting in her boyfriend's endeavors, which was about as effective as if she had picked up a pan and wrapped it around his head. Her wild hair pulled one way and then the other, as if blown by a strong and erratic wind. No longer a wobbly-headed dog, Annie was being tossed about like a tennis ball, though her bounce was more indicative of a brick. Things were out of control and when her head collected the leading edge of the right rear pillar, the quarter window exploded in one great detonation of glass-crumbs. Part of this shower fetched up in her hair, as if sprayed with glitter before a prom. There were gaudy streaks of red running through it, too, for that finishing touch. And the dark pools of fear in Annie's eyes now stared in the ultimate expression of 'You're it.' But for Annie, the game had come to an end.

Her face peeled from the pillar and, on the broken spine of her neck, wobbled once more in the perfect manner of a rear parcel-shelf dog. Annie's body slowly made its way down the seat, her face submerging below the window. One arm flopped to the floor, followed by a leg. Her body seemed to be melting away. The shoe on the wayward leg came free and rolled over against the carpet, like Mickey Mouse's Pluto playing dead.

Paul shot a glance in his exterior mirror to see the balls of white light still in the chase. *And gaining!*

Foo fighters, that's what they are! I've heard of these… I didn't believe in them… now I do! I do! 'Cause I can see them and they're coming for me! The foo fighters are real! And I'm in trouble! OH SHIT!

He then snapped at look into the back of the car. *"Annie! ANNIE! OH JESUS, ANNIE!"*

The Judge skittered hopelessly to the wrong side of the highway, hit an embankment and went airborne. Its tires and suspension hung foul, like the landing gear of a jet on take-off. Its headlights sent beams angling into the starry night. They levelled and, for a moment, remained on that plane before embarking on a near graceful descent.

Ladies and gentlemen, we are experiencing a high degree of turbulence and advise all aboard to strap in, because I'm afraid this baby is hot and coming in hard.

That was when Paul Caulfield, otherwise known as Paulie to his friends and recently deceased girlfriend, began his own chorus of screaming.

Piercing the Judge's shiny sheet metal and glass without fuss, the balls of white light had given up the chase of its brake lights in favor of flooding its interior. They poured in until every bit of space was stuffed full. A mad one became impaled on the shifter and exploded with a suffocated *pop*, its mean little face sinking in on itself. Its rubbery carcass fetched up on top of the shifter like a used condom.

At some thirty feet above terra firma, the Judge had become a beacon of sorts. A lighthouse warning of grave dangers ahead. Its windows cast the soft glow of Black Eternity's insanity and the sound of much laughter.

Not in the least bit interested now in testosterone-driven desire, Paulie continued to holler his lungs out, like a boy in a church choir for the overly exuberant. His eyes bulged from their sockets, his face surrounded in a mad one's scrum.

Their laughter was shrill and that of completely demented little children who thought it funny terrorizing others.

They dragged Paulie, hollering, up through the roof of his car. He kicked and thrashed. Unwittingly and impossibly, his song of terror imprinted across the ionosphere, so that anyone, in the near vicinity, tuned to the radio waves got an early morning blast.

And while he ascended to the stars and beyond, the Judge nosedived to Earth. In a matter of milliseconds, it was nothing more than dismembered parts, shiny bits flying hither and thither, Annie's ragdoll body amongst the spray.

She hit the ground and tumbled. Her useless arms and legs beat the hot night air like a Mixmaster turned horizontal, its blades spinning wildly. Parts coming adrift. An arm flying here. A leg there.

Sue answered the door. Frankly, she was in no mood to talk, regardless of whom wanted to yap in her face. The air was stringently hot for this time of morning—or for any time of day.

The memories of 2011 were resurfacing at a greater rate, like pictures floating up from the depth of her mind to reveal themselves to the bright light of day. She could see it all, the people going mad; that had been the worst, besides her mum dying. But it had been the entire atmosphere. Emergency services were pushed to the point of breaking; and when they did, bedlam had ensued. To stay alive, you had to keep your head down. The fabric of society teased to threads as fragile as gossamer. One thing—*anything*—easily and readily broke a thread here and there. And when it did, the sirens had started wailing. And when they could no longer wail, society had essentially come to an end.

Having done a complimentary job of repressing it all, she hadn't realized the extent to which she'd been left traumatized. Like living in a haunted house, it was okay while you were there, but once you left, you forgot... and when you remembered, the horrors were somehow more vivid in every way.

The pictures, however, were still surfacing, and she knew she still had much of this déjà vu recollection to enjoy in the hours to come. Because, surely, days had become the latest casualty of extinction.

Raoul had said that time was a commodity in short supply. And she believed him, as she'd believed everything else he'd exposed.

One thing kept nagging at her, though. Raoul seemed more of a puppet, a talking head without much knowledge; like a politician who read from a script, he projected all-knowledgeable. But he couldn't completely explain the very things he was revealing. And like any politician of the modern era, when he'd gone off track, he'd started coming off as someone talking out the top of their head.

Nonetheless, none of this distracted her from what affected her the most.

Her men were gone because of some tie they shared. Some common factor.

Bob's past and Joshua's future seemed to be locked together, like a pendant around the neck that you opened to reveal those you loved. On one half, the face of her husband. On the other, the face of her son.

Sue opened the door.

"Hi, there, Mrs. Triplow." The brightness in Leon's voice was totally false, but top marks to the kid for effort. The air seemed on fire as it rushed in. "It sure is hot this morning," he said, both reading her reaction and of the same opinion, the sun biting into his legs.

"Yes, it is," she said, thinking, *I fear it's gonna get a lot hotter.*

"Is Josh ready?"

"No. Oh, it's Monday, isn't it?"

Leon looked baffled but was nodding.

"Sorry, Leon, he and his dad have gone on a vacation."

"They're still in Lake Welland?" *Lucky guy,* he thought.

"Not exactly," Sue said, and immediately regretted doing so. Lake Welland would've been the perfect cover. "They've gone to,"

Hell

"Australia."

"Why?"

Sue could've done without this boy's interrogation. Had he been any other kid, she'd have told him, politely—not like her own mother would've—that it was none of his business. As it was, though, this was not just any kid off the block, but Joshua's friend. A boy whom, honestly, if they ever decided they were more than just friends, she'd not be in the least bit surprised. Of course, that was given to the arrogant luxury of assuming there'd be a tomorrow… a future world. "They've gone to his birthplace. Adelaide, South Australia, to be exact."

"Wow, he never said."

"It was rather impromptu."

"When will they be back?"

They may never be back. But if they aren't, not to worry; time for worrying will have passed. "As soon as they can."

"Okay." Leon's disappointment stifled his false inflections, the brightness evaporating into the heat of the day. "I'll get going, then." He was stalling to see if this was some kind of joke.

"Have a good day at school."

"Thanks, Mrs. Triplow." He got the message; this was no joke.

He called by home before continuing on his way to school. With Sammy missing and Joshua out of the picture, his world had become a wasteland. He hadn't realized just how much he relied on his conversations with his best friend to make all things in life palatable to some degree.

His thoughts went to Old Mister Grouch. What would've happened if he'd come across that murderous scene by himself? He had handled it pretty well with Josh by his side. But on his own... The mangled wreck that'd been Old Mister Grouch... the odor in their air that neither he nor Josh had commented on, because some things in life were better left unsaid. But there had been an odor, and it was that of the recent dead, reminiscent of animal carcasses in the back of a meat truck that arrived at a butcher shop to unload the wares gaily hanging on hooks, and still moving as if to be away from another round of carving knives.

Marlene had offered that he stay home if he wasn't up to going to school. What was one day?

Leon surprised himself when he'd said that he thought it better to be with Ethan and Craig rather than sulk around the house all day. Not even hopping in the pool had any appeal; he'd just bob about, his tan complexion turning the deep-shade of an ancient bronze statue, and think of the things that had transpired over the past week… and he might just go under while the water gently soothed his body.

∽

The door bell rung once again. It seemed to have gone just past 9:00 A.M.

Time's inherent unreliability, however, rendered such judgement to a matter of prediction by the arc of the sun, the fall of shadows, and the blinding glare of the moment.

Not to mention the unbearable heat that barged through, the moment the door was opened, to pervade every room in the house. The person standing at her door wasn't Leon, which she'd fully expected for reasons unknown, except he couldn't cope without Joshua. Standing as substitution, in a Mendoza tag team, was his father.

"Hi, Sue, how's it going?" Zachary wasn't nearly as good as his son at pulling off the charade of '*Oh, what a beautiful morning.*'

"Good," she said, slightly stunned.

"Boy," he started and looked back over his shoulder. "It sure is hot."

Yes, Zach, I've had the same conversation with your son 'bout half an hour ago. "You've got a pool, haven't you?"

"Of course," Zachary said, feeling somewhat ashamed amongst the other goodies churning ominously in his emotional package.

Never let it be said, boys, that your teacher's a pushover.

"Sue, you're more than welcome to come over and use it."

"I know, you've invited us before," Sue returned pleasantly, sweat running over her body. *Christ, I could do with a shower, though I'd just had one. Maybe I could stand under the fucking thing until I dissolved into the network of sewers. And unlike Gordon MacRae's uplifting ditty in* Oklahoma *about everything being just as swell as treacle and candy while bouncing his buns atop a horse, things are surely going my way, whether I like it or not.*

Zachary stared at her intently, making her feel more uneasy than she already did. "I stopped by because I'm, um, a little confused. It's none of my business, but Leon tells me Joshua's not going to school today because he's gone on a vacation to Australia with Bob?"

"Adelaide, to be precise," Sue said, still contemplating Gordon MacRae and his jiggling buns and hoping his faithful steed, Flicka or Mister Ed, would pass under a low branch and shut him up.

"Is everything alright? Because—" He quickly shut his trap. Close. Very close. How easy it'd be to spill his guts and tell all of last night's sordid affairs. His chest tightened and he worried that he would accidentally let it slip when having a casual chat; the type you have, perhaps, over crackers and dips. Just the sort of conversation that got the party started.

"Because?" Sue inquired.

"Oh, well, as I said, I'm a bit confused. I mean, a vacation after going to Lake Welland. How did the sea bass go?"

"The sea bass are *very* safe." Sue refrained from telling him that they didn't do anything of the sort. That a man from the stars put the kybosh on such indulgences.

Zachary laughed, at odds with the entire conversation. "Was this planned?" Only hours before, he'd been ordered to either act or see his friend and his son die at the hands of a madman. Had to be a madman… in that way, his mind could at least go partway to finding reconciliation through appeasement. Now, they'd taken an impromptu trip overseas. *What the hell's going on?*

"Since you've raised it—no, it wasn't," Sue said. *I think I might lose my mind with worry. But thanks so much for asking.* And if Gordon MacRae didn't get out of her head, she might just pick up a 12-gauge and blast the asshole singing cowboy out of his seat… sparing Flicka or Mister Ed, of course. "Zach, as we might've told you, we're from Adelaide and Bob has taken Joshua to visit a family member. We were contacted middle of last week and told that someone very important to the family is on his deathbed. Patrick's his name. Patrick Nesmith. And before he dies, he desperately wants to see Joshua, whom he's never met."

"Huh, I didn't think either you or Bob had any family."

Sue wiped sweat from her face. "He's more a distant relative, but knows of Joshua." *Now, if you don't mind, Zachary, as much as you are a dear friend, can you kindly fuck off?*

Zachary wasn't buying this, especially in light of what had unfolded last night. He cast a nervous eye once more over Chasing Boulevard. The rusting hulk had disappeared as the mysterious man on the phone said it would. *From the government, my ass.* But Zach had to accept the explanation, as there was nothing else. "So how long is he going to be gone for?"

"I dare say as long as it takes for Patrick's wish to be satisfied."

"What are you doing tonight—for dinner?"

Sue glanced across the way, noticing 'Dorothy Evans' was up to her usual tricks. The curtains moved in the upstairs window, which she was apt to use. A face appeared. Even from this distance, Sue believed she could see excitement in her eyes. The face fell away. The curtains fell together again.

"I'll be fine, Zach. There's enough food in the freezer to survive on for a year."

"Yeah, well, we'd love to have you over for dinner. You could take a dip in the pool, make a pleasant evening of it. Please," Zachary added, so that it left no room for Sue to breach the offer with an excuse.

Lucille Goldman's front door burst open and she came running across the road. Of course, her run was more akin to an awkward trot, as if she had indelicately rammed a pole up her butt. "I saw it!" she was shouting.

Zachary's heart leaped into his mouth.

"I saw the old car parked out here *all day* yesterday, and I saw what happened last night!"

Zachary was about to get caught. He'd never been so scared in his life. His body seemed to fall away and the astringent heat suddenly nosedived into the sub-zeros.

"There was a man sitting in the car *all day* yesterday." Lucille was pointing to the road out front of the Triplows. "I tried telling the cops but they weren't interested, said they had better things to do with their time. Well, last night the man in that car stumbled from it, screaming! You must have heard it? He was dancing all over the road, as if swatting away a swarm of hornets. The cops don't know what happens right under their noses."

"And you do?" Sue asked with more than a passing dislike for the woman.

"Of course. It's people like me who keep the streets safe. I report things that *need* reporting. If it weren't for the likes of me, it wouldn't be safe to leave your own home."

"No, but you could get on with your life without being constantly harassed."

Lucille Goldman turned her attention to Zachary, ignoring her neighbor's impoliteness as nothing more than a product of the heat. The poor woman didn't know what she was saying. The heat did that to people of weak disposition.

Zachary continued falling away, while Lucille pinched her eyes down and he waited for the sentencing to be delivered. *You have the right to an attorney. If you waive your right…*

"You saw it, didn't you, Zachary?"

"I—I," he stammered badly, "was sound asleep all night. I didn't move an inch till this morning, and even then I cursed the alarm. I'm sorry, but I really don't know what you're talking about." He had to put a full stop on his raving, lest he reveal his deeds in a desperate attempt to prove himself innocent. *Keeping such sordid affairs close to the chest is gonna take effort and concentration I'd never planned on. Christ, what have I done?*

"No one ever does," Sue said, directing her words towards Lucille Goldman.

The woman was beyond caring for such insults. Perhaps Sue Triplow should take a cold bath; that'd settle her caustic insults. "I eventually got through to the cops about four this morning. If it wasn't for the little prick in the phone, I'd have contacted them earlier, as the man was stumbling about, obviously in terrible trouble, at about one. They arrived about five, but of course there was nothing to see. In the meantime, several people had come along and driven the car away." She shut up for a moment and frowned. "I think they picked something up from the road before doing this, though. There was no good happening right here on Chasing Boulevard last night, and

I can't believe no one knows about it except for me." She once more pinched her eyes down in Zachary's direction.

If only he had another one of those lozenge things. He could apply it to her and get her to shut up. But then, where would it end? This is why murderers had to keep on murdering so that their nasty secrets remained secret. Only they couldn't kill everyone. There was *always* someone who knew. At the end of it, Zachary Mendoza was no murderer.

Fleetingly, the thought raced through his mind. He'd been given just one of those lozenge things some ten years before, in a package that he'd somehow kept beyond all reason. It was as if the darkly spoken stranger on the line last night had had a premonition those years ago… a premonition involving one murderer and one hapless patsy. *Him.*

"You didn't check yourself before the cops arrived?" Sue asked. "I find it hard to believe, Lucille, that skulduggery was unfolding before your very eyes, and yet you chose to hide in your house. So much for the neighborhood watchdog."

"I might've placed myself in terrible danger. It's how they say in First Aid courses: Never become the next victim."

"Lucille," Sue started, "we are *all* in terrible danger. What do you think that little prick in the phone is on about? Did he say something like: *At the third stroke the time will be twelve… twelve… twelve o-one A.M.?*"

Lucille Goldman stared at her, dumbstruck, then said, "How did you know?"

"Have you noticed that's been getting worse? A day ago, there were only two twelves and now there are three. It's going to get worse until you won't get any sense except the number twelve, over and over again."

Lucille gave this serious consideration, before answering, "You must have foreknowledge of such a thing, Sue Triplow."

"I've been keeping my eye on you, Lucille Goldman." She couldn't help herself. She then looked at Zach.

He nodded. "I've heard this, too."

Sue's eyes returned to her busybody neighbor. "What do you think it means, Lucille? After all, you profess to know everything, so you must have an idea as to what the little prick's rhetoric means?"

Again, Lucille Goldman was dumbstruck.

Zachary felt relief seep into his flesh, as it was evident that she hadn't a clue as to what had taken place before her rather intrusive nose last night. Then suddenly she said, "Data collection. We're addicted to our phones, and now the government has woken up and hatched a plan to keep tabs on each and every one of us. They're tracking us through them. They're taking records because they don't want us to live in a democracy. Not anymore. They want to rule over us and tell us what to do and when to do it. And if we revolt, then too bad for you."

Sue raised her eyebrows. "Bravo, Lucille, you've hit the nail on the head. I'll pass on your comments with compliments."

The horror that swept into Lucille Goldman's face, refusing to budge, was more satisfying than either Sue or Zach would've believed.

"I—" she started, stepping back from them as if they'd suddenly turned rogue. "I'll see about that. I'll call the cops."

"They're in on it, Lucille; can't you see? And the more you use the phone, the more they know who to target first and foremost." Sue tutted. "It's a pity all that good knowledge of yours is in peril."

Lucille Goldman staggered across the spread of lawn, almost losing her footing before crossing the road, glancing continuously behind her as if she was being hunted.

Sue Triplow was thinking that maybe she could pull the rod out of her butt and have a good lie down. Damn, it was hot!

Zachary smiled somewhat wistfully. The generator's hum of last night had toned down to a purr. It was going to take some time to master, but he gladly accepted the respite. "I've never seen her stumped," he said, watching her disappear inside her house, impressed with Sue's rejection. He turned to her once more. "What do *you* make of the message on the phone?"

"Zach, I don't know. Not for sure. But I do believe it's the harbinger of bad times ahead."

Zachary frowned. "Why?"

"Because a man from the stars told me so," Sue said offhandedly.

Zachary laughed, unconvinced, once more. Then it dawned on him that, maybe, Sue wasn't pulling his leg. The color drained from him as it had when Lucille first laid her squinty eyes on him. Last night's caller: government operative? Or man from the stars?

"How did the wedding go?" Sue changed the subject altogether.

◦‿◦

Wednesday September 14, 2022
10:35 A.M. Sydney local time

Bob and Joshua entered the jetway to Virgin's Flight 613.

The plane got off the ground without further delays. It was nice to be in the air, even though the destination was anything but.

The pilot said that they had a tailwind and expected their arrival into Adelaide to be approximately at 11:20 A.M. He hoped all aboard would enjoy the flight, and thanked them for flying Virgin Australia. He informed them that the day's temperature was going to be a stinker at fifty degrees Celsius (122⁰ F), and that there was no forecast of cloud cover or rain.

As promised, they touched down a little less than five minutes after 11:20 A.M.

Bob and Josh left the jetway and made their way through a throng of travellers, either being scanned by security or having been cleared already.

"You know, mate, there was a time when none of this had to happen," Bob mentioned. "They were more innocent times, when people could come and go as they pleased without the threat of some lunatic with a bent on blowing up their plane."

Joshua walked by his side, struggling to comprehend what it'd be like to move about an airport without the heightened security.

Adelaide International Airport had a slightly warm, somewhat claustrophobic atmosphere. The contrariness of the hordes assailed them from all sides as they moved about like poisoned ants in a maze. The sounds of families, friends, holidaymakers and businessmen interlaced with the odd disgruntled ticket holder whose flight had been delayed, forming a wearily calamitous revelry.

Wait till it gets into full swing, Bob thought with ponderous gravity. *This is that tip of the iceberg like the one they never saw*

on the Titanic, only more destructive. Carry binoculars if you wish.
Like the lookout guy on the Titanic, who learnt too late that his eyes
were inadequate, you still won't see the final act until your world
is ripped apart.

Off to the side, amongst the drearily animated wallpaper, a
woman was slugging it out with her luggage, screaming at the
top of her lungs, *"Fucking, stinking, fucking cesspool! If I ever*
have to return to this fucking city again, I'll take a gun and shoot
my-fucking-self!" She would've made the perfect partner to one
hostile taxi driver outside, whose besieged passengers might well
be weighing the consequences of throwing themselves from the
car. She landed the ultimate in a drop-kick to the largest piece of
Samsonite in her arsenal. Its latches promptly burst open and its
innards fountained forth like a large party-popper. This didn't
do much in the way of mitigating the woman's ire, fed up with
waiting for one delayed flight after another. If a human body
had the lung capacity to blow its skull clean off the cervical
spine, like a cork from a briskly shaken champagne bottle, then
she was treading dangerously on such limits. *"I FUCKING*
MEAN IT! I'LL SHOOT MY-FUCKING-SELF!"

Someone within earshot, which damn near covered the entire
grounds of the airport, perhaps even a portion of the city, yelled,
"I've got one! Want to do us all a favor?" The woman, who
was having more than just a bad hair day, retorted, *"WHY*
DON'T YOU SHOVE IT UP YOUR ASS AND PULL
THE TRIGGER, YOU FUCKING EXCUSE FOR AN ASS-
WIPE!" It wasn't a question. It was a recommendation of
anatomical rearrangement.

The woman escaped the security guards. The fellow, who'd
called out, did not.

"I was kidding! I don't really have a gun!" he began protesting as he was swooped upon. "Hey! Where are you taking me?"

As Bob and Josh were leaving the terminal, yet another announcement came over the PA system, informing all travellers that flights were once again cancelled due to technical issues.

Bob was pleased they were nowhere near that woman's profanity, as he could imagine that on this latest delay, an eruption was taking place inside Adelaide International that might well rival the last.

A string of taxis was waiting outside the terminal. They were about to get into the second in the rank, because the first had plastered over its side window:

HIRED

A tall slender dark man immediately exited his taxi and tore the sign off, saying, "Please, my name is Malinda and I welcome you. Hop in, although mind your head if you do, as there is not a lot of room between the roofline and ground." He smiled a brilliant white smile and tapped his head, just to get his message across.

"Right," Bob said, a little stunned. After all that'd transpired that morning, this took the cake. "You had 'hired' on the car…?" he started.

"Oh, yes indeed. There is no need for it now, since you are here." Malinda smiled charmingly.

"Right," Bob said again, not quite knowing what to make of the situation, but accepting the taxi because it was there, and all he cared about at this point was getting to Lower Mitcham. Besides, the fellow's personality nullified all reasonable concerns of this being a set-up, and the driver part of the star-man's renegades that had experienced an epiphany, upon which the decision was made to move both he and Josh into their crosshairs.

As he gingerly got in, rather than hopped, thus avoiding a potential lump to the old noggin, he noticed the taxi number: 151.

"How you be today, sir?" the fellow said cheerily. Either he was South African or alike, his accent heavy. "I see you've no luggage."

"We're not intending to stay long."

"Where have you flown from?"

"California."

"Oh, well, that is not far at all." The taxi pulled out of Adelaide International with little regard for fellow drivers, leaving behind horns of anger and the screech of brakes. "I would love to live in California. I imagine the weather is kinder there."

"Nope, it's exactly the same."

"Really? Well, I'll be. I have family that live in America. I think they are in Seattle, but we do not stay that well in touch. I have heard Seattle can get cold, and it might surprise you to know that whilst I am dark-skinned, and people assume that dark-skinned people enjoy the heat, I can tell you we do not. But being snowed in is not appealing, either," he said, filling the cabin with laughter. "I lived once in Russia. The children there drank vodka before going to school. Can you imagine that? Vodka! They did this to keep themselves warm and their blood pumping freely through their veins. I have never seen so much alcohol consumed by children, some of them much younger than your son. At least, I am assuming he is your son?"

Bob nodded and the taxi driver smiled at him in his rearview mirror.

"These days one cannot be too sure. Human beings have become liberal… that is nice, depending on the intentions."

Again, the taxi driver had the ability to derail Bob. "I'm Bob." Hesitation made for a jerky introduction. "And this, as you rightfully pointed out, is my son, Joshua," he carried on in a smoother manner.

"Hi there, Joshua."

"Howdy."

"My, you seem like a nice young boy. What are you?"

Joshua didn't know quite what to say but, "Sorry?"

"Going on to be a teenager, is that correct?"

Joshua returned the driver's smile. "I'll be eleven in a few days."

"Well, isn't it nice to be young with all those hormones. What I would do to be youthful again," Malinda said cheerfully as he drove through the traffic like a maniac, stirring within Bob an image of Ray Charles and the skills he might've applied if he'd ever gotten behind the wheel, as opposed to his rock-bluesy songs and voice.

Bob wished this fellow would look where he was going rather than in the rear-view mirror. If the taxi was in reverse, he'd be doing just fine.

"How long have you been driving taxis for?" he asked.

"Three days," Malinda returned in his unfaltering cheery manner.

"You're kidding me."

"I'm a fast learner. What is it they call this city? A big country town?"

"Something like that."

"It is difficult to get lost here."

"It's easier than you think."

"Right you are." Malinda found joy in Bob's reply. "So where are you two charming fellows heading?"

"Nesmith Drive, Lower Mitcham."

"Very good, sir. Where might that be located?"

"You know Greenhill Road?"

"I… think… so." Malinda took a pause between each word.

"Fast learner, hey?" If things weren't bad enough, the driver's lack of attention equalled his knowledge of the city's roadways. "Okay, go straight ahead take the intersection onto Greenhill Road and keep driving until you see the sign for Unley Road. At that intersection turn right. From there it's straight through."

"Oh, it sounds simple enough. Are you visiting friends or relatives?"

"Haven't you got GPS?" Bob asked, disregarding the question.

"Oh yes, I do indeed, sir. But, you see, it is not working, so I cannot use it." Malinda rapped the taxi's onboard computer. "See, things are crazy. I think it might have something to do with the heat."

"You're probably right, Malinda."

"I have never seen it act this way, though. But I have seen what the heat does to electronics when it is extreme enough. Although I would not have thought it was extreme enough for long enough." Malinda was sounding a tad perplexed. He rapped the taxi's computer again, as if this would magically correct it, wearing his indelibly large and brilliantly-white smile.

"In all your three days," Bob muttered, slightly amused despite the situation. Under brighter circumstances, he reckoned he could've lapped up Malinda's insatiable cheerfulness.

It was obvious that things were deteriorating. Seemed as if Earth had fallen into the grip of the event horizon. Raoul had said that Black Eternity wasn't a black hole. He'd also said that if it was, life would start coming apart.

Well, there was a word for what was happening. That word was 'asunder.' It meant 'to come apart.'

Witnessed in Corona, Sydney and now Adelaide, it was as if he'd been transported back to the beginning, 2011, and all the horrors that it'd encompassed. The 'coming apart' had yet to escalate, to reach the same dizzying heights of terror. But then, it hadn't just popped out of the blue back then, either.

He'd been told that he was a special man who'd walked on the 'other side'… had skipped over the quasi-event horizon and into the yaw of the awaiting hell beyond. Spared memories of that joyous occasion, and without hardened facts, he could only go by gut feelings. Whilst this conveyed elements of that time, it also felt different. More sure of itself. The assessment raised a conundrum he wasn't quite sure how to dispel, but it seemed as if the world had become encased within an atmospheric bubble, suggestive of the volatility of expanding gas in a sealed room.

People were already starting to show the first signs of stress. Cracks in social correctness were opening up.

Scientific investigations of 2011 chalked up the events to solar flares. So, here we all were again, everybody blissfully unaware… going about their daily business because it was just another day… tootling about, getting things done, managing what needed to be managed… comfortable in their knowledge that things which didn't happen today could be taken care of tomorrow.

Bob had always known that such comforts were gravely flawed. For over a decade, he'd carried his wounds deep down inside, and told himself that the past was over. Unlike the lie promulgated throughout the world by those astute scientific boffins, he *had* known better. Theirs was one born of ignorance. His wasn't. That made his lie reprehensible. Regardless of how he looked at it, it *was* a lie—and he'd been lying for a very long time.

What could he have done, though? He didn't even know what he was going to do *now*. To bear witness to the same horrors he'd experienced in Adelaide 2011 was incomprehensible. The terrifying unknowns, yet to unfold, only allowed the past and imminent future to merge. To become one.

"Did Raoul organize this?" Bob asked, wondering of the convenience of a taxi waiting seemingly just for them.

Malinda consulted the rear-view mirror, beaming. He held that pose momentarily, while the traffic dodged and weaved about them, before saying, "My watch is doing the same thing. See?" He removed both hands from the wheel to demonstrate how poorly his watch was doing, raising one wrist and tapping his watch with the other hand.

The taxi squirmed across Greenhill Road.

Bob looked at Joshua, who looked back at his dad. "Mate, I'd like to arrive in one piece."

"Oh, yes sir, I would very much like for you to arrive in that state as well."

"Really?"

"Oh yes, body parts are very messy. Besides, I love my job and would be devastated if I lost it."

"Thank goodness your heart's in the right place."

Finally, and with a certain amount of relief on the behalf of both its passengers, the taxi pulled into Nesmith Drive.

"Well, here we are," Malinda declared. All the moisture had dried up in Bob's mouth and throat, and a wave of dizziness had come over him. Malinda's interesting driving skills couldn't be entirely to blame.

Here they were, indeed. But exactly where was that?

"Where would you like me to pull up?" Malinda asked, his cheeriness shouting contrariness to the situation.

Bob was momentarily startled, thinking, *A church?* It was something he hadn't considered, because hadn't Raoul said that he'd know what he was looking for? Hadn't he? Now that they'd arrived, his confusion was getting the better of him. "Anywhere will do."

"Oh, nonsense. It is too hot to be wandering about. I will drop you at the front door." Malinda was blissfully driving along Nesmith Drive, passing one address after another. The sound of a horn emanated from yet another aggravated driver as he failed to give way to his right at a roundabout.

The driver decided his horn wasn't enough. "You asshole! Can't you see where you're going?"

Malinda waved as he drove on. At no time did his smile waver. "Happy fucking days!"

The taxi reached the end of Nesmith Drive and still no destination had been chosen. "You are sure it is this road you want?" Malinda asked, turning the taxi about.

"Yes. Please go back. We'll look again."

Another pass of Nesmith Drive. Nothing. No church. No parsonage.

Noarlunga. Bob's thought was a dawning light. *We need to go to Noarlunga… Raoul was wrong…*

"Might I make a suggestion?" Malinda asked, parking the taxi and turning around in the driver's seat. "Perhaps you and your fine young son with his growing hormones meet my family and rest for a bit. You look lost. And I have children you might find appealing."

"Thanks, Malinda." Bob said. His puzzled expression was nonetheless carried on a bed of deep appreciation. His invitation seemed palpably out of sorts amongst the bigger picture. "I'm not lost. I simply can't find what I'm looking for."

"And what might that be?"

"A church."

"You want to pray?" Malinda asked brightly. "Then let us pray together, maybe for the weather to get a little kinder."

"Malinda." Bob had to raise his voice, as their taxi driving friend had started some sort of gospel chanting… muttering… whatever they called it. "I don't need to pray."

You should pray, Bobbyyyy, you worthless little shit!

Bob felt faint, the voice of the bitch taking him by surprise.

During this discourse, the one person left aside was the one person who should've been included.

Joshua opened his door and was getting out, on an urge which seemed to be in control of him; one second thinking Malinda was a nice man, if a bit quirky, then the next having to go on foot and scope the local neighborhood.

"Mate, what are you doing?" Bob asked.

"I need to look around."

"What a fine young man," Malinda repeated with great affection.

"Josh, we have to get going. We've a long road ahead of us to Noarlunga." Bob turned to Malinda. "You know how to get to Noarlunga?"

"I'm a very fast learner. I love driving and people. It will be fun."

"Yeah," Bob said, unable to share the man's enthusiasm. "Fun."

He stepped from the taxi and Malinda followed.

"Josh," he called out, "come on, mate." He caught up with him and grabbed him by the arm.

Joshua shrugged it off and crossed the road, Bob following closely behind. "There's nothing here, Josh."

"Something's here."

"What?"

"I don't know. Something."

They walked on further, with Malinda joining them. The heat of the pavement bit into the soles of their shoes.

Josh led. The men followed. Malinda had decided it was appropriate to return to his gospel chanting... muttering... whatever they called it. Bob could've done without it.

Joshua was taking his time, looking with particular interest at signs, glancing over one after the other, moving on with intention until—

"Here it is," he said excitedly.

Bob came around on his side.

Frustratingly, parts of the plaque had been defaced, perhaps in a deliberate act.

This plaque marks the original site of the first
XXXXXXX church in the city of Adelaide. Built in
1837, the church of XXXXXXX served as a place of

worship for 155 years, until its demolition in February 1995. Throughout that time, it attracted a strong congregation.
Whilst all attempts to save the building were undertaken, the original foundation was unable to be successfully restored. The building became unsafe and started deteriorating. One pedestrian, Mary Prior, was tragically killed as a lintel fell from the structure on April 7, 1993. She was 24 years of age.

Amongst much protest from both the public at large and the faithful, as well as much political deliberation, the church was finally marked as condemned on November 1993.

"Do you feel anything?" Bob asked his son.

"Feel?" Joshua returned, perplexed.

Malinda's gospel chanting abruptly ceased when he saw what Joshua had located. "That is some miracle," he said gleefully. "How did you know that it would be here?"

"I didn't," Joshua said honestly.

Bob held out his hand to Malinda. "Thanks," he said. "For being a terrific sport."

"Oh, it is my pleasure. Are you certain you do not want to come with me to meet my family?"

Bob smiled. "Malinda, I think we've found what we were looking for. We've got to do a bit more searching, but it's here. If it was any other time, I'd enjoy meeting your family, providing they didn't chant."

Malinda laughed. "My singing is certainly not the best."

That wasn't it, but Bob wasn't going to further his impoliteness by commenting on his driving skills. Or lack thereof.

When Malinda stopped laughing, he noticed the sprawl before them. "A supermarket. You must be famished after your flight, yes?"

"Not exactly." Bob guarded his words. If he started on about a portal, Malinda might just go into a frenzy of gospel chanting in the fear that the Devil had possessed him.

Malinda finally took Bob's hand and said something odd, "How long does a handshake last?"

"Pardon?"

"A handshake is meant to last for about four seconds. Did you know that?"

The pavement's heat was almost burning the soles of their feet, their clothes clinging like a second skin, as if they'd need to be shed from their bodies rather than simply doffed.

"No," Bob admitted.

"Well, I will tell you," Malinda offered. "There are some that bond you for life." His cheery voice made the surrounding heat seem that little bit more tolerable.

On that note, he crossed the road, got into the taxi, pulled out into traffic and drove away. Tire smoke and a squawk of brakes were left behind as one car managed to avoid a serious accident, which caused a domino effect with several others having to take evasive action to avoid the first. Vitriolic words flew like a flock of rudely-startled birds.

Both Bob and Josh watched his taxi disappear into the heat haze, seemingly immune to the unfolding events it had caused.

"What was that about, Dad?"

"I really haven't the foggiest." Strange words under the circumstances.

Bob returned his attention to the original site of the church whose name had been defaced from the plaque. It'd been replaced by a Duncan's Megastore.

No church. No parsonage. Just terrific buying every day of the week, where the congregations were endless and eager to hand over their cash.

"Feel like shopping?" he asked.

"For what?"

Joshua's dad gave him a wink. "Reckon you'll know when you *feel* it."

It's the heat, Joshua thought. *Dad's going crackers under the strain.*

As they entered the store, Bob withdrew his mobile; time running amok in its screen. He pressed the dial button, but the service had been hijacked: *At the third stroke the time will be twelve... twelve... twelve... twelve o-one A.M.*

He stowed the phone in his pants pocket, once more doubting if anyone was able to make a call, anywhere around the world.

Meanwhile, the gas in the sealed room neared the point of self-detonation.

᪐

Monday, September 12, 2022
6:00 p.m.
Corona, California

Unlike her husband earlier that day, Sue Triplow hadn't heard the news. She was in no mood for the imparting of further doom and gloom.

Therefore, bothering to pick up *The Sentinel Weekly News* that evening was done purely on the off-chance that there had been positive developments on Sammy Debnar. Instead, glaring across the front page was the headline, **THE CITIZENS OF BONATARES CEASE TO BE… ALL FIVE THOUSAND**.

The article, written by someone named Daniel Mayson, reflected on an incident that had taken place several weeks before, at the beginning of August.

She read with sickening fascination about how an entire township, Bonatares, Brazil, had been terribly clumsy in losing every one of its residents. It seemed that such losses had occurred concurrently with other strange events: the sighting of balloons and the sound of bells.

Could such manifestations be attributable to the missing five thousand? Where did they come from? Who was responsible? And who knew of such events but weren't saying?

"I can tell you some things." Sue stood in her sofa room before its expansive front window. "But it'd make your hair stand on end."

Her sickening intrigue hardened into a stare, and her stare turned inwards. The figure moving on the other side of the pane, in the fading light of the tortured day, went unnoticed. She was but an infinitesimal creature soliloquising in the eerie quietness of her minuscule abode, a tiny pile of bricks and mortar nestled on a pinprick on the face of the Earth at 22 Chasing Boulevard. "I can tell you, but you'd have a terror of a time believing me," she repeated, her words chosen with graphic poignancy. They drifted into the quietness like spectres absorbing into the walls.

She'd seen balloons associated with unpleasantries… in 2011.

Everything seemingly came back to that year.

But bells?

That was something she hadn't had the delight of experiencing, but Joshua had said on several occasions about bells.

Sue shut her eyes.

The world was being consumed, only no one knew it. A strange slant on the story of the frog in cold water that was heated slowly until boiling, taking the unwitting frog along for the ride until it became a French delicacy.

She plucked her mobile from the low table at the front window, a vase of wilted flowers sitting square in its middle. Before leaving, she'd reminded Bob to set his mobile to airplane mode, so they could stay in touch.

Great idea, but for one thing.

Lucille Goldman's little prick was at it again, as he had been all day. *You can't keep a good man down. Little prick or not, he was one tenacious bastard,* she thought, and was desperate to speak with her men. To hear their voices. To know that they were alright.

She laughed sadly, worry and anxiety welling inside her. "Alright," she uttered aloud. They weren't alright. Come to that, who was?

They'd flown directly into the eye of the storm. Unlike the world at large, they'd done this with both deliberate intention and, for the better part, a smattering of knowledge. Though Joshua had been spared the details of another dimension; knowledge of that sort was unlikely to be of any benefit beyond overwhelming. Considering Joshua a prophet remained a mother's god-given right to indulgent exaggeration. Whether it carried a gain of truth or not hardly detracted from the facts. She had delighted in observing him, on many occasions, unconsciously wield his powers of insight and reasoning… his ability to adapt… to think a situation through at a moment's notice.

These would have to be the qualities he relied on when in another dimension. They'd have to be good enough.

The doorbell went and she almost hit the roof. The phone went sailing through the air to skittered across the dining room floor on the opposite side.

"Sue!"

She heard Zachary calling out and opened the door, the heat spilling forth like a horizontal geyser.

"You coming for dinner?"

"Christ, Zach, you scared the hell out of me!"

"Sorry, Sue. I only rang the doorbell."

"That was enough. I'm a bit… frayed at the moment," she said apologetically. "I really don't feel all that hungry."

Zachary laid a soft hand on her arm. "Come on, Sue. You don't have to eat. Maybe coffee or something stronger. Up to you."

She agreed with some hesitation and, as she came back through the sofa room with the house keys in hand, and having retrieved her phone, she glanced once more over the front page of *The Sentinel Weekly News* lying on the coffee table: **THE CITIZENS OF BONATARES CEASE TO BE… ALL FIVE THOUSAND.**

The Beatles' 'A Day in the Life' played inside her head as she closed the front door. They sung about reading the news of a man who'd taken his life and how that had made him miss the change in traffic lights… just sitting there with his brains leaking from a botched attempt of lobotomy while commuters built up behind. Though a personal favorite of hers, such indulgences were intrusive in light of the very real possibility that the world at large could soon be on the front cover of a newspaper lying on a coffee table somewhere far out in space, everyone dead while the satellites continued merrily whizzing about in orbit.

The shopping centre was abuzz. Nearby schools were on lunch breaks and there were bargains galore. *But of course*, Bob thought sarcastically. *Give me six Hail Marys and a $200 gift voucher, or a year's discount storewide.*

Something had caught Joshua's curiosity. Bob followed his gaze.

"I've heard that before," Joshua confided in his dad.

"Yes, mate, that's the sound of people spending their hard-earned cash for a moment's thrill," Bob retuned.

"It's… a girl. She's singing."

Bob listened hard. "Mate, there's kids over there. Reckon that's what you're hearing?" It was a question, not an answer.

Joshua shook his head and started walking through the aisles. "It's stronger here."

"It is?" Still Bob couldn't hear a thing resembling the sound of a girl's singing.

"Something's wrong with her." The color drained from Joshua's face, but he pressed on.

"What, mate?" Bob followed closely. He trusted his son's instincts, as he'd been told to. That much he now remembered. Though Joshua was unaware of what he was doing, it was absolute to his father.

The lights throughout the store flickered. Righted. Flickered again. This caused a wave of both excited and concerned jabber, as if none had ever seen lights pulsate on a power surge.

Bob caught more than the odd conversation centring on the day's temperature, as well as the fact that nobody could tell the time with any degree of accuracy. Shopping centres were a bureau in gauging the latest trends on people's minds. He supposed hairdressing salons were the same. Get a bunch of people together and it was the same old conversation starter: *How's the weather today?* After that, opinions ran thick and fast—everyone talking over one another, claiming to be in touch with the deeper meaning of life.

"Bastard's gonna lead us straight into another summer of heatwaves," one fellow, sporting a chambray of delightful sweat patches, chimed to his wife.

"Brace yourself, mate," Bob said as they dove past him and his partner, before coming to a stop. "You remember the summer of 2011?"

The man frowned and his partner went into deep thought. "*That* was a bastard. Bad times."

Bob nodded. "Bad times ahead." He moved on, leaving the man in his sweaty chambray to think it over.

Some older lady was arguing vehemently with a young store assistant that the bathroom scales that she'd come to purchase weren't on the shelf.

"I'm sorry, but they've proven to be very popular," he was replying. "If you like, I can place a set on raincheck for you?"

"I want to speak to the store manager."

"I'm sorry, but he's not available at the moment."

"And how the hell would you know that?"

"Because he's in a meeting."

"How bloody convenient! How is it when you want a store manager, they're always in a meeting?"

"There are other bathroom scales on offer."

"I don't *want* the other bathroom scales! I've tracked halfway across this *fucking* city in this *fucking* heat, I've got sweat in every crack of my body, and you're giving me lip!"

This delightful passage of conversation had drawn the attention of schoolkids and adult shoppers alike. Some found it amusing, others offensive.

"Got out the wrong side of the bed, did we, honey?" another woman said close by, pressing her luck and the woman's buttons.

"Why don't you go fuck yourself?"

"Charming," the woman said, walking off.

Maybe the human race is really just insane, when you get right down to it, and things like heatwaves are just an excuse, Bob thought miserably.

Tills were dinging. Bells were ringing. A cacophony of jabber rose like heat exhaust from the long-snaking lanes of people.

Joshua was otherwise engaged, and so the inner store antics passed without notice. He came to an abrupt halt and Bob walked straight into him, almost knocking him off his feet.

"I can't hear her anymore."

"The girl, who is she?"

Joshua shrugged, mystified.

"You've heard her before, though?"

"When I was at Sammy's, the night he disappeared. At least, I think that's when I first heard her."

"Another part of your dreams?"

"It was a nightmare, Dad."

More dinging, ringing and jabbering. Trolleys were clattering and rattling. A baby was crying incessantly, as his harassed mother appeared on the verge of throttling the little bastard and eliminating the witnesses.

Again, Joshua was in no mind to listen. "There's something about her, Dad, something… important."

"What?"

"Something," Joshua replied frankly, unable to explain himself further. He desperately missed his mom and his friends, especially Leon. For the first time since leaving Corona, the loss presented itself, and now, in the midst of the carousing the bustle, it seemed amplified, and he desperately wished his best friend was right there with them. Kind of odd, really, as he wished this more than he wished for his mom—because Leon understood.

On that, a thought jumped inside his head, as if it'd been standing on the sidelines, balancing on the tip of a springboard, before taking its opportunity. *I love Vegemite… because it puts a rose in every cheek. I really and truly love Vegemite—the stuff that Leon barfs at just thinking about. That's why I love it!* And on its heels, another image from the past popped up: "It tastes disgusting!" Leon had protested, acting out a vomiting motion. "How can you put that shit in your mouth?" In cavalier style, Joshua had returned: "Cause real guys eat shit!" He finished with an outrageous 'this is a belly-rattling yummy' sound, even though he questioned the very mentality of those who stomached the stuff, including his mom and dad.

He turned to his dad. "I'm glad you're here, Dad."

"Where else should I be?" An odd reply, but necessary. Bob squeezed him close. "Tell me that after we've done what we came here to do."

"To find the man in black?" Joshua should've conveyed a tone of profound incredulousness. He didn't.

Banners wafted from the ceiling throughout: **_20% to 60% STOREWIDE SALE! ENDS 21st SEPTEMBER! HURRY – LAST DAYS! YOU'D BE CRAZY TO MISS THIS!_**

"Mummy, I want Baton Destroyer!" One kid, about the size and shape of a large mass of bubblegum, was protesting.

His mom, a bigger version of that bubblegum, was protesting back, "I've got you a box of chips and we're having Pizza Hut tonight, Bruce. We'll get Buton next week."

"It's _Baton_, and I want him _now!_"

"Well, you _have_ been a good boy."

The smaller bubblegum squealed excitedly and wobbled to the fixture, to claim his prize for being an asshole from the stacked shelves.

Joshua pretty much ignored the kid, but he couldn't arrest a slight feeling of envy. Wanting to be the size of a hippo wasn't exactly part of his agenda, but following the song of a haunted girl that was leading him to somewhere not of this world, was, as they said, 'no picnic.'

He led the way through the crowd, continuing his fruitless search, until he rounded the corner into another aisle of toys. "I hear her again."

He hurried forward. "It's stronger here, Dad." He wasn't waiting about and Bob was simply following like his loyal servant.

"Here… down this way, Dad!" He went further down another aisle.

On opposite sides were teddy bears, Tonka toys of any variety you cared for, and dolls. Rows and rows of dolls, each incarcerated within a cardboard box. Each staring through the clear window from their imprisonment.

"Here! Here! Over here!" Joshua's excitement attracted the glances of several shoppers. He wasn't looking at the shelves of toys, but into the floor, as if fascination came by way of the simplest things.

The shelves of dolls all looked on with their unblinking eyes. Impassionate. Locked up. Unable to escape.

The girl's singing seemed to be drifting up through the floor, coming out of thin air. Joshua couldn't pinpoint exactly where it was emanating. The surrounding noise mingled with it, seemed to carry it here, then there, then somewhere else.

In a place far over the rainbow
The Boogaloo is out of sight
In a place far over the rainbow
Everyone's lost in a lullaby…

He didn't see her. But he imagined her. And suddenly he was overcome with sadness.

When did you last comb your hair? When did you last put a band in it to hold it back? When did you last see your mom and dad and friends? When did you last laugh and give up that hideous song? When did you last go to the toilet? When…? When…? When…?

This was the doing of the man in black. This was Sammy's fate. He couldn't bear thinking about it, but he was helpless not to.

In a place far over the rainbow
The Boogaloo is out of sight
In a place far over the rainbow
Everyone's lost in a lullaby…

Would Sammy be singing the same song? Would he do that whilst his hand scribbled away like a malfunctioning electronic typewriter whose type hammers kept stabbing at the paper again and again and again. How long could the human body endure such punishment?

One of the dolls started talking from her imprisonment: *Mommy, I'm thirsty! Mommy, I want a hug! Please, give me a hug!*

The flood of silent tears came unannounced, drawing unwanted attention. Joshua did as much as he could to hide himself.

The bubblegum kid and his bubblegum mother happened to be passing by. The kid looked at Joshua as if he had a curious disease. He was twirling Baton Destroyer between his chubby hands. The remnants of crisps stuck to his chubby fingers and both his lips. He then started giggling, forgetting Baton for the moment. "Look, Mummy, that boy's mental!"

His mother scowled at him over her enormous boobs. At first she put a hand out to give him a gentle slap, but then she changed its course and put it to her mouth. It was rude to laugh at others' misfortunes, wasn't it? "Bruce, stop it," she said with no intention of any real discipline.

Bob wrapped his arms around his son, cradling him like one might cradle a large ragdoll, his arms dangling loosely about him.

"What's happened?" several shoppers asked.

"Is your son cuckoo?" the fat kid chimed in and started guffawing. His big fat cheeks billowed, and his squinty little eyes disappeared into folds of fat.

"Stop it, Bruce," the larger bubblegum was saying, though giggling just the same.

Bob pushed through the crowd, dispensing with the bother of giving some trumped-up explanation. Somewhere in his rush, he managed to say, "He's feeling faint, that's all."

One astute shopper offered knowingly, "It's the heat. The poor child. Gonna see a lot more of that."

The first and only thing Bob could think of was the store's bathroom. Safely tucked within a cubicle and away from others, he could gather he thoughts, decide how to enter the portal. Without doubt, this was what Joshua had led him to.

Once inside, he shut the lid on the toilet and sat his son down. Squashed between the cubicle's side and the toilet bowl, Bob rocked his son as he had rocked his wife in Leonard's garage, tucked deep in Adelaide's south of Noarlunga so many years ago. It should've been ancient history.

Yet, here he was.

Damned if he was going to subject his child to the same sort of horrors. He would allow Joshua to lead him to the portal, and then eject him from proceeding with the horrifying journey. At no time in his life would have he considered abandoning his son, but he was left no option.

Mission of madness, his mind chided bitterly. *After all, what could Joshua do, anyhow? This fulfils* his *part in this story, according to Raoul. Once in the portal, I'll find Patrick Nesmith and help him pass into the light, with my greatest of pleasure.*

The more Bob rocked, the heavier both their eyes became, the exhaustion of the past days taking its toll.

Bob knew he couldn't allow this to happen. He withdrew his mobile from his pants pocket, hoping; but logically, there was no hope.

He dialled at any rate.

At the third stroke the time will be—
Useless. Utterly useless.

The displayed time was completely out of control, more frantic than ever.

He fought not to pitch the technologically useless piece of crap. Gritting his teeth, he shoved it into his pants pocket, for all the good it was.

Joshua had shut his eyes.

Bob let him rest. He'd been a gallant kid so far. He needed to go just that bit further.

 ✺

Adelaide, approximately 3:45 P.M.

The storm was advancing across the southern hemisphere, obliterating the skies and all communications. The electricity buzzed and flickered here and there, to finally wink out altogether.

Bob's eyes snapped open; something was clamped over his mouth. It was quiet, that much Bob did note.

In the surrealistic swill of post-sleep curdling about his head like vanilla mousse, his mind began to lumber the pieces together. What was clamped over his lips wasn't the parasite from the classic movie *Alien,* with the nasty habit of depositing a living embryo in your stomach, but his son's hand. He could smell the scent of his boy on it and immediately his heart conflicted, yet again, with his mind. *He shouldn't be there.*

No child should be placed in such a position.

Somehow Bob had taken a seat on the closed toilet lid and Joshua had ended up in his lap. His butt had gone numb. He rubbed a hand down his face. That, too, felt fat with numbness, as if he'd made an impromptu visit to a dentist. *This won't hurt a bit, Mr. Triplow, just lie back and let me stick you with this ten foot syringe.*

"I think we've had a blackout, Dad," Joshua whispered, slowly withdrawing his hand.

Bob sucked in a harsh breath, his son's voice taking him ridiculously by surprise.

He shifted on his butt and realized it was so numb, it hurt.

Joshua was standing at this point, as if he was going to relieve himself in his dad's lap. This was good; not his position, but the fact that he was no longer weighing him down. "Jesus," he moaned, slowly removing his glutes from the lid. He could appreciate how one would feel if they truly got kicked in the butt. "When did you get up?"

"Just now. I was woken by an announcement over the store's speakers, asking everybody to leave for their own safety due to a widespread blackout."

"Handy," Bob said almost whimsically.

"Dad, have you called mom?"

"I've tried," Bob said shaking his head. "Can't get through. The lines are—" *Are what?* "Out of action."

Joshua had the strangest feeling that while they had slept, they had slipped into his nightmare occupied by the man in black. "Are we still in Duncan's, Dad?" he stammered.

Bob took a moment to sum the situation up. "Yes, mate. The emergency lightning has kicked in. They operate when there's a power outage, like when we were at Sydney airport."

"How long were we asleep?"

"I don't know, but by the feeling in my ass, I'd say seventy-two hours."

Joshua laughed nervously.

"When was the announcement made?"

Joshua shrugged. "Five minutes ago, maybe."

"Okay. We'll leave off getting out of here for a few more minutes."

"Why?"

"We need to find that girl again. That's not going to happen if security come along and usher us from the store."

"Dad?"

"Yes, mate."

"What's the girl got to do with the man in black?"

"I was kinda hoping you could tell me that."

"I can't say for sure, and I can't say why I think what I think, but I think she's with him—the man in black. And Sammy."

"So we need to reach out to her, Josh."

"I let Sammy go, Dad," Joshua admitted tearfully. "I couldn't hang on, so he went through a doorway that led into a place that had no end. At least, I couldn't see one. And it was filled with tables and people sitting at the tables. They were all doing the same thing."

"What were they doing?"

"They were writing."

There it was: the connection. Writing. The incentive, zero-zero, zero-one, which once translated was the same that had overwhelmed communication systems. It seemed highly likely his son had caught a glimpse, seen into the other dimension, the very act of Black Eternity's desire.

"I saw something else, too. It looked like a crazy version of the man in the moon."

Bob's heart tumbled from its lofty position, decoupling from its arteries to perform this most amazing feat. It was a lucky thing he was no longer sitting on the can, else it would've been at risk of floating away in the sewers. "You've seen him before?"

Joshua shook his head.

"Do you know what he wanted?"

"He wanted me to rescue Sammy. But he scared me, Dad. He wore bells."

"Bells?"

"It just keeps getting worse," Joshua whispered gravely, with images of Old Mister Grouch's permanent disfigurement chasing through his mind, and Sammy slipping into a wash of bile-green.

Attempting to comprehend the impossible was getting them nowhere, as testified by his feet that were welded to the toilet's floor, where years of wayward urine would've been spilt and lovingly washed away by a team of dedicated cleaners.

After a moment, which couldn't be counted, Bob said, albeit with some reluctance, "We have to go." He carefully and quietly unlocked the cubicle's door and peeked out.

Everything was in near pitch-darkness, which would've been total darkness if not for the anaemic glow of the emergency lighting.

They walked from the MENS toilet block into the main store.

The contrast from the earlier hustle and bustle sent icy slivers piercing through Bob's flesh. Though his legs were moving, he was mildly curious as to how that was happening.

Surrounded by women's undergarments, a sign hung like dead weight in the emergency lighting's umbra: **20% TO 60% OFF! HURRY, LAST DAYS!**

"It certainly is," he said aloud.

Joshua was taking no notice. He was searching for the girl once more, following her mournful signing about a rainbow, boogaloo and lullaby. Again, he found himself amongst the imprisoned dolls. Their unblinking eyes pierced through the murky darkness, shining like a thousand evil stars.

The girl's singing, once more, strongest here and—

Then he was falling.

The suddenness robbed him of the opportunity to scream. It felt like what someone might experience whilst crossing a road, mistakenly looking ahead, when what they should've done was follow the road rules taught to them when a preschooler. Look both ways. Avoiding the truck that could slam into them, turning their lights out forever in a millisecond.

Maybe that was what happened to Old Mister Grouch. He hadn't been merely flattened. He'd been pulverised into a meat patty... *I'll never eat another Joe Joe's hamburger as long as I live,* Leon was saying in great big loops that went around and around inside his head.

An acidic pain expanded behind his naval and extended into his throat. Joshua's heaved. Nothing came of it but a rasping noise.

He might've been turning bodily, end over end. He might've been falling sideways, or head first. Blackness, blacker than black, surrounded him. He was falling through a vacuum, lost in complete confusion. Pilots navigating the Bermuda Triangle might've experienced a similar loss when all their navigational equipment went into a tizz.

Then out of nowhere came a bright white button of light against the vacuum of nothingness.

And it grew. Expanding like a mouth preparing to consume him whole.

Larger still.

Ever larger.

There was no rushing of air past his ears. For all he knew, he mightn't have been falling at all, but standing on the spot, the light careering towards him.

Perhaps he was still standing on Duncan's floor, and the lights were coming back on in staggered bursts that confused the senses.

Perhaps... but amongst the mental calamity, Joshua thought otherwise.

The white light enveloped him and—

Suddenly he was sitting at his school desk, in his school chair. There was a textbook open before him and a calculator off to one side.

Mrs. Bruckheimer was scribbling on the blackboard. The sound of chalk against it was ominously loud, almost shattering his ears.

She abruptly stopped, gently placed the chalk down, and started talking without turning about. "Nice of you to join us, Joshua Triplow."

Giggling sprouted from his classmates, including Leon, who sat directly opposite.

Joshua felt his face warm and knew it'd turned red, which only served to further his embarrassment.

"Would you like to regale us all with your powers of mathematical genius, and enlighten us of the answer to the equation I've written on the board?" Mrs. Bruckheimer asked callously.

Joshua wasn't gifted with such powers and she knew it, especially when it came to algebra. Basic maths had never posed a problem. Algebra, though, in his opinion was mumbo-jumbo. His strength was in words; and when the world of words met the world of numbers, the amalgamation was akin to an afterbirth from some prehistoric planet.

"Well, we're all waiting," Mrs. Bruckheimer barked into the blackboard.

Whiffling laughter rippled throughout the room once more.

He looked to his left, and Leon was sporting a toothy grin, finding amusement in Joshua's embarrassment.

"I think the mathematical genius of the class should present himself to the front," Mrs. Bruckheimer said. "Don't you think so, class?" She finally turned around.

"Yes, Mrs. Bruckheimer," they chanted in unison.

"Now!" she ordered Joshua.

What the hell's happening? He felt dizzy with all kinds of unpleasant emotions, which seemed to be crashing into each other like water fighting amongst itself to be the first droplet into a drain. He walked between the aisles of kids, the centre of attraction, approaching the board and Mrs. Bruckheimer.

"Why don't you take your time," she said with malice in her voice. "Here." She thrust a stick of chalk in his face. "Regale us." Her grin was pure nasty. Her teeth seemed larger than usual, which kinda matched her rather large eyes.

Joshua faced the blackboard properly and whispered, "Why are you being so mean to me?"

She burst into belly-laughter. "Mean? I'm not the one who strode in all hoity-toity, thinking his shit didn't stink!"

His classmates no longer restrained their amusement. They, too, started laughing without restraint.

He was a stupid little boy. All skinny and in shorts and T-shirt with shoulder-length blonde hair. He was a joke. More than that: he *was* the joke. A certainty to which the bubblegum kid in Duncan's would've agreed with his fat guts jiggling before him and, now, that of his classmates.

They stripped bare his ownership of boyhood through emasculation, while snorting in appreciation of their teacher's chastising.

"I'm not being mean to you, Joshua Triplow," Bruckheimer continued in her tirade. "You're simply a little asshole who needs to take his punishment." Then she bellowed into his face: *"NOW WRITE, YOU WORTHLESS LITTLE SHIT! WRITE THE ANSWER TO THE EQUATION!"*

Everyone had entered a state of ecstasy, tears streaming from their eyes. One girl was laughing so hard, she was slapping her table as an extension to her amusement.

No matter where he turned, everyone was having a cracking good time at his expense. Even Leon, of all people, appeared like a thermometer about to blow its top, as he revelled in the exploitations of his best friend.

By golly, Mrs. Bruckheimer was giving them all a lesson that wouldn't be forgotten in a hurry.

They began screaming, *"WRITE, YOU WORTHLESS LITTLE SHIT! WRITE!! WRITE!! WRITE!! **WRITE!! WRITE!! WRITE!!**"*

Joshua burst from the room, spilling into the corridor just as Mrs. Bitch-Tits was walking in his direction. His mind was panicking, and he sat on it hard, the act like sitting on an explosion and retaining it within limited confines. A lid to a bin within which a nuke had gone off.

"Joshua, why, you look totally mortified," Mrs. Bitch-Tits said kindly.

"I'm… I'm not feeling well." Gales of laughter continued unabated and he imagined the door, which he'd slammed behind him, restlessly jumping up and down on its hinges with the percussion. Any second, their ugly faces would start poking out, all teeth and malice, from between the crack it left around the architrave, their laughter chasing him down the corridor.

Jessica Lane looked at the door to the room. "Has Bruckheimer been at you *again?*" she said, sympathy softening her tones. "Won't be long now…" She smiled.

Just as contrary to Mrs. Bruckheimer's cruelty was Mrs.…

Joshua didn't feel right thinking of her in nasty names, but as he couldn't recall her real name, he settled for "Lisa Something-or-Another's" kindness.

"Come with me," she said, taking him tenderly by the arm. "There's fifteen minutes to go before lunch and I'm on an extended break, so you can stay with me until the bell sounds." She smiled once more. "Then you can go outside to be with your friends."

His friends? Exactly who were they?

She led him away from the chaotic classroom where everyone, including his very best friend, Leon, seemed to have gone mad. Utterly mad.

The lunch bell went.

Crossing the quadrangle, Joshua's shame and embarrassment had given way to anger. He sized his group of friends up, particularly Leon.

"What the *fuck* were you on about?" His words came forth like fire.

"Piss off," Leon said with a sneer. "You're pathetic."

Ethan and Craig were giggling.

Sammy was with them, catching Joshua off-guard. "Sammy?" He swallowed hard. "What happened to you?"

"What happened to you, you little ass-wipe? Heard you pissed your shorts and ran out of the classroom with your dick tucked hard up between your legs."

The retort swiped aside what remained of Joshua's ability to fend off insults.

A couple of boys came up from behind. He thought their names were Nathan and Dylan. Frankly, at the moment, he didn't care. Having become encircled by kids he no longer knew, they pushed him one way and the other. Laughing. He *was* the joke. Around and around he went... where he'd stop only the kids knew.

"Hey, Josh, forget them." Dylan stuck out a hand to steady his friend who was frighteningly unstable on his feet. "They're a bunch of douchebags."

"Watch it, O'Casey," Sammy warned.

"Or what?" Dylan retaliated, knowing Sammy would back down. Either that or he'd hit him one. He wasn't given to violence, but he'd stand his ground. "Come on." He and the other boy beckoned Joshua away from the pack of douchebags.

"They're my friends," Joshua argued.

"Since when?"

"They've always been my friends."

Dylan and the other boy seemed somewhat baffled. "You'll be telling me Bruckheimer's a lovely teacher next."

"She usually is."

"Earth to Mars, come in Mars. Josh, she hates your guts. But only two more weeks and the old bag is out of here. The sooner the better. I swear she's got it in for most kids, but loves that douchebag Mendoza," Dylan said as if he'd sucked on a particularly bitter lemon.

"I've known Leon all my life."

"You might've, since he lives down the road from us, but that doesn't make him your friend, Josh." Dylan looked at him closely. "Man, are you feeling okay?"

"Not really."

"That explains a lot," Dylan said, both satisfied and relieved. "We still catching up for ball after school?"

"Ball?"

This time the other boy spoke. "Yeah, Josh, ball."

With his mind in a spin, Joshua couldn't begin to even pretend that some of this made sense. "You mean skateboarding?"

"No," Nathan said. "I mean *ball*, as in base*ball*."

"That old bag has really done a number on you, hasn't she?" Dylan asked.

"Yeah, I guess." *No* was what Joshua had wanted to say. Everything was getting to him.

"Let me remind you that you hit the ball out of the park so often, we've lost ten this year. You keep going at this rate, we'll need to set up a roadside stall and sell lemonade to pay for them."

"Either that or sell our bodies to the highest bidder," Nathan added with a smirk.

"Well, in your case, we'll be reduced to selling lemonade for the rest of our lives."

Joshua wasn't able to share in their banter, however breezy it was. "What about last year?" he asked. "How many balls did we lose then?"

"'Bout the same," Dylan said without hesitation.

Nathan was shaking his head. "Nope, it wasn't *that* many."

"Well, close to it. Who cares?"

"I do. I'm the one who's gonna have to sell my body."

"What about the year before? We've been playing for a while and I've lost track of how many I've hit out of the park, never to be found again."

"As you've gotten stronger, you've also been able to *really* take a swipe at that sucker."

"So if I started weightlifting—"

"You could become Lou Ferrigno, and then become governor of California like he did. You could influence the right people and our careers would be set for life," Dylan said brightly.

"Yeah? What happened to Arnold Schwarzenegger?" Joshua liked Arnold and couldn't imagine him not doing something grand and glorious.

"Who?" Nathan asked, puzzled. Then: "Oh – that guy who won Mr. Olympia ten million years ago? Don't know."

Joshua played along with the lilt of the conversation. "If I started now and got massive arms, like Lou, how many would be hit out the park then never to be found?"

"A thousand," Nathan said.

"And in five years, which would be…?" Joshua said as if too eager in thinking of becoming the next Lou Ferrigno, whom he knew as the Incredible Hulk in that cheesy old TV show, glowing radioactive green and nothing like a governor of a state divesting itself of nuclear stores.

"Well, then," Dylan said, "by 2030 we might just be playing for real."

This was serious talk for them, to get good enough to turn their love affair of the sport into a career, so neither Dylan nor Nathan laughed.

Joshua's head-spin whirred like a bandsaw behind his eyes. He'd somehow dropped into the year 2025, where everybody and everything was different, except for one thing: him. He was the only thing that hadn't changed. If he kept managing to skip the years, by 2100 he might just be old enough to get his driver's licence.

How he'd accomplished this, he supposed, was all due to the fall. What a fall—

Fell further than you could've imagined, Joshy-Washy!

"Seriously, you're that good. You'll get signed to the Dodgers or whoever's willing to pay the highest," Dylan said rather than asked, breaking Joshua's train of thought.

"Really? I've never seen myself that way." Joshua felt sick. If he puked in the quadrangle, would anybody really care? Would anyone notice? Was any of this real? Or was it all inside his head? Perhaps his head hit the floor in Duncan's and knocked him out and this was his version of seeing the fabled white light.

"That's what's so good about being around you, Josh—you're no big head."

"Dylan O'Casey." Recognition finally set in. The kid who lived right next door to him, whom he'd never gotten to know because of distractions that hadn't allowed for what should've naturally taken place. And did Dylan in 2022 play baseball?

He supposed he could, since he didn't know much about the kid at all.

Nonetheless, three years had passed… time had skipped away from him. As had many other things. There was no *Cha Cha* here, no Leon, just honing his skills in baseball, the sidewalks and Citrus Park making way for the diamond and home plate.

"The one and only!" Dylan punched his arms into the air with enthusiasm. "There's just one hitch this afternoon: I've got a dentist appointment at 4:15 p.m., so mom's picking me up from the park. You can come if you want; it shouldn't take that long. It's just a check-up." Dylan wasn't fond of dentists or people playing around with his mouth, particularly when shiny instruments of torture laid about, ready to go to work.

"Thanks, Dylan, but I'll walk," Joshua said. He had to be with himself so he could get his head straight.

The guys had gone on talking, but Joshua had become distracted. There was a most curious girl across the way. She wasn't singing, but her voice… it was the same. Not just by a bit. But the whole nine yards.

"I'll catch up in a second, guys," Joshua said, walking over to her.

She looked about his age, ten, almost eleven. More than that: she looked like he might have pictured her if he'd had the time to indulge.

"Hi there," he said.

"Hello," she returned pleasantly.

"Do you ever sing?"

The girl looked confused. "That's an odd question."

"Sorry, it's just that your voice…"

"Sometimes. Don't you?"

"Yeah, but I stink."

She smiled and appeared to be searching for what to say next.

"What's your favorite song?"

With a degree of thought and a twist of the nose, she said, "I guess it's the one by The Mad Jugglers."

Joshua had never heard of such a group, but then this was the year 2025. "Don't know them."

"You must. *Every* kid knows The Mad Jugglers."

"Can you sing a bar?"

"Uh-uh."

"Why not."

"I stink, too."

"Betcha you don't."

"Bet I do."

"Come on, just a couple of lines."

"Well," the girl steeled herself. "Somewhere over the rainbow, where the Boogaloo rages, people go tripping, and the lullaby's out of sight."

"Wow," Joshua said, unnerved.

"You've heard of them now?" she asked, mystified by the possibly that someone actually hadn't.

"Yeah, I know who The Mad Jugglers are... now." That feeling of sickness, curdled with putrid dread, was unrelenting, spreading through him with numbing tendrils that had begun wrapping around his organs. Strangulating them. Strangulating him.

"You're a strange boy, Joshua Triplow," she said. "You haven't learned your lesson."

Yes, puking in the quadrangle would suffice quite nicely. A bit of puking and then some time to get his head straight. "What lesson is that?"

"Bruckheimer asked you to give the answer to the equation, didn't she?"

Joshua didn't signal a yes or no, but merely stared at her as if she spoke a foreign language.

"Bruckheimer asked you to do that and you didn't. Did you?" Suddenly the girl's voice had adopted the tones of a spinstery old lady. Perhaps even a diseased man-in-the-moon.

"What does it matter to you?" Joshua said, because he couldn't think of anything better to say, but it required some sort of reply.

"It matters, Joshy-Washy." Her voice sounded older still, like ancient winds that blew through a land time had forgotten. "It matters a whole heap." Her eyes were growing large and dark. Her teeth seemed to be elongating.

Joshua started backing away. "Thanks for The Mad Jugglers," he was saying.

"Forget them. Concentrate of what *you* have to do!" she said, walking after him. "It's little boys like you who should never grow up and have children."

"I'm not that bad. I play baseball," he said in his defence.

"You're a worthless little shit. Isn't that correct? You are what you are. You can't deny or run from it, so you might as well accept the truth. Joshua Triplow is a worthless little shit!"

By now, the girl's screaming had attracted the attention of all whom had congregated in the quadrangle, including his former friends.

Where were his new friends? They seemed to have suddenly vanished, abandoning him without offering the slightest support.

Those strangulating tendrils had wound even tighter around his throat. As the world spun around and around. He could barely breathe.

Chanting resonated amongst the quadrangle's horde. Their numbers had swollen from a couple of hundred to a couple of thousand. Maybe more.

"TAKE YOUR PUNISHMENT, YOU WORTHLESS LITTLE SHIT!"

The momentum self-sustaining. The chanting growing bigger and bigger. The crowd growing bigger and bigger.

One boy, almost eleven, in the middle of an amphitheatre of hate.

The percussion he'd sensed bouncing the classroom door on its hinges was now doing the same to him, as if he were standing before the world's biggest boombox, whose bass had been cranked to molecular-shattering. His teeth rattled and danced in his mouth. His stomach reverberated heavily and his bones quaked. The air was vibrating and warping the surrounding environment. The building beyond swayed, as if its foundations had suddenly become rotten and were falling apart.

He wanted to run, but the kids had reinforced their encircling scrum. Besides, it was near impossible to get a clear bearing with his eyes also rattling in his head.

The amphitheatre was getting smaller. Tighter. The crowd was closing in.

"TAKE YOUR PUNISHMENT, YOU WORTHLESS LITTLE SHIT! TAKE YOUR PUNISHMENT!"

At this rate, his body might self-destruct, detonating in an aerosol of a million tiny fragments.

Gone…

Just gone… vanished… replaced…

He staggered and had to take a rest for a moment against a road sign. GIVE WAY, it read. He slumped down its metal pole, his knees slowly tenting before him.

He must've played ball with Dylan… he must've escaped the amphitheatre of hate… but he didn't know how any of this had happened. And now, he must have been trekking his way home.

Leading up to this most memorable of occasions, he'd had his share of nightmares. In them, things had looked weird, like looking at the sun which shone a syrupy orange, as if a partly dissolved throat lozenge had been spat into the sky where it cast an amazing amount of illumination to all below. The sun didn't shine that way. It was just your regular variety of sunlight.

He felt himself entering a mild form of hypnosis, as he watched the sun bounce off his knees. He could see them as if under a large microscope. The fine lines in his skin were like criss-crossing streets. And speaking of streets, there was not a car to be heard or seen; which was good, because if there had been, the passing occupants would've been forgiven for thinking they were witnessing the destruction of a very sad, very lost and very lonely boy.

He finally got to his feet. Sense told him to stay put, that there was no good in walking home, because, like everything else three years ahead of his past life, that'd be deranged. However, sense also told him that there was no point in staying by the GIVE WAY post for the rest of his life.

Of course, he could find the nearest Duncan's and go searching for another hole in the floor, which didn't exist but didn't matter as it'd still take him under… to another life… another time. It was easy, as he had a knack of hearing the girl sing her mournful song. Because *that* girl, unlike the one he'd met in school quadrangle, was lost as well. At least, she sounded lost... very lost... lost for a long time, if the way songs were sung preceded images. Her singing a prelude to falling into a hole.

And so, here he was, entering Chasing Boulevard, once the best place to live. Now, just another horror story.

Everything seemed the same as everything thus far had. Leon had looked exactly the same. Bruckheimer had looked exactly the same... as had the school... the classroom... this street. But, after initial appearances, they had a habit of turning feral.

The trees and shrubs and houses and lawns and even the cars that sat in the driveways *looked* the same.

But what was deception and what was the real thing? What could he trust? Perhaps an innocuous shrub had the ability to strike you dead with a single drop of its poisonous sap. Or when it rained, instead of a refreshing experience, it'd burn your flesh to the bone.

That probably wouldn't be so, as everything would be dead, including the people who lived in this year. Unless immune to acidic precipitation.

He arrived at what *looked* like his house: 22 Chasing Boulevard.

Everything was in its rightful place, down to the small chip out of a corner of the letterbox's top.

As for the answer to the sixty billion dollar question—*What was he doing here?*—he was going home, of course.

Joshy-Washy was returning to where it'd all started a million years ago with the man in black. Not that he was privy to such knowledge, but if this was a game of hot and cold, such a thought was hotter than he'd ever have believed.

Besides, as he'd already determined, he couldn't simply sit at the bottom of a pole. He couldn't simply keep walking the streets until he dropped in sheer exhaustion. *I could look for a Duncan's Megastore,* he thought again. *But are there any in Corona? For that matter, are there any in good ol' U S of A?*

It was tantalizing. If things spun even further out of control, that would be the next option, after which he had nothing.

For now, that just didn't *feel* right.

On that rather ambiguous appraisal, Joshua started up the driveway, a lookalike which he'd taken ten thousand times. And though he didn't know the writers and singers, Zager and Evans, of 'In the Year 2525,' he knew enough of the words to mark this audacious and somewhat prophetic occasion.

The lyrics jagged parts of his brain with words about ten thousand years, starlight, and that maybe it all came down to yesterday if man was still alive.

He braced himself and opened the front door, his schoolbag sliding off his shoulder and down his arm.

"Where the *fuck* have you been?" his mom shouted as she stormed through the sofa room.

Joshua's spine slammed into the wall of the downstairs hallway as she raced towards him.

"I asked you to be home right after school!" she screamed. Her hair was a mess. The flesh around her eyes was massacre black. And, by the looks of her, she'd been doing a bit of self-mutilation. "I've been pulling my hair out waiting for you!" It'd been fashioned into three distinct tufts or peaks, one to either side and another straight up, reminding Joshua of the man-thing—

forget the moon—in the three-peaked hat who had stalked Sammy's upstairs hallway.

"I'm sorry, Mom. I forgot. I played ball..." Joshua said, nerves warping his voice.

"*I'll* play ball, you little shit! I'll play ball and you'll be a eunuch!" she screamed out of her head. "*GET UPSTAIRS AND TAKE YOUR PUNISHMENT! TAKE YOUR PUNISHMENT AND START WRITING AS BRUCKHEIMER WANTED YOU TO!*"

"Mom?" Utter hopelessness clouded his voice.

"*DON'T MAKE ME TELL YOU AGAIN!*"

Joshua turned and ran upstairs. He slammed his bedroom door shut and threw his bag into a corner.

His chest was heaving, his breaths enormous, hot and blustery. Sweat made his body run both hot and cold. His heart ratcheted in his chest like a fishing reel, whose drag was being taken out a thousand miles a minute by the biggest, baddest sea bass ever to haunt the waters. His clothes stuck so hard to him, they might as well not have been there. He felt utterly naked, stripped bare. *Emasculated.*

What made this so much worse was that it was perfect. Not a single article or item out of place. His room was how he'd left it before catching a flight to Australia.

With his hair hanging in his eyes, he looked over to his computer desk. Well, there at least was something that didn't fit after all. Everything was how he'd left it but for the pens and pencils, which lay strewn across the top. In the melee, he might've been mistaken, seeing things when they weren't really there. But he wasn't. Furthermore, he couldn't stand a mess. He never would've left pencils and pens in such disarray. Someone had been rummaging around in his drawers. Someone had left them there, as if they'd wanted him to see them.

He needed to write. Why did he need to write? What did he need to write? And if he started writing, would all of this horror dissolve away?

Enormous pounding started up the stairs. Items in the room rang and jumped on the spot.

His eyes dilated, as if in response to a megadose of hallucinogens.

The door slammed hard on its hinges, burying the handle into the wall's plasterboard.

His mom was sporting a huge pair of scissors, her hair messier than before. She'd been at it again. She had a mad grin stretched across her face; and though she *looked* like his mom, she was just another deception.

SNIP! SNIP!

"Let's play ball! You want to play ball? I'll help you play!"

SNIP! SNIP!

"You can still write! It won't kill ya!"

SNIP! SNIP!

The scissors were snapping their ruthlessly sharp blades together. They wanted to feed, and needed what he had.

She started her bloodthirsty chase of him around the room, snapping the scissors incessantly, the black flesh around her eyes getting darker. Something was growing out of her head. Taking form. Appearing like some obscene party hat that encased what she had hacked away at in her moments of distress.

The blades lashed out, casting manic flashes off their shiny blades.

"Moooooommmmmmmmmm!" Joshua screamed, propelling himself backwards.

She snatched a fistful of pens and pencils from the computer desk in her travels. Those not claimed went flying to the floor. Scissors in one hand, pens and pencils in the other, a hat with three peaks bouncing atop her huge, toothy grin; she was truly the epitome of lunacy.

"*WRITE, YOU WORTHLESS LITTLE SHIT!*"

SNIP! SNIP! SNIP!

TINKLE-TINKLE-TINKLE

Bells had joined the fray. Why not? Next minute the fat and jolly Santa Claus, who had burst into his thoughts of late, would burst into his room and reach into his bag of goodies, pens and pencils spilling forth as he did so in the hideously perfect addition to the year 2025. *Have you been a good boy, Joshy-Washy? Heard you've been very naughty and need to take your punishment. So I've some writing utensils to get you on your way.*

Everything in the house had begun vibrating violently. Fixtures, from door handles to light switches, picked up the airborne resonance, as if a huge earthquake was passing directly beneath the house, threatening to tear the place asunder. The earthquake's epicentre followed the footfalls of the thing his mom had become.

Joshua bolted from the room and went to run down the stairs, only that in the unfolding maelstrom his feet became entangled, and he went head first instead. It was a miracle that he didn't break his neck. Landing painfully hard at the bottom riser, his teeth clattered and brilliant chromatic sparklers shot through the roof of his mouth and then the top of his skull, while his breath instantly seared the soft lining of his nose in one massive expulsion, and seemed to vent from his eyes in which black spots drunkenly swam. He looked to where he knew the front door was, but couldn't see a thing. Everything was a blur, as if he was deep underwater, looking up to the sun high in the sky.

SNIP! SNIP! SNIP!

TINKLE-TINKLE-TINKLE

Her screaming and the snapping of scissors, cutting the air like she wanted to cut him, were approaching fast from behind.

He scrambled to his feet. Slipped. Got up. Scrambled again for the front door. Got that handle. Missed it. Went for it again. The sweat on his fingers made it difficult to grasp. But this was life or death, and so he grasped it good and hard. The handle turned. No go. The lock was on. His fingers danced manically over and around the lock.

The snapping... the bells... the shuddering house... were after just one thing, and their appetite was voracious.

In a last desperate effort, his fingers got the job done.

The door slammed into the wall running alongside it, just as his bedroom door had when the deranged thing his mom had become stormed into his sanctuary.

She lunged forth, the scissor tips diagonally swiping across his back.

Spilling from the house, as if ejected by it to land heavily on his chest, his screaming was flattened into yet another expulsion of air. His next breath was near impossible to get. Stars swarmed his eyes and his chest was on fire, seemingly rising into his head to boil his brains. Amongst the pell-mell, he found his feet and bolted onto the sidewalk of 'the best ever place to live', where the relentless pursuit begun to gain the upper hand.

Managing the impossible, he ran without a single breath to call upon, the stars swarming en masse until there was nothing but blind panic.

Somehow, he had done enough to avoid his mother's wrath. Her abusive ranting, snapping of scissors, and tinkling of bells had faded into the distance, as if somewhere in Corona, California, 2025, she had taken a dive into her own wormhole, which had hungrily opened in the ground beneath her.

Struggling for survival against a lack of breath and sheer exhaustion, it welled up inside him, the brunt of everything you'd never want to experience in a lifetime, let alone one incomplete day.

His cries weren't merely coming in heavy sobs. He was bawling.

He hid his face in his hands and slumped, once again, in that somewhere place in Corona, burying his head between his legs, with the sidewalk rapidly becoming wet with his tears. Despite the bright slivers of kindness and compassion from Lisa Something-Or-Another, Dylan and Nathan, he'd never been this frightened. This empty.

"Oh my, whatever is the matter, young man?" came the voice of a kind stranger.

Joshua couldn't look up. He didn't want to look up, knowing he'd be seen as a wretched kid. Misery etched deep into his face, his lips curled down while he cried his eyes out. Not a pretty sight. Even in the light of all that had unfolded, there was no point making it worse. So he kept his face buried.

The stranger squatted. "Now, I might be wrong, but it sounds to me as if you are in need of a friend."

Joshua babbled, "Yes." God, he felt foolish.

"It might come as a surprise, but I too have been there. Lost, that is. Yes, I have. You see, not everyone is kind to people with dark-colored skin. They think because theirs got bleached in the process of evolution that they are somehow superior." The stranger's voice was soft and friendly, and carried an accent that suggested he came from South Africa or somewhere like that. It sounded terribly familiar. "Yes, indeed, some people are most unkind, young man. But I do not think you are one of them. In fact, I think you are a very nice boy who desperately needs some help in this matter."

In his emotional tug of war, Joshua was slowly hauling in the rope, and managed to get his bawling down to hitching sobs that were coming at longer intervals. Had he a mirror, he wouldn't have seen such a wretched kid looking back at him. His lips thankfully no longer curled in a pathetic "woe is me" fashion. His chin no longer dimpled.

The sidewalk had almost dried, although the day's temperature was mild, perhaps low-twenties (72^0 F).

The stranger allowed him to come to terms with himself.

"I need to get to Duncan's Megastore," Joshua said, and was surprised to hear the evenness in his voice.

"For what you have been through, you are a most brave young boy," the stranger said.

Joshua, at long last, looked up from between his legs.

"Malinda?" Relief and comfort flooded his heart.

The stranger smiled. "Yes, that is correct. And you are Joshua." He looked around. "We cannot stay here. We must get going. It will be dark in a few hours."

Joshua wiped his face partly dry, the mildness of the day doing the rest.

"How are you here?" Joshua asked.

"I could very well ask the same of you," Malinda returned brightly. "Do you know?"

"Yeah. It's gonna sound crazy."

"I am okay with crazy," Malinda said, his white teeth a complete contrast against the darkness of his face.

"I heard a girl singing and went to look for her and... I fell through the floor."

"Well, come on, then. Let us see if we can find whatever you fell through, and send you on your way." Malinda helped Joshua to his feet and then frowned with some consideration. "What was the first thing you did when you stopped falling?"

"I was sitting."

"Where?"

"At my school desk."

Malinda beamed. "That is, then, where we must go."

"I don't want to go back to Citrus... Elementary, not in this timeline." Joshua rushed his words and they crashed together.

Malinda deciphered enough, though. "Do not worry, I will be with you."

"Have you brought your taxi?"

"Oh, no, my taxi driving days are over."

"After three days?"

"I decided that I had better things to do." Malinda once more offered Joshua a huge friendly smile.

"How did you get here, then?"

"I followed you," Malinda said with such finality that Joshua dropped any further questioning.

This was not a dream; that much Joshua had already figured out. But how they reached Citrus Hills Elementary as fast as they did was bamboozling. His feeling of disconnect was hardly mitigated when he couldn't quite remember what they did on the return to his school. Just as he hadn't been able to remember playing ball or how he'd escaped the amphitheatre… what he'd done for the remainder of the day at school. He had been helped to his feet by this kind man, they'd spoken a bit and then—*hey, presto!*—here they were before the steps leading into the main building of Citrus Hills Elementary.

The wide double doors leading into the building were unlocked. A scattering of staff cars remained in the parking area.

Malinda said to his young charge, "If anyone asks, you left homework in your desk that you need tonight."

"I hate homework."

"Let us then say that there is something left unfinished."

"Bruckheimer wanted me to answer an equation."

"Well, then. That is nice."

"No it's not."

"And I am a friendly neighbor." Malinda's insatiable cheeriness was infectious and readily sponged up, though the seriousness of the matter was greater than anything Joshua had ever known.

Walking through the semi-darkness of the building's corridors and classrooms was eerie in the absence of another living soul. Besides, he had never seen it quite this dark. The sun had started setting, and within an hour it'd be well into dusk. Their footsteps magnified in the deserted quietness, and he got the feeling he and Malinda were the only ones left alive on Earth, despite the abandoned cars in the staff parking area.

Crazy thoughts for the craziest of days.

He now stood before the door which had barely contained the barrage of ridiculing laughter on the back of Mrs. Bruckheimer's personal assault. He really didn't want to go back into that room.

Malinda stuck out a hand and opened it, saying, "We will both enter."

He was a man of his word, remaining by Joshua's side, step by step.

"Which is your desk?" he asked quietly, when he hadn't been at all interested in keeping his feet quiet coming here.

Joshua pointed.

They approached it and Malinda gestured for him to take his seat, which he did.

The darkness within the store had solidified.

The emergency lighting was beginning to fail.

Across the ceiling's vast plain, buzzing on and off, winking in and out in the darkness, several continued lighting up like flashbulbs going off in an old camera.

Bob had returned to the toy section, where he'd turned aside for what couldn't have been but a fraction of a second. However, it was in this sliver in time that his son had vanished, as if vaporizing into thin air, or sliding between a gap that had opened up in that second. A doorway to another existence.

He'd walked the aisle again and again, searching for clues which would come from things not in keeping. That was about as good as he could guess. He hadn't the first notion as to what forms those clues might take on.

Joshua had said he'd heard a girl singing, and so he'd listened intently, hearing only his own breaths washing in and out of his airways. They were unsteady and shallow, stabbing at the air. He hadn't heard the girl then, and he hadn't been able to lock in on anything of the sort now.

So he walked the store, a lonely shopper sans trolley.

What are you looking for, sir?

My son.

Oh, don't worry yourself. Children are always getting themselves lost. Security will manage to find your child. In the meantime, would you like to buy some lingerie for your wife?

Thanks, but she's in excommunication.

He pulled his mobile from his pants pocket. Looked at it. Slid it back home. Nothing had changed.

How he'd relish Sue's pragmatism. She had a fiery streak, no doubt, but her buttons had to be pushed hard to engage it. Even then, the streak was short-lived. Like a shooting star ripping through the night's fabric, it'd come and go and her pragmatism would return.

She'd say something like: *You must go with Joshua and I must stay home.*

Why had she remained rigidly stoic on this procession playing out? Had something happened that he was not aware of? Something more confronting than last Wednesday's revelation? *Indeed, that'd take some beating. After all, men from the stars don't often come calling. And no, he hadn't been selling religion or encyclopaedias. But brother, what he was selling were gold nuggets from asteroids existing in the far reaches of the Kuiper Belt.*

Had he known that while she poured herself a soda water to quench her thirst, she had also picked up the kitchen phone, he might have made the connection. No big deal in itself. Except the little man, whose tinny rhetoric had haunted the lines in

2011 across South Australia, had returned. Had he known of this at that precise moment, he too would have understood that Raoul's warning, of time being short, tended to be somewhat optimistic, leaving no room for adjustments. As it was, even the image of his wife was floating ever further away when he needed her the most. When her son needed her the most.

Lingerie, sir?

Shove it. And for God's sake, shake a leg and get security!

Having returned to the toy section, he found himself moving through the aisle with the dolls' beady eyes upon him.

The overhead emergency lighting buzzed on and off, its incandescent hue a thousand candles in those eyes, extending the full length of the aisle.

The candles were there...

And then gone...

Like his son.

But unlike his son, they returned in the flickering emergency light. Soon, even their batteries would be rendered totally powerless, as would all things not of wick and flame.

He felt those eyes watching him.

The mettle of paranormal investigators in those documentaries, which had become popular viewing, was something he'd often mused on; creeping about the darkness, searching for spectres amongst walls which had seen more than their share of tragedy. So here he was, playing surrogate investigator himself.

Something out of the corner of his eye—that was how it always happened!

He spun round and knocked into the dolls, setting one off.

Mommy, I'm thirsty. I want a hug! Please give me a hug!

He hit the box from which the stupid thing was yapping.

This set off more dolls, *Mommy, I'm thirsty! I want a hug. Please give me a hug!* They were talking over each other, their supplications unstoppable. *I want a hug. Please give me a hug!*

"What do I do now, Malinda?" Joshua asked.

"Listen," he said quietly, raising a finger to his lips.

There was the odd creak, the odd *ping*, as Citrus... Elementary's multi-storey complex was coming to grips with cooling conditions.

"I can't hear anything. Besides—"

Malinda pressed his finger harder to his lips.

Like a radio with poor reception, Joshua began to hear what was meant to be the voice, or voices, of a young girl, or girls, coming in waves. It was the kind of sound that only automation could ruin. Like the GPS woman in mom and dad's car, who delighted in voicing her opinion on their poor sense of direction, and that they might topple over a cliff. It *sounded* close enough to a real woman, but not near enough to actually be one.

"What can you hear?" Malinda whispered.

Please hug me!

"I was in Duncan's... surrounded by dolls," Joshua whispered in awe. "I think I can hear them now."

Malinda smiled his big white smile. "That is terrific." And with that he reached up, as if grasping for something floating above Joshua's head.

In the fleeting interludes of light, the dolls' eyes sparkled before going blind in the darkness. From their rows of plastic mouths, they persisted in asking for a drink and a hug from their mommies.

At full extension from the deep shadows blanketing the floor, a long, slender, dark-skinned arm latched on to Bob's ankle, cutting short the panicky cascade of what he should do next.

"*What the …!*" he yelped.

It yanked with set determination and he went down.

Not merely onto the floor.

Through the floor.

As his son had discovered earlier, he was thrust into a vacuum of utter darkness, a pin-prick of light opening beneath him. Getting larger. Ever larger.

He went through it and, as he did so, found the arm of his boy. He held on tight and they fell together.

The area of Lower Mitcham had a geologically high granite content. This content was at its highest directly beneath the store's foundations. Prior to building construction taking place, or even going on the drawing board, the depth had to be calculated. If the stria was too close to surface, it'd pose a serious hindrance to the development, as extra labor, not to mention machinery, would be required. Even though the location for the proposed store was perfect, dead-centre of a populous without overburdensome competition, cost blow-outs would jeopardize the project.

When the geologists had made their final examination of the data, it was determined that the granite stria sat approximately seven meters below surface level.

There were high fives all around and, subsequently, the centre's doors opened to customers on May 22 2003 at 6:00 A.M. Whilst assuming the typical layout of all Duncan's stores, it boasted additional lines only offered in their 'megastores.' If one was on the hunt for quality products that elicited raptures of having practically stolen them, then this was the place to gravitate.

Cash registers had started rattling minutes after the grand opening, with the store remaining at the pinnacle for turnover across Australia per capita ever since.

However, there were those who vowed never to return. Several had run out, barely waiting for the automatic doors to open and damn near careering into their glass panels, only moments after entering, hollering at the top of their lungs much to the bemusement of other bargain-happy customers. Had a record been kept—although, of course, any suggestion of such a record would've been scoffed at—it would've shown the number to be much higher than anyone reasonably suspected.

The question had been raised to store managers over the years, each attesting to a smattering of such occurrences, yet fast to point out that many had no validity, whilst the remainder often resulted in the customer themselves distraught through extenuating circumstances. Unfortunate incidences, no doubt, with managers always at the ready to extend a friendly hand; gift vouchers were the tried and tested standby. Many had accepted—the bargains at Duncan's had the mystical power of soothing those wounds—and staunch vows of disassociation were reversed.

Others had simply disappeared into the population at large. After all, a store manager's job entailed a list of imperatives as long as your arm; and chasing down one disgruntled shopper, while of great importance, was near impossible when they seemingly wanted to become just one of the crowd.

But there was the odd case which stood out, perhaps going some way toward an explanation, if one could call the mutterings of someone who'd undoubtedly experienced a hallucination going anywhere near to providing an explanation. Invariably corroborating one another, as if in cahoots of bizarre events occurring in the toy section, these folks seemed to have had a vision, in which an overactive imagination, fuelled by a heightened state of suggestiveness, simply filled in the blanks. At least, this was the one proposal that carried the most weight when giving any sort of argument to such behavior.

Several testified that they had seen and heard a little girl forlornly singing a goose-rippling song. It was familiar. Almost like "Somewhere Over the Rainbow." But it was different in that it was dark and full of tears, as if the girl couldn't find her way out of the rainbow. The kind of thing that wrenched at one's heartstrings.

Others experienced a much darker presence. Perhaps they were catching a glimpse of Darth Vader—after all these years, his popularity still maintained shelf status—and their imagination was running riot. These folks testified they'd seen a man, or at least they guessed it was a man, dressed in a hood, his vestiges that of a monk. But his eyes were pools of black oil, and he stared at them while remaining seated at a small desk, the type associated with school classrooms, his hand scribbling away at something. He never spoke; he didn't have to. His very presence was enough. Several shoppers actually fainted, and when they came to, they either told their tale to relieve the burden or withheld it for fear of ridicule and a little vacation with the nice porters at Happy Vales Sanatorium.

The storytellers amongst them all had one thing in common besides the experience; they never returned to the store. Gift vouchers aside, nothing would entice them back.

As one elderly gentleman had said, "If you gave me a winning lottery ticket, I might return on the off-chance of purchasing another, but if you think I'd return anywhere near the toy section, you need to have your head examined."

Still others had an even more terrifying experience.

After tracking down one such witness, the woman finally spoke. The store manager proclaiming his relentless detective work proved himself a hopeless outcast, where his skills were simply wasted on selling the same thing as Joe Blow in another Duncan's.

He hadn't remained in the position long. There were rumors that he'd become a private dick and that, somewhere along the line, he'd stumbled across something that would've been better left alone.

"What happened to him?"

"I believe he's pushing up daisies in Centennial Cemetery."

Regardless of his eventual fate, the woman he'd tracked down had proceeded to verbally vomit. She hadn't wanted to reveal all, but since they were asking, cope this:

"Your advertising tactics need to be reviewed. You need to take responsibility, not simply scare the living wits out of people. How do you expect that to increase your sales? Consideration in what you're doing, and the effect this may have on people, is sorely lacking. This is the toy section, for Christ's sake. We're talking of an attraction to all amount of kiddies. They're always running about the aisles, often blocking them off, so you have to choose another route to get to haberdashery. And to think it's justified or even funny to have a dwarf jester running amok, with a face that is nothing short of a horror story, is both outrageous and disgraceful. You should all be ashamed of yourselves. I mean, what are you trying to sell, at any rate? Nightmares?"

"I sympathize, but I'm afraid I don't know to what you are referring."

"Isn't that just peachy? The fallback whenever we need to worm ourselves out of the wrongs we've perpetuated. No one has the fortitude to say: 'Jeez, I'm sorry, that was my fault. It won't happen again'. Nope, all you people do is shift blame."

"We have no such thing as a dwarf jester running about the toy aisles. Perhaps it's a little kid dressed up for Halloween."

"That's months off."

"Well, I was hoping you'd understand what I meant."

"That's the problem. You lot are in sales, you should know better."

"I'm sorry."

"Can you look me in the eye and honestly state that a dwarf jester isn't scaring the bejesus out of kiddies and adults alike in the toy section? Can you honestly tell me that he doesn't have a hideously distorted face, full of eyes and teeth, wearing a gaudy outfit, including a hat stuck with bells? I bet you're going to tell me that this thing hasn't scared many children at all, if any, since he's been employed."

"No, I can't say that any child has been sacred."

"So, an admission."

The would-be detective-cum-manager shook his head. "There is nothing to admit."

This only served to infuriate the woman further. With her breath seemingly on permanent hold, her face assumed the hallmarks of hypoxia; and the hapless manager, for one insanely frightening moment, was convinced that it'd detonate, leaving her body short from the shoulders up.

The high granite content below the store's floor produced a strong electromagnetic field which fluctuated. At its peak, things came out to play, more than the dolls and characters lining the shelves of the toy section. However, those fitted with simple electronics would start engaging whatever program they'd been prescribed, either attempting to move inside their boxes or talking as if suddenly becoming artificially intelligent.

Other unusual happenings occurred as well, particularly with chronological pieces, which would simply go haywire. And anyone using a mobile phone, particularly in the toy section, would often be quite perplexed as to what transpired:

At the third stroke, the time will be twelve… twelve… o-one A.M.

One man who'd catalogued several such incidences of the girl, the monk and the jester, as well as the effect on both watches and mobiles, came up with a reasonable theory. "The ground is highly susceptible to being charged due to its disproportionately large amount of granite. In regions around the world, similar events are witnessed, the most famous being Loch Ness. It's the Casimir effect."

"The what?"

"The Casimir effect. It's what happens when a ripple in time allows a glimpse into the past or a walkway to another dimension. Theorists are often at odds whether when in a Casimir effect you're transported somewhere else, or that somewhere else is transported to you. Either way it's a portal, a doorway between two disparate times. These people are most likely seeing things that exist somewhere else—in another time and place, perhaps not even of this world. Things that can only be seen when the electromagnetic field is at its strongest."

It was a reasonable conclusion, which was met with the same results as if he'd said, *I saw a cigar-shaped object cruising the skies, and it was obvious that the technology was not that of man's.*

One astute executive of the board had abruptly turned to the panel around the conference table and scoffed, "It would appear the man is in need of some serious therapy."

❧

Wednesday, September 14, 2022
Late afternoon

An eerie penumbra of deep orange, mixed with an unhealthy dose of black, had consumed all in an unworldly presence, bearing more than a passing resemblance to a solar eclipse, in which the moon would barge between the sun and Earth.

Had the power grids been operational, there'd have been more than a smattering of streets bathed in streetlight, as their photo-sensitive chips reacted to the deteriorating conditions.

As it was, traffic had rapidly divested itself of such travels as the afternoon wore into evening, with the heat transforming pavements into inhospitable tracks and the streets into rivers of tar.

The city and its vast sprawl of suburbs appeared like wastelands after an apocalyptic event.

On Nesmith Drive sat just one car. Surrounded by white parallel markers that shone like bones across the parking lot of Duncan's, it laid emphasis to the total lack of life.

From choked trolley bays, several of their occupants had escaped. They littered the segregated expanse like wayward pets abandoned by bargain-happy shoppers, who had renounced materialistic fervor to snaffle an even better deal: their own lives.

Plastered on both sides of the car was a taxi decal, and an advertisement on the trunk told the beleaguered atmosphere travelling from the west that chicken-flavored Pringles were just the thing to brighten up your day.

The taxi number: 151.

Bob and Joshua flew as white misty orbs. The sensation was exhilarating, and Joshua was reminded of the need to wear a helmet while the wheels of his *Astra-Links* sizzled down the steep inclination of Cresta Verde Drive. He'd felt like an eagle then; but now, he was a rocket running on jet propulsion.

No more than mere specks of dust, they cut a path through the darkness of a strange existence; and saw what no other, including Bob in 2011, had ever seen in the existence of everything that ever had been or ever was.

This realm was neither vast nor expansive. In its mockery of such definitions, it defied the senses, overwhelming cognitive processes and rendering these intrusive space travellers to cavemen who'd taken their first tentative steps into the great unknown.

The darkness stretching beyond all horizons was a speculative judgement at best, and one that relied solely on the imagination of just where those horizons might be. They must be somewhere. Out there.

Not a thing existed in the perpetuity except for endless strings that floated like undulating highways on the surface of a gentle breeze, their soft white illumination readily absorbed by the darkness. If Bob could strike a match, would it glow, or would its feeble presence be immediately snuffed out? The darkness was of such totality.

Their bodies of misty white now travelled between the corridors of such strings, like spaceships on autopilot, their destination predetermined.

A small breakaway cluster shot from one and came directly for them at lighting speed, starting way out there somewhere before it was upon them in an instant.

They could see it was a concretion of countless balloon-like entities. Though the cluster was comparatively small, neither would've been surprised had they learned it was made of thousands of individual bodies.

The cluster abruptly came to a halt before hovering around them, laughing. It was a common reaction to laugh when others laughed. But these balloon-like creatures were downright menacing. Theirs was the kind of laughter that forebode stormy weather ahead.

Barely audible was an undercurrent of faint chatter, as if they were communicating to one another, the kind of senseless gibbering possessed by the completely insane.

Each was endowed with a stick-figure face: two black dots for eyes, a vertical black slash for a nose, and a horizontal one for a mouth. These sketchy representations worked in fits and starts at a maniacal rate, the faces contorting within milliseconds, as if by surges of involuntary spasms.

Their interest was that of an army of rabid dogs. They came at Bob and Josh in a brutal assault of coordinated attacks, darting in before sharply turning aside. There was no doubting that these balloons were attempting to find a weakness that exposed them. Then what? Possession. Insanity.

Bob and Josh could do no more than watch on helplessly. They had no voice. They had no body. They had no control over their actions. They were passengers within the misty orbs, which were not in the least bothered by the attention bestowed upon them.

In the distance dawned a disruption.

It stood stark against the darkness and strings of illumination, looking for all intents and purpose like one enormous pus-filled cyst.

Once again, reasoning was stretched beyond limits.

This sure was one nifty ride, the type to send you bugaboo, and running to all quarters while flicking a finger over your lips and making the sound of a five-year-old having a silly turn. Perhaps this could become a regular attraction at an annual fair, where children hollered and whooped all around, while the plasticity of your very sanity was severely put to the test. *Please, keep the change, it was worth every last cent! I didn't lose my lunch but I sure lost my mind!*

Bob guessed that it might be a new breed of galaxy that he could only liken to a cyst, as there was nothing else he could compare it to.

Joshua, on the other hand, saw it more as a snotball of galactic proportions. After all, if those balloons could sneeze, it had to collect somewhere.

As the balloons had previously, it was approaching at breakneck speed.

Things didn't happen at a saunter in these here woods.

But then, weren't they the ones doing the approaching this time round?

While Joshua determined that there was zero comparison to the *Astra-Links'* hyperdrive on Cresta Verde Drive, he couldn't help but continue feeling exhilarated, despite every cell in his body tingling as if charged with a dangerous concoction of electricity.

Surrounding the cyst or ball of snot, depending on whose eyes were doing the interpretation, were more strings of those balloons. Overall, their endless highways, whose routes sinuously washed around the galaxy, bore more than a passing resemblance to the proverbial take-away restaurant that defied yielding to the pressure of redevelopment. Joe Joe's Hamburgers seemed open for business.

A grisly hue of light toffee brown, like rancid fat, reflected ever brighter off the misty orbs as they closed in at frightening speed. If this was a galaxy, the usual players were starkly missing.

There were no stars, no planets, not even the odd asteroid. In fact, it seemed to be entirely enveloped in a membranous film that rippled in the vacuum of space.

Toffee-colored snot, Joshua's mind insisted. *Gross!* He felt himself moan, the expression coming from within, as he didn't seem to have a mouth to speak of, let alone speak with.

Caught in its gravitational field and closing in ever faster, the galaxy devoured everything to become all-consuming. The orbs were on a collision course, and there was not a thing that either Bob or Josh could do about it, except fill their heads with screams.

Bob braced. Joshua braced. The countdown to impact was on. Three… two… one…

Their screams seemingly blowing their minds apart until the spectacularly anticlimactic conclusion, upon which their spaceships nonchalantly slowed for their feet to touch solid ground with all the flare of a cat falling from the tree. There was no jarring, no jolt, just a smooth touchdown.

The Casimir effect had transported them to a place far over the rainbow…

For a very long while, Bob and Joshua stood motionless, lost within themselves, neither able to speak, think, nor feel.

But as if administered an intravenous shot of adrenalin, a slow cascade of their senses began to flow. Like heavy gray curtains parting without any propriety to rush, the flow was both warm and gratifying. The two stared into each other's eyes, coming to the realization that they hadn't gone mad.

Apparitions, Bob thought. *That is what we are.*

Whilst there was no way to verify such a thought, they formed a rather profound segue for developments to come.

"Well," he started, struggling for his senses. "That was an experience I suppose you can raise at your next show and tell."

Joshua appraised his dad with groggy eyes. He couldn't hold his head steady, and the world—wherever that was—continued to sway.

"I've seen those bastards before," Bob muttered. "In Adelaide…"

"Me too," Joshua mashed his words. "In my nightmares, and on Snowbird Lane the day Old Mr. Grouch was found pancaked on his front lawn. They were huddled against houses and under trees here and there. They don't seem to like light."

Bob floundered. Those gray curtains were still parting. "What happened to you at Duncan's? Where did you go?"

Joshua couldn't explain himself. He'd fallen into another reality. Another time. A world where reality and fantasy had no boundaries. One was the same as the other, each having mixed and merged. He supposed it was true of all realities. If someone had a double of themselves in another time and place, what was to say they couldn't do the same thing? Who was to say that this wasn't happening all the time? Only those to whom it was happening didn't get the full nine yards, and so their recollections of such transpirations were merely reduced to their own fantasies, the kind kids have all the time when apt to daydreaming.

And wasn't he that type of kid?

Did he merely go into a daydream? Was that it? Had he stumbled across the answer?

In the end, what he believed, at a pinch
Pinch hitter knocks it out the park!
didn't much matter.

But perhaps, just perhaps, some of that reality had been embellished with a generous dose of shitty fantasy, like an old married couple who never got out of the house, but certainly got under each other's feet; and Joshua's mom was a pretty good mom after all. Unlikely to mutilate her son because he was late getting home from school. And with even sharper pangs, as if he had swallowed broken glass, he could never believe he and Leon would ever share acrimonious feelings towards each other. *Never!*

If all this was true, even if only a sprinkling, had he merely borrowed that Joshua Triplow's body for the day? And for what reason? He'd followed the singing of the lost girl because that meant something. Right?

And why had he'd seen in several of the characters, including his mom, the face of the man-thing in the three-peaked hat?

A mixing of reality and fantasy, Joshua thought again. *For what means?*

"Josh," his dad prodded, breaking Joshua's introspection, whilst the gray curtains within himself parted altogether. Bob's attention suddenly turned from his son to what he hadn't been able to see until now. He shut his eyes. Waited. Opened them. "Oh, no." The expression dragged from his mouth by the same force that softened his knees. "Where have we come?"

God help him. He knew.

Joshua blinked aside the remaining cobwebs of introspection and followed his father's gaze. Like a monument to all the things you'd never wish for, it was both impressive and daunting. And it meant to be both. It didn't try and camouflage what it was.

This was the beginning... the end... the future... for whomever was unlucky enough to find themselves ensnared.

"What is it, Dad?"

"It's where I grew up."

"You grew up in that?" Incredulous. "A... church?"

"It's no church, Josh. But, by God, the children here should've been prayed for."

Taking his son's hand, Bob embarked on the first tentative steps towards the unthinkable which should have been lost in the past. "Stay close. And don't go on your way, even if you hear that girl singing."

As they crossed a large expanse of shiny-white gravel, the tiny stones crunching ominously underfoot, Joshua cringed at the perverse sight which lay off to their right. The image of children even contemplating the large swing set and slipper dip, in an atmosphere cloyed with sinister intent, seemed offensively implausible.

Facing forward, it was necessary to crane his head back as far as he could. Monolithic bricks rising ever further from the ground on their approach was no optical illusion. Set within them were doors that seemed to reach into the clouds hovering overhead like curdled milk, making him dizzy, domineering over his diminutive presence which had no right to stand before them, but would be eagerly accepted regardless.

He snapped his eyes down and shook the oppressive dizziness from his head.

The doors, now of skyscraper proportions, were aged rough, and the wood had started rotting in several places. Each was adorned with gnarly steel hinges and handles, as well as bolts the size of a well-muscled arm. The steel had rusted, over how many years, to set nasty stains clawing their way down to the bottom. The stonework at the base puddled with the same nasty rusty-red. It looked like blood.

Bob reached forward, his hand unsteady.

"Dad," Joshua warned.

Wise to be cautious, but as Bob had thought on several occasions throughout this perilous journey into Black Eternity, his choices were twofold. With his heart pounding fiercely in his chest, and his arms the weight of ten men or more, he struggled to manage the distance between the doors and his outreached fingers… but it was either move, or everything he knew would be lost.

And so he pushed.

The doors opened smoothly and effortlessly. For all the rust, their huge thick-metal hinges emitted not a sound. Their massive bulk gliding back, opening wide...

Onto Bob's past…

And Joshua's future…

RETURN OF THE STORM

~~

Moments prior to Joshua being disturbed from sleep in the MENS restrooms of Duncan's...

> *In a place far over the rainbow*
> *The Boogaloo is out of sight*
> *In a place far over the rainbow*
> *Everyone's lost in a lullaby...*

At an outpost in the heart of the North Pole, a global scientific collaboration was in full swing. The goal was to study the effects of global warming on polar ice caps in the first quarter of the twenty-first century. The group of dedicated men and women had been, for the past six months, collating measurements against a plethora of historical data, which were systematically uploaded into what was building to be a comprehensive compendium. Today was no different than any of the others, until their activities were plunged into silence.

The aurora borealis had been suddenly wrenched from the sky. Its dancing veils of blue and green light, with hints of red, had simply vanished.

The silence lasted but seconds, yet felt like hours to those caught in its grip.

Finally someone spoke and, all at once, the collective scrambled into a hive of activity, needing to make sense of the phenomenon. But what they couldn't know was that the unfolding events were going to get a whole lot worse.

For this group of specialized individuals, it seemed that it wasn't their day. Confusion with an overwhelming dose of frustration reigned, as fingers danced feverishly across computer keyboards and equipment to no avail.

For now, generators continued providing the overhead light for their immediate sight; but otherwise, unless they could receive and send messages through telepathic means, they were blind. Amongst the rows of laptops patched into some of the four thousand satellites orbiting Earth's outer atmosphere, there was nothing doing. External hard drives, monitors and audio/video devices were rendered to junk.

It the middle of each monitor sat an increasingly infuriating offer:

Would you like to connect to the internet?		
Yes	Cancel	Work Offline

This phenomenon was by no means localized to the North Pole.

Sweeping the northern hemisphere with the brutal power of an unstoppable juggernaut, a storm of pitch darkness KO-ed technology back to the age of the abacus, and rekindled conjecture surrounding the eerily similar events of 2011.

Within a short time, all electrical systems failed. Globally.

Once more, the Perfect Storm was being debated in excited chatter throughout rooms of learned souls the world over.

Including those at the North Pole.

Unfortunately, such chatter was isolated to each respective group, as communications had not so much ground to a halt as they had been ripped from the socket. Ironically, this included the very task force that had been established in hindsight from the 2011 event.

Solar flares had been the easiest culprit to blame then, in spite of it falling well short of any definitive explanation of the true nature responsible for the significant disruption. Yet again, everyone was caught blindsided, having overlooked the one critical element. Obsessed with ensuring the safety of the world from incoming incursions, whether it be from the sun, or perhaps a cosmological body such as asteroids, radiation bombardment from pulsars, or even advancing black holes, no one had considered that everybody, everywhere, would be rendered both visually and audibly impotent in the passing of a single second.

Man's absolute reliance was also his greatest flaw.

If this was a storm, it was like none other ever witnessed or recorded throughout Earth's history. In today's rhetoric, people love to say 'It's gone viral.' Suffice to say that this had gone way beyond that.

A darkness had encroached upon both hemispheres of Earth, taking out power grids one after the other, like a billion stars sequentially dying.

Man and the Earth had been thrust into an alien darkness that had snatched the last ray of sunlight from the lands, as it did the last electrical pulse, leaving those who bore witness in stunned silence, many of whom stared agape at the strangely blackened sky, wondering if the sun would shine again.

The Australian Bureau of Meteorology Centre (BMRC) tracked this disastrous unfolding with startling clarity, until their trusty machines of cutting-edge technology were rendered to junk.

One fellow uttered, as much to himself as any colleague standing within earshot, "Do you think we'll come back online?"

From somewhere in the benighted room came, "No, I fear we're down for the count."

The northern hemisphere had been first to feel the full brunt of the storm, which blanketed both the stratosphere and ionosphere before rolling across the equatorial line.

Peruvians had had a peculiar incident only nights before, when their radios had belched forth one helluva scream. On this occasion, the dramatics were much more intense, if less obtrusive over the airwaves, as each was instantly snafued to meaningless static... and then... nothing.

On the outskirts of Cusco, where the city sprawl gave way to ever-fragmented villages and larger areas of barren wilderness, it seemed that Rosa Marquez' El Chupacabra was back to wreak havoc, and leave a trail of mutilated animals as well as human beings in its passing.

Only Rosa's fears were something of the past themselves, as she was in none too good a state to care. In fact, Rosa had joined an instant circus act... and, brother, could she fly! Just add a touch of madness and watch her go, boys and girls! Thrill to the spectacular heights Rosa Marquez can achieve on her flying trapeze! Whoopde-do! Whoopde-do! Whacka-whacka-whacka!

The mad ones, which most described as glowing white balloons with mean little stick faces, moments before joining them, had started falling from the skies in vast sheets. It was rather pretty really... until people suddenly found that they could fly, and the screaming started.

Had those on Anphilan 4 been observing the wondrous transformation of their neighboring inhabitants, they'd have seen nothing. The third planet from the sun in its solar system had simply vanished. But now and again, a blackened sphere could be glimpsed still in orbit, appearing as if something had scorched it barren of all life. Some bright spark on Anphilan 4 was bound to have concluded, after kicking back with a margarita in hand, or a version thereof, *It looks rather dead, doesn't it, my dear?*

But they had stopped observing their neighbors long ago. They had their own lives to get on with, and options to explore in an ever-developing universe. Besides, after a few margaritas, nothing much mattered and observations were purely internal and often incidental.

The only ones from Anphilan 4 who did know about it were caught in the same doomsday as everybody else around them.

The Elder sat speechless, motionless, in his bunker deep below Earth's crust.

Tomorrow... it all came down to tomorrow.

And success...

∽

In a place far over the rainbow
The Boogaloo is out of sight
In a place far over the rainbow
Everyone's lost in a lullaby...

As for real panic on the world's streets, there was surprisingly little.

At the moment.

Primarily, the reason came down to the fact that people were unable to send their messages of dread hurtling across space and time via their mobiles and tablets. There was no Twitter, no TikTok, no Facebook, no Instagram. In fact, many were at a loss as what to do and left staring blankly into screens and waiting for their world to come back to them.

Those in the southern hemisphere had begun to catch wind of the maelstrom blanketing the northern hemisphere before news networks there began failing across the continents, after which they heard no more and so knew no more.

It is said that ignorance is bliss. What people do not know does not worry them. Without a platform, panic cannot attain a foothold. Not knowing what was happening in Uncle Henry's backyard over in the next state, the next country, on the opposite side of the world, left folks wondering, but panic was generally not part of the purview. At least, not at the very outset.

It wasn't just those frostbitten scientists in the North Pole with global warming on their minds who carried serious misgivings. There were many scattered across the world who shared the same sentiment. But at no time would they had considered anything beyond Earth's continued existence, because anything beyond that was inconceivable trollop from the worst of the worst sci-fi schlock horrors.

Profound doubt and misgivings—yes.

Panic—well, that was on the back burner, simmering away quite nicely, like baked beans in a slow centrifugal dance.

Being the CEO magnate of Crystal Bell, Malcolm Edwards was, as usual, burning the midnight candle. Whilst metaphoric, it was also true: he was literally burning a candle, and it must surely have gone midnight. This penchant had fostered much displeasure in his wife over the years. She'd often remarked that their three children—and why had he bothered?— were growing up with nothing more than a photograph for a father.

This too was true, Malcolm Edwards had to concede, which saddened him deeply as he stared from the lofty windows of his 34th floor office into the abyss. Yet for as successful as he was in the role of CEO, he was equally helpless in changing his home life.

"Global warming," he muttered, not believing for one second that this was the cause for the abyss beyond, but unable to fashion what he saw into anything better.

He so wished the air purifiers, compliments of Bob Triplow, were in place and running. Then again, they wouldn't have been, as they too would've been dead as a doornail, so to speak. But it would at least go some way to appeasing his mind.

Man had done a pretty good job fucking up the world and, whilst the bottomless darkness outside his benighted office mightn't be entirely to blame on this, he couldn't help thinking that it might have *something* to do with it.

Whatever *it* was...

The only thing that worked were the phones, if you could call it that. Because usually they were used to contact business associates—or one disgruntled wife—yet all he could manage to get was something eerily similar to the recorded voice of the 'time man' who'd tell you quite faithfully, yet without a skerrick of emotion, that you were letting your children down, yet again, when you dialled his service.

Quite odd, really, as this service had long been put to rest; people had been told that they no longer required such a service. Yet the military still relied on a similar system. Was that what this was? *Odd*, he thought again, on the back of which he added, *Such are the turn of events on this Tuesday the 13th of September 2022.*

Thank God it's not a Friday. That'd have made things doubly bad.

He fiddled with his Rolex. The illuminated hands were quite a fascinating affair in the darkness. Rather spellbinding in the way they flew about the face. Little green specks in helter-skelter.

The building was creaking and twinging, as if traversed by a multitude of restless spirits.

Suddenly, Malcolm Edwards, CEO magnate—except to his family, who thought of him as merely a photograph dad— gasped, dropping his Rolex which he'd removed from his wrist.

On the far horizon were countless white orbs.

"Fuck!" he gasped, once more, before turning to his desk and fumbling about for the binoculars which resided in the second drawer down on the left.

He often enjoyed stargazing when here late at night, and nothing but a pair of Barska Cosmos Binoculars was good enough to truly get intimate with the stars.

More than your wife, hey, Malcolm ol' buddy

He brought them to his eyes with unsteady hands. Looked… and struggled to comprehend.

It would seem that it had begun raining way out south.

Only it wasn't raining water droplets from laden clouds. Nothing so prosaic for this night of thrills and chills.

Malcolm slowly lowered the binoculars, yet continued staring at the far horizon. He swallowed hard, cold sweat breaking out over his body.

He returned to looking through the binoculars. "Can't be," he whispered while the building creaked and groaned with those restless spirits. "How can balloons be *raining* from the sky? It's *impossible.*"

What was more impossible was that they seemed to have been joined by hordes of people.

Helium balloons?

He never did trust those lighter-than-air suckers, especially the great big ones. Always of the belief that they were apt to carry you away, and you'd be forced to hang on and go wherever the winds swept you.

∽

Tuesday, September 13, 2022
11:30 P.M. or thereabouts

Sue Triplow was amongst the extreme few who knew the true cause behind that darkness. She'd done her apprenticeship and she'd met a deranged Englishman who had come from the stars with bad tidings to offer. Unlike Malcolm Edwards, she hadn't had to spend a hefty sum on a pair of Barska Cosmos Binoculars; he simply rocked up on her doorstep bearing haunting condolence cards… the type that were likely to get you killed. Along with everyone else.

She might've hoped in vain—because it was better than not hoping, at all—that it wouldn't get much worse, but life was unravelling at a horrifying pace as she and Marlene prepared cold lasagne for dinner at Marlene's kitchen counter.

Sue was not a callous woman, so she wouldn't say what was on her mind: *They allow a prisoner the right to one bang-up meal before being led away to the gas chamber. Guess cold lasagne's as good as it's gonna get.*

They were working by candlelight.

There were more candles flickering away on the coffee table in the sofa room, around which sat Zach and Leon.

"Dad, I'm scared," Leon said in a small voice.

"There's nothing to worry about, Leon. It's just a blackout." Regardless, Zachary was plenty uptight.

"It doesn't feel like 'just a blackout.'"

"What does it feel like, then?"

"Menacing." Leon didn't hesitate. "I wish Josh was here."

Marlene and Sue entered the sofa room bearing plates of lasagne, and the candles they'd worked by. As far as Leon was concerned it had about as much appeal as hamburgers with heads for meat patties. "I don't feel hungry, Mom."

"Leon, you've got to eat. You didn't have breakfast or dinner, and your lunch was still untouched in the box after school. Again."

"You didn't have dinner either," he countered.

"That's why Sue and I prepared this. It's your favorite." Marlene sat next to him on the sofa whilst Sue took the remaining sofa chair next to it.

"Not tonight." Leon was sounding very scared and alienated.

"You know, Leon," Sue started, "I wish Bob and Josh were here, too, but we're here."

Leon offered a sad half-smile in which his hopes lay bare. "Maybe we can all start getting together every night for dinner."

"Huh—two nights in a row, I'll begin to overstay my welcome."

"Not at all, Sue," Marlene said, appreciatively. "I'm glad you took up our offer as you did last night. It does feel... right. And, I agree, we should do this more often. *All* of us," she was quick to add.

Sue didn't dare think too far ahead. "It sure does beat knocking about in the dark by oneself and the candlelight does add that certain something," she said, not ungratefully.

Zachary approached the same question as he had tried on yesterday morning. "Where have they gone?"

Sue took a moment and it was obvious that she was thinking things over. "I told you before."

"I know. It's just *I'm not buying it* things seemed to have gotten very strange, very fast, and it just so happens to have coincided with their sudden departure to Australia." He paused before adding, "Patrick Nesmith... a family friend, right?"

Sue's determination to remain closed-lipped was evident, and Zachary had had enough. It was time for the adults' version of 'truth or dare.' "Several nights ago—Sunday night, Monday morning—I received a phone call from a man stating that Bob and Josh were in the gravest of danger. He asked me to help prevent this from happening." *Well, honestly, he hadn't given me any choice in the matter, even if I'd wanted it.*

Marlene sat astride the chair in which her husband sat, her mouth agape. Her eyes, like her son's, made large pools of astonishment in which the light of the candles danced erratically, the way lit candles did even when there wasn't a breath of air to stir the flame.

"What did you do?" Marlene managed to ask... as if the night's peculiarity needed any assistance.

"I prevented the gravest of dangers from happening..."

"How?" Her breathing had increased to such a state, one could've been forgiven for thinking she'd returned from a brisk walk around the block. The sheen of sweat adorning her face was the perfect compliment. All she needed now was a Fitbit to tell her the success of her accomplishments.

Sue merely observed Zachary, as if he'd suddenly become a pinpoint of interest.

"I used a—" He had to think fast. "A lozenge."

"A lozenge?" His wife's stunned amazement was hardly mitigated by this unbelievable revelation. "On what?"

"A man."

"How do you subdue a man with a lozenge?"

Zachary wouldn't say *exactly* how the man was subdued, but he did say, "It relaxed him, allowing the clean-up crew from the government to step in and take charge."

"Zachary Mendoza." Marlene was both perplexed and not at all convinced. "The government called *you*? Of all people, they decided to pick up the phone and dial you, asking for a stranger to take a lozenge."

He nodded. "I asked the same of the man on the phone, and he said if I didn't, it'd be too late by the time the officials arrived. That there'd be only cadavers to wrap up and cart away."

"Where did this 'exchange' take place?" Marlene was lost in the numbness of utter wonder, looking at her husband as if he was someone she no longer knew. Her fictitious Fitbit might have sounded an alarm warning her of a heartbeat that had gone out of whack.

"Outside Bob and Sue's." Zachary's tone was a strange mixture of both guilt and justification.

"The man who called you, who was he?" Sue asked, thinking: *Raoul.*

"He didn't say, except that he was from the government."

"How could you be sure?" Marlene asked.

"Lucille Goldman's midnight dancer," Sue interrupted introspectively, yet speaking aloud.

Zachary was nodding.

"*What* did you *do?*"

"Nothing. As I said, I merely offered him a lozenge." Nerves jangled Zachary's voice.

"How did you come by it?"

"It was… mailed to me…"

"By this mysterious government man?"

Zachary nodded, sensing his beloved wife backing him into an inescapable corner.

"What was in the lozenge?" Marlene's eyes had grown even larger. The flickering candles were like a city of tiny campfires scattered throughout them.

Zachary looked at his friend's wife and said with a heavy dose of compassion and dread, "Bob and Josh went to meet Patrick Nesmith, who was dying… so you said. I can't help but feel there's a connection between that and the phone call I received."

"Zachary Mendoza, I'm asking you a question." Marlene's voice sent a chilly current through the stifling heat.

Leon sat amongst this discourse, spellbound. Listening to the adults chatter around him was both frighteningly entertaining as well as draining. A movie couldn't have done so poorly. *Top critics rave: 'The characters lack vitality whilst wading through nonsensical dialogue. The confounding problem: how to star-rate such a tawdry mess?'*

Zachary looked at his son, who was staring at him in a rather curious manner. "I don't know what was in the lozenge." He licked his lips. The lasagne was so yesterday sitting amongst them, like the painful aunty who'd popped in unannounced with bowlfuls of that unappealing porridge. "It subdued him. That's all."

"Then what?"

"He was listening to Jefferson Airplane's 'White Rabbit,' and then he disappeared down a rabbit hole. The next day his car was gone, and both Bob and Joshua were safe."

"You don't know what happened, do you?" Marlene asked.

"Not for certain." It'd be rather foolish of him to reveal what *did* happen, so best to leave things as they were. "But it's the only thing I do know. It's what I saw."

Marlene brought a hand to her face, not knowing whether she wanted to cry or wipe the sweat from it. Her conviction remained in tatters.

The mercury in the hallway barometer had the ambient temperature at a staggering 120 degrees Fahrenheit.

"I had to act, Marls. The alternative, if I hadn't, I could never have lived with. If it means anything, I do believe what the man said on the phone." Zachary then returned his attention to Sue, no longer able to look his wife in the eye, and feeling less relieved from breaking his silence than he'd hoped.

"You want to know who Patrick Nesmith is?" Sue asked.

Zachary nodded; but frankly, the look in her eyes made him think it would be better not to know. She too had campfires flickering in them, but there was something else, wasn't there? Something ominous.

Before she answered, she claimed her mobile phone from the coffee table and dialled. Without listening, she held the phone out to him.

He took it with the care someone might take when handling fine crystal or an unstable hand grenade and put it to his ear, because what better place to secure a dodgy relic of war?

At the third stroke, the time will be twelve... twelve... twelve... twelve o-one A.M.

Peep! Peep! Peep!

At the third stroke, the time will be twelve... twelve... twelve... twelve o-one A.M.

"I don't understand. Is this *really* the government eavesdropping?"

"At some point in a history lost to this universe, something went tragically wrong with Patrick Nesmith. He started inviting this darkness in." She loosely swept a hand about her. "The invitation that he used was 'zero-zero, zero-one.' Funny how it's been slowly infiltrating our phones until that's all we can hear, isn't it? Funny how nothing works, but we can still hear this incessant repetition. It's like it doesn't belong to this world; yet there it is, in our phones." Sue had her legs curled up on the sofa chair, looking casual in her repose, not at all like someone giving last rights. "And even that is deteriorating, with more twelves than a just hours ago."

She glanced at her watch, Zachary his.

Neither Leon nor his mom wore watches, but if they had, they would've followed suit. This cosy little get-together seemed to require this ritual to be performed.

Sue smiled and said, "Guys, if you want, look at the Karlsson on the far wall."

They did this and Zachary forgot his watch, preferring the company of his family's gaze on the Karlsson.

Behind its cipher of glass were drunken hands verifying the little man in the phone's ominous rhetoric, before they whizzed off around its face, spilling forth all amount of times, only to once more tremulously hold at one minute past midnight.

The antics transfixed the family's gaze.

The hands rocked around the clock yet again, perhaps in search of Bill Haley and the Comets.

In the universe of darkness, the ember of hope fluttered, threatened to puff into non-existence, then caught. Blown by dark winds determined to snuff it out, Sue found herself on a rollercoaster of violent loops, each supported by the rails of pure desperation for her own family. Though she was lucky to be with friends, she realized, and wondered how many across the world would be enduring this ordeal alone. And in the dark.

Sue recalled, for the second time in as many days, The Beatles' 'Day in the Life,' something which felt like she had mulled over a very long time ago. Following the man who had blown his brains out, the mental jukebox of yesteryear coughed and, in doing so, carted The Beatles away, before dropping another vinyl disc into position and settling its needle into place. The latest offering certainly summed up the state of affairs, with Phil Collins' foreboding chords opening 'In the Air Tonight.'

I can feel it alright, as I've seen what it's capable of. And whilst my pain doesn't show, how could I forget the moment I seem to have been waiting for all my life? How could have I forgotten?

The dead man's masquerade had gotten underway, the dance building to a deadly crescendo. And again, she wished for nothing else than to be with her family.

But she couldn't, and that was all there was to it.

"He's the man in black," she finally said, nodding at the Karlsson. "What you see in the clocks, what you hear on your phones, comes compliments of the man himself."

Leon's stomach had begun cramping, his lips numb. "Josh's gone to *meet* the man in black?"

"Yes, Leon, that's exactly where he's gone, along with his dad." Sue smiled tenderly and then took a mouthful of lasagne. Boy, she was feeling suddenly peckish. Might as well dig in. After all, could well be her last meal.

"He lives in Adelaide?" Zachary asked incredulously.

Sue laughed softly. "Not exactly. He disappeared down a rabbit hole, too, and both my husband and son have gone down that hole to meet him."

"To save Sammy?" Leon asked.

"To save everything." Sue took another mouthful of lasagne.

The Mendozas stared at her, as Marlene had stared at her husband moments before.

They did this while Sue relished the scrumptious mix of pasta and tomatoes, with just the right hint of herbs to give that authentic mama's touch, before swallowing and then asking, "Marlene?"

The woman yelped a little. She was hanging onto her son and he to her, wondering, as was Zachary, what was coming next. "I do enjoy cold lasagne, but this is exceptional," she said, stabbing a fork in its direction. "Where *did* you get the recipe? Or is it another Marlene special?"

⌒

Sue went to the bathroom, hanging onto a candle. Its soft illumination set an eerie atmosphere amongst the darkness. And people actually found candlelight romantic? Maybe shards of glass under their fingernails would be appealing. She shut the door.

The window was open. She went to close it, but then jumped back with such a start the candle went out.

Her heartbeats and breathing were enormous instruments in her head. No room even for Phil Collins' dirge-like procession. She remained dead still. Either that or she'd die.

The bathroom was lit by a soft white glow that cast moving shadows amongst its fixtures as it slid past.

She couldn't see them, but they were close, just beyond the window's view.

Balloons… glowing and laughing.

And they were on the hunt.

She remained a statue until the light faded altogether, then belted from the bathroom, following the candlelight into the sofa room.

"Shut all the curtains, as fast as you can. And be very quiet," she said in a hurried whisper.

She approached the candles sitting on the coffee table and blew them out.

"Close the curtains, *now*."

"What the hell for?" Zachary said, feeling his stomach tighten into a knot before rolling over to play dead. "We can't see a thing."

"Good, then *they* can't see us."

"*What* can't?" Panicked.

"Corona is being visited by things you want nothing to do with."

Sue wasn't exactly keen on the idea of flying through the air, whilst imparted with utter madness.

Kill me fast, she was thinking. *At least allow me that.*

An avalanche of splintery rungs swept down from above—wherever that was—and out of an impregnable darkness that, like the clouds outside, seemed to shift in curdled currents. The staircase spilled into yawning dimensions that swallowed you the moment your feet passed the skyscraper doors and entered *the rainbow*

a place of no return.

From the corner of his eye, there and then gone in a transient wisp, Joshua was gripped by what passed through his vision.

Bob misinterpreted this reaction and, without averting his attention from the hallway disappearing into the lightless depths to his right, urged, "*Stay close.*"

Joshua dared not blink. He turned his head aside, because it was said that the peripheral vision was more sensitive to surreptitious transpirations. Nothing. Yet. He could have sworn he'd seen his friend, Sammy Debnar, running up those stairs. Fanciful thinking, perhaps, on the back of wishing too hard.

"Dad." Fear had tightened Joshua's throat to a pinprick, through which he could barely speak. "We need to keep moving."

"Welcome to my nightmare," Bob uttered breathlessly, unable to rip his eyes from the hallway.

"Yeah, mine, too."

"Alice Cooper," Bob said offhandedly.

"Who's she?"

"A singer. And a man." His tone was flat and seemingly coming from miles deep within. "And in one of his songs, he sung, 'Welcome to my nightmare.'"

Joshua looked at his dad in a rather curious fashion, the type often reserved for those slow of mind.

With tears shimmering in his eyes, Bob admitted, "I shouldn't have brought you here."

"I had to come. It's me the man in black is after. Isn't that why we're here?"

"Christ, you're so like your mother," Bob said with a swollen heart, before returning his attention to the hallway.

"Actually, Dad, I'm a boy," Joshua said, thinking of Alice Cooper who was a man with a girl's name.

Bob snorted a single laugh. It conveyed no humor. "Now that we're here, I'm not sure if you're the one that the man in black *is* after." He swallowed hard. There was a click at the back of his throat. Then, in a whisper his son could not fully discern, he said, "She won't allow us to approach him, at any rate."

"She...?"

"The bitch takes care of her charges, Josh. She doesn't look after them; she takes *care* of them."

Mother's Care Orphanage had somehow escaped time to survive like a blackened heart whose arteries pumped pure evil. Having staggered backwards and come close to losing his footing, Bob now took his first tentative step towards that hallway.

Behind them, the massive doors stood ajar by his own actions. But they also seemed to stand ajar in satisfaction.

"Who, Dad?" Joshua didn't understand. "Who's the... bitch?"

Was the bitch waiting for his son? No—not his son. Joshua didn't know this place, but he did. It was part of him, and he part of it. They'd been transported here through the portal, because dimensions were thick on the ground, baby, and these days one could book a vacation to anywhere amongst the existences of other worlds and other times.

"The bitch chased me through the hallways of this orphanage."

"This is... a what?" Stunned.

"She desired hatred and a passion for inflicting the worst of pain." He looked down at his boy. "No child should ever experience what happened here." He then stared off into nowhere. "I wonder if the apple grove survived time? It wouldn't surprise me."

Joshua maintained an inquiring look, and Bob laughed humorlessly, once more. "Oh—it's a place where the dead get buried."

"You grew up here? Amongst all this?" Joshua was finding this hard to accept.

"Mother's Care Orphanage kinda looks the way it should. But when I was here, the sun did shine now and then through one of its many windows." He nodded to those set ridiculously high on the outer wall of the hallway. "It wasn't quite this bleak and dilapidated. Nonetheless, it suits. Black as the bitch's relentless pursuit of pain on the children. Inspections happened, but when the governing bodies came to determine that all was in order and responsibilities were well-entrenched, the kids were too afraid to speak the truth. The facade of a happy place for children who'd otherwise be homeless and unloved was carried off to perfection. She should've been known as the matron, and she was amongst the social and support workers. But to the kids, every kid that walked through these doors, she was known as the bitch. Few uttered that. I was one."

Bob continued on, keeping a tight grip on his son's hand, and getting a sudden blast from The Eagles' 'Hotel California.'

How true it was… he'd never checked out. He'd only thought he'd paid his dues and gotten on his way.

Seemed those wounds that Raoul had brought to the surface were the symptoms of being bound here. You could live a lie so completely that the lie became the undeniable truth. But it always had a way of catching up with you.

Welcome to my… Hotel California…

The interior was by far worse than the exterior. Age hadn't been kind to it. Then again, in light of the misery and havoc wreaked within its pitiless and fortified walls, it was just.

On the Earth that Bob knew, this cesspool had been razed to the ground on the jaws of bulldozers. Could the litany of Earths absorbed into Black Eternity have each carried a Mother's Care Orphanage? One concentrated pool of pure malevolence on the surface of each? The concoction brewing and gaining strength with each subsequent absorption? A relic for the trapped souls of the young and vulnerable?

The air and walls oozed malevolence along with profound sadness in loss. Great swaths of dark brown, varying to grays and blacks, and festoons of gaudy green hung here and there from the stonework. The floor shone like poisonous gas. Unsanitary cerements both hideously and perfectly justified down to their low-rank odor of long-spilled bodily fluids. The years of torture and pain so imbued into the walls that, each brick was now like a time capsule, slowly exuding the emotions and apparitions of those trapped within.

Maybe he'd never know the answers to these questions. And maybe he didn't want to know.

One thing was clear, though: something nasty, as usual, was on the brew at Mother's Care... and everything started from here.

Joshua glanced back to the doors that seemed to disappear into the curdled overlay. In comparison to the dinginess within, the light cascading through them was the type that made you squint. Its lack of substance was enough, however, to declare the same ravages extended, only more so, within. At bottom of the backside of the nearest door, it appeared as if someone or some *thing* had tried clawing through... to escape into whatever served as freedom beyond. Perhaps it was all the children that his dad spoke of.

Joshua shivered at the thought that somewhere in here was both the man in black as well as the man-thing in the three-peaked hat, the bells teasing his friend Sammy as they stalked him through this grime and what surely must be disease. Perhaps chasing him up that staircase into the hideous depths of the upper levels.

The smooth skin over his knees jerked up and down. Stepping further into the hallway, his curiosity was now drawn to the inside of the outer wall. "Water, right?" he said, peering over his shoulder at his dad while reaching out to touch it, noticing the same on the opposite wall. "Why's water dripping down the *inside* walls, Dad? A busted pipe?"

Bob was shaking his head. "Not water, mate."

There's was plenty of room at Mother's Care Orphanage, just as there had been at the Hotel California.

Joshua snatched his hand away from the slick fluid with a grimace. While he stared from the wall to his hand and back again, his dad was saying, "Innocence was butchered here, and the walls still cry."

Despite Joshua's revulsion, curiosity would not be satisfied until he touched the wall again, running his fingertips through the slickness there. Seemed the more he touched it, the more he wanted to touch it.

He brought them away and was momentarily mesmerized by the way they glistened. When common sense struck, he frantically flapped his hand, then wiped it down his T-shirt.

Again, he chanced a look behind, into the breathtaking cavern of the staircase, and then understood that this place must have been riddled with hallways that cried. Those he could see in the lustreless light, spilling through the entrance, created mouths of dense black in the encircling wall of the cavern, indicative of tunnels to mortuaries rather than thoroughfares where wailing children once roamed.

Now fully immersed in his dad's chosen tunnel of misery, a series of lights marched overhead from a high ceiling. They hung uselessly on their long chains. And whilst the first few were visible, the rest gradually disappeared into the murky darkness, along with the lustreless light. Those closest to the entrance swung gently on their chains in the mild breeze that fingered lazily through the open skyscraper doors. The ceiling too was coated in patches of that same shitty goop and gaudy green, smeared like a crazed plasterer's handiwork across the walls.

At regular intervals there were more of those huge gruesomely dark doors on the inner side. Though lacking the size of those at the entrance, they nonetheless made Joshua wonder what in the hell they were meant to have ever locked in.

Children? Surely not. How bad would you have to have been to deserve this?

His feet were rocking to and fro and his eyes were finding the back of his head. There was sudden pressure on either side of his shoulders and he swallowed a harsh breath that instantly hit the back of his throat with the taste sour mud.

"I'm sorry, mate," came his dad's voice through the nightmarish scene.

"I'm okay, Dad," Joshua said. Nightmarish but no nightmare. This was for real… whatever happened here, he knew there'd be no waking up in a cold sweat and eventually sitting down to Cheerios or blueberry muesli and orange juice… no goofing off with his friends and pretending to be a skateboarding wizard.

There was no morning after the dark here. Just darkness… the forever darkness.

As if compelled to do so, Joshua turned towards the entrance, once more. The breeze kicking up strands of hair. There was a special kind of something about it. A lack of vitality. The perfect companion to the light and its weary sheen. On the acute angle at which he stood, he could see a street in the far distance, upon which sat a decrepit house, masquerading as something people might have lived in many years ago, but where life would no longer be found. There was no Duncan's. No glimpse of Lower Mitcham.

Everything seemed surrounded by a thin haze, like fog but not as thick.

His father followed his gaze. He didn't see the house, just a curdling ether where nothing good could come of it. "We're trapped in a nightmare, Josh," Bob said. "The worst of nightmares. Only here, the way out is not the way in."

"This isn't a dream, Dad." Joshua had no doubt, but potentially waking up to a bowl of Cheerios and orange juice was still mighty appealing.

"No, mate, I guess it's not." As simple as that.

"You said that you grew up here. Did the man in black live here?" Before his dad could answer, he added, "Did you ever hear bells?"

Bob shrugged almost imperceptibly. "Besides not recalling bells, you're asking questions once again that I've no idea how to answer. I might as well be the dunce of the class given a complicated mathematical equation to solve."

"What made you say that?"

"A metaphor. I was never that good at math."

Joshua didn't much care for the metaphor. Next thing his dad would be telling him was that behind one of those huge doors was Mrs. Bruckheimer, still awaiting the answer to the equation scribbled on the blackboard.

He joined his father's undivided attention to the hallway's ominous and secretive depths. "We have to go in." This was no question, but a resignation from a child who had no business being here, and yet was compelled by the laws of fate to be nowhere else.

A vague movement disturbed the darkness beyond.

"Dad?"

"I know," Bob said. "Enough with the photograph album of childhood pleasantries. As you said, we've got to get going—*now!*" He took hold of his son's hand, once more, and led him deeper into this unimaginable place.

A small whine escaped Joshua. His dad didn't react. Joshua hoped he hadn't heard, because he needed to be there for his dad as much as he needed his dad to be there for him.

The lustreless light rapidly fell away. The brooding shades of long-suffering and woeful misery were stronger here. The pitapat of countless waterfalls of tears down the walls and against the stone floor was a symphony of echoes speaking for the doomed. It was impossible to tell where the original sounds emanated, each taking flight in an endless flurry, beginning strong and gradually losing volume, the antiphony of a bunch of musical artists stoned out of their minds.

Further along the hallway, the surroundings had become darker than winter poor in the dead of midnight. The eyes' miraculous ability to adjust allowed for muted sight, which was both a blessing and a curse, because in the dead of midnight there was further movement. A shadow moving within shadow.

And something else: a noise they both heard differently.

It came to Bob's ears as:

CLACK-CLACK

Joshua recognized it immediately. He'd heard this recently when Sammy was standing before the doorway in his house, and on his own in the year 2025. Both memorable occasions had one common factor: the bells had come for him.

TINKLE-TINKLE

Bob came to an abrupt halt. Joshua was tugged back by his weight. The floor here was particularly slimy and his Nikes skid across the mucous overlay, laying shallow trenches in their wake.

"What is it?" he asked, a little annoyed and very afraid.

Having no sooner asked the question, Joshua was jerked forward, scrambling behind his father like a dog on a leash.

"Wait up, Dad! I can't keep up with you! Your legs are—*wait up!*"

Their hands detached and Joshua went forward with all his weight. Thirty-five kilos kissed the floor and sailed ahead like a stone in a game of curling. Joshua yelped, as one door passed by and another was coming up to take its place. He was more startled than hurt, and every bit disgusted. His legs and arms, hands and front of his T-shirt were besmirched in slime that seemed to build in layers.

The wave of disgust broke apart to expose the raw element of fear in being left alone. It sunk into his belly like a fist of ice.

His dad was running ahead, leaving him further and further behind. *"You can't be! I know you can't be! So why are you?* **WHY?**"

The tones of his father's unimaginable hurt sent a tsunami of fear surging though Joshua. *"Dad, we've got to stay together!"*

Instead of his dad answering, there came a boy's crying. Through the echoes of tears and his dad's running and yelling, it rolled along the high ceiling like dangerous thunder, swamping the lights that hung from their long chains and whose globes mightn't have shone in decades, if not eons.

"Sammy?"

Joshua carefully got to his feet, the desire to rush tempered by the knowledge that it'd only end in another fall. His trainers had little traction against the slime. He reeled back, then forward, his arms doing a dance to either side. The thought of reacquainting himself so personally with what lay at his feet revolted him. Though his trainers squished amongst the muck, that was different, less personal, if you like—than actually *touching* it. The entire front of him was covered in it and still dripping, but one full-body slippery slide was more than enough.

He gathered his strength and began down the hallway, supposedly towards his dad and the crying boy.

It must've been Sammy. No crying was ever good to listen to, but this was awful. It staggered through the darkness from up ahead, from on his right… left… maybe even from behind. Again, noises travelled as if omnipresent. He was being approached. But from what direction? It seemed in front of him and had begun picking up the pace. His dad's footsteps and frightening screams were graying out, while something had taken upon itself to stalk him in this place that had once, unbelievably, been an *orphanage* and home to his dad.

It's Sammy and he's being chased by the man-thing in the three-peaked hat!

As Joshua peered into the darkness, desperate to see, a powerful impression rammed into him with the energy of a lightning bolt: he was losing his dad, and that was exactly what was meant to happen. It wasn't Sammy coming at him, of that he was now certain. *"Dad, wait up!"* His legs seemed awfully heavy, and when he resumed his attempt at running, it took all his effort and several strides to get into some sort of rhythm.

He slipped and slid, his trainers searching for what precious grip was on offer, the crying surely no more than an arm's length away.

"DAD! WAIT UP! PLEEEEAAAASSSSEEEE!"

He turned a bend that veered to the right, running on the hot fumes of growing terror. The heavy shades of the cumbersome lights, pressing from the gloom overhead, didn't move here as they had near the entrance. He was deep inside the bowels of misery. And going deeper.

In a repeat of events, one minute past midnight seized the bones of time. There was no more dancing across clock faces of every variety known to man. The little hand pointed to the hour of twelve, whilst the big hand held firm at one minute past the hour.

The last healthy beat anywhere just so happened to tick over in Adelaide, South Australia, at the heart of where it'd all originated, in some other time on some other Earth, by the hands of one family.

Time succumbed to fatal arrhythmia seconds upon a man and his boy moving into Mother's Care Orphanage and all things unknown.

Whether switched on or off, from every phone spewed the unrepentant dialogue of some twelve years before—and perhaps millennia before that—churning out with ever-increasing fervor: *At the third stroke the time will be... will be... twelve... twelve... twelve... twelve... twelve o-one A.M.*

Beep! Beep! Beep!

At the third stroke the time will be... will be... twelve... twelve... twelve... twelve... twelve o-one A.M.

Beep! Beep! Beep!

When you're so far over the rainbow, the Boogaloo is always out of sight!

Within the primordial vapors of the most ancient of instincts, its land, of sorts, stretched ad infinitum. A land never once kissed by a sunrise or sunset, whose topography was near billboard flat in areas as vast as ten galaxies. Like shattered glass, its barren surface was crazed by fathomless fissures, and punctuated here and there by mountains, some towering to heights that rivalled planets on the grandest of scale.

The infinitesimal anatomy gleamed, by Bob and Joshua in their spaceships of misty white, of perpetual darkness with endless strings of balloons, akin to those wild ape-like beings inching from their caves for the first time. Their only line of defense against the incomprehensible monsters in stars and moon were the stones they threw and the sticks they wielded. And they did this while the very patch of ground, upon which their hirsute feet were planted, hurtled through space at some sixty-seven thousand miles per hour without them having yet the wit to conjure the idea of fire.

Whatever Black Eternity was—a black hole, a parallel universe, the anti-universe, the unwritten epilogue of the entire universe's existence, some of these, all of these—forces were at work that it was bound by. The laws of nature that operated outside man's understanding.

The attraction to Earth—and all the Earths that had come and gone—beat stronger than ever from the toffee-colored pathogen. Of galactic proportions, it was a cancer that had altered Black Eternity's DNA and, therefore, the laws of nature.

Fooled once by the father, not to be fooled again, the Dream Sorcerers had Their own set of instincts. The bounty had to be protected. The endless supply of food had been good and readily accessible. In the early epoch of infestation, the larder had suffered long famines, and not until the very first Patrick Nesmith's possessive sickness was it understood that this could be abolished.

They'd grown fat, Their numbers disproportionate, as They gorged on the consistent flow of human souls not lost to the mad ones. As parasites of the most ancient of existences, They'd thrived through adaptability. Readily learning from past errors, They were the ultimate opportunists.

The incitement had been disrupted just the once; the bounty had come perilously close to permanent disruption; and then the father had had a child...

"It can't be! You can't be! I know you can't be! So, why are you? **WHY?"**

"DAD! WAIT UP! PLEEEEAAAASSSSEEEE!"

Fooled once...

Never to be fooled again...

Deep underground, in the loneliest room on the planet, amongst a complete absence of people and sound, a small white candle sat on the table. Its calming little flame danced on the wick hypnotically. The oldest of the Dark Suits, known as the Elder, sat before it, his fingers calmly interlaced on the table, his pensive face aglow in the candle's yellow-orange cast.

He hadn't moved a muscle in hours. He might've even been meditating, the way he stared ahead into the opposite wall.

The core group had disbanded; seemed they'd all held the same deep-seated emotions, to be with their families in this time of crisis. Families they had created since coming to this planet.

What had any of it been for? Advanced Earths must exist whose civilizations had mastered star travel. Earths which no Dark Suit had descended upon or knew about. And even if they had, the longer the years passed, the greater the dilution to the Dark Suits' old and defunct ideals. After all, they were a dying breed in themselves, their numbers forever dwindling. For all the Elder knew, those on this Earth might be the last.

As for the likes of the Gillespies and the Lithgrows, good riddance to such evil. Their radical and downright malicious behavior had been abhorred even amongst the core group.

And then there were the likes of Reynell and Raoul. Such individuals had striven to avert the annihilation of an entire species—even if the chances of success were but a mere sliver. And, of course, there was Malinda, who had come closest in turning that sliver into a very real possibility. The Elder had last heard from him, at a guess, roughly eight hours earlier. It came via a text message, which simply read: Happy fucking days.

The Elder inhaled. His breath both deep and shuddery.

Anphilian 4 would always have competition in the universe. He could see that now... he'd always seen it. Or so it seemed now. What began as an obsession, fuelled by an ideology, was truly at best quite stupid. The longer he had remained on this Earth, the more the fuel's potency degraded, and with it the burning aspirations to see the end to this world.

With such insight came enlightenment: he was a relic, and the best he could do was play his part. And play it he had done to perfection.

He laughed once, sadly. Even his own kind had long since disregarded such ideologies. Nonetheless, he'd blindly travelled to this Earth a much younger man, full of pride and full of shit.

The universe's fruits were indeed bountiful, and two like species could coexist potentially without ever crossing paths, let alone robbing one another of a possible addition to the homes they'd already established amongst the stars. This was true. It had always been true.

Whatever the Dark Suits had done had had little impact on events that'd transpired in the past, and those that would arise in the future. They'd invested a lot. They'd lost even more, all because of the fear so passionately embraced at the core of that stupid ideal.

People like himself often became fascists and joined militias. Wasn't that what he'd effectively done? Worse, they sometimes assumed leadership to propagate their stupid ideals. Unable to think beyond narcissistic self-righteousness, they really were despots, when you boiled it all down, robbing both themselves and others of life. Full of rage and hatred, they were incapable of embracing the joys of life and the differences in others, and how those differences complemented and strengthened such joys.

His philosophical thoughts didn't end there.

If everyone on every planet could embrace such enlightenment before shedding a single drop of blood, there'd be no wars... no dying... no crying mothers and fathers... no crying siblings...

If such a world existed, it'd be truly paradisaical.

Fancy anyone, young or old, overcome with such pompous brashness, they'd even conceive and believe in their ability to change the course of future events of worlds.

To that point, could Bob Triplow and his young son, Joshua, have ever carried out this most impossible of tasks? Albeit sans the pompous brashness?

Supernova eruptions occurred throughout the universe, as did time warps and wormholes and pulsars... the colliding of planets... galaxies... the voracious appetite of black holes. The universe wasn't given its lofty name for no reason. It was the grandmaster. Had been since the hands of time started ticking... at least, in this universe.

Bob had managed to disrupt events, so it was conceivable he could do it again. Wasn't it?

And his son only further enhanced possible success with the nightmares of Patrick Nesmith. The man who seemed at the very centre of the gruesome, long drawn-out events.

But which Patrick Nesmith could lay claim to starting Black Eternity's incitement? Surely not the contemporary Patrick, or the Patrick who'd died on this Earth hundreds of years ago. Perhaps some other Patrick, on some other world, passing on his unique set of skills across time and space, was more to the point. *Inheritance.*

Fact: Black Eternity had been summoned by the hand of *a* Patrick Nesmith, at some point in history, on some Earth. Fact: Black Eternity was, in all probability, always going to take this world. So why even bother with ensuring this happened? Great question.

Pity the young, who are full of shit and pompous brashness.

The Elder made his first move in hours: he shook his head. Inconceivable.

The how-tos and what-fors were complete unknowns, as they almost always would be. And now, father and son were hopelessly pitted against an unimaginable force. Another universe.

Aboveground, a nuclear storm of sorts had enveloped the world. This wasn't the extinction of the dinosaurs, in which ninety-nine percent of all species had been either fried, suffocated or starved to death. This was extinction of totality, in which the Earth itself would cease to exist.

So sitting his ass in a chair deep below the surface was hardly of any advantage. There was no recourse, just a finality that had yet to play out its hand.

As he sat and thought his grisly thoughts, the neurological network across his brain imparted one further piece of information, the kind that was so undeniably implicit that to do anything but agree would be manifestly a lie.

And, frankly, he had done enough lying.

Whether the father and son had somehow found a way into the belly of the Black Eternity was inconsequential. Mere grains of sand within another dimension; what could they ever possibly do or have done?

The Storm was here.

And he was all alone, playing solitaire.

With just hours… minutes? …or even seconds to endure his loneliness, the Elder reached down and withdrew from his lap, not a lozenge to sooth his aching bones, but an old faithful .45, lovingly crafted by human hand. So much for not spilling a drop of blood.

Without interrupting his stare, he raised the muzzle to the right side of his head.

He hesitated for a moment. A smile flickered across his lips, the little candle merrily burning away.

There was an explosion. The .45 fell to the linoleum floor with a remonstrating clatter, while the Dark Suit's head crashed to the table with a meaty thump.

A rapidly expanding pool of thick maroon began edging towards the table's edge.

The little candle's base looked like some pristine-white lighthouse in a macabre sea of red.

The expanding pool found the edge and began dripping to the floor.

$$\sim\!\!\sim$$

In a place far over the rainbow and one step from the Boogaloo, Joshua had frozen midstride past yet another of those monolithic doors, when the crying went flying past and something ducked into the room off to the right. "Sammy?" His heart pounded against his ribcage.

Whimpering talk was filtering from the room, fingering its way into the hallway, just as ghostly as the figure itself. Joshua swallowed hard and approached the door.

"*I'm sorry, Bobby, I can't be with you... I can't take it anymore.*" The boy produced a knife, his face etched with the tears and misery of years beyond his own. Joshua guessed he might've been about Sammy's age, but wasn't his friend who testified the inconceivable of actually liking school.

The knife glinted in the winter-darkness, which made no sense, but neither did anything about this godforsaken place.

The boy was holding it out to his side and repeated, "*I'm sorry, Bobby... the bitch made me do this... I've got to leave you now... I've left a note...*"

He abruptly turned to face the opposite wall, to hide what he was about to do. There was a sickening *SWAT.* The sound was like someone taking to a cut of meat in a fit of rage.

There was more pitapatting coming from the room; a thickish rain fell about the boy's feet.

He slumped. Held. Then slumped further, until he collapsed to the floor.

Joshua went into the room, despite all his senses telling him to take flight. He fought against it, as the boy needed help.

"What have you done?" he asked in a strangulated voice.

No answer.

Joshua was feeling faint; he uttered again, knowing it'd get no better response, "What have you done to yourself?"

The boy was dressed in school uniform as if he'd just sneaked out of class.

What kind of lesson had he escaped?

Joshua stepped closer and his trainers *thwacked* into more goop, only this was sticky unlike the slimy stuff that covered his lower legs.

He lifted his foot and it dribbled a dark matter. He could smell it, too, a strong odor of iron.

The dark matter, seeping around the boy's crumpled body, grew to the size of a halo, from which his closed eyes seemed to float. His left hand was holding something... what he'd cut off.

"*What made you do such a thing?*" Joshua whispered, his revolution mixed with wrenching sympathy.

The knife rolled onto the floor as the fingers on his right hand spasmed and then unfurled. It made a pathetic metallic sound and just lay there like an innocent artefact in this sad tale.

Joshua was staring at the boy's left hand. Most of the arm was caught beneath him. In his fingers was squeezed something.

They, too, eventually unfurled as the last of the boy's life force evaporated from his crumpled body. The object rolled away from them and Joshua yelped before recognition approached and smacked him in the face.

Pencils.

There was a handful of them, when you really only ever required one, unless you were a genius and could do multiple writings at once.

Joshua backed up, remembering his computer desk in the room of his house in the year 2025, and the images, that had tormented him for months, of a jolly Santa Claus foisting presents upon him with which to serve his punishment... because he'd been a bad boy... and the imperative urgency to write.

Answer the equation, you worthless little shit! **WRITE!! WRITE!! WRITE!!**

What was the connection here? Was there a connection? And why had he used his dad's name? Was he referring to his dad?

In the churning of thoughts, like reference books blown by erratic winds, Joshua was in no mind to sit down and analyse a single one of them.

He retreated into the hallway, his eyes never leaving the sad image of a boy who could no longer take it. This place... his dad had spent his childhood... unbelievable...

The boy, who Joshua's dad could've told him went by the name Douglas McKenzie, remained lying in his death pose until things seemed to shift. There was a quirky buzz-like effect around him, like a television station battling to hold on, and then he was gone.

He didn't miraculously get up from the floor and run from the room. He simply vanished as if the TV set had suffered a malfunction.

Moments later, somewhere in the distant gloom, he could hear a boy crying as he ran terrified through the darkness.

Once again it came closer... ever closer...

"*Not again!*" Joshua retreated slowly.

A figure rushed toward him. "*Fuck!*" he yelled and almost slipped as he whirled about. He was desperate to get away, but the slime and his trainers conspired against him once more, and all he managed to do was run on the spot like he was an actor in a comedy show. *Ah... cha-cha-cha...*

The figure ducked into the room where the boy had given up being tormented by demons—the bitch, perhaps—in preference to taking matters into his own hands. Literally.

Whimpering talk filtered from the room, fingering its way into the hallway just as ghostly as the figure itself.

Mesmerized by terror, Joshua approached the doorway and peered in.

"*I'm sorry, Bobby, I can't be with you... I can't take it anymore...*" The boy produced a knife. His face etched with the tears and misery of years beyond his.

The knife glinted in the winter-darkness.

The boy was holding it out to his side and repeated: "*I'm sorry, Bobby... the bitch has made me do this... I've got to leave you now... I've left a note...*"

He abruptly turned to face the opposite wall. There was a sickening *SWAT.*

His body deflated upon the floor in hitching stages.

The knife fell from his loosening grip in one hand, followed by pencils in the other. Joshua shambled from the door, whose lintel towered above him, shock numbing his flesh.

So this is what they hide. What type of place was this—ever?

It's where I grew up... pray for the children 'cause the bitch is on the prowl.

The figure winked in and out of reception, and the macabre broadcast was gone.

Through the darkness came a boy's terror. It approached at rapid speed.

A figure went flying past Joshua and into the room, where whimpering talk started up. Yet again.

Numb from head to toe, Joshua forced himself deeper into the winter gloom. Whatever that boy was running from was what Joshua had to meet head on.

He rounded into another hallway, certain that even if he wanted to find the entrance before that seemingly never-ending staircase, he wouldn't be able to. He wouldn't be *allowed* to.

Though he couldn't hear his dad, the faint cries of a terrorized boy drifted like black ice amongst the pitapat—as well as something else. Bells. Beginning softly, they soon filled the diseased environment in the manner of a creche whose endless bundles of joy had found the delights of wielding their rattles to get exactly what they wanted.

Joshua slogged his way through the darkness, struggling with the strength to keep moving, as this place seemed to heave from its very bowels, stimulated by the peal of a thousand infants shaking their rattles. The more he pushed forward, the more his trainers threatened to go from under him. The more those infants shook their toys.

To his left came a dim light through the series of windows set high in the wall.

Something was passing surreptitiously on the outside. The tears, streaming from the walls, were hideous drapes to the daunting developments.

Joshua froze on the spot, despite the darkness and its hallways swarming with man-things in three-peaked hats.

It was a balloon. And he imagined it laughing, because that was what that kind of balloon did. Perhaps amongst them were the restructured bodies of a mother and her baby.

Who would've once rattled its own toy to have their mother accede to their beck and call! There was no escaping. You were either in this hellhole or out in that hellhole.

Roll up! Roll up! Roll Up! Boy and girls! Take your pick, it's a lucky dip, fancy your luck when the choices don't ever get any better!

If Joshua was asked for his honest appraisal, he'd have said that the sun had never shone in a place like this, regardless of what his dad had maintained.

TINKLE-TINKLE-TINKLE-TINKLE

This jolted him into moving his ass. He shouldn't have stopped. *Why had he stopped?*

He was surrounded by a hundred, maybe a thousand or more man-things gravitating towards him as if he were a magnet, the single point of their undivided attention.

"What do you want, *BITCH?*" Bitch! Bitch! Bitch! Bitch! His dad's shrieks barely managed to break through the maddening peal, rolling away into whatever had become of Mother's Care Orphanage.

"*Dad!*" Joshua yelled. His own echoes ran hither and thither amongst the catacombs.

With his breath soured by the weight of fear, he came to another bend, to another hallway. The windows continued above him, casting their dreadful light ahead and into the asylum.

His dad's shouting had given way to the odd footstep of him rushing ahead. At least, Joshua hoped that it was his dad he was committing himself to following.

With the infants' rattles squeezing in from every direction, he grimly stuck to his commitment, else he'd simply start going around in circles, and the bells would carousel him as they surely wanted to.

⌒

Sue was giving the Mendozas a hand to close the curtains throughout the house. If memory served correctly, if those balloon-things couldn't see you they were inclined to leave you alone. They didn't seem clever, but what they lacked in the upstairs department they more than made up for in their ruthlessness.

They came from the skies and they took their prey into the skies, and there was little she'd seen anyone do about that except for the thrashing of limbs. Pretty useless, really. Taking on a monster with a feather duster would've been more effective. At least tickling your foe into submission was an option. Not great, but better than slapping the thing to see if you couldn't further enrage it.

She was at the downstairs dining room window. The curtains were closed, but she couldn't help herself. She had to have a peekaboo. Christ, she'd suddenly become Lucille Goldman.

Kill me quick, she thought again.

Chancing the smallest of cracks at the edge of one of the curtains, she stuck her face through, very much in the same vein as Lucille Goldman.

Chasing Boulevard seemed awfully quiet. Too quiet. Mind you, she couldn't see a thing. That was good.

She kept staring and wondered if her busy-body neighbor was doing likewise, at the ready to call the cops, her efforts entirely frustrated by the little man in the phone, what Lucille likened to as government interference, taking charge of its citizens.

"I wonder what you think of this shit, Lucille?" Sue muttered at the front window.

As if on cue, and several doors down—it was hard to tell in the solid sheet of darkness—there came a muted light.

Could've been someone totting a candle like Florence Nightingale. Maybe those infamous pigs, reputed to fly, were at it again, too—and when they needed to take a dump, sister, you better run for cover.

A balloon casually rounded the corner on a house adjacent and one door down. She could tell this by the way the letterboxes reflected the light. She could also see its mean little face twitching as it floated through space. It was on the hunt. It was searching. It had yet to claim victory, which was good. It continued cruising down Chasing Boulevard like a dim headlight that had lost its surrounding metal.

Sue dared not breathe, but of course she had to, else she'd go blue and die. Call the paramedics… call the hospital… call anyone you liked, it'd do you no good. So—breathe.

She took some solace in the fact that she could see no other activity. The good people of Corona were obviously a highly intelligent bunch. They must've already figured it was best to lay low in the darkness lurking outside. Of course, they lacked her insight, but the darkness was eerie, and why would you light candles and sit around them in front of your open window for any Tom, Dick or Harry to have a perve? One might've even taken it upon themselves to indulge in a bit of self-pleasure, either a solo act or with your spouse. Hell, why not? Of course, there was always those who'd take it further... a threesome under the cloak of darkness. Hey, what about a family orgy?

What was going through her mind, especially at such a time, was both out of character and hard to credit. "Jesus, Sue, there's a time and place... and this ain't it," she softly berated herself. Nonetheless, a little self-indulgence would help pass the time. Take her mind off things for a moment. Whilst tempting, it'd be difficult to explain to Leon and his parents, should they happen in on her at such an intimate moment.

I was trying to adjust my contraceptive because one never knows when it'll be called upon. Yeah, right, that'd go down a treat, and here they were weeks out from Halloween.

Trick or treat, kiddies. What would it be? She laughed in the face of her fears. Some kids, boys likely, would stare on in stunned amazement, while girls might stare on wondering what that might feel like. Not the kind of thing a responsible adult should do when answering the door... better to hand out choccies and candy. *Here, take this and that. Stuff that in ya gob until you're big and fat and die of a big fat disease.* She bit down hard to stifle her laughter. Tears had started squirting from her eyes.

What the fuck was in Marlene's lasagne? She assumed it was spinach, but it might just have been a heavy dose of weed.

Now, Sue, I can't begin to imagine how distraught you must be, so I've whipped up a little motherly comfort.

Oh, thanks so much. A roast?

No.

Oh, a nice pot of chicken soup?

Afraid not.

A cheesecake! I love cheesecake, especially the baked variety.

Bake in this weather? Are you fucked in the head?

Yes—yes, I am.

Well, then, you'll be pleased to know: tuck into this and you'll get a mouthful of Uncle Larry's attic homegrown best. Grab a bunch and have a munch. Need not for lunch as you'll be punched!

Sue needed to pee. She moved away from the dining room window and hurried towards the downstairs toilet by the light of the silvery moon… no, afraid not. Try candles, which had been relit now that the downstairs curtains were all closed.

Upstairs, Leon was starting to close his bedroom curtains when he saw what was at once familiar.

"Old Mister Grouch," he uttered.

He was referring to a time and place, rather than being literal.

The balloon cruised along the street below and on the opposite side before disappearing from sight.

He flicked one curtain over to its central point and grabbed the inner hem of the other, when the balloon sprung up in front of him.

Leon's scream fetched up in his throat, and, as he threw himself away, his feet tangled, sending him crashing to the floor. If he could've exchanged notes with Joshua, he'd have found that this was one thing his best friend had become quite accustomed to.

The balloon's face was moving weirdly, which was rich when you put it in context.

And it was laughing.

Leon didn't much care for that laughter: it signalled something bad was about to happen. To him!

He scrambled to his feet, but before he could reach his bedroom door, the balloon had slipped through the window's pane and latched between his shoulder blades. Its lunatic laughter pressed against the back of his head, its sickness cackling directly into his ears. In both shock and rude surprise, Leon finally found the scream that had become locked within.

It took Zachary and Marlene less than a few seconds to reach him, as they too had been attending to the upstairs curtains. They burst into his room and stopped cold, stunned into doing nothing. For there was their son surrounded by a riotous mob of balloons, as if he'd decided to throw a party, only it'd gotten out of hand and the guests had become unruly.

They kept pouring in as if someone was standing outside the upper storey window and releasing them in droves. No invitation required and no need to open the window, as they simply slid through its glass. Their bodies so tightly packed, they squeaked the way balloons did when rubbed together.

Marlene felt her heart momentarily pause, only to restart with a thud at the sight of the terror in her son's eyes.

"MOM! DAD!" Leon was screaming, out of his mind. As usual when the balloons introduced themselves, it involved a new type of dance craze, where mindless arm waving and running were mandatory moves. But for all his efforts, he was being dragged towards the window.

Several of those balloons had already passed through the glass to the outside. How was that even possible? Were they really able to drag his son through the window? Impossible, but true.

Zachary lunged at them and batted a few aside, but they kept pouring in by what seemed like their hundreds.

The room's confines rapidly filled with a pulsating madness, which turned on Marlene in an instant, as if she'd poked a stick into a beehive and threatened the queen.

"*ZACK!*" she screamed.

Overwhelmed by their sheer numbers, Zachary's valiant retaliation was both futile and unintentionally provoking them into a higher state of revelry. *But what else could he do? Start singing 'Happy Birthday?'* Their high pitch and unnervingly childlike cackling vibrated the eardrums, before they rebounded and came for seconds and thirds...

With the new dance craze shaking the walls, Zachary seemed pitted in a warped game of Twister where he shoved his hands one way only for them to follow... before placing a foot another way to be matched... poking his face somewhere else and rubbing noses. Forget dunking for apples when celebrating with the demented—that was *so* passé.

One... two... three... a dozen or more had captured his arms, then surrounded his body. The rescuer had become the victim, the game out of hand. He could feel a hot warmth seeping into his flesh, as if doused with an overdose of Deep Heat. And it seemed he could feel his brains peculating, as if being sautéed on a skillet, little bubbles of fat squeezing from beneath his intelligence and going off in satisfying pops.

Give me more onions, for what's a barbeque without onions?

He struggled to reconcile the fact that part of him was actually enjoying the sensation when all his mouth was doing was screaming in abject horror.

Whilst he batted and thrashed, he whined with effort, but had no resistance to these things that came with a bag of tricks, and an unfair advantage that he couldn't compete with.

Having heard the commotion upstairs, Sue rushed from the toilet. Paper had caught under the waist of her jeans; the roll was unravelling fast, jigging on its holder, finally coming loose to skitter on the toilet floor.

She went straight for the knife block in Marlene's kitchen and snatched the longest carving knife she could see at a glance *nice, Henckels, good edge, handy* and flew upstairs with the toilet paper streaming behind until it broke, leaving a ten foot trail like a kind of cheap bridal train.

She burst into Leon's bedroom wielding the knife.

Pop!

The balloon erupted as if blowing air through pursed lips.

With that, Sue Triplow went on her own rampaging Twister. The carving knife sliced through the air, making a whistling sound that went unheard amongst the commotion. It slashed open one balloon after another.

The popping came at such a rate, it mimicked a machine gun unloading its deadly wares, until it blended and became seemingly one.

She made her way first to her son's best friend, because they needed to have a chance to grow and develop, and he was close to being pulled through the glass. If she struck these things down as his body was both in his bedroom and hanging foul from the upper storey window, there was every likelihood that the glass would reknit and slice him in half. She had to take care, though, and aim her strokes with precision, to avoid contact with the boy, which was easy said than done as his arms helicoptered about.

His face was now free.

More slashing. Finally his body was removed of the balloons.

Thank God for good kitchenware, Sue thought as she continued the task ahead of her.

Despite their unbridled madness, the balloons seemed momentarily hesitant, and in the distant reaches of Sue's mind she supposed even in madness there was some breed of recognition and organization. Madness, after all, didn't denote stupidity. A mad man could still add and subtract, just not in the way one would expect.

The bodies of countless balloons had begun piling on the floor.

Sue slipped on a thick layer, but not once did she and Henckels cease their slash-and-gash attack. As she went to her knees, Henckels whirling above her head, she struck one rubbery body after another.

They rained down like featherless birds dropping through the air.

She managed to get to her feet and free both Zachary and Marlene, before fanning the knife in huge swoops at the window, slicing open every balloon that slipped through, the drift of bodies surpassing three feet in depth.

After a time out of mind, the balloons stopped coming. The party had come to and end.

Exhausted, drenched in sweat, Sue began to snag the remaining curtain closed. "And that is why we must keep these shut," she panted, each word separated by a breath.

A straggler popped in, thinking it terribly funny as it went for her face.

She stepped away and shouted, "Trick to treat, you mutant bastard!" Henckels' blade made short work of it.

Her breathing was rapid, her hair wrapped around her face, as if she was emulating a semi-seductive shampoo ad for a company to grab more of those precious consumer dollars.

She blew a thick strand from her face. It hardly moved, glued into position with sweat, so she gave it an agitated flick of a finger.

After a moment of staring at her friends and them at her, she looked down to see the trail of toilet paper hanging down her leg. It was markedly shorter than before, having broken apart in the melee, not that she was aware of it being there in the first place.

With the bodies of mad ones thick on the floor and up to her knees, she said, "A coffee would go down well. Maybe the power will return soon."

Of course, if power grids came alive, her biggest wish would come true, one which a shot of caffeine could never rival.

∽

In a place far over the rainbow
The Boogaloo is out of sight
In a place far over the rainbow
Everyone's lost in a lullaby...

He came upon the door through which the bitch's voice had taunted him. Sitting halfway up its towering length was a plaque.

It too was begrimed by years of neglect and the surrounding misery.

Bob reached up and rubbed it like a genie bottle. Only nothing magical was about to spring forth and grant him a favor, just the name: **MATRON**.

This was the bitch's office.

The room he'd taken his worst beating ever.

The day before Douglas' disappearance. And if the apple grove was dug up, there would be the bones of his childhood friend.

He pushed the door to. It went without the slightest protest. As he walked through, he could hear the heartbeat of clocks. They were faint, and yet he could have sworn they were just on the opposite side of one of the walls.

The ticking and tocking heralded his arrival into the most hellish room of his life, but he had returned home and the most fitting song by Pink Floyd, 'Time,' filtered about him, coming either from inside his head or from within the walls. He couldn't tell which.

'Hotel California' had given way to the stark reminder that what went around kept going around until it was met. He was on the patch of ground he had walked as a small boy; and whilst he had run, it'd done him no good. So here he was, filled with both dread and purpose, upon the threshold and much, much closer to death than he had been when last here.

"Come, Master Bobbyyyy! It is time for all worthless little shits to get their comeuppance. Douglas was unfortunate. If only he had realized that it was not as bad as he imagined. Come!"

The voice was distinct, the words dusty and ancient but no less potent. The bitch was toying with him, speaking from behind a corner here or there. Bob couldn't see her, but she could see him.

When she had last threatened him with these very same words, she'd been in hot pursuit and not nearly as relaxed. Coy, almost. When she had caught him in 2011, it'd done her no good, but this time round she was playing a different game. Her projected whisper came from the furthest recesses of this room.

Having ceased the chase through his tainted childhood, Bob's breaths were hot and blustery. The buzzing in his head, wild and rambunctious, an electrical storm sizzling across the surface of his brain. But thankfully, an apocalyptic sun of rage had risen to overwhelm his emotions. He embraced it, because rage was a useful tool. The power it conveyed he could use.

And just why had he been running? Had he fooled himself into believing she'd ever left his life for good? What a jackass. Run... walk... it didn't matter... as neither would've standing on the spot, because she was always going to catch up to him. Or allow him to catch up to her.

And just why did she want him so badly? What made him the subject of so much of her attention? He was nothing special: born Bobby Triplow to loving parents, Helen and Godwin Triplow, until some son of a bitch had mowed them down on the first minutes of the new year in 1973. At just three years of age, he'd been unable to comprehend the situation he'd been suddenly and violently thrust into. But as he grew and his mind explored, his loss of love also grew until it consumed him, tightening around his memories with vicious tenacity.

So, what made him the objet d'art to her? His own profound grief throughout his growing years? Or was it that he'd been able to defy her—to turn his back and walk away from her?

"What do you want, *BITCH?*" Bob shrieked.

Bitch! Bitch! Bitch! Bitch!

When she walked, Bob didn't hear the sound of bells but that of

CLACK-CLACK ...

her insectile feet hitting the floor.

She was nothing but a psychotic murderer feeding off the fear of children. She thrived on it and ensured, with a passion, that Mother's Care Orphanage operated according to her malicious episodes of unjust punishment.

Those insectile footfalls were ridiculously fresh in his mind, as if 2011, the last he'd heard them, cut its own jagged swath through the storm and anger raging across his mind.

He was, however, a different man from then: no longer afraid of stepping into the light, of being taken as a worthy individual amongst society, rather than someone of ridicule. He would not cower or take a backward step, not ever again. He wouldn't run from the bitch. She could play her stupid games and he'd play along, but only so far. He meant to face her and end all the misery she'd ever perpetrated.

Was this what Raoul had been referring to without knowing the true identity himself? It seemed to have thrown a spanner in the works in 2011. He hadn't known what he'd done then to stymie Black Eternity's assault on the Earth. Was it due to the fact he'd more or less conquered the bitch? Though he'd done so in a rather unintentional way.

He had another power besides anger. He had more knowledge, and that was better than having none at all. He would go toe-to-toe with her, see what eventuated.

Something kept nagging at the back of his head: Joshua's man in black. How he figured into this Sunday jaunt along the boardwalk, he didn't have the first notion. Could it be, if he went toe-to-toe with the bitch, that Joshua's man in black could be relegated to the compartment of all things unimportant?

While Joshua was trying to find his legs, Bob was trying to find some sort of reasoning. But to reason out of mayhem was tricky; there were just too many unknowns.

Not for much longer, the more you keep dilly-dallying. Keep your mind on the job. Your nose to the grindstone.

The storm intensified. Lightning cracked and sizzled with incessant violence, and hurricane winds howled throughout Bob's cerebral synapses, while the molten sun domineered from a distance.

Bob Triplow was going to use his own form of bulldozer until Mother's Care Orphanage was no more. Not in *any* dimension.

If the one memory that kept this hellhole alive was appropriately dealt with, surely the bubble would collapse? Close the wounds that had never healed, because they were merely the symptom of the memory. They remained while the memory had seemingly been long cast adrift. Forgotten but not to be forgot.

In this bubble of horror sat the man in black. Since he was here, according to Raoul, he resided with the bitch. Were they one and the same? Had he passed this onto his son through the Triplow gene pool, an insight to something that he had been blind to? If that be true, then if he took care of one, the other would be taken care of.

Was he prepared to die to save the world? The magnificently prophetic question had an equally demure answer. Yes.

Everything would return to normal. Earth would be spared. Six billion souls would continue with their lives. Pissed off and put out, they would, nonetheless, get over their air-dryers and electric toasters having gone on the fritz for a while.

We believe the sun caused all these disruptions, as it did in 2011. You'll find that there are no long-term effects. Rest assured you can go about your daily affairs comforted by the knowledge that the integrity of all services has been enhanced. This pandemic affected each and every one of us, its magnitude unprecedented. Further steps will be taken to avoid any such future disruptions to your toasters and air-dryers, as well as your flights to destinations out of this world.

Using the power of his own storm, he followed the sniggering tucked away in the dark depths. Though a clumsy attempt to draw him ever closer, Bob had decided his shoes had done all the running he intended for them in this place. Pink Floyd had said that he had come home again and it was time to rest his bones by the fire.

And that he would.

A watermark pressed in high-relief from the darkness. *"Why don't you take off that stupid fucking hat?"* The hatred in his voice was thick.

"Tsst! Tsst! Mind your language, Master Bobbyyyy; you do not want your punishment to be worse than what it already is, do you?" The bitch paused. *"Then again, maybe you do. You want to feel me, Master Bobbyyyy? You want to know what I am like, and there is something I wish to impart upon you. So we have something in common, do we not, Master Bobbyyyy?"*

"I'll never stop loathing you for what you've done to me and all the other children. For what you're *still* doing." His expression was both guttural and low.

"And what might that be?"

"You're still punishing the children."

The bitch found an amount of humor in this. *"Yet you felt compelled to remain connected to me for all these years. Why do you think that is, Bobbyyyy?"* Huge teeth gnawed away in the gaping 'say cheese' mouth, glimmering in the near complete darkness at the back of the room—at least, Bob supposed the bitch stood near the back of the room, for it was impossible to tell in the dimmest of light.

In this place, where there was no recourse, he took another stand and chose not to answer.

"You think you have made something of your life, but you have made nothing of the sort, you worthless little shit!" the bitch spat. *"Had you accomplished the impossible, you would not have been drawn here time and again, using me as your excuse. You, Bobbyyyy, are the one who could not let go of your past. For it was here that you found safety and security—a sanctuary—from the unpleasant vagaries of the streets that you would have otherwise wandered alone and tender at age. You are home, Bobbyyyy; you have always wanted to come home."* The bitch spread her stick-like arms wide, the fingernails a-glistening, spectral circumference about the dull sparkles from her swollen eyes and planks of teeth.

He could see she was clutching something in one of them.

"It is here that you have always belonged, and though you can fool yourself, there's no denying the truth."

In a classic Mexican stand-off, they eyeballed each other until she said, *"Come... come close, Master Bobbyyyy, because you want to know, am I correct? You want to know what I know—and so I will tell you, because I know what is eating you up from the inside out."*

As Bob stepped forward, he thought, *Dear Watson, the difference between strategy and invention is a fine line, to say the least.*

With the distance closing, he became aware of an object in the room with them. For a moment, he believed it to be the bitch's desk, the helm of Hell Ship. But that wasn't the case. In fact, it was quite innocuous. And instantly recognizable.

At the third stroke, the time will be... twelve... twelve... twelve... o... one A.M.
At the third stroke, the time will be... twelve... twelve... twelve... o... one A.M.
At the third stroke, the time will be... twelve... twelve... twelve... o... one A.M.
At the third stroke, the time will be... twelve... twelve... twelve... o... one A.M.
At the third stroke, the time will be... twelve... twelve... twelve... o... one A.M.
At the third stroke, the time will be... twelve... twelve... twelve... o... one A.M.
At the third stroke, the time will be... twelve... twelve... twelve... o... one A.M.
At the third stroke, the time will be... twelve... twelve... twelve... o... one A.M.
At the third stroke, the time will be... twelve... twelve... twelve... o... one A.M.
At the third stroke, the time will be... twelve... twelve... twelve... o... one A.M.

It was a school desk.

The bitch sniggered and advanced. **TINKLE.**

No more *CLACK*.

Bob looked down at her insectile feet and instead saw that she had donned shoes. And no ordinary common garden variety of shoe at that. These were special: they were ridiculously long and curled at the toe, each ending in a bell.

Her leering face pushed further through the umbra. She was either stooping very low or had shrunk over the years, because in that hideous watermark, she was a diminutive creature and not as nearly as tall as Bob had remembered.

She'd downsized in other ways, too. The bitch had always carried the weight of a behemoth who stomped about the halls of Mother's Care in the fashion of a cheerlessly brutal Fairy Godmother in stilettos. The floor vibrated beneath her burden, adding to the fear she instilled. Her shoes clacked against the floor in search of a thrill to fulfill her lust.

She ground her teeth. Had Bob shut his eyes—which of course he'd have been a fool to do—she would've seen a deranged chef, eyes hang-dog dark and bottomless pits of contamination, sharpening his knives on a steel in his kitchen, preparing to slaughter. *"Like what you see?"*

"You're still the bitch." Bob's revulsion was offset by sickening fascination.

"Your persecution is unfounded, Bobbyyyy. The heroine of which you speak was treated at the senseless hands of hick rednecks. They tore her world apart, Bobbyyyy. Their hysterics rallied supporters of weak substance, and vilification grew until she lost all she ever had, all she'd ever built. Did they care, Bobbyyyy? Noooo! They came at her with their bulldozers and buried her life, and then erected a playground for the kiddies before standing back, admiring their handiwork. They basked in their hypocrisy, proclaiming they were just and moral, of high ethics. But they allowed the kiddies to play, is that not so, Bobbyyyy? Oh yes indeedy, they allowed them to play, when what they really needed was guidance. How else were the little shits ever going to learn?" The bitch began laughing, and if her teeth were the deadly sound of sharpening knives,

then the laughter was the blood spilled thereafter. It was thick
and diseased, something that had no right to be, just as this
hellhole had no right to be—a mutation of a massive nuclear
catastrophe.

"So you *concocted* another *hellhole!*" Bob trembled viciously.

TINKLE-TINKLE

Two extra steps forward… out of the black and into the
dark gray. She rounded the school desk, sitting lonely, awaiting
company, like a dog waiting for its master.

Shaking his head, submerged in his growing revolution, Bob
struggled with his words. "You took them for your own means,
to serve a life of relentless misery and torture at your hands.
This… this *hellhole* was nothing but a latter-day gulag. It had
nothing to do with providing love and sanctuary."

"*I am not the bitch of which you speak.*" Amused.

Bob was in no mood for deceitful proclamations. "A graveyard
for the living's no substitute for the streets beyond. They were
right to bulldoze this *hellhole* into the ground. And, by God,
had I known, I would've been the one sitting high in the leading
bulldozer and grinning from ear to ear, while crying out against
all the evil that had gone before the day."

"*Those I take care of are given all they had ever wanted. All
they had ever dreamed of. They are safe, Bobbyyyy. All of them.
And that is the way it is going to be forever. They will not have
to fuss over getting old, trying to provide for family. They will not
have to worry about grades or who their friends are. They have got
everything they deserved. They got exactly what they had desired.*"

It was Bob who laughed this time. In fact, he began to
laugh so hard, he was finding it difficult to catch his breath.
"They razed Mother's Care Orphanage and you couldn't stop

them. You couldn't stop them because out there—you're just a powerless little piece of shit yourself."

"*Why not do yourself a favor and let go of your pent-up fear? Your anger?*"

TINKLE

"Outside these dirty little walls that incarcerate your dirty little secrets, your own existence is meaningless. The world still turned and no one cared about you, beyond wishing your body rot as fast as nature could dispose of it. But the children—that was another matter. How people must've cried over them, for what you'd done to them." Now his laughter had dried up and the inner storm and rage had reclaimed his emotions.

"*I gave them a future.*"

"You took away their innocence, their lives. You ruined anything that might've become of them."

The bitch started singing, the song as instantly recognizable as the school desk had been: "Dream a Little Dream of Me."

Despite this, he went on. "My parents didn't *choose* to die and leave me. They were returning home because they *loved* me."

"*They chose the easy way out, choosing to run the red light, to end it under the wheels of a prime mover. I only ever helped those who were in need of help.*"

The bitch went on singing 'Dream a Little Dream of Me.' She was moving in a way that made the bells' sparkly percussions adorning her release as soft and wistful as colorful kites riding high on a breeze.

"You truly are hopelessly insane." Bob noticed the bells on her stupid hat and the sudden urge to take a seat had him swaying on his feet. Seemed jetlag had doubled back to syphon the strength for his legs, while applying eyeshadow made of lead. A moment's rest… couldn't hurt. Might make things better… A clear head paid dividends of clearer thoughts; and frankly, he sure needed that by the bucketload.

The storm raging across the hemisphere of his brain lit up with snarls of lighting; and all matter of recollection, whether real or imagined, churned ever faster as the winds increased. But hell, it was a walk in the park. A tap dance in a rain shower. The bitch's outrageous sanctimony had bought it on the blade of a bulldozer, with some fat jock eating a pie and spilling sauce down the front of him, while farting a complete rendition of 'Waltzing Matilda.'

Bob staggered a little. Corrected.

Embrace the storm. Yes—that was what he needed to do. Take a good hold of it and allow its power to surge through him. Forget clear thoughts. He had to act or he would be acted upon. Like a kid in a candy shop of poisonous offerings, he was struggling in knowing what to do, how to act or what to think. He wanted to sit down. He wanted to rip off the head of this bitch. He wanted to go home and… fly a kite.

The bitch grinned. *"Just a few steps from where you could find yourself in a place where nothing else would be of concern, where nothing matters—just as all the others have discovered. They are to be envied. They have what you so richly desire."*

Bob wasn't going to give the bitch the pleasure of asking what that might be. He snapped his eyes open, reminding himself to seize the moment. Or tap dance alongside a fat jock whose flatulence skills were truly breathtaking.

"Freedom," she crooned, *"is what you have searched for but have never found. It is a matter of will, Bobbyyyy!"*

"Trapped in a world of your own delusion can hardly be called freedom!" Needing to keep his head on his shoulders, Bob managed the storm despite the jetlag.

The bitch had continued singing. The kites hovered above his head like colorful helicopters against a bright blue sky.

Out of the dark gray and into a lighter shade.

"*Your son is just beyond this room, roaming about without direction because his father abandoned him. Tsst! Tsst! A boy needs parental direction.* Guidance. *That is fair to say, would you not agree, Master Bobbyyyy?*"

Bob's anger swelled through his growing stupor and confusion. "You leave Joshua out of this!"

"*I am afraid Joshua's been coming to my front door for some time. You did not you know? Of course. Poor Master Bobbyyyy. You are not even aware of your own son's whereabouts.*"

The bitch tried on that grin again as she danced around him.

"Patrick Nesmith sought him out." But then, hadn't he considered that he might have been talking to the man himself, in drag?

"*That's what you think? You might at long last have something right. It makes a change, but doesn't change the fact that your son has had to come through me to get to Patrick Nesmith.*" The bitch's face took on the appearance of deep thought. "*Isn't he the one the children call 'the man in black?'*"

The jetlag coerced Bob further down to where an inviting seat awaited, appearing in the form of plush sheets and pillows. "It's time to take care of things," he said, fighting against opposing desires.

"*You have always been wrong, Master Bobbyyyy! Whoever you think I am, you have been wrong. You were wrong when just a teenager and escaping the orphanage, you were wrong as a young adult, and you are still wrong. Tsst! Tsst! All that worry. All that turmoil. And for what, nobody will ever know."*

"You're just the bitch." Bob shook his head. "The man in black."

"I have never been anything of the sort. After all, this bitch that you speak of, you honestly believe she had the power to infiltrate your most private of moments? She could not have, because she too enjoys endless peace in her own world. She is just down the way, with all the children, all the men and women of your world... eating and growing fat. But not for long, as they will be lost if not claimed within their dreams first. Those who have found such pleasures are the opposite side of this wall. Why not you go see for yourself?"

"I'll finish this then go find my son and leave." The bitch was messing with his head, as she had always done. He shouldn't have allowed her the conversation he already had, but he had needed to know. And now he was more confused than ever.

"You must at long last take your punishment!" The bitch held out a clenched hand. Within it were a number of pencils and pens. *"Take your pick. It is easy... easier that you have ever imagined."*

Bob staggered away before his inner resolve had him once more stepping forward. His knees buckled. Straightened.

She lunged at him, this diminutive leering monstrosity.

The kites ducked and weaved in a sudden gust.

His knees buckled once more, and his feet slipped, threatening to bring him down. He corrected this near-miss only to whirl about to protect himself, as something shuffled up to him from behind.

Through the oblong patch, marking the entrance into this room, he could make out a figure.

"*Get out of here, Josh!*" Bob bellowed, slurring his words like a man who had drunk his way to the bottom of a whiskey bottle.

Out of the winter gloom walked a finely-framed child. A bespectacled boy whose arms and legs were no more than pipe cleaners. He had donned a striped T-shirt for the day and a baggy pair of shorts. These clothes Bob knew well. The boy he knew intimately.

He cast an eye down the scrawny figure before him. His knobby knees interrupted the skinny decent into white socks and sandshoes. His face was awash with a pallor that suggested he'd seen the sun only in fleeting trysts throughout his short life. There was a sprinkling of freckles across the bridge of his nose, and a timidness bordering on fear shifting beneath the thinnest of films.

As the adult and child stared into each other's eyes—and saw themselves—time seemed to stand still.

"Time for your punishment, Bobby," the bespectacled boy said, holding out something in his hand. His fingers were curled over them. More pencils and pens.

Bob stared down at the frightened little boy and his heart cried a little.

"Please," the boy begged, his hand trembling badly.

After a moment, he got the message and scampered from the room. His silhouette broke the charcoal patch of the doorway, and was gone in an instant.

"*You were always a frightened little boy. You're still a frightened little boy.*"

Bob spun to face her and finally saw a jester standing before him. Not the bitch at all. Nor a man in black. Just a jester, caricature or not, the type of comical relief for aristocracies from far in history.

"*How long has it been since you truly tasted and felt freedom? Never... ever... never ever... You should have taken the punishment that was offered when just a scrawny little boy. You were given a way out, as many have been. They took their chance. You still have yours... punishment is merely a figure of speech... a bit of writing for so much freedom. It will continue to wait until you take it. You can run forever and ever and never ever run fast enough or long enough to stay far enough ahead that it will not catch you up, Master Bobbyyyy. For wasn't it you who thought you could run but you would always come home?*"

"You've been reading... my *mind*?" Bob uttered. His eyes shut. A moment lingered before they snapped open.

"*Your time to take the long outstanding* freedom *is now at hand, and you will take it as you should have when just a boy, sparing yourself the agony and anguish. You should never have had a child... passing on your genes so that one became another. All you have done is assigned your only child to his own* freedom."

The jester slow danced, and recommenced 'Dream a Little Dream of Me.' It swooned about the godforsaken room, stirring the rich odors of rank and rotting algae, and perhaps the last breath of forlorn children that cloyed the senses.

A pencil slipped from the jester's grasp, landing on the floor with a rather innocent wooden clatter, its spidery fingers clutching the rest.

Another fell... then another... the jester was sprinkling the floor with love

'cause they make you taste oh-so sweet…
The toffee-apple tree, the toffee-apple tree…

offerings.

Waiting for Master Bobby to get his comeuppance.

Bob had to get to his son. He should never have left him, breaking his promise. *Oh God, what had he done?*

He ran for the door, but it kept dodging his advances, before slamming shut with a sonic boom and sending him reeling towards the desk behind.

In the moment following, a delirious silence overcame Bob. The storm dissipated and he felt at peace. He'd never felt so restful. Strange—a moment ago, he was torn between ripping some motherfucker's head off its ugly shoulders and getting to his son. The transition, both dramatic and powerful, was accompanied by a dry scratching, rather like dragging a fingernail down your cheek when it sported a day's stubble.

Had he been running from the very thing he should've simply accepted all his life? Had he simply misinterpreted what he had been running from since childhood?

It seemed highly probable. If not absolutely possible. If not downright factual.

The most poignant point to all of this was that he should've heeded the signs and not born a child, because by doing so had led his only child, his beautiful son, into this labyrinth of hell—

Peace.

Yes, it is peaceful here. I'm a bit silly, aren't I? Guess that makes me a silly-Bobby, rather than a silly-Billy: always jumping to the

wrong conclusions. Instead of running, I should've come here earlier.
Much, much earlier, because if I had...

"G'day, mate!" It was his dad's voice and, by the sound of it he was incredibly happy to see him. Bobby hustled about as he had been looking in another direction, although there wasn't much to see there.

"We've been searching high and low for you, mate! Where've you been? Your mother's been beside herself, as you might've guessed. And may I say you've grown a bit over time." Godwin marvelled at how he and Bobby were almost on similar eye level. "You're gonna be a strapping young man!" With that he clapped Bobby on the back.

"*Dad?*" Impossible!

"Either that or I'm a poor substitute for the Easter Bunny."

"*Mum?*" Impossible!

"Oh, dear!" Helen Triplow bent a little, took hold of her son and hugged him tight. "It's been a while," was all she could say. She thought she'd have said a lot more after all this time, but words failed her and that was okay.

Her fragrance, cherry blossom on a spring morning, filled Bobby's senses, and his tears streamed forth. She was real; the pads of his fingers played gently but firmly over her to confirm what he never thought possible.

"Good to have you back, mate," his dad was saying. "Don't know how much more of these bloody green fields I could've taken in search for you; reckon I've turned over ever fucking blade of grass there is."

"Godwin," Helen chastised on auto-pilot.

"Agh, honey, we can give up our proprieties a smig, just this once. It's been an adventure, mate. Like looking for a runt amongst thickets of hairs on a bald man's ass." He was laughing. "Every one of them green!"

"I dreamt of green fields. I dreamt about you … For decades I dreamt all these things! But I haven't dreamt them in years."

"That's strange," Godwin said. "So when *did* you stop dreaming them?"

"I thought I was in my twenties."

Goodwin and his mum turned to one another, each wearing a smirk that both hardened and softened their faces at once.

"Decades, hey?" his dad continued. "Don't go trying to grow up too fast; we've got a bit of catching up to do as it is, mate!" With that he disappeared into the green fields. After a moment, he reappeared—and he'd brought a few things, which he shook excitedly before him.

For a moment, Bobby ignored this, suddenly remembering what had been forgotten. "I had a son," he blurted.

His mum drew herself away a little. "Oh honey, I don't know where you've been, but you're what? Eleven?" Her breath was pepperminty fresh.

"You had a dream, Bobby, that's all," his dad was saying.

"But I did," Bobby protested in his striped T-shirt and baggy shorts. "I also got married."

"Uh-huh. Perhaps in another life, but not in this one, sweetheart," Helen said, smiling. Her teeth were so white, it invoked a jingle from an ad Bobby had seen long ago. Or was it?

He frowned, then shrugged.

The ad asked if your Macleans were showing… stating that if you brushed with Macleans, you'd have knockout white teeth. And Bobby's mum had knockout white teeth.

He giggled. "You're probably right; must've dreamt the whole thing."

"As your dad said, don't try growing up too quickly."

"Though you *are* growing up," Godwin added. "No one's ever too old to fly a kite!" he chortled like a kid about to wet his pants with excitement. "One's for you, mate!"

"I only ever dreamed of two!" Bobby said, marvelling at the two kites remaining in his dad's hands. In all the nights he had dreamed of flying a kite with his mum and dad, he'd only ever seen two. And now there were three! *Why not?* He'd also dreamt that he'd had a wife and son. Anything was possible when you dreamed!

Then, coming over the green field's horizon, he heard: "*Dad!*"

"One each is what we shall have!" Godwin broke into Bobby's distraction. "Come on, then!" he yelled over his shoulder, running away with his kite trailing behind. It caught some air and lifted, then dipped. Godwin put on a bit more speed, and the kite caught a good lot of air and soared high and bright into the endless blue sky.

Wearing a broad grin that seemed to touch each earlobe, Bobby chased after him.

And the three of them ran over the bald man's ass with Godwin yelling, barely able to keep the laughter out of his voice and make himself decipherable. "Let's see which one of us can get their kite the highest!"

Bobby was running so hard and fast, his hair flailed back on his scalp, and his glasses were in peril of slipping from his face, hanging askew on the bridge of his nose. His kite soared way above, its magical colors in full flight.

"Who decided you were blind as a bat?" Godwin asked.

Helen was running by the side of her men, giggling like a pre-adolescent who'd just heard a naughty story.

"Dunno!" Bobby yelled as he ran. "I love you so much!"

Helen Triplow started crying.

"The orphanage they sent me to was terrible. I never want to go back."

"*Orphanage?*" Godwin had a few tears of his own. "Don't worry about that now, mate!"

The banter from there on was the type of stuff Bobby wanted to sponge up and bottle. It was beyond rapture.

He went running into the distance with his dad and mum, into what had once been a dream that teased his sanity.

He ran hard and he ran fast.

And when the Triplows' got tired, they finally went home, only to fly their kites again and again...

For the moment, the peal from those rumbustious infants had gone silent. Or was it that he'd been deafened by them?

Joshua couldn't possibly hope to have evaded the man-things in three-peaked hats, but if that was the case, it had happened by design. They hadn't gone. They simply waited in the darkness, their bulbous eyes watching his every move.

He had no sooner reached the door when it had slammed square in his face, placing a rather nasty full stop to his searching, and damn near rupturing his eardrums in the process. The percussion had sent a shockwave through his stomach, as if the fist of an angry tyrant had found its target, winding him yet again. The habit had become a little overdone for his liking, and something he'd rather edit from the script.

With his ears still ringing, he began ramming the door with his shoulder, since all attempts by the usual method had failed. His fingers were slick with sweat and the brass knob was covered in greasy slime.

However, the skinny body of a boy against an ancient slab of wood, held into position by industrial-sized hinges that bled rust, was hardly a match.

"*Dad!*" Yelling might well attract unwanted attention, but he had to get to his dad, who had become locked in this room.

Drawn here by his dad's muttering, after his footfalls had abruptly stopped, Joshua had not been able to decipher his words even as he approached the door. But when his dad had received a reply, he had been left shockingly in no doubt to whom his dad spoke.

"*DAD!*" All within had gone quiet, except the pitapatter of tears, like raindrops on a depressingly gray day, in which the clouds had dispensed with wearing masks of human faces for outfits of bruised and moldy cauliflowers, interlaced with rotting aubergines.

A man-thing in the three-peaked hat and his dad were locked inside. Together. And conversing on a subject that carried dangerous undercurrents.

When this had happened at Sammy's…

Oh please, I can't lose my dad. Just as soon as it had come, Joshua renounced the whining of that weaker self.

What had the man-thing called itself? This did seem important, so it required some attention. Because the man-things were hardwired to each other. The chasing bells had been a team effort. When one stopped, they had all stopped. When one started the chase, they'd all started the chase.

Just like drones.

When your thoughts were the debris churning and blocking the drains upon that depressingly gray day, it was difficult to be yourself and just let yourself do what you normally would. He needed to think, but time was ticking away

As his father had learned

and the more he debated the ins and outs, the more his desperation grew.

"The Dream Sorcerer," Joshua said aloud, because it was easier for the memory to make its way through the blockage.

What did that mean? This *wasn't* a dream, unless when he and his dad had fallen asleep in the Duncan's toilet cubicle, they hadn't actually woken up.

Joshua had determined before that this was no dream, and remained steadfast to the conviction.

So where did that leave him and his dad?

Questions, Joshua. Too many questions and not enough answers. Not enough time!

His dad and his childhood misery, the man in black and his cohort of man-things, Sammy and himself... there was a common factor, and the Dream Sorcerer was weaving them all together. Or had already woven them altogether. For what purpose?

His own. None of this served any other as it did the Dream Sorcerer, including very much Sammy's abduction.

He'd been afraid of the man in black, but did he have a hand in stealing his friend from his mom and dad, from his friends, and sweeping him from the life he knew?

Joshua stood amongst the dripping echoes of lost childhoods in a cold sweat. For all he'd been through—and such stuff receded into the depths of his own history when he had started dreaming of the man in black—such uncertainties had never occurred to him.

Ultimately, the man in black had the answer to ending this. The Dream Sorcerer, on the other hand, had been desperate in the last nightmare to have him rescue his friend. Why? Because he was meant to follow him into that place beyond the doorway?

Running with cold sweat, breathing hard, heart a rat-a-tat-tat, he reached forward, clasped the brass knob once more, the slick coating squeezing between his fingers, and held on tight.

The handle turned. The door opened smoothly, as had the entrance doors… no hoary squeaking as you'd expect.

What it opened on completely, and in an instant, assaulted the mind. No matter what configuration it raced to, it couldn't do it. The more frantically it tried, the colder Joshua became, until he and all else froze over.

Because, somewhere in the slideshow of configurations, something unthinkable had taken shape. In the dingy depths of this room was his dad. He was obviously tired after all the running he'd done, and the long flight to Australia. Finally, he had found the opportunity to take a proper seat… at a school desk, no less.

His dad was staring directly at him but not seeing him.

"Dad?" Joshua's mouth cracked open a sinuous fissure in the ice-pack.

No response, as he had feared.

Because his dad was somewhat preoccupied with the task at hand. Since he was given to an archaically orthodox habit, as was Joshua, he had an item clutched between his right fingers, with which he furiously scribbled away.

Skittery-scratch... scratchy-scratch...

∽

1987
Kapunda, South Australia

Within Mother's Care Orphanage—and in the very room currently occupied by Bob Triplow, the adult, whose scribbling denoted that, at long last, he'd accepted his punishment—his *dream*—a conversation took place.

"Anthea, the Order is concerned with their aegis being misappropriated."

"It's nothing to be concerned with. You need to focus on your own shortcomings."

"There's much talk of your ability to run this orphanage in the nurturing and harmonious style we all value and support."

"You, Patrick, I'd have credited with more intelligence than to listen to idle, malicious gossip."

"What of the missing children over the past years?"

"Have they ever been found?"

"I hardly have to tell you the answer to that."

"Well, then, malicious gossip," Anthea said with great justification. "If a child wishes to hide, they're masters at it. Children who come here are often traumatized beyond help, and all they want to do is to run away and hide from their past. Whilst we have quality social workers, counsellors, support workers and people such as yourself, we can't be there twenty-four hours around the clock to soothe away their torments and pain. If you bludgeon a dog mercilessly when its young, it'll always grow up with unsavory baggage."

"All the more reason why it's imperative that you be the motherly figure."

"What makes you think I'm not?"

"Most children are too frightened to tell me the truth, Anthea. But I see enough to know that something is not as it should be at Mother's Care. The children I speak to are doubtlessly hiding something—"

"Their past."

"No, Anthea, I do not believe that is so. There's more than that. It's fresher..."

Anthea laughed with pretentious sarcasm. "You've come up with this startling conclusion?"

"The Order has come to the conclusion."

"Have any of the

Worthless little shits

children ever said anything that implicates me as someone who'd know of such allegations?"

"They're too frightened. But then it seems you're not the most pleasant of women when watchful eyes are averted, and your fitness to care for the children appropriately is under serious question."

"Whose question?" Anthea retorted. "I don't have to remind you that I'm held in high esteem, and don't appreciate your accusations."

"Children may well be running from their past, but they shouldn't have to feel they must do that once here, should they?"

"You're looking too hard for a scapegoat, and I'll be damned if I'm it!"

"The Order thinks not."

"Patrick Nesmith, both you and the Order are delusional. *If* the Order even know of this, *which* I highly doubt. How would they feel if I told them of your little interludes when you're in your hidey-hole? I see you scribbling away." Anthea paused for a moment. "What are you writing, Patrick? Your memoires or the confessions of a torn man… supposedly caring for the children, yet interfering with them?"

"I abhor the suggestion."

Anthea laughed her sarcastic laugh once more. "Oh Patrick, have I not been forthright enough? I suggest nothing; merely stating facts. The disappearances coincided with your incessant scribbling. You say the children here are hiding something nasty. What about you, Patrick Nesmith? Is there something you'd like to get off your dirty little chest?"

"Doodling is cathartic. It allows me to

Appease the demons within and the images of a lost world into which souls are snatched

think."

"The look in your eyes, Patrick, tells me you're lying." Anthea tutted sadly. "Such a sin."

Anxiety had become a garotte, its steely cord pulling ever tighter, threatening to suffocate him or break his windpipe, whichever came first. It was all Patrick could do to look the woman in the eye. Anthea had a point. God Almighty, she had a point. He desperately wished he could undo what seemed to have overtaken him.

One day, he had been just normal Patrick Nesmith, man of God. The next he was scribbling. And whilst such scribbling had the appearance of nothing more sinister than the doodling of idle hands, there was more to the 'zero-zero, zero-one' than met the eye. The scribbling was a sickness he couldn't escape, as it was buried within his very makeup. You could say it was part of his DNA.

Often such episodes would become so exhausting, he'd faint in a pool of his own sick sweat, pen dropping to the floor. Waiting… forever waiting for him to pick it up and use it at will.

But that wasn't the way it was at all. He had no will over it, therefore he had no control over the sickness.

Indeed, he was a sick man with a sick mind… but not in the way Anthea projected. He could never be like that. Never. Could he? Oh dear God – help him!

On his grandmother's deathbed, he'd discovered that the sickness was more than happenchance. Decades earlier, well before the scribbling sickness had started, his grandmother had confided the deed his great grandfather had left as a slanderous legacy.

He, too, had an addictive penchant for scribbling.

"What did he scribble, Grandma?"

"On face value, rubbish. But I can tell you it is by far more than the stuff you stow in the trash. The bins would overflow with pages of the same scribbled contents."

"What was he writing?"

"Three zeros and a one."

Patrick had been utterly dumbfounded. "What does it mean?" he had said, pulling a face.

"Lost," Florence had gasped. "The devil's curse. You must promise never follow in his footsteps."

"Why would I?"

"You must *promise*!"

Patrick had nodded. "Of course. Why would I?"

Why indeed? I'm not that sort of man! Am I?

Destiny… fate… a family inheritance… the Nesmith curse… nothing to do with the Devil. Mind you, it just might conjure the Devil.

"You speak of this to no other. The family name would be destroyed." These were the last words Florence Nesmith had uttered before taking her final breath.

For years, it'd been nothing more than a confounding memory: what could be so heinous in writing 'zero-zero, zero-one?' He'd researched books, papers and the internet for its meaning, to no avail. It was just a story made up through the failing mind of one at death's door.

Until that day happened along and yanked the rug out from under his feet.

Night after night, day after day—now that the sickness had settled in for the long haul, his right hand had never done so much writing.

The sound of pen against paper

Skittery-scratch… scratchy-scratch…

was enough to drive him further into insanity.

On the outskirts of Kapunda, South Australia, some fifty-three miles from the state's CBD of Adelaide, it stood as the only building along the aptly named Solemn Street.

Birds sung here and there from invisible perches and the sun cast few pools of shadow. The day was mild, but the western horizon looked threatening. A storm was on the rise.

The immediate surrounds to Mother's Care Orphanage resembled a postcard from the 1950s, rather than the late 1980s. Had a couple of old geezers been hovering about the Hudson Terraplane that sat out front, they'd have fitted in seamlessly.

Long flaxen weeds surrounded the Terraplane. They blew fitfully in the errant breeze. Scrawled across its ample flank was:

WHY DON'T YOU ALL GET LOST
JUST DISAPPEAR

Typical sheet metal from the late fifties, this Terraplane personified what everyone feared in a gangster: big, ruggedly handsome, slick and unpredictable. If you weren't kissing ass or steering clear, your chances of having made the top ten on the hit list were disproportionately high. Many locals had complained to the council about the eyesore and the attraction it created, especially drawing the attraction of the wrong sort of character to the orphanage. This fuelled further interference and mischievous acts. Often, disparaging comments could be heard shouted from open car windows as they passed. Once a Molotov cocktail was hurled at the orphanage, which required the immediate intervention of the local fire service. One officer had said that the orphanage was a light to moths, only it attracted the wrong sort of moth.

When asked to explain, he clarified that in no part had he been referring to the children themselves.

"Poor little blighters need a helping hand," he'd said morosely. "A fresh start not associated with such a place. Living under the banner of 'orphanage' puts them behind the eight ball before they've got started."

The Light Regional Council argued, and rightfully so, that the children at the 'orphanage' needed a home. Mother's Care was that home, and they weren't about to suggest a relocation, as if the children were less than acceptable citizens of the council's jurisdiction.

"Why don't you remove that eyesore out the front of the orphanage, then? You say one thing and act opposite. If these children are so precious, get rid of that bloody car!"

This too was a reasonable argument.

Nonetheless, the Terraplane remained with its slanderous slogan, emblazoned in heavy-handed black paint, that had run as mascara might do after a particularly sad story. The dubious accompaniment to the orphanage, within whose towering walls almost all wished they could dictate their own 'getting lost.'

The boys were hiding from the matron's attention. Her whereabouts were easily detectable, if not always avoidable, as her shoes clacked against the stone floor, portending trouble on the way. She was big and fat and she had a particular disliking for boys.

Those between the age of eight and fourteen were high on her hit list. And hit she did, with a leather strap she'd affectionately titled the Official Marker. Forever champing at the bit, its malicious tongue would lash out with relish, stimulated by the screams it evoked.

At the age of twelve, both Douglas McKenzie and Bobby Triplow were in her crosshairs. They had met with her Official Marker often, and could still show the results it'd left from those past acquaintances.

Officials would come to the orphanage for a surprise 'inspection' and leave none the wiser to the brutality handed out. Sheer fear of more of the same kept the children in check. That and an unhealthy dose of understanding that promises made could be easily and readily broken. Go blabbing to the outsiders in their finely-cut dresses, shiny shoes, suits and ties, smelling of expensive perfume and cologne had the potential of backfiring. They would smile sympathetically, as if they knew it all and walk away... leaving the blabber to have a change of heart upon subsequent interviews and admit to telling dirty little lies to get the matron into trouble because they had to blame someone for their wretched life.

None, including Douglas or Bobby, held any trust in those who waltzed through the doors, nosed about for an hour or so, poking here and there, asking a lot of pointless questions, before slipping away, not to be seen until some other kid went missing. With clipboards and notepads in hand, as well as a lot of 'umming' and 'arring,' they were about as effective and inspirational as sudsless dishwashing liquid.

"What do you think has happened to all those kids?" Douglas was asking his best friend.

"Some say the Norton twins went to their grandma's. They're real lucky."

"You think that's what really happened?"

"I guess. Don't you?"

"Nope. Look at it, Bobby. They supposedly left for their grandma's just when kids have been leaving this place in droves. It doesn't figure that they're all going to their grandma's who've suddenly become remorseful over losing their grandchildren somewhere along the way. So leaving the grandma's aside, don't you find that somewhat of a coincidence?"

"I guess. What do you think happened to them?"

"She murdered them, Bobby. Their disappearances are too coincidental. And I reckon she hid their bodies on these grounds, and when they eventually have to dig it up because of a busted water pipe, they're gonna dig up more than dirt and the odd worm or two."

"Man, no way could she get away with that."

"You for real, Bobby?" Douglas couldn't quite believe what he was hearing; maybe from one of those sudsless dishwashing clipboard characters, but Bobby? "She gets away with close to murder in front of everyone, and who dares to do anything about it? No one, that's who."

"She couldn't get away with murder, Douglas," Bobby repeated himself in an act of self-conviction. If he said it enough, he might just believe it.

"Okay then, what happened to horseman Billy? She couldn't stand him because of his size... you know what I mean?" Douglas said as if he was implying a secret. "I reckon she had her way with him until she either accidentally or intentionally killed him. It's still murder in either case." Douglas shivered.

His arms wrapped around his legs as they sat in a small closet, discussing the horrors at Mother's Care Orphanage.

"How many do you think have disappeared this year?" Bobby asked, not wanting to know the answer but macabrely fascinated at the same time. "I reckon about half a dozen."

Douglas' eyes grew large. "Some say there've been fifteen kids who have left this orphanage, but that they never did so walking out by themselves. And that's only the ones officially known of. Kids come here, Bobby, who are already lost."

"If she buried them here, on the grounds, where could she possibly do that?"

Clacking footfalls had entered the hallway outside. They got closer, the boys sweating, barely able to take their next breath, before they moved away.

Each boy exhaled with relief.

"That was close," Bobby whispered nervously.

"The apple grove," Douglas said finally.

Bobby nodded. Everybody knew of the apple grove, because it was a place that bore big red shiny apples that many came and paid for. Their reputation for making the best apple pies on the planet was legendary. That was not how the children of Mother's Care knew so well of the apple grove, though. Stories had abound for years about happenings down in the apple grove.

Children doing naughty things.

Adults doing naughty things.

Adults doing naughty things to children.

And, sometimes, children doing naughty things to adults.

Such stories were rife. Most were born of urban myth. Most, but not all. Other than the big juicy apple ones, none of them were at all pleasant. Seemed to be the more sinister they became, the more sinister threads the stories took on.

"Those apples grow so well down there, Bobby, and it's no fluke. It's not as if anyone gives a shit in caring for them, pretty much like no one gives a shit about caring for us. But apples just don't naturally grow that way, because they're not cared for in some way."

"What are you getting at, Douglas?" Bobby asked, knowing exactly what he was 'getting at.'

"The bodies are what those trees are tapping into... their juices oozing through the ground feeding the trees. Betcha if we dig, we'd find horseman Billy and the Norton twins. Their stinking rotten flesh providing for those big red apples that people pick then peel and cook. They eat them, Bobby, whilst saying, 'Oh, what a lovely pie, don't think I've ever tasted any this good. I simply must have seconds.' That's what makes the difference, and no one knows. And if they do, no one cares, 'cause they care more about the apples than they do about the children."

Once more, the air agitated to footsteps that went off like penny bombs along the hallway. The footsteps came closer and the boys feared that they would be caught by the matron having a merry little chat in this closet. If so, there'd be merry hell to pay, and her Official Marker would do some walloping and they'd do some hollering. Moments passed, as did the penny bombs.

"You want to go down there?" Bobby asked, but not before complete silence befell the hallway.

"There's a spade behind the gardener's shed. For some reason he never packs it away," Douglas returned excitedly.

"If you're right, it'd be in high demand, Douglas. Maybe he never puts it away because it's just too inconvenient to go fetch all the time. Best leave it somewhere handy so it's always at the ready. After all, have you ever gotten a load of that weirdo? If there's murder going on, I reckon he'd have to be stopped from committing his part of the deed *right* in the middle of town. It's his lack of intelligence that scares me *more* than the bitch."

"You reckon that's what they're using to bury the bodies?" Douglas asked, shivering at the slobbering image of the gardener toiling away whilst laughing as a dead kid lolled by his side.

"If you're right, there's no way the matron could be doing this all by herself. She's so fat, she wouldn't have the energy to dig a hole big enough, let alone carry a body down to the grove and then fill it in."

"So she has an accomplice?"

"It makes sense. *If* you're right."

"Let's get the spade and do some digging."

"Douglas, if we get caught, forget the Official Marker. Our balls will be her next day's breakfast."

A funny look came over Douglas' eyes. "Kids do go down there to… you know?"

"I know."

"Ever wondered what that'd be like?"

"I suppose. But for now, let's get the bitch into deep trouble, the kind not even she can escape."

"When?"

"Now. It's Saturday. We don't have to be anywhere in particular. It's not as if we've got to hurry 'cause we've got an invitation to a party, or our folks are going take us to the movies. We might as well dig."

"What if we find something?"

"Then we run, 'cause it'd do us no good coming back here. She'd only manage to cover it up and then turn her attention to us, Douglas, and that would be very bad," Bobby said ominously. "We find anything, we run to the police."

"I've got a Polaroid Instamatic. We could take some happy snaps of the apple grove at Mother's Care. The shit would hit the fan and this place would get what it deserves, as well as the matron."

"How have you got that, anyhow?" Bobby knew they were expensive.

"One of my relatives—not my grandma, don't even know if I have one—with a guilty conscience," was all Douglas was willing to offer.

"Lucky you."

Douglas shrugged. He didn't feel that lucky. Having assholes for relatives was hardly a blessing.

"It'd be good to give the bitch what she deserves," Bobby said with mean spirit. And why not? If there was one person on Earth who 'deserved it,' the accolade went to the bitch.

"Bobby, you should be careful saying that. If she heard you, she'd—"

"Punish me? That's a laugh, Douglas."

"Come on, then, let's get going."

The boys had snuck out back and made their way around the gardener's shed. The spade was there, as predicted.

They hid it the best they could between themselves as they made their way down to the grove. It'd have been manifestly ridiculous to start digging at the leading edge of the grove where everyone could see what they were doing, so they continued deeper in. Since the grove covered roughly half a hectare, there was ground enough to hide plenty of bodies.

Partway through, they disturbed a group of kids not from the orphanage, who quickly left without wanting to exchange words.

"What do you suppose they were up to?" Bobby asked.

"Take one guess, Bobby."

They walked on a little further. The overhead branches formed a thick canopy that was interrupted by small corridors through which the sun fell. Red apples hung plentifully and resplendently all around them like Christmas baubles. Leaves crackled and crunched underfoot.

Douglas looked up through one of those corridors and saw clouds building in the sky. "I think we might be in for a storm," he commented.

Neither boy had the slightest inkling as to the ferocity of the storm to come.

"Where would be a good spot to dig?" Bobby asked, then added, "How far down do you suppose we have to go? If the bitch has an accomplice, it could be deep; if not, you'd think the bodies would be left lying on the surface."

Douglas offered a nervous laugh and they walked a little further into the grove.

"There's a clearing here." He pointed. "Perfect spot." He started digging without further delays. He meant to find the answer he had come searching for.

It was easy going. The spade sliced into the friable soil without much resistance. Having reached about a three feet down, Douglas was becoming a little dejected. He wanted to hand the matron her just desserts for all the atrocities she'd unleashed on all the children at Mother's Care.

Mother's Care, huh, what a ripping joke!

They kept digging, taking it in turns when the other got tired in the arms. There was a surprising lack of tree roots to stymie their progress, which they thought odd since the place was practically choked with trees. On the other hand, perhaps their roots didn't have to spread too far to find all the necessary ingredients to satisfy their needs.

Big red juicy apples, compliments of the children at Mother's Care Orphanage.

The hole was nearing, at a guess, four to five feet deep, its diameter about six feet. Suddenly Douglas said, horrified, "It's a bone." Despite his disgust, he was unable to hide his excitement.

"A what?"

"A fucking *bone*, Bobby!"

They dug a little more and found yet another bone. It was long and, in their eyes, rightly or wrongly, a human bone. Most likely of the leg.

"Oh fuck, Bobby, what should we do?"

"You should put the shovel down," came the matron's sweet gravelly voice from behind.

The boys spun about, both sucking in harsh breaths. How had she approached them without them noticing? Her weight couldn't have traversed silently through the groundcover. Their focus had been their undoing.

For one hysterical moment, Bobby thought, *While one dug, the other should've remained as lookout. But we didn't. We didn't because we were too engrossed in digging the hole to bury the bitch.*

And what a hole they'd dug.

"What are you worthless little shits up to?"

They stared back at her like rabbits caught in the glare of headlights.

"I asked you a question, and I expect an answer."

"We were—" Bobby started.

"Careful. Lying will only make matters much worse than what they already are. And I must confess, they don't get much worse."

"We were just digging," Bobby finished. The cold hand of utter dread coiled around his entire body and squeezed the breath from his lungs.

"For what?"

"We thought it'd be fun to dig a hole."

"Tell you what will be fun; you both coming back with me and I watch you both squeal and squirm, while the Official Marker takes a shine to all your soft bits," the matron said with a wicked smile.

"Please, matron, we weren't meaning any harm."

"Two boys at once. I can't wait. By the time I'm finished, you'll be hard pressed deciphering if you are boys are not. But then, why would a couple of worthless little shits such as yourselves ever be allowed to be anything but worthless meat?"

Tears welled in the boys' eyes, their senses totally nullified into a cauldron of cold numbness.

Her enormously fat body rolled towards them. "Just digging to have fun, you worthless liars? You were snooping. *That's* what you were doing." She snatched the spade from Douglas' trembling hand. Not once did her smile wilt. "You might be thinking now of running from me, and that I can't catch you. But you should know that I always catch up with worthless little shits. Here's an idea—run to the nice policeman and tell them your tales of woe, and they'll come to see that you are worthless little shits, as well as worthless little liars. The Official Marker will still be standing at attention and ready for welts and bruises. So, run if you dare. Run and know that I will be true to my word."

She turned about and started leading the way out, knowing they'd dare not run from her. She stopped and without turning around said, "Thanks for digging the hole. You saved me the trouble. What a shame there won't be another living soul to shed a tear." She tutted mockingly and shook her head before her massive weight lumbered on.

∽

A storm had rolled in over Adelaide. Lightning lashed molten trails across the city from beneath the brooding clouds, and thunder thumped overhead. The ground reverberated and windows shook their thin panes at what had overtaken the skies, while Anthea had taken power over her charges.

Her Official Marker had never been worked so hard. It came down stroke after stroke, careless in what it hit or where, just so long as it landed on the boys. She spent five minutes on one before turning her vengeful lust to the other. Each boy was made to endure the five-minute intervals between their punishments while watching their friend being butchered.

Most impacts occurred around the buttocks. Some to the lower legs. Others higher.

Massive welts and bruises were being raised on tender flesh. Welts developing on welts. Bruises growing ever larger. Blood started to run here and there.

The boys' cries were those of sheer mortification. They rattled around Anthea's office while the storm rolled overhead.

Anthea was, indeed, a woman of her word: she kept her promises, because ethics wouldn't allow her to stoop as low as the dirty little liars. Boys and their *filthy* ways. The Official Marker would right that quick smart.

Bobby and Douglas had been reduced to crumpled piles of pitiful cries. To off-cuts that had landed haphazardly on a butcher's floor, where they got booted about just for kicks. Just for the thrill of it.

But still the rain came down in Anthea's office.

Her bastard doctor had advised her that she'd needed to increase her cardiovascular output, as her heart and lungs weren't in the best condition. She needed to do more walking to get both her heart and respiration rate up. But walking couldn't compare to a solid round of beating. Of course, her bastard doctor couldn't have advised such radical measures—but she knew what he'd been driving at. Boys that lied needed to be taken into hand.

She allowed herself to take a breather, making her way to the office door, the boys hobbling after her.

"Just where do you think you're going?" She was feeling right perky. Why, she had even raised a sweat. She turned the handle as double insurance that she'd locked it. No good getting interrupted in the midst of her workout session.

On the back of that, she reckoned she could go another round with each.

Good job the little bastards had dug that hole; she just might need it.

And while the storm continued to rage across the skies of Kapunda, Anthea, aka the bitch, continued hers within her office, the storm the perfect camouflage for the humiliation and crimson screams unleashed by the Official Marker.

The lustful pummelling concluded only when exhaustion set in.

Twenty minutes of aerobic exercise was recommended as a daily dose by the World Health Organization. Anthea released the boys, proud of her thirty-minute fix.

Neither Bobby nor Douglas could walk, so they shambled, Bobby forming a crutch for Douglas who was doing worse and kept buckling at the knees.

The blindingly excruciating pain in their groins, buttocks and legs were cohorts of the lightning that split apart the gloom beyond the windows set in the walls at a lofty height. Gateways to the heavens, but no salvation to freedom.

They'd managed just ten or so feet from her office when she said, "I feel better than I have in months." She shut her door and Douglas burst once more into tears, his small-framed body heaving with the exertion.

Bobby somehow managed to get them almost to their room on this relaxing Saturday afternoon, where invites to parties were substituted by rollicking good times with a leather strap, the stonework and windows rattling and rumbling around them.

"Oh fuck, you look like shit!" a boy passing by stated the obvious, and leant them a hand to go the remainder of the distance. He didn't have to ask about particulars. He knew.

As they lay in their beds, pain blossomed in breathtaking bursts. Exhaustion graciously overcame a night of otherwise exquisite restlessness.

Bobby cried himself into deep sleep, the type the body demanded so that it could embark on a desperate bid to heal itself.

Douglas, too, slipped into a deep sleep, on sobs that saturated his pillow. At the ripe old age of twelve, however, Douglas had decided that he'd had enough, and that his two-faced relative could shove his Instamatic wherever he chose. He wasn't fit to be a boy. He wasn't fit to be amongst the human race. He was nothing but a worthless little shit as drummed into him by the matron.

And so he dreamed of planning his escape.

By two that morning, his eyes snapped open, his head roiling with the weight of festering depression. He didn't see the light of morning.

A gruesome betrayal was taking place in the depths of the room.

Joshua wanted no more to look at it than he could pretend it was a figment of his distraught imagination.

Some things in life didn't bear witnessing—this was one of them.

He went to rescue his dad—any which way that came to mind and hand—but couldn't.

Because they weren't alone.

Behind his dad, who scribbled away

In the same frenetic style of the man in black

was an abstract picture that instilled unadulterated fear. And it *moved*.

"*Like what you see?*" came the crooning inflection he recognized from Sammy's house. "*Daddy's finally accepted his destiny.*"

Joshua's lips were quivering. He had to wipe the tears from his eyes, fearful that he'd miss the man-thing's approach. Because surely that was what this was about.

"*This is your destiny, too, Joshy-Washy.*"

Perhaps Joshua could've replied with something profound, but he couldn't, as his world had detonated and the ground had fallen away from his feet. Again. He struggled to remain upright, and was doing so purely on his autonomic nervous system. Had his bladder been holding any amount of fluid, he'd have added to that overall coating of sweat, as bodily functions were desperately clinging on.

His dad's eyes kept staring at him, *through* him. He had become invisible to his dad, and whatever was happening inside of him was his own secret.

From far away, he could hear clocks, the old-fashioned sort you had to wind up to keep going. They faded in and out, mixing with the pitapatting from beyond the room.

The man-thing held a hand out. Clutching something.

Joshua stared at this, as his dad stared at him. But he could see, unlike his dad whose eyes had turned inward.

"*Time for your punishment, you worthless little shit,*" the man-thing crooned, taking a step forward, singing 'Dream a Little Dream of Me.' "*What type of son are you, to turn your back on your own father when he needs you more than ever? Best take a seat next to him and keep him company in his moment of need.*"

Joshua staggered from the room. There was nothing to be saved within it and everything to lose. His outstretched arms found no purchase between the architraves of the door, and he almost toppled into the hallway.

A rush of bells immediately came at him. He turned, his mind compressing into a singularity: *run*.

Where to, he couldn't know. He just knew if he didn't run, he too would spend the rest of his life sitting at a school desk, writing. And he hated school... so *fuck* that!

Beyond the blinding objective was a dull awareness, that from every conceivable space between these rotten, miserable walls, those infants' mind-numbing rattles had become an unrestrained tantrum, and that the walls to either side were contorting as if made of soft rubber. Everything was awash and swirling. Yet it all seemed merely part of his own coming undone.

Behind him, doors flew open, many exploding from their enormous hinges and careening into the hallway like falling monuments of death.

Ghosts of many a lost child began drifting from the rooms where they'd been long incarcerated. Each one was caught in their own time loop, lost to Mother's Care Orphanage rather than the Boogaloo.

Lights swung with ever-increasing violence overhead. Like suicidal dive-bombers, they began breaking free of their long chairs. Bulbs exploded throughout the labyrinth of hallways with deadly assertion, splinters of glass finding Joshua's exposed flesh and peppering it with countless bee stings.

The way out is not the way in... came the frantic memory. *The way out is not the way in...*

The bells had manifested into a freneticism from which toll-like reverberations threatened to dismantle the limestone bricks, many the size of compact vehicles, and bring the walls crashing down. The floor had begun shaking violently. Flagstones were popping up like solidified jagged volcanic outcrops, forcing Joshua to run a gauntlet between glass shards, the cast-iron scrolls of light fixtures, shrapnel in the form of wooden doors, and the possibility of taking his own dive.

He slipped and slid between, and past one obstacle after another, still of no mind as to where he was going. It didn't matter. What did was that he had to pursue his own preservation.

Another door emerged from the winter gloom, launching into his path like an escape hatch on a Luna pod, only much bigger. Just as his awareness of the disintegration was realized on a level that could only be described as narcotic, he sensed the powerful disturbance punch through him and into his spine as it cannoned into the wall opposite, releasing its precious cargo of lost souls.

In their lack of corporeal solidarity, Joshua careened through them as he might have through pockets of fog.

From high above, windows buckled and bent, before their panes became showers of lethal shards. Amongst the perpetual darkness beyond, balloons cruised by as casually as if each were at helium filling station. Now and then, one would take a hit and go shooting off as air jettisoned from within. The rest of the pack continued unaffected, always remaining outside, and of no intention to mount an invasion.

Running to an unplanned destination, with just enough mind to take care of the grunge underfoot and the scrapyard of obstacles, Joshua caught a glimpse of a leg here, an arm there, amongst the clusters.

One woman peered through her envoy of balloons, her face a mask of utter terror, her mouth wrenched apart by her incessant screaming. She could see the boy way down inside the stone mansion through one of those windows and reached out for his help, because she was desperate to get away, as if she hadn't gone far enough from all her worldly loves and possessions already.

"*I can't!*" Joshua shrieked

The way out is not the way in!

leaving his dad further and further behind in the ravages.

Then he started his own brand of screaming, with tears running into globules of sweat and chasing down his cheeks.

In a sudden jolt, her terrified face was ripped aside. There was an increased flurry of balloons. Amongst it, her thrashing arms and legs shrunk to stubs, and then were gone. Her screaming subdued while her mouth dissolved and her body became rotund. The woman's transcendental experience concluded in a ball of soft white light, stuck with a stick-figure face.

Its stick-figure mouth worked a mile a minute; but instead of terror, it was laughing like a lunatic.

Despite clear excretions drenching his body, Joshua's spit had found an inner sinkhole into which it had poured, leaving his mouth a shrivelled mummification of its former self. He was burning up, his heart pounding hard against his eardrums. Any second now, they, too, would go off like hatches on Luna pods, and his brains would shoot from either side of his head in cartoon-like fashion as it took a crash landing. Its parachutes having not been deployed.

He was one boy fumbling about and lost somewhere far over the rainbow. For wasn't that what the girl's song had been imparting?

If Leon were here…

Well, he ain't! Get over it!

His dad… what about his dad…

Get over that, too!

There was every chance he would end in the same predicament. Either that or become one of those balloons. But while he could, he had to try and do what he'd come here to do, which was—

I don't rightly recall! Am I looking for the girl?

Sammy?

How about the man in black?

Out of the darkness wandered another door to intrude upon his rampaging resolutions that were about as rocky as the hallways he ran.

This one was different, though, its size radically demure in its statement, and lacking the splintered and aged appearance of wood, diseased beyond repair. Its glossy white surface was free of slimy festoons, as was its handle. A rather pristine ball of stainless steel sat comfortably against its background.

In fact, this could have been Sammy's door. *At least, the exact sort of door in his house.*

Have I gone full circle, cutting through 2025 and returning to 2022, at precisely one bedroom from Sammy's parents and two from his? Have I never left where Sammy slipped through? The terrifying thought that he had been caught in his own time loop came at him with the same force as the rampant bells.

The man-things were approaching fast—the infants were in a fit of rage. If he turned, he'd see those huge eyes and teeth everywhere, leaving no opportunity to indulge in such hideous speculation.

Déjà vu then came at him with all the trappings of a moment that had transpired on his doorstep in Corona, 2025. Joshua lunged forward and clasped that ball of stainless steel. For one cataclysmic moment, he was certain he would not be able to turn it... that he'd find it locked and his fingers helplessly inadequate due to sweat. While this ditty was playing out, the sensation of a thick-steel nail sizzled across his back. He shrieked like a trapped animal, grabbed the handle and burst through, slamming the door closed as he went, and expecting to find himself dashing blindly onto a sidewalk to get away from his deranged mother and her scissors.

But for all his fears of having unwittingly become lost in his own time loop of one arrangement or another, like the boy he'd left behind to end his life over and over again, what he came up with was a lock on the inside of the door's handle. How quaint.

Joshua turned it doubly hard to ensure that nothing could come through.

He leaned his forehead against its smooth paintwork, crying for the loss of lives and from exhaustion.

Moments went by in the hot winds blowing through his disarray, when he finally observed the door's white paintwork. It was high gloss, acting somewhat like a mirror. Whilst things were indistinct, he could see movement behind him, and its surface glowed an eerie green.

He gathered himself and slowly lay his back against the painted surface. Sweat dribbled from every pore, though the surrounding atmosphere was as if someone had cracked open the lid on a long pent-up freezer.

The moment Joshua Triplow burst into the heart of the Boogaloo, chronological arrhythmia deteriorated into fibrillation...
People were being stripped from their lives by the thousands...
Madness was taking over the world.

At the third stroke, the time will be... twelve... twelve... twelve... twelve... twelve... twelve... twelve... twelve... twelve... twelve... twelve... twelve... twelve... twelve... twelve... twelve... twelve... twelve...twelve... twelve... twelve... twelve... twelve... twelve... twelve... twelve... twelve...twelve...

CLOCKS

~

Spilling over the horizon and out of sight like strange clouds, clocks of every imaginable shape and size choked what substituted as the sky, the air dully churning and reverberating with their antiphonal

TICKING

and

TOCKING

It soaked into Joshua's flesh, vibrating his teeth and churning his stomach. Tending towards a high pitch, with the odd deep bass bonging, the overall quality lacked a certain something Joshua couldn't quite come to terms with.

His breaths expelled in comical white balloons, as if words should've been written in each. The air here was frigid, and his attire of shorts and T-shirt was totally inappropriate.

He'd learnt about Edmund Hillary's journey to the summit of Mount Everest, and often referred to it, as he did now, reminding himself of how that had made him feel: frozen inside. It was as if the words had leaped from the pages and gotten inside of him just for that hands-on experience. This was the type of air that bit into any exposed flesh with its icy teeth. He even imagined the little air sacs in his lungs cringing, just as surely as if they'd been doused with dry ice.

He'd have to be careful, but the very notion raised the prize-winning question: exactly how was he meant to do that? The classic response: he couldn't. He had what he had, and he had to be satisfied with it, and that included his choice of wardrobe.

While his mom, best friend and folks huddled around a coffee table in another dimension, candles burning merrily around them with the mercury shadowing 50° C (120° F), Joshua stared at the alien sky, blowing condensation through his mouth and nostrils.

The tumultuous hotchpotch of sky-clocks was hypnotic, and it was all he could do but stare. Some rolled over here and there, slumberous in their actions. Others skated through. Generally they were smaller and fleet of foot. There were yet others billowing to dizzying heights, like thunderheads.

With so much commotion, there was bound to be the odd coming together; and when this happened, there was a good deal of metallic remonstration, as their cogs clanged and gnashed together. Their hands drunkenly swooped across their faces until finding where they were supposed to be.

If this sort of cloud got fat and gained weight, like water-laden clouds that struggled to stay afloat, they'd start sinking, the air beneath compressing under their ponderous weight. Any sort of fog in this alien place would surely knock you frigging head clean off your shoulders.

Vertigo was threatening to send him to his knees. He quickly looked away. Head spinning… mouth hot and dry… his tongue a wad of bologna while his stomach was a bag of pus and poison. It was touch and go.

He was raising a hand to his mouth to stifle a retch when the glow of his skin caught his attention. He should have recognized it the instant he had seen it, but he had a good excuse in being somewhat out of his mind. The fine hairs on his arm looked like saplings in a forest, the way they shone in the light. He raised the other arm to within inches of his nose, and understood that this glow was radiating from the sky-clocks. To avoid vertigo, he kept his head down and rolled his eyes skyward.

A soft luminescence of bile green issued from the untold assortment. Some glowed from within, like spectral apparitions floating in the darkness, while others seemed to have a spotlight shining on them... though from where, Joshua couldn't imagine. Still others glowed at the hourly intervals around their faces with the green luminance of radium, their hands skeletally etched in the darkness of their own faces.

Joshua realized two things at once: he'd seen these delights before, at the end of Sammy's upstairs hallway; and he'd seen more on that occasion than he'd known until now.

So, tell me, Joshy-Washy, are you sure that you aren't in a time loop?

As sure as I can be. His comeback failed to quell his disquiet through a dearth of conviction.

And the second realization was more a case of recognition: all clocks pointed to the same moment in time. Fancy having missed such a detail... whatever could've come over him? He was often praised for his attention to detail. Seemed that he'd allow this whopper to slide on right by without a second thought.

Seemed that in this realm, you were nowhere if not at one minute past twelve.

As a mark of mocking emphasis, a bank of old-fashioned wind-up clocks, the kind he'd only ever seen caught between the pages of an encyclopaedia, the kind that sat beside the bed of sick people in the middle ages with a bowl of chicken soup, approached.

They had mice drawn on their faces, running towards the top of the hour. Those at the very top had their little mouths open in glee, and their tiny hands reaching for their prize—

Hickory, dickory dock…

TICK-TOCK

The mouse ran up the clock…

TICK-TOCK

The clock struck twelve…

TICK-TOCK

And the mouse was dead…

TICK-TOCK

Hickory, dickory dock…

TICK-TOCK

He snapped his eyes down once more.

Stupid! Utterly fucking stupid! Did I not say to take care? Well, this ain't taking care! The anger Joshua was experiencing from his own shortcoming was good, in that it helped him regain some sort of composure and focus.

Standing on the spot, spellbound by what he saw, wasn't what he'd come here for, as entertaining as it was. He had to maintain a clear objective now that it had reacquainted itself to him. People who had no goals were lost. He couldn't afford that. What had started as a confrontation with the man in black was something he needed to hold firmly to.

Moving forward required making a start, though.

Besides briskly rubbing those saplings, he needed to get his size nines marching, mindful of keeping his eyes low and fixed ahead, though this proved equally fruitless.

The purview was, yet again, not entirely a surprise. He had neither seen nor heard it over the dull yet insistent rhetoric of the sky-clocks, but it made for a weirdly harmonious orchestral undertone. If the sky-clocks were symbols and drums, then these were the bows across the strings of violins, the tone both frenetic and intense in a dull kind of way, like walking from a heavy-metal thrash band into an elevator playing Mozart.

And they stabbed their bows at the strings, playing:

Skittery-scratch... scratchy-scratch...

The man in black's haunting tune rose from the mimicry of ridiculous proportions. Rows and rows of school desks stretched back endlessly until, just as the sky-clocks, they disappeared over all horizons, each accommodating just one student.

As he'd witnessed in his dad, they were a studious class. Though not given the special treatment of solitary confinement, they nonetheless toiled away, heads bowed, hands working feverishly. There was no rambunctious chatter here, just:

Skittery-scratch... scratchy-scratch... for the ghost-dancers that might well revolve throughout the aisles between the desks... twirling... laughing... hand in hand... from here to eternity... all of them lost... Just as the ghost-children he'd left behind, that's all they'd do... that's all they'd ever do.

There didn't seem a seat to spare. Perhaps in row number one trillion, six hundred and fifty-five million, there might just be one available. And, perhaps, it waited for *moi*.

But please do hurry it along, there's work to be done; and as you can see, time stops for no one.

A grandfather clock on the scale of a small apartment block came waddling from the crowd, typical of a grandfather that'd seen too many days riding a horse. Its bassoon-like chimes were dinging and donging in a jumble of morbid tones, a dirge gone horribly wrong.

Joshua yelped, even though he was in no immediate danger.

Grandpa flipped upside down, wanting to show off his voluminous underwear, before rising into the sky-clouds and eventually disappearing. The jumbled array of chimes barked down at him, as if in protest at being dragged away against its will.

The violins continued playing.

The sky-clouds continued to churn.

The countless rows of school desks penetrated lands beyond sight.

He turned to face the door he'd come through, just ten feet or so behind. The space between he and it represented the only sizable free space on offer, with the school desks spreading away from it and positioned in such a way that allowed enough walking space between them at a squeeze... for the dancers to spin and kick up their shoes.

If someone was to fart, they'd blow everyone away, like a nuclear bomb going off. Joshua wondered how far such a shockwave would reach. Twenty rows... thirty... depending on what you had for dinner? Beans or onions or maybe a potent combination of the two?

What the hell was he thinking?

This realm did more than derail the senses; it set out to totally demolish them. Even something as mundane and innocuous as that door assaulted reasoning in a way that simply couldn't be reckoned with. But there it sat, propped amongst the neat rows of desks, merely a minuscule disruption to an otherwise unspoilt landscape of men, women, girls and boys, all taking their punishment in a neat and orderly fashion. And that in comparison to the hellhole he and his dad had travelled, only served to add to the irreconcilable senselessness.

It also lacked that certain something Joshua hadn't quite been able to figure out until now. Vibrancy. Just as the light spilling through the skyscraper doors had had no substance, the clocks ticked away wearily, the skittery-scratching a product of thready bows dragged across frayed strings, its quality crispy-dry and somehow plain worn-out.

Oozing fatigue, as if bleeding out, this realm continued barging ahead, like an interstellar cargo ship whose very inertia sent it barrelling ahead with no hope of stopping.

Behind that pristine white door, Mother's Care Orphanage continued on a path of self-destruction.

Never again would another tread this way.

Having been left ajar since Bobby Triplow had run from its confines so many years before, its purpose *amongst the rainbow* was spent, now that the boy had finally taken his punishment.

The Dream Sorcerers' lair, either a galactic cyst or ball of snot, depending through whose eyes it had been seen from afar, held solid.

The parasites and all Their needs safely contained within the Boogaloo.

Amongst Mother's Care's walls of historical misery, the bells had finally fallen silent. The unruly infants had ceased with their rattles. The years of childhood debauchment now at an end.

Fooled once... never to be fooled again.

Ever...

⌒つ

Pressing on, even the floor mocked Joshua's every step as he stared through it.

His feet seemingly floated above infinitum: the perpetual darkness with its endless highways of madness he'd seen when a misty white orb. Clusters were making their way towards many of those highways, within which were trapped the bodies of human beings. They were desperate to flee, but like sprats caught in the paralyzing tentacles of anemones, the more they struggled, the more excited the predators became. He was a tourist on a glass-bottom boat, looking at all the wonders below.

Do you see that starfish, Mommy?

Oh, honey, that ain't no starfish, that's a young man thrashing for survival. He's being eaten alive.

That's terrible, Mommy.

Nature needs to carry on. Those balloons have to eat as well.

Sweat coursed from Joshua's face, leaving watery bullet holes at his feet, as he traversed, unknowingly, the very same floor over which his dad had as a younger man, a place Bob had come to think of as *The Terminus of Death*. He'd confided this to Sue and no one else. Visitations had abruptly ceased when he'd confronted his fears and the horrors of 2011 came to a close. Bob had never given this place a second thought. As far as he'd been concerned, the theatrics formed on the mind of the little boy he'd once been, and all he'd endured, had ended. For Joshua, the similarities it shared with 17 South Lincoln Avenue, when he'd dipped his toe into the sofa room's floor, sure that'd it come up wet, were horribly confronting.

Everything related to his encounters at Sammy's. Once again, Joshua couldn't dismiss the very real possibility that he'd never left, and that he was merely cycling through a moment in time which somehow encompassed the year 2025. Or straddled the years 2022 to 2025!

I left a note… SWAT!

He *had* to stick to his goal… to stay on the move… to accept what he saw, because dusting off one's hands sure beat popping your brain. It might seem appealing, an easy way out, as often was quoted; but what if he hadn't become trapped? What then? He'd be made to endure the same harrowing torments of everyone else for as far as he could see.

This was not living. This was not life.

This was some kind of engine room, only the workers were students, heads bent to the task at hand. Hands flying across pages.

None were truly alive.

As this entire realm wasn't truly alive.

It existed.

It didn't thrive.

And they wrote because that served a purpose. Otherwise there'd be no point.

So, what *was* the point?

He wasn't exactly sure, but he was certain that he find the horrifying truth—if he didn't know it already.

༄

Clocks of every conceivable shape and size—and then some—rose like bubbles of methane gas, and in Joshua's face-to-face with the man in black, he had thought he had seen something float away from his desk before dismissing it. What he saw now left him in no doubt.

He glanced to his left—

Skittery-scratch... scratchy-scratch... Skittery-scratch... scratchy-scratch...

—where a little boy sat, dressed in a style that evoked images of when the fashion was kind of frilly and the streets dirty. When horses' clip-clopping provided transport and gas stations were a distant reality. His pants were tucked into long socks, and he wore a white shirt that looked more like a woman's blouse, a beret upon his shoulder-length hair. A pencil, whose tip seemed to never need sharpening, was clasped between his smooth fingers, and his hand was going ten to the dozen.

This kid can write, Joshua thought sadly.

What he wrote, Joshua was in no doubt, was the same as everybody else scattered to the far horizons: a series of three zeros finalized by a one.

Line after line, as if serving his punishment for talking too much in class (something that Joshua himself had received once or twice... although on the last occasion, he'd been stitched up by an asshole kid who'd done the deed and had since left Citrus

Hills Elementary without fanfare), he wrote until the page was near full.

At which point, something began emerging from it.

Joshua withdrew with a gasp, knocking into the desk behind, sending it out of kilter to the neverending rows.

It wriggled and wobbled, like a newborn exiting its mother's womb. It grew larger and larger, fatter and fatter. This was no ordinary run-of-the-mill newborn, but a massive clock tower. The sheet, tarnished with age, and perhaps tired from the act of birthing, gave rise to the structure that continued pushing higher until it reached its limits.

Pop!

Full born, it lazily drifted to the sky, where it submerged into the chaos.

A momentary kerfuffle ensued as a Napoleon clock, born on steroids, slammed into its limestone girth and went blathering off, the small boy's hand ceaseless in its action.

What they write, they produce, and what they produce are set at one minute past twelve: zero-zero, zero-one.

What did it mean?

This is where it all ends, Joshua thought again. *Caught in a time loop.*

No! He wouldn't allow that to be. He *couldn't* allow that.

He left the little boy from an era long past to his endless task, the school desk he'd errantly knocked out of kilter readjusted.

Order was maintained.

Exhaustion infiltrated his body. The most seriously affected were his legs. His feet wanted to entangle. Again, he found himself having to will his body on, to get past such barriers.

He had to find his friend, and could do this only by finding the man in black.

He'd gotten many rows further on when lactic acid in his thighs could no longer be ignored or denied. He pressed his hands into them, trying to force the stinging from the muscles there.

Anthea, the bitch matron of Mother's Care Orphanage, had once recalled the World Health Organization, stating that a daily pill of twenty minutes of aerobic exercise should form part of one's diet. Joshua Triplow, not quite eleven, had done more walking and running in the past few hours than most would've contemplated over several months.

Forget the frigid air, or the fact that he wore little more than shorts and t-shirt. His thigh muscles were on fire. His lungs were on fire. His face seemed ablaze, though air kept blowing from his mouth in long white plumes.

He couldn't breathe through his nose; he was plain too tired.

Taking care was easier said than done when confronted by the components of that mind-bending machine.

Doubled over, he hung onto his thighs. He tried. He couldn't. His feet were stuck to the spot. Strings and clusters of balloons floated in the perpetual darkness beyond them. Sweat cascaded from him to litter the invisible floor.

Joshua Triplow had been courageous, but he was in bad shape.

His eyes slipped to the wooden legs of a nearby school desk. They had the same aged appearance as the doors throughout Mother's Care, gray and splintery, sans the rusty scrawls.

Why was he bothering with such incidentals? Because it was the best he could do at the moment.

His energy had drained from him, as if it had been captured by the sweat escaping his pores.

"Oh Christ, is this how it's gonna end?" It was a dismal case, but his body had raised the white flag, whilst his mind clung on and remained willing.

He couldn't run entirely on his brain, though. He could make his brain dictate to his legs; but since they'd packed their bags and gone on vacation, nothing was doing.

Someone really needs to take to those school desks with sandpaper and a pot of vanish. They'd scrub up real swell, he thought. And though he should've been unnerved by such trivial distractions, it seemed comforting.

Maybe if he just sat down for a while, things would improve.

In a place far over the rainbow
The Boogaloo is out of sight
In a place far over the rainbow
Everyone's lost in a lullaby...

It cut through the engine room's lacklustre cacophony. Joshua dug deep and found strength from somewhere. Compelled to move forward, to follow her voice, the white flag was quickly withdrawn, the pole left bare. But before he took another step, she faded into the machine as no more than a tantalizing fragment that cruelly wet his appetite.

If he had any chance—*any at all!*—he had to reconnect with her.

Forcing himself through 2022's—or was that 2025's?—Class of Obedience, he passed people of black skin, pink, gray, yellow... you could have blonde hair or hair in a bun... what about brightly-dyed hair?... Then there were others who wore hats: top hats, bola hats, bonnets, fezzes... as well as berets, as he'd already seen. One lady over yonder was wearing a visor, like you see people do when attending a tennis game, so that they can see the furry yellow ball getting the living daylights smacked out of it, and the opponent who made a mistake smack the living daylights out of the racket

You can't be serious!

because a tradesman always blamed his tools. There were others who had only one arm or none, the writing implement clamped between their teeth. He caught a glimpse of someone wearing an eye patch and looking suspiciously like the Klingon, General Chang, in *Star Trek VI*.

Is this where people disappear to when they go missing? Are the pilots of Flight 19 amongst this, rubbing shoulders with all the other pilots and seafarers lost to the Bermuda Triangle?

What about a boy, and friend, from 17 South Lincoln Drive, who lived just four streets away? Commuted by skateboard in a jiffy, upon which fun times and high-spirited malarkey at the park or Cresta Verde Drive was the order of the day, and when chicken salad sandwiches would be devoured either with or without the chicken.

Further along, there was seductive lady who'd have been better suited to strolling along a beach in her bikini and dark sunnies, rather than cramped behind her third-grader's desk. Anyone standing taller than a metre was finding it extremely awkward, with their knees around their ears and arms trucked between them. Their writing hand looked like a caged bird, desperately attempting to find a way to freedom.

He stumbled on and bumped into a man with a long beard and long hair.

"I'm sorry," Joshua muttered lethargically, straightening up against the tautness that seemed to have calcified him from head to toe. He inhaled a deep, slow breath so as not to frostbite his lungs. "How long have you been at this?" he asked.

Skittery-scratch… scratchy-scratch…

"That long, huh?"

The man merely stared at his paper with his left hand flying across it. But there was something about him. A presence that seemed unique to him.

"Lefties are called southpaws, did you know that?" Joshua asked politely. There was also something comfortable about this man, something he couldn't define, just that his unique presence, as well as his own talking, made him feel as if things were going to be okay. "I happen to be right-handed myself, which makes me dead boring, 'cause I don't think any right-hander is given a title. You're just a right-hander. Right?"

Skittery-scratch… scratchy-scratch…

Besides long brown hair and beard, the man wore beads and a Hawaiian shirt. Flip-flops surrounded his feet and his jeans were bare at the knees.

"You're a hippie, aren't you? I've read about hippies, they're meant to be real groovy. Do you feel real groovy?"

The stainless steel handle on the door jiggled. Turned. Rotated.

The door cracked open a little, creating a fracture in the orderly rows of desks.

Just enough to let a diminutive body slip through.

Then closed.

After all, door locks were entirely unnecessary, as no one was about to leave, just as The Eagles had determined in 'Hotel California.'

⌒◦

Joshua frowned. "Hippies were around in the 1970s, weren't they? They use to drive VW Kombis with flowers stuck all over them. Reckoned that looked pretty cool... what we now call 'sick' or 'wicked,' some shit like that. Reckon you had a better way of describing things, mister. I mean, 'sick'—what the fuck does that mean, unless your head's over a toilet bowl?"

His one-way conversation was continuing to normalize things, or at least help him to feel not as alone... the kind of loneliness that could easily swallow you whole, until there was nothing left of you but a cold empty shell.

The hippie's writing was giving rise to a most interesting clock. It looked rather 'stoned.' It lazily wobbled and staggered from the page as the lines were reaching its end. If it didn't get a move on, it'd be caught on the page. And then what?

With a jerk this way and that, it managed to remove most of itself. Its face was like it had melted, and Joshua imagined it saying something like, *Jeez, man, had a trip... what a trip... still having that trip... and who the hell are you, and where the hell am I?*

The top half folded over itself, like a calzone, before struggling to lift up once more, not sure as to where its hands should be. It was somewhat amusing, considering the sky-clocks were all pointing to one minute past twelve regardless of their shape, size, genre, era or whatever else you could assign to them if you searched an online thesaurus.

It slipped to the man's flip-flops and dragged itself away, like it'd rather be anywhere else than where it was. A few feet on, it wriggled and shook its butt, where the number 6 was stamped.

There, it rose above the desk beside it, only to fall back to the floor's invisible plane, where it emitted a half *tick* and dissolved, as if it had never been.

~

Several rows behind, a hat with bells and three peaks was slowly making its way past one school desk after another. Its progression was that of a predator stalking its prey. It was stealthy, and the little bells on Its hat and shoes didn't tinkle. Not once.

It rounded a corner and came into another endless row of desks, silently making Its way toward the one person who had no right to be standing amongst the fare.

He needed to take his seat.

He needed to learn his lesson.

The hat continued cruising along one desktop to the other. A long pointed nose and chin protruded into the narrow gap between each, followed by a horizontal crescent-moon beaming with white teeth, and eyes that defied the size of the head they were nestled in.

~

The hippie's hair hung in his face, and was more or less held into position by a paisley headband. His beard hung halfway down to the page, tarnished the same aged patina as all others, which he'd already gotten a third of the way through before his hand began slowing.

Decades had passed since he'd torn his eyes from his punishment and, depending on the Earth he'd been abducted from, maybe centuries or longer. Much longer. His eyes were barely hidden behind small round tinted glasses the size of dimes.

He turned and faced the boy standing on his right. "Hey, little man," he said, as if waking from a coma.

"You talked! You can see me?" Joshua rasped. A flutter ran through him, like the seeds of a rain man's stick that gaily sifted down its hollow tube before coming to rest.

"Overdosed on LSD. Like the greats, but not as famous, I've reached my limitations," he said with somewhat of a slur.

"Like Satchmo?" Joshua asked.

"Don't know no Satchmo, but I do know a Jim Morrison… took a bath and never woke up," the hippie said. "I'm gonna take a bath. Do ya mind?"

Joshua was shaking his head, wondering how the hippie was going to do that.

"Good on ya, little man," the hippie said, giving Joshua a wink, after which his face slammed into the desk with a resonant clunk, his beard crumpling beneath his chin.

Before Joshua could ask the man if he was alright—which, of course, he was anything but—he started shrivelling. The skin on his arms wrinkled badly, as if he had stayed underwater for about a week, but instead of swelling it collapsed. The radius and ulnar poked through, as did the wrist and finger bones, whilst a massive clock reminiscent of London Tower, with ornate doodads adorning it in overkill, perhaps three stories in height, rose from a desk two rows away.

It should've shattered in an explosion of ancient splinters. It didn't. Its legs should've buckled ominously before relenting under the titanic weight. But they didn't. And how was it that the clock of such proportions fitted between the woman's slender hands producing it? It filled the sky and, for a moment, Joshua could see only its underbelly. It was gnarly, like the thing had been ripped from an even bigger structure. Steel girders hung foul, and parts of the stonework fell away, yet somehow evaporated like snowflakes on a hot day.

Crouching beneath in fear of his life, whilst everybody in the vicinity carried on, unfazed and unaware, Joshua could feel the air getting tighter as it was squeezed into an ever-decreasing space. It had grown very dark beneath it.

Clouds that had both mass and power to rip your frigging head off!

The thing swayed precariously. Joshua dropped to his knees. Blooms of condensation ejected from his mouth in rapid bursts, as if he were attempting to blow smoke rings.

In the penumbra, just two rows back, a three-peaked hat was closing in.

Higher and higher the thing went, penetrating its massive bulk further into the green bile, before its stupendous mass took flight. Its reflection in the glass floor slowly moved inwards until its edges met and was gone, the muted glow of the sky-clocks occupying the space once more.

The three-peaked hat came to a standstill.

Joshua steadied and returned his attention to the hippie.

His Hawaiian shirt, adorned with big bright hibiscus of reds and yellows, had deflated. His paisley headband had gone limp, like a rubber band without purpose, because it had none. You wore a headband to keep your hair in place on your head. When you had neither hair nor head, it was rather a useless garment.

Like the debris that had crumbled from London Tower, the hippie and his clothes evaporated. It was both fast and unspectacular.

With his passing went the hope that he'd reignited within Joshua. The void filled with the cold dread of utter hopelessness that had rolled in, menacingly dark and with an insatiable appetite.

Joshua stared at the seat vacated by a man who'd once gotten high whilst watching the sun set on a balmy beach.

Wonder what you dreamed? Did you talk too much to the sun? Joshua gazed around. "Why any of you?" He felt himself slipping again.

Skittery-scratch... scratchy-scratch...

From far in the aisle's distance, a blur sped towards him. It lacked all features except for a fussy ball of gray shades that propelled toward him with vicious vibrating movements.

He threw himself into a desk behind, disrupting the order once more with a hurtful yelp, and found himself in the lap of an old lady.

His blue eyes stared into hers whose, like everybody else's, had the curtains closed with nobody home.

His head lay in the path of her hand, which kept bumping into his ear as the unstoppable force running through her veins would not be deterred or interrupted.

He prized himself away. The tension in his muscles was worse than ever, and he noticed a young girl filling the hippie's seat.

"Kylie?" he said, but the girl's hand was the only thing doing the talking: *skittery-scratch... scratchy-scratch...* She had long blonde hair and was really good at math. How did Joshua know this? Because she sat in his class at Citrus Hills Elementary.

⁓

"There's nothing we can do but ride out the heatwave," Kylie's dad was saying in the glow of candlelight. "Normally I wouldn't suggest this, but you need to sleep, Kylie. Christ, you haven't slept in the last three days, worrying about all sorts of things."

"Dad, I can't help wondering what happened to Sammy. It's so close to home... he went to my school. He *dreamt* of that man..."

"I know he did, honey. I know he did. And for that reason, I want you to take these."

"What are they?"

"This terrible heat... the blackout... the worry... you need to swallow these tablets. They'll put you right to sleep. And when you wake, you'll do so with a fresher mind and an upbeat outlook. At the moment, you're harassed by all kinds of things that are set against your well-being and impacting how you judge things. Everything seems negative, but they won't."

"Are they sleeping tablets, Dad?"

"Yes."

"I don't want to."

"I want you to." Kylie's father handed her the tablets and a glass of cool water. "It's impossible to get to sleep in this heat, and without any air conditioning... well, as I said, you *need* to sleep. Heat or no heat. And when you wake up, the blackout should be over."

She swallowed them.

"There," he said, all-knowing that in the morning, everything would be right as rain.

"All the kids are talking about Sammy. They keep their voices low, fearing they'll be next."

"Of course, sweetheart. It's not something you simply overlook, unless you have a heart of stone. He went to your school, and whether you knew him personally or not, he was part of your neighborhood, both at school and outside of it. It's never easy when something this tragic happens, and especially when right on your own doorstep. Makes you feel weird inside, vulnerable, and gets you wondering who's next."

Kylie was nodding, comforted by her father's deep insight and logic.

He bent down and gave her a gentle kiss on the forehead as she lay back in her bed. "You'll sleep well," he said. "They're rather potent little suckers." He smiled and left the room, never to see his girl again.

∽

"Not you, too," Joshua moaned, upon which he caught the spectral wash of singing.

Singing, he thought wildly. *Don't let it get away! It's what brought you into this... it's what you need to follow. Follow your dream!*

The thrills and spills remained profound, messing with his every sense, with his every muscle fibre. They had seduced him into feeling as if he were becoming inured to the whole thing, when in fact he was being anaesthetized against it.

He was more than drained. He too had become dull, and hadn't realized this until now.

⤳

Rarely did the parasites venture into the Boogaloo.

Feeding from the spoils within from outside; this was how it'd been since the first Patrick Nesmith had made it all possible.

Let the child of the worthless little shit find what he's looking for.

By then, he'll be weaker… easier… accepting…

The Boogaloo was wearing him down, worming into his soul and eating it away.

He would either sit or succumb.

⤳

Joshua was being guided, wasn't he?

Either that or lured.

What should we use, Dad? The blue or the silver?

The water's deep blue, so use the silver one. It'll be eye-catching to predators on the hunt.

He looked at Kylie, regretful that he had to leave her, but understanding that while hovering by her side might be the moral thing do to and quite valiant, it was also about as useful as the recently departed hippie's headband.

Kylie was a new class member of 2022—or 2025—, but her eyes were as dead as all the others. There was little point saying sorry for leaving her, but he did so, because it was the right thing to do.

Guided or lured? That was the game-changer. The question to which there was just one answer.

Joshua knew there could be no more distractions, and focused on the only matter that counted. His trainers walked a floor that constantly threatened to open beneath him.

Screw the clocks, the desks, the sound of all that scribbling... screw it all.

His eyes were set, his teeth clamped in gritty determination.

His heart was beating rapidly and loudly in his chest and ears.

He pushed aside his ravenous dread and followed the girl's singing.

April 23, 1987
The morning before the night Patrick Nesmith went missing

He awoke in a thick layer of sickly sweat, his hair adhering to his scalp as if he'd taken a shine to Brylcreem, and took satisfaction in looking almost bald in a skull-cap.

His breaths were rapid and hot. And it smelt. He screwed his nose against his own malodor, before staggering from the bed to his study where he immediately began his sickness in earnest.

It'd gotten out of hand, just as Anthea had accused, but she hadn't known the half of it. 'Worse' wasn't the exact term... he'd been possessed by something he had no defence against. This wasn't a case of ducking down to your friendly doctor to have him examine you, before prescribing an antibiotic to rid the nasties from your body.

His great-grandfather had brought shame onto the family name and whilst Patrick had promised his grandmother he'd never do likewise verbally, there was no doubting he was doing it physically.

His hand was hot and aching, as if affected by a ravenous infection. But what of the rest of him? His mind ached, as did his muscles and bones… but they ached for a different reason. He couldn't help himself. He couldn't control what he'd become. He so desperately wished he could, and so he ached while his hand scribbled 'zero-zero, zero-one'. Over and over.

Wherever this led, it'd be nowhere sane.

Satan's playground, Patrick thought for the umpteenth time, in fathomless misery.

If only this was true, he had the skills to deal with that, didn't he?

Having taken desperate measures one afternoon, he'd succumbed to performing self-exorcism. To rid the evils from his body. The antibiotics he could administer.

For a day or two, it'd seemed to have worked. He'd felt rather chipper, bolstered by the notion of life getting back on track. He had been able to proceed with confidence and vigor in his duties to the community, and those poor little children at the hands of that wicked woman.

The sensation, sadly, had soon extinguished, leaving nothing more than a wispy trail to tease him with things that had slipped through his fingers. Dejected beyond redemption, he hauled his victimized body to his desk… to his writing…

The first tendrils of morning light had begun filtering into the study. The air was warm for April and heavy with his ravaged persona.

Having become something he abhorred, he finally forced himself away from his scribbling, fetched the car keys and took himself for a fifty-mile drive to Kapunda, north of Adelaide.

"Might as well have it out with Anthea once and for all," he said through gritted teeth. Sweat continuing to rivulet over the contours of his gaunt face, his body spurred on, from when it had begun during the night, by the kind of dangerous anxiety that required nothing less than locking yourself away and throwing aside the key.

But then, what good would that do? He could still write— and *would*—even if using the tip of his right index finger until it rubbed the flesh down to the bone.

At one point, he had screamed in terror, partly waking himself from his tumultuous slumber, only to slip right back into it. Whatever the sickness, it was relentless in its pursuit. The more he gave, the more it took. The more it wanted. And God only knew if it wasn't associated often with the manifestation of bells. Dainty and innocent in tone, he'd come to think of them as monsters in the dark.

He stepped from his Holden Commodore, having pulled out front of Mother's Care Orphanage, wrung through of mind and dripping wet. He had trouble walking a straight line, and appeared every bit a madman, whose sobriety had been left months in the past.

On what would be his last journey to Anthea's office, under the bright light of day with a mild breeze shifting around a pleasant autumn morning, something caught his attention. He squinted, holding a hand above his eyes, and diverted toward the Hudson Terraplane. "That bastard needs to go," he said once, if not a hundred times, whenever visiting the orphanage, always in the style of a gunslinger more at home in a spaghetti western than at a church's pulpit. Lights Regional Council needed to take responsibility.

Which was kinda rich, coming from a man of God who couldn't keep his own affairs in check.

With all vexation sidelined, he leaned against the driver's door. To be honest, it was a relief to take some weight off his feet.

Had the young occupant been looking in the exterior mirror, albeit its chipped, mirrored background rather degraded, she'd still have seen him approach from behind. As it was, she been rather preoccupied, pretending to liberate herself from this place of torture. And when on any journey, especially one where lofty feelings made you a bit giddy, singing was par for the course.

The girl didn't know what she'd been singing. Not exactly. She had cobbled together the words and tune some weeks ago, just after the self-mutilated body of Douglas McKenzie was discovered near the apple grove, to ward off the evils that prowled the land both inside and outside. The warped version of 'Somewhere Over The Rainbow' had stuck in her head.

"Hello?" Patrick uttered in a soft tone.

The girl jumped with fright, her eyes wrenched open by fear while her lips had welded tightly shut.

He smiled. She noticed how wet he was, as if he'd walked under a sprinkler and gotten drenched. "You seem to be having a wow of a time," Patrick said. A fly buzzed around his head. He swatted at it unintentionally. "What's that song you were singing? It sounded..." Patrick broke off.

The girl remained frozen in her stare.

"I'm not here to chastise you. I used to like playing in a car that sat out back of an uncle's of mine when I was about your age. I always pretended to be going on great journeys, and I *always* felt safe in the car. Because when I was in *that* car, it was as if nothing could touch me. I drove to many a place I could only dream of as a child. I suspect that's what you're doing now."

Hesitantly, the girl said, "I was driving away from here."

"And why is that?"

"Because it's cruel and makes you do horrible things."

Patrick's smile wilted. The girl's honesty was brutal. "Yes, well," he stammered, "that's about to change."

She looked at him with an expression of hope, her hands clutched white to the steering wheel, which hadn't turned a corner in years. "Can you *really* make that happen?"

Patrick smiled and offered a confident wink.

He stepped away to recommence his drunken walk to the imposing front doors of Mother's Care Orphanage, before turning around for one last look at the girl in the car. His heart broke. She was pretending to get away from this cruellest of places when the very car in which she sat screamed derogatorily:

WHY DON'T YOU ALL GET LOST
JUST DISAPPEAR

The girl waited for the religious man to make good on his promise. But she never saw him again, and his promise was as effective as the suits who came in and took notes in appraisal of the orphanage's management and the care it delivered to its children, especially after one went missing. Or was buried under the pale of solemn gloom, the casket lowering into the ground without a single McKenzie by its side to mourn the pitiful waste of a boy who would never laugh or smile again.

She lost all hope, and so she ventured to the Hudson on a daily basis, singing her interpretation of 'Somewhere Over The Rainbow.'

Somewhere far over the rainbow, the Boogaloo was out of sight, and everyone was lost in a lullaby. The exact sum of what every child at Mother's Care Orphanage endured.

Because lullabies, like everything else she had foolishly trusted, hid their true capabilities until you learned that it was too late.

Unbeknownst to the girl who sat at the Hudson's steering wheel for hours each day, singing her song of desperation, the religious man Patrick Nesmith had gone missing himself.

Just five nights later, on the night of April 28 1987, the girl unwittingly followed in his footsteps.

There was the usual inquiry. The usual inspection. The sudsless dishwashing suits came with their clipboards and took notes before departing and…

Nothing changed.

Neither Patrick Nesmith nor the girl were ever to be found.

Just as the car demanded: they had disappeared.

The boy was weak. Running on the fumes of willpower, he was easy prey.

Joshua had made good on his intentions. Having followed the singing, he now stood before the girl, seeing her for the first time.

She was perhaps a bit younger than him, and her light-brown hair was in two plaited pigtails, held together at the ends with dainty white bows.

Behind her, and one row over, sat someone with a monk's hood over their head. *The man in black.*

"Thank you," he whispered to the girl, whose eyes held the same quality he'd seen in the hippie's. "Can you hear me?" he asked tentatively.

"*Yes,*" the Dream Sorcerer answered from behind, walking directly to the boy. "*You need to take your seat and enjoy a rest.*"

Joshua flung himself around. His shoes momentarily slipped on the picture-window floor, to the delights of Black Eternity.

The girl's singing, a spark of life in this otherwise lifeless place, continued without disruption.

The Dream Sorcerer took another step towards the boy, the bells on Its shoes and hat tinkling. "*I have got something for you that your daddy learnt too, too late. Something he should have done many years before. You do not want to be doing that, Joshy-Washy.*"

"What… are you?" The man-thing's entrancing stare seemed to extract those remaining fumes that kept Joshua afloat.

The Dream Sorcerer approached further still, pens and pencils clutched in Its outstretch hand.

Fooled once… never again.

"*You want to save yourself a life a misery and heartache, and learn from your father's mistakes. Is that not what children are meant to do? To learn from their parents' mistakes? You know you want to save yourself the life your father endured. You know you want to, Joshy-Washy. Yes, you do. So spare the punishment of years in denial and take your pick. It is easy. So easy. Whatever you prefer: ballpoint or lead. It matters not, just so long as you are at peace, Joshy-Washy. At peace is what you want, Joshy-Washy. Peace and to forget all the traumas of late. Because it has been very, very traumatic, and you know if you refrain from taking a pen or pencil, the traumas will keep coming, and that you will not be able to escape this place, but instead die wondering what it would have been like to take the pen or pencil and start—dreaming."*

Joshua's head was swimming as if through quicksand. Having grown arms and legs, it paddled for dear life, but an inch of headway was negated by two inches as the quicksand pushed with greater force. It fought against being dragged under, constantly bobbing up and gasping for breath.

"Here," the Dream Sorcerer offered kindly, showing Joshua a spare school desk. *"Take a load off your mind, Joshy-Washy. That is what you want to do, is it not? To take a load off your mind and legs, and take the weight of the world off your young shoulders? Take a pen or pencil and take a seat. Sit down and give yourself a well-deserved rest. That is what you are thinking, Joshy-Washy."*

Joshua wasn't sure if he was reaching for the offering or stepping to the one person he'd come searching for. He had to admit, the temptation to sit was enormous, as was the desire to write an epic. If any of the others thought they were producing any sort of mind-blowing clock, wait until Joshua Triplow got onto the case.

The Dream Sorcerer smiled; Joshua couldn't fathom how those teeth fitted inside Its head along with Its eyes. Perhaps It wore that hat for a reason… maybe it was full of teeth and eyeballs. *"You are looking for your friend, is that not so, Joshy-Washy?"*

"Sammy," Joshua uttered colorlessly.

"*Yes—he needs to find his way home, so that he can be reunited with his mommy and daddy, and you can all go living into the future in happiness and comfort. All you have to do is take a seat and you will find your friend. You will find everything you have ever been looking for, and the things that torment you will be driven away.*"

Joshua's fingers yearned to busy themselves, and began to clasp a Bic pen, because when you were about to embark on a lifetime of writing, you might as well choose old reliable.

Gleaming with bile green, the gelatinous orbs of the Dream Sorcerer's eyes, dark pupils and no iris, reflected the actions of the man in black just a desk away. But to Joshua, he felt a million miles distant.

The girl intensified her singing, lifting from one octave to three higher. Penetrating. Insistent. Whilst she sat in a Hudson Terraplane, as she had since her abduction in April of 1987.

Manipulated with the tenderness of a loving caress that would not be denied, the Bic was pressed into Joshua's palm.

As the Dream Sorcerer persisted, It began trembling violently, as if suddenly overcome with a terminal seizure. The act was not dissimilar to the blur that was Kylie, when racing from her life in Corona 2022 to a life in the realm of dead scrolls and multiplying clocks.

It bulged here and there, the seizure intensifying before a sudden fragmentation and increase in the infants' rattles, upon which the long spidery fingers of two Dream Sorcerers hypnotically danced around Joshua's smooth flesh in an obscene embrace. Heavily wizened, theirs were the ancient bearers of no goodwill.

Just as the girl had surmised of those who oversaw Mother's Care, Their promises were false and empty. They offered a sanctuary that soon became vulgar… starting as a pleasant, maybe even magical dream, to become burdensome as it played out over and over and over again, until you departed the ordeal. Just like the hippie who had succumbed to a long overdue heart attack on one too many crazy nights of LSD.

For others, such as Douglas McKenzie, no good dream had ever been—their spirits absorbed into the brickwork that was supposed to offer a place of protection and safety. A place of home.

Mother's Care Orphanage was no less a parasite.

The girl had known this for a very long time: two sides of the same coin you didn't want to go playing with, but came for you anyhow, out of the blue and unsolicited. One of bricks and mortar, the other of bells and funny clothes.

So she sat in the Hudson with its black-scrawled letters of ill-intent, driving to a place that had long lost all appeal, just another Mother's Care in a different guise, knowing of a skinny boy in T-shirt and shorts and his ability to change events.

That sliver of Mary Booth, which remained intact and unmolested, she had protected with vicious tenacity, whilst driving the highway without end, the Hudson's wheels rolling over a well-trodden path. Her hands turned the odd parabolic curve, the very same time and again.

The boy was her ticket out of the misery, which had to do with the religious man who'd promised everything and delivered nothing, besides the loss of what could have been.

Now, as she worked her vocal cords harder than ever, sweat— not having graced her skin for the term of this life sentence— coursed down her forehead.

Without exception, the definitive proof would be found in the result:

In a place far over the Rainbow,
The Boogaloo is out of sight
In a place far over the Rainbow
Everyone's lost in a lullaby…

She could describe it no better. Though succinct, it said everything that needed to be said. *Make it happen. Joshua Triplow. Set us free!*

The Dream Sorcerers vibrated violently once more, and suddenly there were six. Their hands around the boy, like flies upon a carcass, pressing the Bic into his palm and curling his fingers around it. Gone was the former tenderness, their intention leaving no room for doubt.

Make it happen. Joshua Triplow. Set us free!

Joshua somehow resisted the temptation. He could sense the girl's intensity rather than hear it. It was as if she'd crept inside his head, had started running amok in the passageways of his mind, her fists banging loudly on all its doors. Not because she was angry, but because she had something of vital importance to impart upon him.

He stumbled into the man in black's desk.

The man's sickness would never relinquish, his fingers and pen the strikers of a typewriter, snapping at the page faster than ever, cranking out 'zero-zero, zero-one.'

The pace was contagious, spreading horizon to horizon and beyond, forever and ever to each and everyone.

Skittery-scratch scratchy-scratch... Skittery-scratch scratchy-scratch... Skittery-scratch scratchy-scratch...

Skittery-scratch scratchy-scratch... Skittery-scratch scratchy-scratch... Skittery-scratch scratchy-scratch...

Skittery-scratch scratchy-scratch... Skittery-scratch scratchy-scratch... Skittery-scratch scratchy-scratch...

Skittery-scratch scratchy-scratch... Skittery-scratch scratchy-scratch... Skittery-scratch scratchy-scratch...

Skittery-scratch scratchy-scratch... Skittery-scratch scratchy-scratch... Skittery-scratch scratchy-scratch...

Skittery-scratch scratchy-scratch... Skittery-scratch scratchy-scratch... Skittery-scratch scratchy-scratch...

Skittery-scratch scratchy-scratch... Skittery-scratch scratchy-scratch...

The maddening noise was registered by not a soul, long lost in their lullabies; and though Joshua was going under, the quicksand filling his nostrils and all but clogging his ear canals, he dared to remain standing in defiance of the awaiting chair.

Clocks had begun spewing forth in a torrential rain, rising from the school desks to the sky of mechanical mayhem.

They clanked and bonged, like metallic thunder without much punch, as they collided overhead and to all horizons. Bits went flying, cogs spinning in all directions, as if giants had decided they had had enough slumbering for the day and that it was time to expend their energy in a boisterous partaking of Frisbee.

The massive clock that had risen from between the woman's slender hands, with its steel girders hanging foul beneath, was a juggernaut which a bank of Napoleon Hats was about to discover. The contest should've been decidedly one-sided. Indeed, the Hats detonated like exploding stars. Napoleon only thought he'd had a bad day in history. The survivors whimpered off, only to be wiped out in further chronographic volleys. Hands went flying, as did their internals in sprays of untold mechanical parts.

The tower's immensity absorbed the brunt of the impact, yet escaped not entirely unscathed. Several girders came adrift and somersaulted into banks of clocks nearby, crushing their faces and leaving their numbers in shambles.

Hickory, dickory dock...

TICK-TOCK

The mice ran up the clock...

TICK-TOCK

The clocks were struck...

TICK

And the mice were mangled...

TOCK

Hickory, dickory dock...

The tower itself rolled ominously end over end, taking huge swipes at a menagerie of clocks fashioned into the form of animals, cudgelling each and every one with its ponderous blows.

Its jagged ass was up, then down, its face pointing to the sea of devoted writers then away.

Somersaulting into the distance, it continued taking everything that dared to stray in its path.

❧

00:01... 00:01...

The ticking.

The tocking.

The white noise of the skittery-scratching.

The destruction across the skies.

The mass birth…

A collage of both sight and sound that defied boundaries. A collage of speed and freneticism whose clarity was faded like parchment left in a desert for eons, yet conveyed a power of unimaginable magnitude.

Make it happen. Joshua Triplow. Set us free!

Sweat now dripping from the tip of the girl's nose and eyelashes, she blinked once. A small spray gaily arced away from her, before coming down to land on the paper between her hands. Her lungs filled to capacity and forced her song with the desperation of someone needing to find salvation, to end the misery, to finally escape the ordeal… and to get as far away from Mother's Care Orphanage and the Boogaloo as possible. To jump over the rainbow and *be free.*

Somehow, Joshua had managed to avoid the Dream Sorcerers' increasing barrage of coercion.

"*Take the pen, Joshy-Washy. Take it and be free,*" They whined in unison, their unshakable confidence having fetched up on rocky grounds.

Joshua's fingers and those of the Dream Sorcerers were in a mass entanglement.

"*End it, Joshy-Washy. Take your seat and free yourself. That is what you want. That is what you need. That is what your heart desires. Take it and be free… be free… be free…*" Their collective voices were a seething hotchpotch of jabbering and yammering in his head, chasing the girl as she ran through its passageways, insistent on getting her message across.

Make it happen. Joshua Triplow. Set us free... free... free!

His attention veered to the man in black, with his hood shrouding his face as if in shame, his eyeless sockets staring ahead, his hands continuing what his forefathers on a distant Earth had begun in a time lost to the history of the universe.

"Stop," Joshua said, quietly, yet with firm deliberateness.

The Dream Sorcerers went silent for a split-second before yelling, "*Free yourself and spare the misery! TAKE YOUR SEAT AND FINISH THE EQUATION. BRUCKHEIMER'S WAITING! MOMMY'S WAITING! YOUR FRIEND IS WAITING!* **THEY ARE ALL WAITING!**"

> **In a place far over the Rainbow,**
> **The Boogaloo is out of sight**
> **In a place far over the Rainbow**
> **Everyone's lost in a lullaby...**

Mary Booth fired the words from her mouth.

"*Why don't you stop?*" Joshua now yelled.

The man in black ignored him.

Make it happen, Joshua Triplow. **SET US FREE!**

Joshua bit down on his bottom lip, drawing blood. "*Just stop it, you fucked-up asshole!*"

The man in black's hands and the incitement to Black Eternity remained unchecked, on track, and spiralling further out of control.

Skittery-scratch… scratchy-scratch… emanated across a hundred lights years and more from a septillion human hands. Row after row. Aisle after aisle. On and on and on. Over the horizon and throughout the Boogaloo. Southpaws, right-handers, between toes, between teeth, rapping, hitting the parchment with the ferocity of pit vipers on the attack.

Throughout the expanse, desks and their students were pinned against the picture-window floor, under the invading flood of clocks, but their hands continued striking viciously until the last. The pulverization of bones and wood crunched and gnashed like grisly pockets of air rupturing amongst the squeeze. Spatial saturation nearing critical.

His sickness had always been his fate, his destiny, as it had been for all the Patrick Nesmiths that had come and gone before him. Perhaps, somewhere out there, was another Patrick Nesmith. Perhaps, like the hippie, he was coming to the end of his tether, his best days of writing having well and truly past him by. Having served his purpose, he would fade as all others had before. Without fanfare.

Or be crushed under the weight of time.

Out with the old and in with the new.

So how was it that the son of the worthless little shit was ignoring them?

Stop the girl. The girl needs to be silenced. She is the one urging him on. Stop the girl and the boy will take his seat.

Transfixed by the man's hand, Joshua could hear and see nothing else, even though an elderly gentleman's skull was undergoing radical transformation just five rows over, the weight of his creation elongating and narrowing it against the floor. His false teeth became a projectile that portrayed the total dislocation of his bottom jaw.

The Dream Sorcerers' attention turned to the girl who sung at the top of her lungs. This was no 'Dream a Little Dream of Me.' This was deception.

Make it happen, Joshua Triplow. **SET US ALL FREE!!!**

Fingers scrabbled over her lips like a nest of agitated spiders, some pinching them together, forming bony sutures. When that failed, they mutated into a garrotte that began squeezing what remained of Mary Booth, for she had to be silenced.

Watching the bastard scribble away caused Joshua's infuriation to escalate, like feeding it with the type of fertilizer one might use to watch their carnations grow and bloom bright and fragrant flowers.

"How, nice, Penelope, I've never seen such healthy colors. How *do* you do it?"

"It's no secret, Matilda. Just shove on the poop."

"I'll be... is that all?"

"Not quite. It does make for a rather awkward time in the toilet!"

MAKE IT HAPPEN, JOSHUA TRIPLOW!!!

The boy prized his fingers from the remaining scrum and France's answer to modern-day scribes: Bic.

Silence the girl and get the son of the worthless little shit writing... *He must take his seat...* **HE MUST TAKE HIS SEAT...**

Joshua bit his lower lip harder. A trickle of blood cascaded to the end of his chin, where it formed a small droplet. Attempting to stop the man and his scribbling had become more of a struggle than what he might have thought. It wasn't as simple as snatching that pen from between his fingers. The strength this man possessed was that of one who had lost their mind and therefore all inhibitions and restraints.

However, if Joshua put an end to this, all the souls would be spared. They would be... *free!* He didn't know how he knew that. He just did. The very thought overwhelmed all others in a blinding assault. They would be spared and Sammy and Kylie would be liberated. As would the girl whose tune ripped forth as if between the bags of titanic bellows.

It all ends here, he thought wildly again. Though a trivial player amongst the main assault, it carried a potent message.

Sick with dread and numbness, as well as rage and blinding purpose, if he couldn't put a stop to the man in black's hand, how about holding his arm? It was bigger and therefore he could get a firmer grip.

Sweat shimmied across Joshua's forehead and dangled like dew on a frosty morning from his cheeks. The small droplet of blood detached and fell to the floor, to be replaced by a larger drop, the trickle becoming both wider and thicker.

With blood filling his mouth, he took a firm grip of the man in black's upper right arm, condensation streaming from his mouth like a charging bull, before: "*Stop, you sick son of a bitch!*"

"*Stop, son of worthless shit!* **BE FREE...!**"

Joshua gave a firm yank.

There was a sickening **CRACK,** and in Joshua's mind's eye, he wondered where the branch had come from. He hadn't seen a tree before. And whatever tree it had broken from must've spent umpteen summers under the baking heat of a relentless sun, its limbs becoming bone dry and brittle.

Then comprehension struck like a sledgehammer against a thick steel shutter. He stared agog at the thing in his hands, his lower jaw seemingly hitting his chest. This was no branch, for goodness' sake! And the proof was right before his eyes, in the form of a human body part. A right forearm, complete with upper arm, to be precise! It was dry and brown, and might've even been mistaken for a branch by the unwary. Having parted company from the man in black's shoulder blade, here it was, inches from his face, finishing at one end in a fork of mummified fingers, between which a pen was clasped. At the other end was a splintery mess. Seemed the upper arm bone had broken near the top, probably due to overuse and a little too much force on his behalf.

Joshua had learned basic anatomy in Mrs. Bruckheimer's class, and so he knew he was observing the humerus without the ball that articulated with the shoulder blade, known anatomically as the 'scapula.'

A dirty smudge of canvas was wrapped around it, or at least what might've been a dirty smudge of canvas. But then, only the unwary would've not known the truth to be skin.

His threw it aside with a grimace.

The repercussions of what he'd done had become universal in an instant.

Following the breaking of bone, there was
Silence!
There was no ticking.
There was no tocking.

There was no scratching.

The scribbling had come to an end, and so had the torrential upload of clocks it had produced.

Whilst deafening in its own right, the absence of noise would not hold for long.

The door standing magically amongst the school desks opened.

Then closed.

Fooled…

The door imploded on the Matron's office. With the force of a guillotine, it sliced through the air, missing Bob by fractions and certain decapitation by tenths of an inch. The sheer force of its wake sucked the pen from his hand, marking the only occasion that any good had come Bob's way within this room.

The glaze fell away from his eyes while the pen flew across the room.

The walls, the floor, the ceiling, the very air, shook to pounding reverberations, as if an air-raid strike from every country with the military might to do so had gathered to unleash their deadly payload.

Either that or one helluva fat jock, with a pie shoved in his face, on the biggest baddest bulldozer in history.

With strength and presence of mind—out of the black and into the blue—Bob staggered to the doorway. The floor was rupturing, as if the dead wanted to make their way from under the bedrock. Great jets of dirt and steam shot into the air with the force of laser-cutting beams. The door frame contorted hypnotically before him, its architrave buckling and splinters firing in all directions.

Staggering into the hallway, he could've turned right or left. He chose right and eventually stumbled upon the small white door that had reminded his son of the type used in his friend's house.

As he opened it and stepped through, he was left in no doubt that his son had accomplished what he had been never able to do—and never would have. Without the luxury to absorb or react to the gravity of this achievement, he pressed ahead into the ensuring pell-mell and helter-skelter. He held an arm to his face to shield it against the blizzard of acrobatics formed of people, school desks and clocks. Only, as with the Matron's door, any incursion would swiftly nullify such a feeble barrier.

The floor had begun opening in great swaths. Desks plummeted into the infinity beyond, taking their students with them. Pens, pencils and parchments flew like confetti at a grand wedding.

Many spun through the perpetual darkness, as if a cartwheeling competition had gotten totally out of control, while others remained unaffected. For now. The students, like good children who'd learnt how to behave, simply stared ahead and awaited their turn. Each wore a bedraggled appearance, suggestive of having completed a 400-yard dash just seconds before, after which some kind soul had hurried along to douse their faces with water to cool them off.

Bob recognized in a instant that he stood on the same floor from his nightmares of years before. This was *The Terminus of Death*—but with one major difference: there was a life here that he would not leave without saving.

The 'coming apart' was gaining momentum and moving through those school desks, which had yet to join the somersaulting fraternity, their cargo lost in a lullaby, involved a generous dose of Lady Luck. Desks were falling away like little flour particles through a sieve, leaving increasingly larger expanses of nothing. Each step could be his last, but Bob's single presence of mind was to find Josh and get the hell out of here. Somehow. Before they too became lost.

The girl, as she had been for Joshua, was his beacon which he needed to follow. Her song steering him through the melee, then, out of the blue and into the light, he heard, "*Dad!*"

Bob stopped cold in his tracks, condensation snorting through his nostrils and mouth, eyes looking every which way before locking onto his son—the boy who had saved the world. He rushed toward him, mindful that the floor was shattering at a greater rate, and that balloons had begun drifting up through.

The air was filling with their demented laughter, the muted radium glow giving way to their soft white luminescence.

Clocks dive-bombed the floor. Starburst formations of shattered glass glittered amongst the desks and their students as well as clusters of balloons and their recently acquired quarry, many of which straddled the clocks' pathways beyond the starburst formations. Those who hadn't transformed were abruptly dismembered… arms and legs, like winnowed matchsticks, joining those of the recently departed Class of Obedience of 2022—or 2025...

The huge clock tower, with its jagged ass of steel girders and stonework, thundered past Bob. He spun with an acute sense of mortality gripping his heart. It rapidly descended into the perpetual darkness and out of sight, after spearing through a string of balloons to send it scattering. Their mean little faces turned end over end, each a macabre caricature of a happy face.

The victims of the Dream Sorcerers were now easy pickings for the balloons, sans the usual thrashing and screaming. They were simply plucked off like feathers in a poultry abattoir, their souls forever lost.

Without fanfare. Without hoorah.

But at least the enduring ordeal of worn-out dreams had come to an end.

〜

Wednesday, September 14, September 2022
6:30 A.M.

The streetlights of Corona, California, winked on in the late hours of morning like strings of ornamental Christmas lanterns, the type often festooned between porch posts to add a splash of festivity.

Beneath them, front doors began to tentatively open and disgorge their human contents into front yards and onto the streets, as if setting forth wind-up toys that had seen better days. Others tottered about the sidewalks, though there wasn't a single car to be seen.

Each was the survivor of a night not to forget in a hurry.

And, for some, like Kylie's father, it'd never be forgotten.

The Mendozas were no exception. Zachary, Marlene and Leon staggered into the sprawl of lawn that led to the verge in a state of shock. Behind them, a light blazed from the sofa room where cold lasagne sat unloved and ruined.

Sue Triplow followed closely behind, clutching a Heckles carving knife, at the ready but with little belief in its requirement.

As observed by Leon and Joshua at Old Mister Grouch's, balloons were piled wherever the day's first rays of sunlight had yet to reach. Their manic laughter was rendered to pathetic whimpers. Only, unlike the morning at Old Mister Grouch's, having been stranded outside Black Eternity as the feeding frenzy was in full-swing, their numbers had accumulated in deep drifts, like hailstones deposited by streams of cyclonic storms.

Whilst deep in the south to the equator, over the plains of such lands and continents such as Australia, they soared towards the stars in search of refuge, where they would simply pop in the atmospheric pressure like zits between the fingers of a frantic teenager.

A faint smile caressed the corners of Sue's lips.

Leon turned to her. "Does this mean I'll see Joshua again?" The hope in his voice was that of one holding back their tears.

Sue ran her eyes over the bluing sky, then down to the boy she'd rescued just hours before, his parents watching on intently. "Yes," she said rather matter-of-factly, "I believe that will be the case." The streetlight adjacent then switched off in the growing light of morning, and she frowned with deep consideration. "I reckon it's time for a coffee."

Her hand went to her mobile.

The time was just after 6:30 a.m.

So she waited for the best call of her life.

Mary Booth continued to sing while plateaus of the Boogaloo, some as large as planets, collapsed around her, because that was the way it had to be.

Her song had changed somewhat, but its purpose hadn't.

Behind this door exists a dimension unimaginable
Dare to step through
And fight for reasoning and sanity
Amongst the sound of time
Of madness
And that of cruelty
Exposed to the Dream Sorcerer
And the skittery-scratch of the man in black
Lost with no way back
You have stepped into the Boogaloo…

Remaining at the wheel of the Hudson Terraplane, the highway between here and there had to remain open.

Just for a little bit longer.

Bob and Joshua had momentarily abandoned the galaxy's collapse within Black Eternity for a love that surpassed all else, until

You have stepped into the Boogaloo…

Joshua pulled away from his dad's embrace. "How do we get out of here?"

In a steely lasso of fingers, Bob took hold of his son and ran the gauntlet. Ducking and weaving between the floor's planetary gaps, he threaded their way along needly veins of glass that floated amongst infinity. Soon, there'd be nothing left of it. And that was fine—in fact, that was breathtakingly liberating, but the door which stood contrarily amongst the mayhem had to hold firm.

Maintaining his eyes on it as much as the sinuous and decreasing veins, it forecast his need to make haste.

Its pristine white panel, with its delicately shining stainless steel handle, teetered on the brink of becoming lost to the perpetual darkness. And for one spectacular moment, Bob was rudely drawn to the similarities between it and the opening title of *The Twilight Zone*.

He reached for it.

"*Dad! You said...!*" Joshua got no further before the wind was ripped from his lungs and he was falling, his dad's hand never letting go.

The Casimir effect had opened once more between dimensions, Black Eternity and the universe as known to the human race, for one final celebration.

More to the point: between Black Eternity and Duncan's.

The last door standing within Mother's Care Orphanage detonated in a spew of aged splinters and rusty bolts, creating a hole in the continuum of dark matter, which it would soon reclaim.

The parasites were running to all quarters, and it seemed an endless army of overly zealous tambourine players had been unleashed. The tiny bells on Their funny shoes and hats manifested into a cacophony that projected profound bewilderment. Huge streams of toffee-colored matter ruptured and belched into Black Eternity, taking with them entire populations of Dream Sorcerers.

The outpouring spun, wheeled and ran, but were no match for the descending madness. One by one, the bells went silent in spheres of soft-white illumination.

The dreams were no longer.

And the message that had intrinsically tied Black Eternity to all Earths

00:01

had ceased to exist.

⌒⌒

Sue remained with her friends because the company was good. Healing.

The coffee was good as well, a cascade of golden-brown bliss. The best tasting coffee that had ever touched her lips.

The phone call that followed was out of this world.

"Bob?"

"Yes."

She burst into tears. The woman who'd valiantly saved the Mendozas was reaping the rewards for her efforts. Her bravery.

"Providing there's no issue with flights, we'll be home in about a day, even if I have to pay triple the cost to get seats," Bob was saying. "We'll have to wait at the airport for a few hours, though." He paused before adding, with great emotion, "How are you doing, babe?"

Sue was listening, but she had something to ask, and it couldn't wait. "Can I speak to Josh?"

Bob smiled, tears shimmering in his eyes, and passed his son the mobile outside the Duncan's megastore. Its parking lot was otherwise empty but for abandoned shopping trolleys and one white taxi.

He couldn't help noticing the number stamped on the front guards: 151.

"A handshake for life," he muttered under his breath.

"*Mom!*" Joshua cried.

It was just after midnight, the 15th September 2022, in Adelaide, South Australia.

HOME

~

California

Since the blackout, and the traumatic events that had come about seemingly because if it—or at least while it prevailed—Californian authorities had deemed that schools and many others services would remain closed until the following Monday, September 19, 2022.

A dreadful amount of people had gone missing, almost fifty residents within Corona alone.

Numbers across the world were likened to those of the Black Plague, in which entire townships and cities had been ravaged. How could that be in today's day and age? Where did they go? Who or what was responsible? Such outcries swept across all continents and races from Russia to China, Afghanistan to Australia.

It was difficult to categorically put a figure to such losses, since they remained in constant flux on a near riotous fusion of consternation, frustration and fear. Perhaps it wasn't as bad as first thought.

Then again, perhaps it was far worse.

One elderly lady wailed and snorted on national news broadcasts throughout America over the waste of life, only for all five members of her family to be discovered huddled in their Winnebago out back of their residence in Jackson, Wyoming. This divine news came to her as she was filling her second white handkerchief, which she promptly flung into the face of one reporter, before dropping to her knees and praising the Lord for His merciful blessings.

When asked by a journalist, sporting a microphone the size and shape of a chihuahua, why they hadn't come out of hiding after noticing daylight behind their closed curtains, Steven Chastain, husband and father, replied, "I thought the balloons had come back en masse. We saw them take people into the sky... at least, it looked that way. That was when I told the family to take shelter in the van."

Stories of balloons being somehow responsible threatened to escalate into global hysteria.

Confiscated specimens had been summarily secreted within cloistered laboratories and underground black operations. The official statement, promulgated by the leading powers, warned: Should you be in possession of a balloon from the recent blackout, it's a matter of urgency that you lay them within the sun to purge potentially lethal pathogens that pose a risk to mankind.

The scientific community covertly hedged toward the presence of undeniable life from another world, whose survival seemed dependant entirely on darkness and an extreme gravity field. The same element speculated to be intrinsic to black holes, and capable of near instantaneous disassembly of every molecule within the human body.

⌒

Friday, September 16, 2022

Though their reunion the night before, just as soon as he and his dad had arrived at Chasing Boulevard, had been one of high emotions, Joshua hadn't had the energy to tell his story to Leon. Not then. Not immediately. This hadn't stopped both boys behaving like kids on Christmas morning, and Joshua's spine smarting in the aftermath of both his mom's and Leon's hugs. However, it might have been worse had Leon's dad not given him a hearty slap on the back that almost sent his teeth flying from their sockets. In that way, he had probably done him a service.

That night, sleep had come easy and deep. Void of a man in black or those bells from that fucked-up man in the three-peaked hat, he dreamt of nothing, his mind totally at peace.

And now, in the bright light of morning, Joshua relished the exquisite vitality of the surrounding birdsong and all things blissfully normal. The air danced refreshingly across his skin and excited his nostrils. He had thought about his *Astra-Links*, but it had seemed somehow more fitting just to walk the short distance between his house and Leon's. To feel the ground beneath his feet. Mind you, if he heard an infant's toy rattle ever again, he'd take to the fucking thing with a sledgehammer until it was obliterated.

With the sensation of having been reborn, his bones and muscles tingling with youthful energy, he told his story to the one person he entrusted it to. And tell it he did.

After the better part of an hour—although no one was counting—in which both boys had become so absorbed in the reveal that time had slipped by in a blur, Joshua arrived at: "When he went through the doorway, his eyes were bright, Leon. I saw that and didn't recognize it until now. Everybody in that realm of madness had nothing going on in their eyes. They were the eyes of the dead, except for the hippie—and the girl," Joshua added remorsefully.

Fear tightened the flesh across Leon's face. "I've never seen someone with dead eyes."

"Neither have I, but I imagine them to look that way."

"So what does it mean?"

"It means he's still in that madness somewhere."

"But you said it was destroyed."

"I don't know if it was *completely*," Joshua said, horrified by this part of the story. "He's caught there, Leon. Doing what, I don't know. All I do know is that he's caught and I didn't find him."

"It's not your fault, Josh."

"I saw Kylie, too."

"From our class?"

Joshua nodded.

"Does that mean…?" Leon trailed off, thinking, *Her face will be in the newspapers and on the TV…*

Joshua nodded, again, solemnly.

Leon swore as a shiver ran the length of his body.

"I had to leave her." Joshua looked at his friend intensely.

"What were Kylie's eyes like?" Leon pressed. "Were hers... you know?"

"Dead," Joshua returned flatly, suddenly intrigued by his hands bundled in his lap. "Sammy's lost somewhere that nobody wants to ever be lost in."

"There's not a thing you could've done more, Josh. And besides," Leon started with great consideration, "you started in this place called Duncan's—"

"It's a supermarket."

"Whatever," Leon dismissed this trivia. "You then woke up in Duncan's."

Joshua's intense gaze had returned. "Dad and I didn't 'wake' up, Leon: we were already awake. It's like we dropped out of the sky right back amongst those dolls in the toy section."

"What's the chances that you had a dream?"

"Christ's sake, Leon. Were those balloons in your bedroom a fucking dream? And what about those left after the blackout?" Joshua levelled with him. "Please don't reduce this to a dream. It was no dream. Alright? None of it was a dream. This wasn't one of those movies or mini-series where whatever you've been watching has all been in the head of the main character." Joshua had to get his point across. "It wasn't a collective dream or hallucination or some shit brought on by too much heat. Alright?"

"Alright," Leon agreed, holding his hands up. "I believe you. I really do. I'd be a liar otherwise. But, Josh, you can't go beating yourself up because you couldn't find Sammy. From what you're saying, you could've been in this place your entire life until you grew old with a beard down to your ass and still never have found him."

"I only found the man in black because of the girl's singing."

"Well, then, you've answered your own stupid misgivings. Say, for example, if she hadn't been there, what do you think you'd have done?"

Joshua shook his head, staring at his hands once more. "I don't know, Leon. I honestly don't know."

"Exactly." Leon reached out and gently laid a hand on him. The touch of human kindness felt good, reassuring, for both boys. "From everything you've said, it's a miracle any of us are even here. Those balloons we saw at Old Mister Grouch's when he was flattened against his front lawn—"

"He was dead, Leon."

"Yeah, flattened. If those balloons we saw and those that came through my window—" Leon broke off, wearing a cheesy smile. "Your mom was really good. She's not the type any asshole would want to go messing with?"

Joshua recalled—*snip-snip*—the year 2025. "I met mom and you on my way to the realm."

Leon felt rather proud of this. "Really? What was I like?" he asked eagerly.

"A total jerk. You made fun of me, and so did the other guys."

"Thanks," Leon said. "Was Sammy there?"

Joshua nodded.

"Anyhow, it's obvious that place you went to screwed with your head, because it wouldn't matter when you met me or where, I couldn't be anything like a jerk." Leon feigned haughty offence.

"On this other Earth, everything looked the same, but nobody acted the same except—"

"Except?"

"For the taxi driver."

"Malinda?"

"Right. The fellow who drove us to Duncan's."

Leon shrugged. "Guess it's possible there are all kinds of ourselves across the universe. At least, it's possible."

With great relief and love, Joshua said, "I'm glad I know you, Leon. On *this* Earth."

"Back at ya," he said endearingly. "At least, I think I know what you're driving at."

A weary smile touched the tips of Joshua's lips.

Leon shifted on his bed, sending waves through it that made Joshua wobble. "Those balloons... from everything you've said, and from what I witnessed, it's possible they would've taken everybody. You put a stop to that, Josh. You ended that and saved billions of lives. Think about it." Leon raised a hand to stop any interjection of modesty. "No adult could've have done any better, and I reckon most would've failed. Those balloons *wouldn't* have. You're the ultimate hero, Josh."

"Funny, I don't feel like the ultimate hero."

"Jesus, Josh, if the Debnars knew what you conquered, do you suppose, just for one second, they'd blame you for not finding Sam the Man?"

Joshua huffed, head down, his bundled fingers moving restlessly. "Sam the Man," he repeated softly.

Leon answered in place of his friend's reluctance. "No." Final.

Moments of silence passed. It was comfortable—and necessary.

Joshua was sitting cross-legged on Leon's bed whilst Leon had his legs dangling over the side.

"Do you think it'll ever come back, whatever *it* was?" Leon asked in the quietness of his bedroom.

"No," Joshua said with such surety, there was no denying his conviction.

"How can you be so confident, since you're not sure if you completely destroyed it?"

"Because it all had to do with the man in black, Patrick Nesmith. He was the one that had somehow caused all of it. When I accidentally broke his arm," Joshua was saying with a sense of guilt.

"You should've smashed his fucking head in." Leon left no room for guilt.

"When I broke his arm, I stopped him from writing, and when I did this, everything fell apart." Joshua flopped back on the bed and stared at the ceiling. The invitation was almost too much for Leon to resist. "I don't think he was here to cause us any harm."

This was met with an amount of sarcasm.

"No, really, Leon. I don't. I think he was trying to warn us. I think he wanted to be stopped from what he was doing, and since he couldn't do it himself, he needed outside help."

"Have you spoken to your dad about any of this?"

"Some."

"What's his take on it?"

"Like me, he doesn't really know. He did say that it was somehow mixed up with where he spent his childhood."

"Where was that?"

"Mother's Care Orphanage."

"He was an orphan?"

"Apparently. His folks died in a car crash, and there were no relatives to take him in, so he became a ward of the state."

Leon didn't like the sound of this at all. "Where's Mother's Care Orphanage?"

"It *was* in a place called Kapunda, Adelaide."

"Where you and your dad went to confront the man in black?"

"Yeah, but it's a long way from the city, and nowhere near Duncan's."

"Then how did this have to do with his past?"

"He doesn't know for sure, and certainly not how the man in black figured into it, besides getting to me. He mentioned that the orphanage was frequented by a reverend, or pastor, at least someone dressed in black pants and white collar, but nothing suggestive of a monk." Joshua's eyes widened in awe and, as he bolted straight up, he laid them on his friend, who quickly averted his eyes from his shorts. "The orphanage teemed with those man-things, and the walls cried tears of lost ghost-children. It's hard to know what fits where, and how to make sense of it."

Leon remained quiet until a slight blush subsided from his cheeks. Speaking beforehand might have made him sound like he was experiencing an erotic moment. At least, he reckoned that was the way his tone and warbling would have been interpreted. "Maybe you're not meant to," he finally said with the forced inflection of the profoundly wise.

"Dad said he escaped it just before it totally collapsed." Joshua shrugged. "Since I reckon it had to do with the man in black, and dad reckons it had to do with this creepy old orphanage, and since the scribbling and school desks all came to an end, you'd have to think there's no coming back."

"Good. I don't want any more fucking balloons sliding through my window, Josh. I mean, I like playing with balls, but they weren't the kind you go messing with."

There was one exquisite moment in which both boys appraised the other, absorbing what Leon had admitted, with the boy himself a human thermometer projecting from boiling water, before the floodgates released a gale of laughter from both.

Silence fell between them, but not before their faces ran with tears.

After a while, Joshua asked, wiping his face dry, "You reckon I should tell the other guys?"

Leon was shaking his head firmly. "No," he said just as firmly. "Craig would throw his guts up and Ethan would more than likely make fun of the whole thing. Besides, neither of them have to know. *Nobody* has to know. The same with Dad and his involvement before you and your dad flew to *Australia*." The country was given special emphasis as if it held exotic and, perhaps, dangerous secrets. Ones best left cloistered in a vault beneath mega-tons of cement after transportation to the heart of Eris where even the dimmest of sunlight took a whole nine hours to reach.

"What was that all about?"

"Just as your dad doesn't know, neither does mine. He says it was a good thing, though. I agree." Leon reached out to his friend again. "We can't say anything."

"You know the ultimate bummer?" Joshua asked.

Leon waited, paddling his feet back and forth, hands now palm-down on the edge of his bed.

"We've got to go to school on Monday."

"Let's veto all school polices unless they include another summer break." Leon expressed his dejection.

Joshua half-laughed, half-smiled.

"Dad says we're all going to Lake Welland the weekend following."

"Where *I'll* catch the biggest sea bass."

"Bullshit, my good fellow. It is I who shall snare the grandest," Joshua said, affecting a stiff upper-lip British accent.

"In your dreams," Leon retorted with a pure Louisianian drawl.

The boys froze for one stupendous moment before losing it entirely once more. It seemed laughter that morning was a must-have accessory. Nourishment for the soul, and anything was up for grabs.

The bed squeaked, which set them off yet again.

With eyes watering and stomachs sore, they decided to hit the pavement and give the *Cha Cha* a go.

Sammy's absence left a decided hole in their lives; but having caught up with Ethan and Craig, the four boys were determined to make the most of it.

Leon and Joshua especially.

And that was all that counted.

KALEIDOSCOPIC SHADES

Within Black Eternity

Twelve years after a cataclysmic event ripped apart the state of South Australia, the Triplow family has finally found peace. Settling down in Corona, California, has ensured that the horrors and madness remain relegated to another time, another place.

On the morning of September 7th, 2022, that false perception is shattered when Bob Triplow is compelled to take his son on a journey back into the horrors of his childhood. To a place well beyond their old home in Hastings… well beyond South Australia… a place truly out of this world, where Bob will learn that the past always finds a way of catching up.

While Bob Triplow struggles for his own sanity within this dark, boundless dimension, his son, a mere child of ten, will have to make decisions upon which six billion lives depend.

Kaleidoscopic Shades – Within Black Eternity is a mind-bending collision of horror and science fiction, perfect for any fan of Stephen King and David Lynch.

AUTHOR PROFILE

Born in Adelaide, South Australia, David A Neuman was gifted a vivid imagination. In the late seventies, he walked out of Norwood High School an underachiever to embark on a scholastic journey before graduating from Flinders University in Behavioral Science.

Some thirty years ago, disenchanted by the rigidity of life's endless stop signs, he first penned *Kaleidoscopic Shades - Within Black Eternity*, and if not for a chance meeting with a man of poetry, this Literary Titan Gold Book Award winner would have remained a secret passion. Though he has written several other novels, yet to be released, he admits that each production is a two-year dedication and similar to stumbling over a rough diamond and looking into its heart.

Neuman continues to live in Adelaide with his four-legged companions: Saffron, Cinnamon and Ginger – his very own Spice Girls. It is here he feels at home, especially when exploring its ghostly past, understanding that, regardless of our backgrounds, we are all in this together and always will be.

Kaleidoscopic Shades – when a book becomes an experience.

It is my sincerest desire to provide you the ultimate escapism, opening worlds within your imagination.

Thanks so much for choosing Kaleidoscopic Shades and running with the characters within.

David A Neuman

<u>Publisher Information</u>

Rowanvale Books provides publishing services to independent authors, writers and poets all over the globe. We deliver a personal, honest and efficient service that allows authors to see their work published, while remaining in control of the process and retaining their creativity. By making publishing services available to authors in a cost-effective and ethical way, we at Rowanvale Books hope to ensure that the local, national and international community benefits from a steady stream of good quality literature.

For more information about us, our authors or our publications, please get in touch.

www.rowanvalebooks.com
info@rowanvalebooks.com

Ingram Content Group UK Ltd.
Milton Keynes UK
UKHW012041050423
419711UK00004B/109